Domicile

Enter the dystopian world of modern children.
Since Dickensian times,
No author has conceived so damning a commentary,
concerning contemporary childcare.
This book is based entirely upon known fact.

John Morris

Fiction and fact muddled so closely together,
It is difficult to tell one from the other.

Charlotte Greene
Dorset, England

Also by John Morris

Fractured Series
Inner Sanctum
Conspiracy Theory

Star Gazer Trilogy
The Gatekeeper and the Guardian
The Twelve Tribes
The Wrath of Gaia

Stand Alone Novels
Islamic State: England
Domicile

Published by Charlotte Greene, Dorset, England

Editor: Susan Dewey: http://beeberrywoods.com/FiberEtc/

Cover Image: Carol Knowles
Full Cover: Boris Junkovic:
http://www.charlotte-greene.co.uk/Agents_BorisJunkovic.htm

Acknowledgements: Christopher Booker, Ian Josephs, Professor Alexis
Jay, Andrew Norfolk, Camilla Cavendish, and other journalists.

Dedicated to:
My mother, Dorothea Jane Orr.
She taught me the difference between Good and Evil, as applied in daily
life. I follow a Christian morality, but I do not believe in an omnipotent,
preternatural, and all-seeing God. Moslem, Christian, and Hebrew faiths
all rejoice in the same godhead. These are the words of man, at the
exclusion of women, that differentiate the various religions of The One
God. That in turn is used to control of the populous.

Proceeds:
Profits from the sales of this book, will be donated to supportive charities,
helping UK children caught up in similar macabre, including Muslim
children threatened with FGM and Forced Marriage.

Official author website: http://www.john-morris-author.com
Publisher website: http://www.charlotte-greene.co.uk

ISBN Print: 9781910711125
ISBN eBook: 9781910711132

Table of Contents

References

Unusually for a book of fiction, this novel contains references. This is to assist the reader independently check information in the public domain. It also supports details of the story some may think to be fiction, but are indeed fact, or based in fact.

Copies of the Printed book and EPUB are identical, except the printed book names links to the reference. This reference is square brackets, containing the chapter and chapter entry number. An example would be: [R 3.1], [R 30.12].

In the EPUB version, the link should work. Full references are again available after the end of the book proper.

Prologue

Isabella Waites had been stabbing her ancient teddy bear with the curved point of a metal nail file. Humphrey had belonged to her beloved grandfather when he was a child. She loved the bear, which had been a part of her young life for as long as she could remember. Now the milky soft stuffing was oozing from fresh wounds, and the ancient straw skeleton had been exposed.

Issy worked determinedly, until the second eye popped out and rolled across the cold tiled floor, coming to rest against a pile of ripped photographs, and the remnants of clothes she loved, shredded. Her anger flared again as she worked seams and removed both legs from her saintly bear — it was much too much for her to cope with, alien, hostile.

She threw the remains of the bear away from her in disgust, as her anger flamed once more. Memories of recent events flooded back like a tsunami, overpowering her raging hatred, and breeching her resolve. Amongst the debris of devastation rose a new and harsh emotion, utter isolation. She curled up on top a bed, and wept bitterly.

It was not her own bed. It was somebody else's bed. It just happened to be in the room where they had put her.

Issy looked at the mess of her favourite cuddly toy and cried. Wracking sobs welled up from deep within her. Aspects of her heart she never knew existed before, flared like deep, livid welts.

She ignored the knock on the door, but it came again. The gentling voice of a man said, "Your dinner is getting cold."

Isabella smashed herself into the door, jabbing the nail file into the centre panel and yelled with mounting venom, "Get lost! Take me home!"

The release brought silence from outside. She wrapped up in a ball on top of the alien bedding, seeking succour, needing desperately to feel her missing parents' protective arms around her.

In time, she drifted into a nightmare world, one where happy memories and horrific events collided, each emotion struggling for prominence to control her future life.

Isabella could not understand why strangers had forcibly taken her from her parents' loving arms. With the aid of armed police, she had been physically prised away from her mother's protective grip, as her father fought desperately to keep her safe at home. He had also been arrested.

At eight years of age, Isabella could not understand what crime she had committed. What she had done that was so terrible, a gang of police felt it necessary to break down their front door and arrest all of them at six a.m. Her little brother included, and he was only a baby.

It got worse the next day: Isabella was in prison.

Chapter 1 – Bilty Steadman

Bilty Steadman put down the telephone, and looked out of the window, his mind lost within torturing thoughts. Rain battered the glass pane with the vehemence of a car wash. His eyes were momentarily blinded, when a whiteout of lightening silhouetted eerie buildings in the foreground. A neon sign flickered nearby, as people ran for shelter. Counting two seconds, thunder rolled like a damnation of the fates, obliterating all other sound.

He mused aloud, "Two miles. About the same distance between Isabella Waites and this office. But is this omen, this atrocious weather, marking a passage to, or from danger?"

His gaze returned to his desk, and his mind to that phone call. He eyed the files he was working on, and others newspapers wanted him to look into. Being an independent investigative journalist was an interesting life, and he was one of the best. Everybody wanted him to investigate their passion of the moment. He had a nose for a story, and the nous to discover the truth, a rare commodity in contemporary London. At times he felt more like a modern-day Philip Marlowe, at odds with the world around him, and sometimes with himself.

Rising from his leather chair, he closed the blinds, and returned to his desk with a bottle of whisky and lead crystal glass.

"Isabella Waites." His eyes looked into the distance, unfocused, as he sat back and sipped from the glass. He repeated the name, before glancing at his notes, taken during the last phone call. There were few of them: a mobile phone number, and an address.

He felt indebted to her. She alone had the balls to challenge, and browbeat a system so Machiavellian, as to make the Devil himself drool with delight. The fervour had since died down, and 'enquiries were ongoing', mostly out of the public eye. The moment had moved on. Or had it? This would be their second meeting, the first as brief as two trains passing in a tunnel. She had left for the orient, but it appeared she was back, and eager to rekindle the flames of injustice.

§

"Bilty, how delightful to see you again. Hurry inside, the weather is atrocious tonight. Something to drink before we start?"

"Likewise Isabella. Yes whisky on the rocks, it's almost nine p.m. How was the orient?"

"Different, it gives one a larger exposure of life. I loved it, well, most of the time. But let's get down to why I asked for this meeting. I thank you and others for following through on what we exposed. The thing is, nothing of substance has changed."

1

"Not true. They locked up several gangsters, ringleaders, and that is only because of you."

"Agreed, but it's nothing like the thrust put in by Operation Midland, that Metropolitan police hotcake to find dead people guilty of crimes it is impossible to legally convict them of.

"Meanwhile, I guarantee, that on any given night, thousands of seriously underage, white, British girls, are still being used as unpaid prostitutes. They remain in thrall to their Muslim grooming gangs, and nobody has acted seriously to stop it. I am mad as hell. They are still making a mountain of free money. Nobody followed that up. And the SS are still up to their old tricks, backed by closed courts. So Bilty, tell me what has actually changed for us ordinary girls. Eh? Fuck all.

"I tell you Bilty, I expected the prisons to be full of Pakistani Muslim child rapists by now. But nope. They carry on as if nothing happened. I'm determined to do something about it. Will you help me?"

"Yes of course, but what?"

"That's what we're here to discuss. I want it all documented, and promulgated far and wide, so that everyone has access to the facts of my life. Well, except for the private stuff."

Isabella smiled, and her two accomplices, Zoë and Melanie tittered nearby. "You mean like a film?"

"No, not a Michael Moor type exposé. I was thinking of more like a literary testament of fact."

A serious discussion, interspersed with flippant chitter-chat, and asides of innuendo ensued. Bilty stated, "Isabella, you need to write a book. I'm thinking a work of fiction, but based upon your life, and those of your friends."

"Me? Write a book. You're joking. I barely have time for me."

"Isabella, I can record your words, all we need is a voice recorder. I'll run a transcription application after each session. How about it?"

Melanie spoke for the first time, "Issy, we can do this. I'll video the interviews, and I have the latest, and British, text to speech software. Bilty, I'll give you a copy, how about that."

"Great, and a copy of the video — it helps frame the scene, shows the emotions. If we agree, I'll bring in a trusted ghost-writer I know very well: my wife. Do we have a deal?"

"Yes. But this will be written as an exposé, understood. I retain final say on the content of the video copy you receive, the transcription, and also the book. OK?"

"Deal. When do we begin?"

"Tomorrow at two, just after luncheon."

"Okay. I'll be here. So tell me, what is this place..."

Chapter 2 – World Perfect

Project Domicile
Interview: 01
Location: Fiddlers Court, The Oval, Holborn, Central London.
Time: 14:08 hours, Monday, 9th October.
Subject: Isabella Waites (IW).
Others Present:
>   Melanie (Mel) on camera and computer.
>   Zoë as friend, go-for, and minder.
Observations:
>   IW presents as a well groomed and highly educated young woman. She firmly shakes hands on entering the room, then chooses a straight backed chair. Her hands are clenched in her lap. Offered wine, whisky, coffee, or tea, she requests iced water.

Bitly Steadman
>   "Please relax Isabella, and tell me about what happened to you."
>   "Hmmm. So many years ago now, yet sometimes it feels like just moments ago. I've thought about how I should tell this, and have prepared some notes to help me keep on track. I'll use my childish words of back then, unless it breaks the flow. Where should I begin?"
>   "From the very beginning please, that would be ideal."
>   Isabella grouped her thoughts, and looked at her notes. She spoke her memories as if a monologue. She was recalling what had happened.
>   "Isabella, wait. I want to hear this from your heart, not a vaguely recalled memory. My wife was insistent. Can you cast your mind back into that past, and relive it? Be a part of it, and not with us here now."
>   "Cripes. I guess so. Yes, I can do that, but you'll get the warts and all. Zoë, I'll need a proper drink, and a spliff just in case. I'm about to put the record straight. To boldly go where no woman has gone before."
>   Isabella giggled, but it was false mirth. We all knew she was about to expose her personal trauma to the world at large. She moved around the room, before settling in an armchair near the coal fire. Feeling comfortable, she talked around the subject, before hitting the trail and trials of her life head-on. The transition was instantaneous, like switching TV channels.

Isabella
>   How did it all begin?
>   I'm about to tell everything, but I doubt anyone outside the system would believe me. It was all so innocuous at the beginning. I was at school and we were playing tag in the playground. I was the hit. I dodged several kids, as I squealed with delight. It was great fun.

3

They set a trap for me, but I saw it and again dodged away. I tripped over my own feet and went flying. My knees jarred into the gravel, as my outstretched hands sought to break my fall on the nearby grass. My palms hit and skidded, and my left eye crashed into the concrete retaining strip, that was essentially a low set kerbstone.

I had been tagged, but I was also bleeding. My knees were a mess, and I would end up with a black eye. Someone brought a teacher, and I was sent to see the Headmistress. My head hurt, and my knees had stopped bleeding, but were sore. They needed a wash with clean water, and some antiseptic cream.

The Head seemed overly concerned, due to what I now know as the possibility of a civil action. So she sent me to hospital for a check-over and treatment. She was only covering her own back; there was nothing wrong with me, save a few scratches that would soon heal.

A taxi was called to take me to hospital, and the driver was most sympathetic towards me. He touched my knees above the grazes and cuts, and peered at the injuries. He told me he was sure they were only minor. I was relieved, and did not realise his hand rested on my exposed thigh until he had to use it to change gear. I did not think it was strange. I thought that was a very caring endearment — at that time.

I was giggly, because the driver was quite funny. I thought he was either Pakistani or Indian, probably the former, but I wasn't sure in those days. He kept overemphasising his native version of English, and saying absurd things. He called me 'Princess', and I guess I told him quite a lot about myself, and my family.

By the time we got to the hospital, we were friends. He dropped me by the door and moments later, came in with me after parking nearby. The queue was interminable and we were there for hours. Don't ask me now, why I didn't think it strange, that he stayed with me. He even took my picture on his mobile phone, and we did 'selfies'. I thought that was great, because I wasn't allowed to go near my parents' mobile phones.

He wasn't happy with them, so we went to a stairwell where the light was better, and he had me pose while he took several more pictures, and a short video. He seemed pleased with his shots, and after checking the slowly diminishing queue, he treated me to an ice cream.

We returned to the waiting area just before my mother arrived. She was clearly distressed, thinking something bad had happened to me. I was fine and wanted to go straight home. The wounds had stopped hurting by that time, and I was all right.

I introduced the driver as Sufdar Hassan, and my mother was outwardly delighted to know he had looked after me so well. However, there was a shadow in her eyes until he charmed her also. "Your daughter is extremely bright, and she does you proud, it has been my pleasure to assist her in her time of distress. Unfortunately, I must leave, as my family are expecting me home for dinner. Please accept my business card and I will be pleased to be of future service. Thank you."

He stood, placing the card in my mother's hand. He bowed his head to her and began to depart. The shadow left my mother's eyes, and she asked, "What do I owe you?"

Sufdar said, "Nothing good woman, it is the will of Allah that brought me to your daughter's aid today. I am merely his servant."

I now realise, when a Paki doesn't ask you for money, for either services or produce provided, they are up to something. I later learned that most white people are exactly the same.

Sufdar rose to his full height, and turned to leave. My mother ran after him, and they had an argument about money. She was not only determined to pay for the taxi fare, but also his time spent watching over me. Sufdar, to his credit, only accepted the cost of the fare, but my mother pressed his palm with a large note as a tip. He smiled, nodded his head, and innocuously left with a large smile playing across his face.

I am sure we would have left the hospital, had the school not sent me for treatment. The time dragged, until finally I was called and attended to. We all agreed my injuries were minor, but they were dressed after a doctor's inspection, and soon after, we left for home.

It felt like an escape to me. We were late, so stopped for a take-away. It was from a Balti house, which seemed fitting with regard to Sufdar's generosity of the day. How little did we all know at the time.

[Bilty interrupted: "Is this where it all started?"

Isabella, smiling wryly said, "I know, it sounds quite normal, doesn't it. And what happened the day after next. Well, I forgot about it all, until years later, when one image resurfaced in a very strange place. I'll come to that much later. Let's move on."

Bilty asked, "How old were you?"

"I was eight, clever for my age, but not worldly wise."]

One knee was still a bit sore the next day, and it took me a few minutes to walk properly when I got out of bed, but with time it eased. The next day I was fine, and we were running late, as mother had to meet a client after she did the school run. It was her turn to take four of us to school that Friday. Outside the school was full of cars, so she dropped us off a little away from the gates. We had all done this before, and it was only a walk of fifty yards.

I was lost in talk with my friends when I heard the voice. We all ran for it, but my school bag was off my shoulders and I couldn't keep up. The next thing I knew was my collar being yanked from behind, and blackness. I woke up in an ambulance. That time I was seen quite quickly at the hospital, a different one from before.

5

The doctor asked me what had happened, and I said, "The bully-gang from school attacked us, and I was hit. I blacked out after that."

He looked at me in consideration for a moment, before he asked me how many times I was hit. I said, "I don't know. I was unconscious after being yanked back, and my head hit the pavement."

He asked me about my black eye and mused, before calling a nurse to send me for X-Rays.

When I returned to the cubicle, the doctor and a head nurse were talking quietly. They stopped speaking as soon as I entered. The doctor was charming, and the nurse over-indulgent. I knew something was up.

However, I was distracted by an examination, and in time told them about my home life. They were asking me questions, but sort of giving me the answers as well. At first I thought that was cool, but later, I realised that what I was telling them, was not the whole truth. The two were not the same thing.

From that moment, I stopped listening to their suggestions, and told them what I wanted to. The doctor dismissed me and I left.

I had nowhere to go except home. My school attendance had been cancelled for the day. I managed to use a hospital telephone to call my mother, but her line was still engaged after the third attempt. The receptionist stated, "You've used up my goodwill. You need to find another solution. Goodbye."

I was faced with walking home, and it was a very long way, perhaps two miles. Trust me, when you're eight years old, have a heavy school satchel to drag around, and have a slightly groggy head, two-miles is a very long way to walk.

I had been walking for what seemed like hours, but in reality it was only half a mile. I was lost within the drudgery of trudgery, when a car pulled up and pleasantly hooted its horn. I turned to look, and saw Sufdar smiling back at me. I hopped in his cab and he took me home. We stopped on the way for an ice cream.

By the time he dropped me home we were firm friends. He had been there for me twice, when even my parents had been too busy with their own lives. He thanked me for brightening his day as I left the cab, and I thought him a true gentleman. He said he would wait until I was safely inside. Bless him.

I turned and waved to him as I reached the path to the rear of the house. It seemed natural he would reverse and wait until I unlocked the side door. He was so caring and considerate. I found the hidden spare key out back, and within moments, waved to him again as I entered my home. He waved back and moved off immediately.

[Isabella: "It never occurred to me until just now, Bilty, that Sufdar discovered we had a key hidden in our rear garden."

Another piece of the puzzle fell into place as Isabella downed her drink. "I have no idea if Sufdar, or another, ever found the key, or used it. Knowing the human species, I would guess that he did. Did he enter my bedroom? Sniff my panties? Oh My God! I have no idea, but the thought repulses me. This is sick stuff."

Bilty added notes to his pad. "Please continue, I'm listening."]

In those days, I wasn't paranoid. I knew somebody was looking out for me. That was a treasure my parents gifted me, as was Sufdar. For a few weeks, he always seemed to be around when I needed help. I got used to his taxi honk, him pulling up, and I hopped inside because I trusted him. He was my best friend after all. He bought me treats and always made me laugh.

Today, I do not believe in coincidence. He was stalking me, grooming me in fact. Sometimes when he stopped for me, there would be another girl in the car, but she would always be on the back seat looking glum. I was always in the front. Those girls never spoke to me, even when I tried to make small talk. They were all going to a big school, like they were thirteen or fifteen. After a while I ignored them.

I'm not sure how long it was, perhaps a few weeks, I don't know. What I do know is that one day I was called out of class because somebody wanted to have a word with me. The woman looked old, although I guess she was in her early thirties. There was another woman in the room, who I guessed was mid to late twenties.

At the time, I thought I liked both of them, but afterwards I wasn't so sure. The lead woman asked me some really stupid questions, like how often my father hit me. I told her neither of my parents had ever hit me, or even spanked me, even when I knew I had been naughty. The younger woman loved my answers, and encouraged me to say more.

I told her a couple of secrets, like when I blamed the baby for something I had done. She was nice to me, and asked what else I had done. I told her daddy and I fought sometimes, and she said, "What did you fight about. How hard did he hit you?"

"Daddy never hit me. We were arguing about my pocket money."

I thought it strange when the older woman stopped us, saying, "But you fought with your father. Is that correct?"

"Yes, quite often."

I had expected them to ask about our rows, which were sometimes about my bedtime. But they seemed happy when I told them I had been fighting [R 2.1] with daddy, and they never asked for more details.

Somehow, they made me speak for a long time. I know that what I said, and what was later presented as evidence in Family Court, was not the same thing. The difference between us was, I did not have my own recording to disprove it. I did not realise the interview was being recorded. They were choosing which bits to use as evidence, editing out the context in which my words were said.

The older woman spent most of the interview writing things on a long form. The younger one asked most of the questions, and kept making me laugh. The time passed quickly. Near the end, the older one asked to take my picture, and I thought nothing of it. She had a proper digital camera and took several, just in case one did not come out right.

I was released, but the bell had already gone for lunch. I remember being a little upset because I had missed five minutes of break.

That day mummy picked me up from school, and told me she had seen Social Services [SS]. She told me they were supportive and helpful, but she had been advised to complete some forms. I told her about my interview, and it was clear she was worried. However, she hugged me and said, "You did well. Don't worry about it, it's just a misunderstanding."

Bilty

"This is horrendous, Isabella. I take it Social Services were responding to the second Doctors report to them."

"Hmmm. One would presume so, but I now know that was not the case. They were asked to pursue it by a third party I didn't know anything about until years later.

"I don't want to give the story away just yet, so let's assume it was because of the second Doctor. Then everything that happened fits neatly into place. He did submit a report later, when asked to by the SS.

"I'll pick this up again from the end of the week, but refresh our glasses first. This is thirsty work."

"Please, but coffee for me. Your memory is very good."

"Yes, it always has been. I can remember like replaying a video."

Bilty:
Personal Journal:

Notes:
1. This is most unsettling, and especially knowing something else was going on, but what?
2. So far, there is nothing of any worth, so how did it lead to life-changing events. Ah, IW has returned and we will resume.

Chapter 3 - The Courts of Injustice

Isabella

The rest of the week passed and I tried to forget about it, but mummy and daddy talked about it downstairs when they thought I was asleep. I was worrying about them, as they worried about me. I didn't sleep much that week, and felt tired every morning. I knew something was very wrong, but no one spoke properly to me about it, because I was a child.

Some days later, we were asleep when the gang of thugs arrived. It was 6 a.m., and men with guns were banging their demands on the front door of our home, "Open up!"

My father had answered bleary-eyed, and stared into a face he had never seen before, but would always remember.

The woman waved a piece of paper in the air, and demanding, said, "I have come to take Isabella Waites to a place of safety. This is an Emergency Protection Order, which you must comply with. You must hand her over to me, now!"

Dad replied, becoming conscious of many police officers behind the woman, "I will not unless you show me the warrant properly, and specify exactly why you are removing my daughter."

She spat malignantly, "You have already seen the warrant, let us in or we will break the door down."

She pushed the door with her hand, but it caught on the chain. My father slammed the door shut and yelled to my mother. She had already rushed into my bedroom and was picking me up from the bed.

I was groggy, disoriented, and we were all frightened out of our wits. I wanted to pee, but there wasn't time. It was still the middle of the night for me. I threw on some clothes as quickly as I could, my mother ordering me what to do as I tried to come awake. She was panicked, and I was responding. We raced down the stairs moments later, hoping to reach the back door and make good our escape.

We made it into the kitchen before mum saw a shape near the back door. She turned at once and we ran for the dining room window. Glass splintered behind us as a police officer put his elbow through the kitchen door and unlocked it from the inside. They were inside as mum opened the window to send me outside, and to safety.

It opened and hope remained, until the police gun appeared. The man said, "Stop where you are, or I will fire."

His gun was pointed at my head. I was terrified. I wee'd and shit my pants in fright. Mum backed away, and picked up a letter opener from the table. We backed away as policemen with guns rushed through from the kitchen, pointing them at both of us. Mother threw down the letter opener and grabbed me, holding me extremely tightly. Police overpowered and handcuffed her. I tried to stop them, hitting anyone that got in my way, until I was also put in cuffs. That didn't stop me biting any flesh that came within range of my mouth, and I made several incisive bites, until they taped my mouth as well.

Once we were secured, I could hear sounds of fighting upstairs coming from the baby's room. There was a loud crash and people were shouting. A woman took me to be cleaned up in the bathroom, and when I returned my father was also in handcuffs. The baby was the only one not cuffed. We were taken out to different cars, and I stayed with a foster family for seven days.

It was hell. I hated them, just because I had to be there. I cried. I missed my parents so very much. What had I done for this to happen to our family? I could not find an answer, except that it was all my fault.

One week later, I was delighted to see my family once more, and we celebrated being together again. Later, I was to learn that after we were arrested, mummy had been kept in a police cell overnight, and was charged with threatening a police officer with a lethal weapon. A letter opener, come on! They were pointing loaded guns at her, and me.

The SS kept in touch as the days passed into weeks. There were meetings and assessments with my mother, forms were completed. I didn't find out about most of it until a long while later.

I did not understand at the time, why they chose late Friday afternoon to come and take me away from home. I now know it was because we would not be able to get legal representation until Monday morning, by which time we would already be before the Family Court. Meanwhile, the Social Services team had ample time to polish their reports and complete their case file. It was a complete set-up.

At 10 a.m. on Monday morning, we had to go to something called Family Court. They tried to make the place look child-friendly, but it looked and smelled all-wrong: phoney.

Mother was only allowed to speak to answer a couple of mundane questions, her name and date of birth. Dad was also there, but kept apart, and <u>never allowed to speak</u> [R 3.1], other than to confirm his identity, and that of us children.

Social Services presented their initial concerns to Judge Selwyn Lewis, making a case for me to be 'At Risk of possible physical and mental abuse in the future', if I remained at home, or even in the area.

No one in the <u>family</u> [R 3.2] was allowed to challenge what was said. My mother tried to present the school statement, and that of the first doctor, but neither were allowed because there was no chain of evidence. She shouted, "You are distorting the truth, telling lies, and making things up!" She was ordered to be quiet or she would be removed from Court.

The prosecution made a damning case against my father, citing my black eye as proof of physical abuse. He defended himself, stating what had happened and told the Court he could prove it. He was told to be silent, as his outburst would only harm his defence.

Social Services provided an expert medical report stating that the (unqualified) 'expert' *expressed the opinion*, "The black eye is an injury *consistent* with being hit by her father."

[Bilty glared, "Consistent? Where is the proof? This is at best conjecture, and full of holes. It means nothing, other than supporting one reason how the injury could have occurred. There could be one thousand other explanations. Ridiculous!"

Isabella replied, "Yes it is. But these are the tricks they use. We are not allowed to challenge them, or present our own reasons or proof in defence of the allegation. Why? So the court accepts the preposterous, and set's that above the truth. This is how they twist information to kidnap us into care."

"Agreed. And on extremely spurious grounds. Pray continue."]

Dad shouted, "I have never hit her. She did it at school."

He refused to be quiet, was held in Contempt of Court, and led away to prison.

I was also shouting out what had actually happened, and my mother continued protesting after I was ordered to shut up. She challenged the next lie told, and was taken from the courtroom by force.

The Judge granted a Provisional Care Order, and I was to be taken away to a new home. I cried out that I wanted to be with my parents, but was told by the Judge to be quiet. I spoke again, and kept shouting the truth, until the Judge ordered I be removed from court.

"The needs of the Child remain paramount."

Huh. A load of bollocks if you ask me. But then, I was never allowed to speak in court. Why not? That is supposed to be my right in law: British Law, European Law, and United Nations International Law.

I was denied by the court, my right to speak at all.

The two women who had been allowed to say a lot of things came for me. I screamed as loud as I could, "I hate you all. I love mummy and daddy. I want to be with them." I threw my best ever tantrum and was still yelling and lashing out with fists and kicks as they grabbed my arms, and physically dragged me from Court.

That was physical, mental, and emotional abuse, in court, deliberately caused by the SS, and sanctioned by the court itself. It seems to me, that both Social Services and Family Court, think they are above the law, and have zero understanding of the immense anguish they unnecessarily inflict on young children.

It would not have been a factor, if they had left us alone.

I should have listened to what was being said in Court, because then I might have known what was about to happen to me. As it was, I did not know the Judge had supported their recommendation of a physical examination to support the allegation of *possible sexual* abuse. Therefore, I was a bit shocked when we pulled up at a private clinic. I was put in a room that smelled awful, told to completely undress, and put on a hospital gown.

I refused at first, but the SS told me the Judge had ordered it, and it was a way for me to prove my daddy was innocent. I faltered, and one of them offered to take me for a burger treat if I behaved myself. Even though I was starving, I said, "I'm not hungry."

I was left alone in the room, and sat and stewed within the depths of my dilemma. My tummy started rumbling, and I undid my trainers. A nice nurse came in at that moment, and she was light and breezy. She almost made me laugh, but I did my best to remain glum. She coaxed and cajoled me into the hospital gown.

The nice nurse left, and was replaced by a female doctor a few minutes later. She was chatty, and showed her concern for me. She asked me about my cut knees and fading black eye. I told her the truth, and she accepted it. She even wrote it all down on a form just like I said. I knew she was not one of them, and that I could trust her.

She ran several tests and had me do things. She never stopped talking, except to listen to what I had to say. She made me feel important. She felt all over my body, before asking me to sit in a strange sort of chair. She told me not to worry, and examined my Fairy. I thought that was very strange, but she only took a moment and was happy, telling me I was perfect and had nothing to worry about.

[Bilty: "Why on earth did they do that?"
"Ah. Wise up, Bilty. I now realise the whole point of the examination was to check if my hymen was intact, which it was."
"For the love of God!" Bilty shook his head.
Issy continued, "I know the full facts behind that, Bilty, and will relate it all in due course. Meanwhile, you have a think about the why of it. Why checking an eight-year-old girl was a virgin, should ever be important—That is, to a Family Court or the SS. Remember, sexual abuse was never mentioned."
Bilty looked up, Locking Issy's eyes, "I guess they may have been looking for evidence of sexual abuse?"
"No Bilty. The real reason is far more sinister, as are the actual workings of the SS and Family Courts."]

I was allowed to dress and went out when I was done. I found four women waiting for me, and was told I had to go with the new people as my case was now transferred. One of the ones I knew gave me a bag, "Here, Isabella. We packed your rucksack for you, with things we thought you would need."

I peaked inside, and was not sure if what they thought I needed, and what I knew I needed, existed in the same universe. I closed the zip, whirled, and hit one of them hard; like me, our family, she had not seen it coming. Before I could get the second one, strong arms locked me down, and I could not move.

"Now, now Isabella. I hope you're not going to be troublesome again. This would all be so easy if you'd behave yourself."

"Then take me home! There never was any trouble, until you lot barged in and took me from my parents. Where's my mother?"

My outrage was futile. They were much bigger and stronger than I was, back then. They settled me by tying me up. I still looked for ways to get back at them, and complained about the burger treat they had promised me.

The younger of the two new women said, "We'll head off at once. But only if you promise to be good."

"I will. I promise."

"Good. I'll take off the ties, if you mean that?"

"I do. I'm just very upset right now."

"It's always hard at the beginning, but you'll..."

My anger started to resurface, and the SS officer changed tack mid sentence, "I know. Have you ever had a King Burger?"

I hadn't, but some of the kids at school raved about them. I said as much, and was at last able to look forward to something. I thought they would take me somewhere local, but instead we drove out of Manchester and onto a motorway.

We were on the M6 headed south for Birmingham, when after half an hour, we pulled into the services and I had my first ever King Burger. It was great. We continued heading south, and I was so bored, I half-slept on the back seat. It was dark when I was shaken awake. They had stopped by their office first apparently. We were minutes away from the house I would stay in that night.

The place turned out to be a care home, and while the older woman talked to the person in charge, the other took me through to the restaurant. The cook was clearing up and apologised, but said there was no food left. I looked around. Some big girls were lauding it across the room, picking on younger fry, and they looked real scary.

I wanted to leave right away. I was frightened.

We went outside, much to my great relief, and I had my second King Burger of the day. It did not last long, as all too soon I was returned to the building, and shown to my room. I decided not to go outside, because the bullies would be sure to target me.

Instead, I locked my door and sat on top of the bed. I was all alone, and could not stop crying. I missed my mummy and daddy so very much. I even missed by little brother. My heart hurt, and I lay awake for hours feeling utterly worthless. I did not understand what I had done that was so terribly wrong.

> [Bilty: "You did nothing wrong, Isabella. You know that?"
> "Yes, I do now. I did not back then. That is important.
> "I blamed myself for what happened, not realising how wicked the Family Court and SS were."
> "I'll log that as emotional abuse, inflicted in full foreknowledge, by the Court and Social Services.
> "That you said to them, ' I'm just very upset right now.' Also demonstrates emotional abuse, by the SS."
> "At the time I was frightened stiff, and extremely unhappy by the all of it. That was abuse. I'll continue."]

I missed breakfast the next morning, because I had been awake half the night. I was woken when the supervisor came in, and I had to go with the two women from yesterday. We went to a different court, and I remember the Judge looking long at me in an extremely odd way. His name was Judge St. John-Smythe. I couldn't put my finger on why he made me feel extremely uncomfortable, but he did.

He seemed to be looking at me constantly, and so much so, I stopped looking at him unless I had to. I answered a few questions, like my name and age, and said little else. I wanted to say a lot, to tell them what I had gone through, and how wrong everybody had treated me and my family.

I never got the chance, and it was like this had already been decided before I got there. It was incredibly quick, and I was transferred. The Judge reserved my case to himself, and granted an Interim Care Order.

I was taken away to a foster home. I hated the place as soon as I set foot inside. The woman in charge was overly pleasant to Social Services, but changed into a demon as soon as the door closed behind my captors. I remember she made a big show of locking the door with a large key, from the chain she wore round her midriff.

That night I destroyed Humphrey, my Grandfather's teddy bear.

Bilty

"This is horrendous, Isabella. I know the Court of Protection, of which Family Court is a part, are zealously over-protective, and to the point of secrecy. But, they cannot ignore the rules laid down in law. Can they?"

"You wanna bet? They believe they are above the law, and act with total disrespect for the laws [R 3.3] and prescribed channels of guidance they should be following. I believe that before I left for the Orient, I proved this. Nothing has changed since."

"But Isabella, surely you were allowed to challenge the Expert Witness. There must have been corroborative evidence, without doubt."

"No. Disallowed in Family Court. As are the rights of the child. I was not even allowed to speak!

"What the SS state is accepted without any challenge being allowed. It is a kangaroo court. Later I'll explain the why of it, but not yet. This is a part of what we girls, abused by Family Court, call The Courts of Injustice."

"I remain most unsettled by what you have told me so far, Isabella. There seems to be a hidden form of judiciary applied to Family Courts, one that appears to be at loggerheads with its stated function and practices."

"Yes, that would be correct. How observant of you.

"You're supposed to be the best, so prove it. A judge cannot be sacked, or barely reprimanded. But they can be prosecuted and imprisoned. That appears to be the only means to get rid of these low-life scumbags.

"Or, they can be killed."

The icy stare that followed IW's last words, sent a chill through Bilty's heart. In that moment, he knew she was capable of murder.

"We are done for today, Bilty. This stuff takes its toll you know. I'm sort of feeling my way into this quagmire of human decrepitude, and it hurts deep inside. Even now. You as well I guess."

"Okay, Isabella. That suits me fine. About the same time tomorrow will be good for me."

"No, I need to work tomorrow. Wednesday it will be."

Bilty:
Personal Journal:
This is all most unsettling, and a clear dereliction of approved points of evidence. Much admitted as truth, is at best hearsay, but it is allowed in Courts of Protection. It is not admissible in criminal court, except under extreme and specific circumstances. Even then, Hearsay is not regarded as reliable, but perhaps at best, indicative.

Notes:

1. I am horrified that armed police were deployed, and yet this appears to be standard practice. I will review the rules of deployment.

2. The mere fact Isabella emptied her bladder and bowels, indicates extreme emotional distress. Surely this could have been avoided, handled differently, and it should have been challenged in court.

3. Why was the Waites family not allowed to challenged unsupported evidence, as supplied by third party 'experts'?

4. "Were consistent," is a prejudicial statement based upon nothing of fact, nor of probable fact. At best, it could be construed as an unlikely possibility. That should never be allowed as a ruse to tear children away from their parents. There must be a legitimate reason. Family court appears to be bereft of any legitimate reason, except substantiating itself.

5. Why was that 'evidence' accepted by the court without question?

Follow up:

6. Research the rules of Family Court. Plus relate to how these courts function in practice. Compare those practical functions with EU and UN Human Rights Acts.

7. Also obtain a copy of The Children and Families Act, given Royal Assent on 22nd April 2014.

8. Then: Compare these to the way Isabella, and others were actually treated, by said courts.

9. Follow/discover the money trail. I remain unsure just what IW means by this, but I will try.

Chapter 4 – Wednesday

Project Domicile
Interview: 02
Location: Fiddlers Court, The Oval, Holborn, Central London.
Time: 13:57 hours, Wednesday, 11th October.
Subject: Isabella Waites.
Others Present:

> Melanie on camera and computer.
>
> Zoë as friend, go-for, and minder.
>
> Vikki, another friend, but older, more worldly wise perhaps.

Observations:

IW seems much more relaxed today, and again she chooses comfortable seating, as if in soirée. We chat around irrelevant inanities, and she insists this part be called 'Wednesday'.

Moments later, Vikki hands IW a long glass of brackish liquid, and whispers something. Then without another word, but within a long slug and aberrant flick of her head, we begin.

Isabella

I was dead to the world when someone opened my door with a master key. I was dragged from the bed, sound asleep, and dumped on the floor, like a rag doll nobody cared for any more. The pain of my mouth hitting hard tiles replaced my dreams of safety at home. My elbow jarred into the tiles, breaking my unexpected fall. I was yanked up by my hair, without concern, like flotsam or jetsam, salvaged from a ravaged shore only the un-forgiven have ever glimpsed.

I looked up into the eyes of my tormentor, a woman of middle age. She was a monster. Behind her hovered a male who also seemed afraid of her. I was waking-up quickly to this new world, but not my fate. The pain in my head from being so roughly woken, only made my heart hurt worse. I was far too young to compete with her, my resistance faltered when the strange woman shouted at me.

Just days before, had I lived happily with my parents. That day I was in prison––foster care they called it. I was being bullied by much older people I had never met before, and hated. I cried.

Above me stood the matron who dispassionately pronounced, "You missed dinner last night. You will not miss breakfast, except to suffer my wrath, child."

She twisted my ear and it hurt. I scrambled to dress quickly, deciding to comply, at least until I understood what sort of hellhole I was sentenced to live in. I knew it was a very bad one. I reasoned that by keeping quiet and doing what they wanted, might just see me through it—until I could escape.

I did not know what to do, except to do as they said. I didn't even know where I was, except it was many hours by car from where I used to live. Everything smelled and tasted different. It was scary.

In the meantime, my mind was working on all sorts of atrocities I would inflict on them, if only I were bigger and stronger. At eight years old, I could only be smarter than they were, so that became my plan for survival. I decided I needed to slip into the background somehow, like being a part of the furniture.

That thought vanished as soon as I sat down at the breakfast table. I sat opposite another inmate who was a few years older than me, and who completely ignored me. I said, "Hello, I'm Isa…"

The horrible woman, my jailer, instantly cut off my words of friendship; "I do not know how you were dragged up girl, but in this house, children only ever speak when spoken to, and we never speak at table."

Chastened, I looked at the place setting. Before me was a glass of orange juice. I tried it, but it was rancid, not sweet like orange squash, and tasted foul. Beside it was a slice of grapefruit, which was sour and tasted just like the juice. I chewed through the first chunk slowly, wanting to be sick, before swallowing large chunks as soon as they entered my mouth, rather than eating them properly. That meant I didn't have to taste the fruit, it was horrendous.

The other girl took all the plates and put them in the kitchen by the sink, and I had to help her. By gestures only, we returned to table—she sat there, remote and unreachable. I was looking around, examining this new place. It was not like my old home, and I felt my heart hurting again, like somewhere very deep inside.

I did not cry, because proper food appeared for the first time. It was an egg in an eggcup. The top had not been removed like mummy always did, and beside it lay a teaspoon. I tried to copy what the other girl did, and eventually managed to gouge the egg open, but many bits of shell fell inside. The worst of it was the yellow runny yoke seeping down one side. I turned that part to me, and when no one was looking, swept it up with my thumb.

I began to reach for the cruet, but there wasn't one on the table. I raised my hand and was allowed to speak, "Can I have some salt and pepper please?"

Matron glared at me before shouting, "You will always address me as Matron child. Know salt is wicked. It will clog up your arteries, and kill you. Neither do we use white pepper, except on special occasions. You will come to love the taste of pure, fresh, organic food in time. Now eat, and never speak again at table."

I had been hoping for toasted soldiers spread thickly with real butter like at my real home. But instead, I ate the most tasteless egg I had ever been given. It was gross. Later this was replaced with four small quarters of toast in a toast rack. The crusts had been removed for some strange reason, and each quarter was identical in size and shape. There was only one piece each, and a small pat of olive oil based margarine, that barely spread over one corner of the slightly browned, whole-wheat bread.

I finished and was still hungry. I hoped there was more, but nothing appeared. Instead, I had to dry dishes and put them away, while the other girl washed up.

I tried to whisper to her as we worked. She pulled an electrical device from her pocket, and stabbed me. My arm seared with pain, and trembled uncontrollably. The device disappeared at once, when Matron came in and issued orders, before leaving to get ready.

Otherwise, the girl completely ignored me, as if I wasn't there. For no reason, I decided to call her Wednesday. Even with three other people close by, I felt completely alone.

I felt my tears rise, and was about to bawl my eyes out; I was so very lonely. But just then, matron came in again and issued instructions, and in fear of her, the moment passed.

After we had wiped the surfaces down, the matron stated, "Now children, it is time to get ready for school. Hurry-up or we will be late."

I went up to my room and found a uniform laid out on the bed. It was used and smelled of someone else. I put it on and the skirt fell down. It was far too big for me. I cried. I had never had to wear anybody else's clothes before. The thought of it made me feel sick.

Matron arrived, ordering, "Shape-up and behave, girl."

She pulled up the skirt and used an industrial stapler to take in the waistband at the back. She did the same with other clothes until they sort-of fitted. I felt a mess, and hated whoever had worn the uniform before me. I hated the bitch matron even more.

I was given a bag with someone else's name etched on it with indelible marker, and told to go to the car. I never spoke once, but inside, in that place where everything my parents had taught me about as being pure and my destiny, I was being ripped apart.

I expected to leave with the other girl when we reached the school, I still did not even know her name. However, she went to school, and I sat in the back of the car as we travelled a few miles. Matron said, "We will go to see the Headmaster later, for your official induction."

There was a lot of traffic on the road, much more than I was used to. My jailer parked on waste ground near a main road, locked me in the car without a word, and left in a hurry.

My mother would never have done that. She always took me with her. I hated the place, wherever it was.

I hated every person I had met since I was kidnapped. There were no happy faces, no laughter, and no fun. This time I broke down and cried

19

for ages, alone. The court had said that I suffered the 'possibility of future emotional abuse', if I was left with my mother. I was suffering extreme emotional abuse, because they had taken me away from her.

> [Bilty: "They are hypocrites, Isabella. I believe they did inflict severe emotional abuse on you, in order to save you from 'possible and future emotional abuse' by your parents. I'm seriously not getting this aspect, and will pursue it through the national media. This is so unjust."
>
> "Thanks Bilty. But better you wait until you hear the all of it. Zoë, another glass of the same, if stronger this time. This really hurts me, for the second time—going back through it all again.
>
> "Ah, thanks, Zō. To continue, Bilty. I was in the car..."]

My tears eventually turned to anger, and in temper, I tried the door handle. It opened. I was shocked, because I did not know I could do that. I opened the door a little further and the car alarm sounded. I knew matron would be furious, so pulled the door closed. The alarm continued to sound. I knew I was in deep shit.

The street nearby looked busy. I opened the door and ran for safety in the crowd, just like they do in the movies. Nobody bothered with me. Everyone, except a couple of old men, ignored me.

I met them in the park, after going on climbing frames in the kid's area. They seemed quite nice, and were very helpful, once they knew I was from out of town. They told me I was in London, in a place called Hammersmith. I had never heard of it before, but they said it was a very good area and had a famous Odeon and flyover. I looked around and was not convinced.

At least I knew where in the world I was, and it was a very long way away from my home in Manchester. Well, I was born in Liverpool, my parents were Scousers, but we moved because of Dad's work.

The old men made me laugh, and even offered me a sip of their wine that was hidden in a shopping bag. I felt like an adult when the strange fluid invaded my mouth. I was feeling proud of myself.

For no apparent reason one of them nudged the other, and they left me in a hurry, almost in mid sentence. I was told to hide, and then follow them at a good distance until it was safe. I had no other plans, and didn't know anyone else, so did as I was told.

I imagined I was in a spy movie, and darted for cover, sometimes peering around for potential bad guys. All I saw was a park warden doing his rounds. Real life is not like in the movies.

A little later, we were out of the park, and onto the streets. The old men stopped and waved me back to them. They were a little crazy, even for old people. They were also really good to me, you know, like grandfathers.

We passed a burger bar and I said, "I'm really hungry."

I hoped we would go in. Grandpa always took me for a burger treat. They spoke quietly for a moment, before one of them said, "Have you ever been to a pub?"

I said, "No."

Although they looked at each other, it seemed innocent enough, as they talked softly about which pub to go to. I got a little bored and wandered off to look in a shop window. I was wondering what I would look like in one of the dresses, when I grew-up, when they came back. Fred said to me, "We were going to The Prince William. We better hurry."

I was going to my first pub. I was thrilled as we walked in a new direction. They talked about the Royal Wedding, which was years old, and kinda cute. They told me I was their Princess, and I believed them. I felt so old and daring.

They hailed a cab, and at first I was put between them in the back. The driver said, "Only two in the back. Girl, sit in front and put on the seatbelt." The driver was a black, middle-aged woman, and was very chatty. I liked her immediately. The old men in the back were talking quietly, and the driver was sometimes watching them in the mirror.

Somehow, we were talking about me, and I told her I lived in Hammersmith, London. She looked at me for some time before whispering, "This is Shepherd's Bush. Your accent, Liverpudlian. You're not from around here, are you Hon?"

I immediately shut up. I had been rumbled. I was thinking what to say, when a voice from the back said, "Driver, please take the road on the left. I need to go home first for my pills. We can walk from there, it's just round the corner."

The driver did as instructed, and I followed the men into the house. I had expected the driver to pull away immediately we got out, but instead she was speaking to someone on her mobile phone. I heard the taxi pull away as the front door closed.

Once inside, Fred said, "Ken, Mable has moved my meds again. Give the girl something to drink while I find them. When I do we'll go to the pub for lunch."

Ken was the kinder of the two, and came back with three glasses of wine. We joked that I would get drunk, and he encouraged me to drink. I stated, "Only this one glass, naughty Ken."

I took his toast, chinked glasses with him, just as I had seen grown-ups do. I was an adult at last. I took a long drink. All breath left me as fiery syrup seared my throat. I coughed, but the liquid remained inside me. Ken held up his glass and took another swallow, telling me, "It is only like that the first time me-dear. Try it again when you are ready. It is elderberry wine, and I made it myself."

I did not take another drink straight away, because I thought I was not stupid. Fred, the older of the two came back and offered one of his purple pills to Ken. All I saw for certain was a large 'V' on the packet, before he put it back in his pocket. Anyway, they both swallowed one pill, and toasted each other.

Ken offered me a white pill with a pretty crown design on it, and encouraged me to finish my glass after I downed it. The drink was sickly sweet, but quite nice, after I got used to it. 'Only experienced drinkers know this', I thought at the time.

They put on some old music, like ancient stuff, and Ken dragged me up to dance. It didn't really work because he was much bigger than I was. He told me to stand on his feet, and he danced with me aboard. A slower song came on, and he said, "I'll teach you how to Waltz."

I was feeling very friendly, more than usual. I thought it was the company. I let Ken kiss me, and it felt great—not like when mommy or daddy did it, it was grown-up somehow, and so was I.

Abruptly, he put me down and asked to look at the back of my school skirt. He showed Fred, and they talked all knowledgeable like about clothes and fashion design cuts.

The result was I needed to take it off so Fred could sew it together properly. Apparently, he used to be the best tailor in London, Savile Row no less, and I had heard of that. I had to thread the needle for Fred, because his eyesight wasn't all that good, but he knew how to sew.

They noticed my school blouse was several sizes too big also, and kept talking about how useless my mother was. I found my voice, and told them about my life. Soon I had strong arms around me. They made me feel safe. After they cuddled me, Ken undid the buttons of my shirt, and soon Fred was working on that as well.

Ken refilled my glass and we toasted again. I was getting to like the taste. He made some jokes, and I found them ever so funny.

Fred produced a rickety old camera and started taking pictures of anything and everything. I think it must have come from the Stone Age, it was so ancient. He had to stop to put a new film in. Ken took the camera from him to reload, while Fred topped up my glass. Soon I was dancing again.

I was enjoying myself a lot, and the thrill every time the flash of the camera came. I was acting as a model for them. And then I fell over. I was lying on the carpet. Ken picked me up and put me in the middle of the settee between them.

I remember, there was a loud bang, and then the room was full of Police. My mind switched-off, and I woke up in a cell. I think it was the next day when I was sober enough to face the Bussies' [police] interrogation, but I am not sure.

First, a doctor checked me over, and wanted to Section me.

I didn't like the sound of that word, so refused. It seemed I passed his test, because I was soon languishing in a cell, again.

The food was not brilliant, but there was a lot of it, and they used salt. I was coming to like the place, except for the smell and The Bussies.

Everything changed later. I was taken out to a new area, one where there is a room they use to torture people. They do not use wet boarding to make you crack, or pliers to pull out your fingernails. Instead, they use words: Adult words.

I was taken to where a nice policewoman, and a real jerk of a policeman were waiting for me. I felt like I was on trial for murder. We had to wait for matron to flounce in, her anger at me volcanic. I knew I was in for a beating later. I did not understand a lot of what was said about me, in front of me. Again, I was not allowed to speak.

They all talked quietly before there was a loud buzz, as an antique tape machine began to record: My interrogation began. I was still suffering my first-ever hangover, drug overdose, and felt like crap. They threatened to charge me with 'soliciting', before realising I was too young.

I told them, "I've never wanted to be a Solicitor. I want to be a pop singer when I grow up, just like Rihanna."

I knew they did not believe me, but it was the truth. For my cheek, I got an official police caution, whatever that is? At the time, I thought it meant that they know you are special.

Bilty:

Personal Journal:

I don't know whether to admire Isabella for being so resourceful, scold her for being so stupid — which she already knows herself, or question the actions of others that brought this about. The latter is most viable.

What remains is a lucky escape from two known paedophiles, and the wits of the taxi driver, presumably. This could get interesting.

Notes:

1. I'm still not sure why she entitled this session 'Wednesday', unless it means today. It does not. She named the other girl that, as if it meant more, but what?

2. I have one idea, but surely she is too young to know about that. Or is she? Isabella can be quite devious, so time to wait this one out, and learn more about her character in the process.

Chapter 5 – Howard's Inn

Isabella

Matron looked angry at me. She never spoke to me as we drove back to her home. It could never be my home.

I was locked in my room and left there to think about my conduct, until she decided I had done something called 'repentance'.

This seemed to consist of saying I was sorry, and that I would never do 'it' again. I had no idea what she meant by 'it' either, but I promised anyway, just to get the old cow off my back. I played along with her game, and the beating I expected never came. The following day I was taken to school for 10 a.m.

I was told to sit outside the Headmaster's office, while matron spoke to the Head. They shook hands as if best friends, and as the door closed the Head gestured at me. I knew this was going to be bad, real bad. I had to escape, the whole place smelt wrong. They were in the room a long time.

The receptionist told me off for banging my heals against the chair legs. I stopped for a moment, before deciding to do it more, and louder, simply to annoy her.

I told her I needed the toilet, and offered to stop banging the chair, but she refused to let me go. I made a run for it, but she was quicker, and caught me. She threatened to slap me, and told me to sit down. I hated her, and told her, "That's against the law. I'll report you."

We argued, well until she got me by the ears, twisting them and pinching hard. I had to retreat and be a good girl, if only just.

Eventually I was called into the Headmaster's office. His name was Mister Conway, and I was made to stand, even though there were several empty chairs. They were talking about me, in front of me, but not to me. I sat down regardless, and they didn't notice for a while.

I presume they reached a decision about my fate, and the Head looked up to address me. He realised I was seated and shouted at me. I stood at once, but a curious smile played over his face. He put his index finger into his nostril, and appeared to spend time working on a bogey. He removed his digit, inspected it, and flicked it at me. Gross.

I dodged to one side, stuck my forefingers up my nose, and flicked one back at him, and the other at the bitch matron.

I got detention for that, and I wasn't even enrolled in the school. How does that work?

As far as I can see, if an adult does it to you first, then you can do it back to them—like their lies with words that have other meanings you don't know about.

For me, if the headmaster wants to pick his nose and flick his snot at me, I am going to fight back and flick my own back at him, simple. Matron tut-tutted and told me I was disgusting.

I said, "He did it first."

I was soon to learn, there is one set of rules for adults, and a completely different set of rules for kids.

The Head started speaking, and he droned on and on for hours. Well, it seemed like it at the time. Matron was enthralled, but I tried hard not to go to sleep on my feet. The bell rang, and he stopped, stared at the wall clock for several moments, as if recollecting which reality he was currently resident in, and called for the receptionist.

I was told to report for Maths in room 11C. The work was so easy I finished miles before everybody else, and got 100%. The rest of the class were more interested in shag-bands and fixing 'dates'. Apparently, it was the latest craze, although very old to me.

The next morning, the non-speaking-girl and I were delivered to the same school at the same time.

School was not a nice place. The buildings were old, the teachers young, and mainly inexperienced. They all seemed to be behind where I was academically. My previous education did not go down well with the other kids.

Outside of class, I was useless with the thuggish street culture, to begin with, but quickly learned how to survive.

On my first full day, I got bullied. I wore the school uniform, when most of the other kids did not. A gang of older kids targeted me, and I ran for a teacher's protection. I almost made it, but he was looking the other way. He went off to sort out another squabble, as if he ever could.

One older girl grabbed me by the throat and demanded money. Another tried to snatch my schoolbag, saying they were hungry. I kneed the first attacker as hard as I could between her legs, as I had just seen another girl do it to a thug.

It worked, so I threw a punch at her jaw, and caught her ear. I knew I was no good at fighting, but they did not. The bully staggered back clutching her hands between her legs. I kicked the girl trying to take my bag, and unexpectedly, they were gone.

The teacher had reappeared for playground duty, and was headed for me. I hurried away, but was called back to answer for my crimes. I got detention, the thugs did not.

Yeah. First proper day at a new school, and I got detention for defending myself. My record read: days at school: one and a half, number of detentions: two. I'd never had detention before, ever. My head was full of confusion in that alien world. I hadn't done anything wrong. I had no answers, only questions.

The deputy Headmaster called me to his office the next day. I was awarded an unofficial caution for conduct unbefitting a pupil. I told him exactly what had happened, and the outcome of our row was that I ended up an Official Caution and more detention. Some school, eh?

Day three, my third detention. But the good thing was, I had an hour less to spend at the prison I lived in. Meanwhile, I endured.

Next day, Maths was with a different teacher, and at a slightly higher standard. I had still done it all before, and hung back to tell the teacher after class. It seems that he was as good as it got in that school. He even apologised to me.

I knew I was being dumbed-down.

He offered me extra tuition, that I accepted, and we called it detention to get around the Head. At first, it was great and I really came on, but over time I noticed he liked to touch me a lot, and later I had to sit on his lap while he explained things about Mathematics.

Sometimes, I noticed his trousers seemed to pulse, as if there was something inside trying to get out. He also took to tickling and prodding me, which was fun at the time, but later it became a problem for me.

I stopped going. I wasn't sure what it was at the time, but there was just something very wrong about it, him.

On Thursday afternoon, I had English, and again, I was moved to the highest group. They were still lamebrains, but it was slightly better. There I made my first friend at the school, the teacher. For a while, she became the nearest thing I had to a mother.

The kids were gross. I seemed to end up in a fight every day, and always got detention for defending myself. I cried each, and every night, alone in an alien bedroom. The next day it would repeat, like a vinyl record caught in a groove, counting down the days. My life was total misery, and I knew I was the only one who could stop this meaninglessness, nothingness taking over the entirety of my life.

Social Services has inflicted this daily physical and mental abuse upon me. The emotional abuse I lived with was much worse. The SS remain, Un-forgiven. I learned to hate every one, and every thing. That was the only thing Hammersmith, and the school ever taught me.

I learnt never to take any money or valuables to school, because they would be robbed. Most teachers were completely useless, and seemed to know less than I did.

Sometimes I watched the boys fight, and they did not scratch and bite like the girls. They punched, but not wide-armed like the girls. They punched straight and true. I decided to fight like a boy.

I practiced in the prison cell they called my bedroom for hours every night. It was hard at first, but I kept the image of boys punching in my mind, and checked my stance in the mirror. I managed it, even though it took me a couple of days, but the next time I was bullied, I laid out my attacker with a single punch to the jaw.

She was a lot bigger and older than I was. I didn't get detention for the first time ever. After that, the bullying virtually stopped. I learned not to wait, but attack first, as soon as anyone I did not know or like, approached me. I learned how to do the trips and throws the best fighters used, and I even bashed-in a couple of boys a year older than me, and that felt really great.

Unexpectedly I had new friends, and I thought that sucked more than any of the other horrors of this childish hellhole. It seemed to me, that only pond-life inhabited that particular school, both as peers and teachers — they were all bottom-feeders. Neither disappointed my appraisal.

I needed to wise-up, and quickly. I learnt to act stupid, most did not, and already were.

Most of those initial days were horrendous, but I dumbed everything down and started to make deliberate mistakes in my work, aiming to come down to the same educational level as the cretins and teachers. It appeared to work, because they lost interest in me.

The English teacher worked out what I was doing, and spoke to me kindly. She gave me more advanced homework, and encouraged me to read books. Otherwise, the teachers appeared to be more disinterested in class than their disruptive pupils.

I had hardly spoken more than a word to the other girl in the foster home, Wednesday. She ignored everybody, but liked to tease moths with lit candles, and was making a taser to use on frogs. She tried it out on my knees at breakfast one day, and I kicked her. She was well-weird.

Sometimes I caught her momentarily staring at me from across the playground. As soon as I looked at her, she always turned away, and pretended to be busy doing something completely different.

I noticed she was never hassled at all, and decided to be like she was. I watched her, when she was not watching me. In time, I copied some of her moves and ways. It seemed like a means to survive. But then I stopped. I did not like her, and refused to become like her.

As I adapted to the new and seemingly dysfunctional school, so I tried to adapt to life in a foreign household.

It was not going well. I usually cried several times each day, and wondered why my parents did not come to rescue me. I was all-alone in the world. I was planning my escape, and with vivid dreams of family reunion multiplying, yet was getting nowhere fast in my real life.

Soon the rows at the foster home escalated. We had the same breakfast every single day, except Sunday, when we were allowed a small variety pack of cereal, a little low-fat, UHT milk, and no sugar. My lunchbox usually contained one crust-less Spam sandwich with lettuce or cucumber, an apple or orange, and a tomato. The only other item was a very small pot of cheap jelly.

I put up with it for a few days, before telling matron what I thought. I also knew she was making a bomb out of keeping us. It changed from being a daily issue, into an argument every time we met. She usually finished these encounters by slapping me hard, but seldom on the cheek unless it was Friday or Saturday.

I started deliberately disobeying her, and saying, "No."

I told her she was not my mother, which led to a long lecture on how lucky I was to finally find a loving family to look after me.

I spat in her face, and tried to claw her eyes out, literally.

I was grounded forever. That meant room imprisonment, except for meals. That was all we were ever allowed to do anyway, so nothing had changed. The bitch was just too stupid to see it.

I began to put a leaving draw together, and it was pretty empty, the sum of my life so far. I determined that would change, and people would remember 'Isabella Waites'.

I sewed Grandpa's teddy bear back together again, but like me, he was irreparably damaged.

Nevertheless, nothing changed.

Dinner was the only meal that varied. Whole or sliced boiled potatoes, assorted greens, and a little meat. I was always hungry, except on Sunday's.

On 'The Lord's Day', after breakfast, we went up to change into our Sunday best, before walking a mile to church. It was mega-boring, and they did a lot of God posing stuff, outside. Afterwards we went to the same carvery every time. I know matron took us there because it was cheap, and filled in her tick boxes. Nevertheless, this was the only meal of the week where we could have seconds, and the next week I had a third plateful. I was that ravenous, I could have eaten a horse.

The following Sunday I wised-up. I took extra meat to replace the Spam in my sandwiches. I also took extra rolls and small packs of butter, and loads of salt sachets. Hiding in a secluded corner near the servery, I put the food into a plastic wallet inside my bag. The next Sunday the head chef caught me, and I knew I was in big trouble.

I expected him to expose me as a thief and call the police. Instead, he pulled me to one side and asked me a few questions. I ended up telling him why I was starving.

Once said, he stared through me for a long while, before patting my hand in a fatherly way. He looked me in the eye and said, "Next Sunday, I will make the package especially for you — just come and see me. My name is 'Chef'. But you young lady, can call me Howard."

I was so happy I started to cry in relief. Finally somebody was caring for me.

His honesty and kindness gave me hope, something to cling to, like a beacon shining through the darkness my days had become. I hugged him in thanks, and he patted me gently on the back as if sealing our forbidden friendship.

The next Sunday I did not expect him to keep his promise, or even remember me. But when I went up for thirds, the carver told me to go through the door to my left. I entered the kitchen and Howard greeted me enthusiastically. I had been extremely worried, but he remembered me, and that was all I cared about.

He handed me a package and told me to hide it well. I could not see inside, but it felt very heavy.

Later, I opened it in the room they said was my bedroom, but it never could be. Howard had vacuum-packed meat for six days. There was a note telling me it would keep outside the fridge until opened. There were rolls, butter packs, and loads of sauces and spices. He even included plastic cutlery, paper plates, and thick tissues. At last, I had a new friend in that foreign land. I ate some of it the next morning after breakfast, putting a bit more in my bag for school. I felt good for the first time since the SS had kidnapped me.

That feeling was shattered on Thursday, when Wednesday spotted me eating in school, and for the first time spoke to me.

"I'm telling mother on you, and I will electrocute you when we get home." That was all she said.

Those were to be the only words she ever said to me.

Mother? She meant 'matron' surely. Or was she their daughter? Adopted daughter? I knew she had moved on to tasering cats and small dogs. And I was to be her new guinea pig: No. Never.

Wednesday was one seriously fucked-up kid. I needed away from her, and her home, her parents. I knew it was time I stepped up, became myself, and escaped into the unknown. Surely it couldn't be worse than living a half-life, as I had been doing. Sure, I felt like a zombie.

She walked away without a care in the world, and I knew I was doomed. I tried to leave school by the back way, but was caught by a teacher and dragged kicking and screaming back to class, and detention once more. Matron was there to collect me for the first time since day one. She slapped my face so hard I passed out.

I woke up in my room, and tried the door. It was locked as usual, from the outside. I packed my bag for the last time. I was ready to leave. The door was made of wood. I reasoned if I used the bedding to set fire to it, I could get out.

The bedding lit easily, but instead of flames, the room filled with acrid smoke. My breath started to catch, and I was soon coughing in convulsions. I headed for the window, but tripped and fell. I lost consciousness when my head hit the corner of the dressing table and the room filled with obnoxious black smoke.

With my last conscious thought, I knew I was going to die. I willed myself to live.

Bilty

"I'm gonna finish here for today Bilty. The next chapter of my life will begin tomorrow, if you are free?"

"Yes, I will be here. Same time?"

"Good. That will be about when I escaped. And when I first realised how divisive the Family Courts and the SS had been. It'll get lighter for a while, before we get to the real crimes they committed. It should be a longer session, but this hurts me, very deep inside. I gotta go, save my sanity.

"Zoë, a stiff drink if you please.

"Bilty, I'll see you next time. Byeee."

Bilty:

Personal Journal:

I cannot relate the Court's acceptance of a charge of 'possible, future, emotional abuse' to what she has suffered since being taken into care. There appears to be extreme emotional abuse. Even now, more than a decade later, she cannot retell it without a very stiff drink. I tried a sip when she was otherwise engaged: Very strong Bacardi and cola.

But, there are other ramifications. IW's previous academic excellence was cruelly compromised by the decision to remove her from home. I know that today, she is highly educated. She was also, for her age, in Manchester. In London, she was in a very poor school, and her academic development was severely hindered. This was most definitely not in her best interests. Yet, Family Court and Social Services condoned it. It appears, they were condemning her to a life of low expectations, when her own, and her parent's was of the highest. That is unforgivable.

Point:

After all these years, it remains her yesterday, and IW feels it today, as if were happening all over again. Regards my wife's ghost-writing, this is excellent, but I remain most perturbed by Isabella's revelations, and we haven't got to the bad bits yet.

Notes:

1. The most notable point of this session, was the immediate change in IW's bearing when she talked about chef Howard. She pointedly stated, "At last, I had a new friend in that foreign land."

"His honesty and kindness gave me hope, something to cling to, like a beacon shining through the darkness my days had become." Those are not the words of somebody who is happy, they are an anathema.

2. I eventually got her play on the name 'Wednesday', and so typical of her requited sense of humour.

3. Or, am I dealing with facts, as yet to be revealed? Thinking deeper, Isabella was stating that the foster home was like living with the remnants of a fictional TV series, there can be no mistake.

4. She is talking aside now, to her friends, and yet, she still holds an air about her none other does. As if she had endured the impossible, survived, and yet had the perspicacity to come out the other side.

It is rare to meet an Alpha Female, one who is so laid back. Most are in your face, challenging men in their own domain. But not Isabella. Instead, she is challenging the entire system. On the other hand, she remains unassuming, but assumes complete charge.

I called my wife and made a date for dinner. Isabella's story, the woman herself, was becoming most unsettling. I also needed to speak to Candice about it; so many things were wrong. Isabella was just a child back then. I cannot imagine.

Chapter 6 – Kidnapped

Project Domicile
Interview: 03
Location: Fiddlers Court, The Oval, Holborn, Central London.
Time: 14:12 hours, Thursday, 12th October.
Subject: Isabella Waites.
Others Present:
    Melanie and Zoë. Others of her clique come and go.
Observations:
    The interview room is becoming familial. People take their places, and we are soon to begin. A routine has been set it seems.

Isabella

I was only knocked-out for seconds, otherwise I would be dead.

I came to disorientated, as the bedding started to burn properly. The window. I knew I had to get there and take my chances. I realised I would break a leg if I jumped to the ground, but the carpet was smouldering, and the room again filling with poisonous black smoke.

There was a garage set to one side, and I thought I could make the leap onto the roof. I threw my rucksack down and balanced on the window ledge. I heard hammering at the door, and jumped for my life.

I didn't quite make it. I landed with some of my chest on the roof, and most of the rest of me dangling in thin-air. I tried to dig my fingernails into the roof tiles, but started to slide. I couldn't do anything about it. I was headed into a black abyss when my fingers tightened on the edge of a cast iron gutter. The sharp edge really hurt, but I held on for dear life, until it began to give way.

I knew the drop was now six feet from my fingers, and I let go. I landed easily, picked up my rucker, and ran for my life.

I made the street, and ducked behind hedgerows and parked cars when I heard sirens approaching. They never saw me. I was free at last. I missed mummy and daddy so very much, and knew they missed me. I was going home.

I intended to head for Howard's Inn, but was being driven by sirens and circumstances in the opposite direction. I had no idea where I was, except I was lost. A clock told me it was almost one a.m.

I was tired and needed to sleep. I heard another siren and ducked down an alley. Around the corner at the far end, I found a cardboard city, and chose one of the empty berths for the night. I pulled someone's large coat over me, and used my rucker to pretended I was bigger.

I slept badly and intermittently. I was awfully scared.

The next thing I knew, I was brought awake by the sound of bin men as they emptied the nearby skip. I jumped awake and hunkered back away from them involuntarily. I stretched out, my arm under the makeshift pillow, and found a bump in it. I looked. It was a cobblestone hidden under the cardboard mattress. I pried it up, and found a plastic bag beneath. Inside was an envelope full of money, a lot of money.

I knew stealing was wrong, so promised to come back one day and repay the guy. I argued with myself that if he had left it behind, he could be dead, or locked-up for life in prison.

I did not believe myself, but it was enough of an angle to allow me to take what I needed; several hundred pounds of money — he had a lot more. I almost put it back, before thinking I would need some smaller notes and change. I cleaned him out of those.

I got the Underground train to Euston, and made it to the real railway station on the moving pavement. I loved it. I wandered into the large ticket hall and eventually worked out which train I needed a ticket for. It was most confusing.

I was headed for the ticket office, when I was plagued by a sudden doubt. I realised a young girl on her own would soon be spotted and questioned. Police and security were everywhere, and I was at last wising-up. I didn't have any answers, so sat by an elderly couple for a while, and we chatted.

Later, a businesswoman passed by, and I heard her say into her mobile, "I'll be there for the meeting in Manchester as planned, so long as this train runs on time. Have a car ready to collect me, and I'll advise you if we are delayed. I should have 'railway internet' in ten."

I decided she would have already gotten her ticket online, because people with loads of money to spare, can claim a discount that way. The poorest always have to pay top price at the ticket office. I knew I had to speak to her, she was my real ticket to getting on the train.

"Excuse me miss, but I want you to know that when I grow up, I want to be just like you. What do you do?"

She was startled, indifferent. I continued speaking to her, and she spoke to me for long enough for others to notice. I grabbed her hand, beseeching, "Where do they sell train tickets, my mother's not well enough, so I have to go."

She pointed, but I made out I didn't know. I grabbed her hand and said, "Show me."

She grabbed me by the arm, and it hurt. She hustled me to the door. "In there! Now leave me alone."

Again she pointed, and the clerk saw us. That was all I needed for my ruse. I kept my palm flat, and shook her hand, appearing to put something in the pocket where my money was stashed. We both hurried away, our destinies to seek. By then she was on another call.

I got my ticket, and waited until she blustered past the ticket kiosk, headed for the platform. She was still talking into her mobile as if her life depended upon it.

I followed at her heels, but she was aware of me. Glancing back she said, "Don't you dare, young lady."

Perfect. I said to the ticket checker, "Mother's always like this." I rolled my eyes and yawned. He laughed. He wished me a safe journey, and within minutes, I was on the train home.

During the journey, the Guard checked my ticket, and asked why I was alone. I said, "Mummy's gone for some food. I'm really hungry."

He accepted my ruse. I also moved around, so I was never in one place too long. Nobody was interested in checking me when we reached Manchester Piccadilly Station, they took passenger's tickets and waved everyone through.

I was home, and it almost smelled right.

Manchester Piccadilly Station was massive, and as big as Euston. I had found it easy to get into the latter, but getting out of that station in the right place was becoming a problem. I worried my face would already be appearing on news boards: 'Missing child'. Huh? I was trying find my way home to my parents.

I paid a rip-off busker £10 for his hoodie, and went undercover. I made the streets, and had no idea where I was, except knowing I was still a long way away from my real home. A horn blared nearby, and turning, I noticed a police car headed slowly my way. I walked in another direction, changing streets and direction as I went.

I lost the Bussies, and in time, I wandered back the way I thought I came, but nothing was remotely familiar. Day turned to evening, and eventually, into night.

I was lost.

The road was quiet, so I pulled my hoodie back to get fresh air and shake my hair. I walked a little further, but froze when I heard a horn hoot and a car pulled up just in front of me. I started to run in the opposite direction, before I heard the friendly voice of our neighbour. His wife called my mum, and she arrived within fifteen minutes. I never thanked my rescuers properly, because I was awash with tears and relief. Soon, my own mother was holding me in her arms once more. She never stopped telling me how much she loved me, and missed me.

I have never, ever, again, been so happy since that night.

The kindly neighbours left, and after our tears subsided, mum called Social Services. They had finished work for the day, the number was never answered. We sat in the car, and Mum decided we should go home and work out what to do. I just loved being with her, my real mother. After the horrors inflicted upon me recently, I was so happy and relieved.

When we were home, I looked in on my brother, but he wasn't there. Mother said he was with my Grandparents, and my father was working away. I accepted her words at face value. I later learned she was trying to protect me from other atrocities Social Services, in collusion with the police, and Family Court, had decided to inflict upon our once happy family. Their wilful abuse of power was destined to empower my hatred of them all.

I asked my mother, "Why can't we be together anymore?"

She was evasive, which was not like her. She said, "It has to be this way for a while, but I will get you back soon."

We were very close after that, and being held tightly in her arms meant the world to me. For the first time in ages, I felt loved and secure.

[Bilty: "I think that says it all regards emotion comfiture versus abuse. Go on."]

I wanted to turn the clock back, but Mum explained why it was impossible. Her voice was flaky sometimes, and she cried too often.

She left a message on the SS' most senior operator's telephone, "Isabella Waites, my daughter, has turned up here, and was walking the worst streets of Manchester at 2 a.m. tonight. I have her, and she is safe. I am too drained to return her to Hammersmith tonight, so will bring her back first thing tomorrow. Do not worry. I will comply fully with the Court Order, although I totally disagree with it. You should be taking much better care of her. Sabrina Waites."

I knew mum was worried, as the lights were low, and she kept glancing out from behind the curtains. In between, I snuggled into her warmth as we cuddled close on the settee. I loved her with all my heart.

She spoke gently as we hugged, explaining why she had to take me back. Unexpectedly she broke from me, at a noise on the street, and watched from the curtains again. I knew something was wrong, very wrong. I said, "Why don't we leave here and hide our trail?"

I thought she had not heard me, but she had been thinking. She looked at me and said, "We leave in two-minutes, fill a bag, but leave anything important behind."

We were in the car minutes later and were away. She diverted several times from the straight route. She told me it was to avoid the new traffic-cams, the ones with instant number-plate recognition.

We made it to the M6, and I had begun poking her to stay awake at the wheel, but she insisted she had to do this for all of us. By that, I knew she was including father, and my baby brother. I hugged her, and opening the window, she came more alert. On the M1 we stopped once for a break. She got us burgers, chips, and drinks from a fast food place, which we ate in the car. She fell asleep just before I did.

Apparently, she woke when a car full of rowdy joyriders pulled in to park alongside us, with loud music blaring. She pulled off as soon as her mind was in gear. I came to when we were off the Motorway, and onto the streets of London. Traffic was light so early in the morning, but it was still a lot more than I was used to. I was napping, awake for a few minutes, asleep for another couple.

I later found out from a friend of a friend, that at that time eight armed police had broken down the front door of our home searching for me. They completely ransacked our house in the process, looking for evidence. By that time, we were long-gone.

They caught us in Shepherds Bush, if only because some moron failed to see a red light, as we passed through the green go. It was awful, and our car was totalled. I hit my head hard on the passenger window, and my neck hurt. I told mum I was OK. She was bleeding, so I offered her tissues, but she seemed not to hear me.

The cops arrived, followed by paramedics. The first was a normal patrol car and they were OK, for cops. Minutes later, the armed police screeched to a halt and they ran from their van to surround us. They bravely pointed their pistols and machine guns at us. Mother was still disorientated from the accident, but grabbed me and we fell to the tarmac. This time it was exactly like in the movies — it was extremely frightening, horrifically real. I thought they would kill us both.

They didn't kill us, which was wonder. They applied handcuffs to my mother, and me. They weren't proper ones, but strips of zip-lock. I wasn't impressed. We were put in the back of different patrol cars and they asked me a lot of questions.

Soon, more police arrived, but these were in unmarked cars. Two men who looked and acted like street thugs or bouncers, took me to their car for interrogation. They seemed pretty shifty for police officers, and apologised that there wasn't a woman present. I looked out of the window, and nodding, stated, "Well I can see three just outside, and my mother is just over there, so bring one of them in."

"They are not acceptable in your situation."

"Well what about either of those two policewomen over there?"

They said, "Shut up, " so I did. They told me they were Detectives. I did not believe them because they smelled kinda funny, and looked like thugs dressed in suits. They asked me why my mother ran a red light, and I sat there dumb.

They told me to answer the question, and I replied, "Will you make up your minds. First you tell me to be silent, and now you want me to talk. Which is it?"

One of the gorilla's face reddened, and his fist muscles tensed. The other exclaimed menacingly, "Just answer the question!"

I said, "We stopped for the red light, pulled off after it turned fully to green, and this jerk ran into us. I bet you already know that from the traffic cams, look there are several on this junction. Morons!"

I thought the bigger one was going to hit me, but his accomplice put out a restraining arm.

I was taken to Hammersmith high security police station. It was not like a normal one from the TV. It was a prison where they interrogate Al Qaeda terrorists, serial killers, and Isabella Waites.

I never saw my mother again, and don't even know if she was in the same police station. I hoped she wasn't. It was very scary.

I was treated like a guilty criminal caught in the act, and put in a holding cell. Time passed and I got loads of time to plot what I was going to say. My hands took on a life of their own. I became aware I was subconsciously wringing the backs of my hands, rubbing my palms together, and pulling or clenching my fingers. I forced myself to stop, only to start pulling my hair. Nobody came. I had just fallen asleep on the awful bed, when the door clanged open, and I was dragged half-asleep to answer questions.

I was put in another cell, that one had "Interview Room 3" written on the door. It looked about the same as where they had just taken me from, except for a table, some hard plastic chairs, and a strange machine instead of a bed. A female police officer asked me if I would like something to eat and drink. I said, "Yes please, I'm starving."

The woman didn't need to go to the door to ask, so I knew they were listening in on us. I looked around to see if there were any sniper positions hidden in the ceiling, as she tried to be nice to me. The cell door opened, and I was handed a paper cone of water, which I had to hold in my hand. I was also given a pack of stale, dry, plain biscuits, which needed two hands to open. I spilt some of the water in the process of prying the hard-sealed plastic wrapper apart.

That was the very first time I had proof adults say one thing, when they mean something else. I said so at once, and again as soon as two goons came in, and started the tape machine. It was so old and decrepit I had to laugh. They stopped the recording and told me off, telling me I was in deep trouble. They restarted the machine once they imagined I was cowed. There were only four of us in the cell.

I didn't understand what they were saying, but it seemed I was in deeper shit. I screamed, "You are frightening me. I want my mother?"

The machine was turned off again. They gave me another lecture on how I had to answer their questions. I was so bored, I stared at the walls. They rewound the machine to scrub my last comment. I stared at the ceiling and hoped they would go away quickly. They did not. They continued to bully me.

I don't think I was any good at their game, because they seemed to know the rules, and I did not. They also knew the answers I was supposed to say, but I did not understand the questions. I didn't like them a lot, and told the truth.

The antique machine was turned off, again, and I remember the very long buzzing sound it made. I knew they were going to beat me up, so I dived under the table. They tried to catch me, but I was quicker and a lot more agile. I ripped one tape out of the machine when they went in the wrong direction.

I ran for the door and turned the handle with little time to spare. I knew I was out, except they had locked the door. I banged it with my hands and kicked it with my feet. It was metal so I knew somebody would hear me. I hoped it would be my mother.

One of the gorillas wrestled me to the ground as I tried for freedom. He was so leery. He sat astride my tummy and held my arms to the floor above my head. I had no idea why. He has very heavy, and I coughed because it was hard to breath. I was handcuffed, again, and informed I was a dangerous prisoner.

I screamed back, "Get Real! I am an eight-year old girl, kidnapped from my family, by you!"

I kept saying that over, and over, and over again, but nobody believed me. So much for 'Law and Order'. I knew from that moment, I was destined to be an Outlaw.

I was put back in a cell. It was horrendous and worse than the last one. The door would not open from the inside. I cried, but nobody came

That is physical, mental, and emotional abuse, as administered by the police. I was only there because of Social Services. I hate them all.

Bilty

Isabella immediately stood and walked away, Zoë going with her. She turned in the doorway, and with the force of a Californian Governor stated, "I'll be back!"

Bilty:
Personal Journal:
Yet again I note the physical, mental, and excessive emotional abuse inflicted on this very young girl. She had committed a minor wrong. For her, she ran away, back home, because that is where she wanted to be. The Family Courts ignored her wishes.

The use of armed police, again, is totally unjustified, as is her interview in the car. These are clear breaches of <u>PACE</u> [R 6.1], the Police and Criminal Evidence Acts of 1984, and subsequent amendments, such as the Serious Organised Crime and Police Act 2005, and the <u>Police (Detention and Bail) Act 2011</u> [R 6.2].

The search of the home in Manchester would be illegal, given Social Services already knew the child was being returned. Their competence to look after IW I seriously call into question. Again, why were armed police sent. This is a mother and young child.

Then we come to Hammersmith High Security Police Station; it is not a nice place. I have been there to see an informant, and I am sure IW was terrified. That she stood her ground does her great credit.

Point of note:
IW was eight years old at the time.

Notes:
1. People do not run away if they are happy.
2. It is obvious the SS did not believe IW was being returned by her mother. Yet, not enough time had elapsed for this to be proven as abduction, perhaps escape.
3. The immediate, and total overreaction by SS on discovering the situation does great discredit to Child Services.
4. Significantly more worrisome, is the unquestioning obedience of the police, as if thoughtless puppy dogs, in actioning SS whims.
5. Surely, armed, specialist police units, were completely unnecessary in all incidents. The friendly face of a beat bobby and WPC, would have been far more appropriate. Therefore, the objective could only be intimidation, plus mental and emotional harassment.

Afterthought:
I wonder if the systems used against her, weren't creating a bigger threat for the future. It only takes one person to stand up and fight, before many others join them.

I remain extremely worried by the fate of IW, and many thousands of other young girls, who found themselves in similar circumstances. Except, that as I finish my notes, I see her return, as if nothing is untoward. She is talking, laughing with friends; is this all a front? I know she survived, but at what cost? I will soon to find out.

She came to me, "Time to finish this part, and all of it for today. I'll go as far as the Streets of London, so if you are sitting comfortably, I'll begin: My first time in Hammersmith High Security Nick. Listen-up."

Chapter 7 – A New Prison

Isabella

I had been crying, and sometimes my anger made me shout out things like, "Set me free," and "Take me home. I want my mother."

I think it was hours later, but anyway, it was a very long time, before a man I did not know opened a grill thing and looked at me. He yelled, "Shut the fuck up or we will make this even worse for you."

I imagined his implications of torture and beatings. I knew they must have a rack for wrenching off people's arms and legs. I decided to play along with their games, at least until I escaped.

After the most wonderful night, when I was held severely tight in my mother's arms, I was now back in hell. My same friend of a friend later told me mother was treated exceedingly roughly by the cowboy cops, and charged with kidnapping [R 7.1], and motoring offences. I was held for 'my own protection', from my mother. Can you believe that? I do not, because it was totally ludicrous!

Eventually some moron from Social Services, Hammersmith, bothered to come and collect me. It was not the same bitch that I saw before, but she took me to be interrogated in a sort of childish, comfy area. I spat at her all the same, and made to run for it the first chance I got. I escaped the room, but the bullyboy Bussies captured me despite my boy punches and kicks. They rugby-tackled me to the ground and handcuffed me, again. They started calling me 'Wildcat' after that, and I sort of liked it. It buffed my ego, the little remaining sense of being 'me'.

My respect for any form of authority, except that of my parents, had been ripped out of me, by the system that continued to abuse me.

My mind was in turmoil. I had done nothing wrong, nothing that a free man could not do. I realised I was a woman, and a young one: Different rules applied.

"Is this going to be the story of my life? Handcuffed and incarcerated for doing nothing wrong," I asked myself. The new woman carer refused to take me in, so later that day I found myself in Hammersmith police cells, yet again.

The next day at seven a.m., I had to pass the stupid doctor's inquisition once more. There was a policewoman nearby who never spoke. It was a different doctor, but the questions were identical.

That time I was not suffering a hangover, or Ecstasy overdose, and brought the medic up to speed quickly. That almost worked to my disadvantage, but I was young and got away with it. I learned a lot that morning. Before determining his report, he received a phone call, and I was immediately signed-off.

I was referred to 'Counselling', but that never happened. Instead, a suited woman, who told me what I must, and must not do, talked at me.

Afterwards, I was put back in the police cell with instructions to think deeply about my conduct. Everything they said was a lie, and I knew it. They were just the same as matron, imbeciles, but too dumb to see it.

Hours passed and I gouged a chunk of plaster out of the wall behind the door, as I tried to escape. I was working to free a brick, and getting nowhere fast, when the sound of keys jangled, before metal came into the lock. I rushed back to my bed and concealed my weapon, a short bit of broken bedspring. I had tried to unlock the door with it first, but real life is not like a spy film. Some of us know this.

The policeman, and policewoman that never spoke, entered and took me to an interrogation room. I was told to sit and wait. The woman stayed with me, and I knew they were preparing the 'waterboard'. I was expecting the wires and snorkel at any moment.

I tried to speak to her, but she said, "Shut up child." I did not like her at all and told her so. I continued speaking, but she was deaf. After a very long time the door opened, and the SS woman came in with another woman. I did not like her at once. Her smile appeared and she told me her name, and that she was there to take me to her home. I wanted to run, but the door was locked again. I screamed at her, "I hate you!" and broke down in tears.

The SS bitch put a piece of paper down on the table and told me to sign it. I refused. I had never, ever, signed my own name before.

She said, "You will never leave this room until you do. Make a cross if you do not know how to write yet. Your mother does not love you [R 7.2] and wants rid of you, she wants to kill you, that is why we have found new parents for you."

I railed at her and let flow a stream of big words. I didn't know what most of them meant, but they sounded good. "...I know my mum loves me, and you are lying. You have kidnapped me. You have caused me extreme emotional distress, and I demand to go home!"

She started shouting at me before I was finished. She said all sorts of nasty things about both my mum and dad, and I shouted back at her, "You are a liar!" I even tried to bite her, and marked her real good, just before she hit me. My jaw really hurt, and I thought it was broken, but I carried on speaking out against her, "That is physical abuse. I'm gonna report you for hitting a child. I can't hear properly anymore."

That was physical abuse. She had hit me. But I was too emotional at the time to use the fact against her. I was also too young to fully know the implications. But she hit me very hard, and that remains a fact.

I crossed my arms over my chest, and looked straight ahead at nothing. Exasperated, the woman asked for the policewoman's assistance. After a lot of talk, they made it clear I had to sign the form. I knew it was a trick, but what could I do?

I picked up the pen, and stabbed her hand as hard as I could.

She screamed with pain, and later frustration, and hit me again. I tried to stab her in the heart, but missed because she moved quicker than a snake. We ended up in a mess on the floor, with her easily overpowering me. However, I had made a good dent in the wooden chair she had been sitting in, and taunted her with my mark. Her pen was wrecked, and she scolded me. I laughed in her face.

Undeterred, she nodded to the unspeaking policewoman, who shackled me with handcuffs. The bitch even told me I was a dangerous criminal. The interrogator produced a second form, filled in my name, and asked the officer to sign it as witness. I was physically dragged out of the room bawling and screaming, and put in the back seat of her car, my wrists and ankles bound by police zip locks.

[Bilty: "Words fail me. Sorry, Isabella, but I'm losing the plot here. They physically hit you, twice. Bound you, typically meaning you were under arrest. And from what you related, you were kidnapped; I refer only to legal definitions I know of.

"I'll research these fully, later. Continue, please."

"It's the truth of what happened, Bilty. You have my word. But, we were never allowed to complain about our treatment."]

I was bundled into the back seat of a car, and as she drove, I started kicking the back of the driver's seat as hard as I could. I made a tear, but that did not last long. She pulled over to the pavement and stopped the car. I knew what she was doing and tried to open the passenger side door to escape. She had activated the child locks, and stood outside laughing at me. She threatened to put me in the boot and started to drag me out of the car, until I wised-up and promised to be good.

I was not good. I was very good. I kept working the tear I had made in her seat. It felt great at the time and kept me occupied. I covered it with my body when we arrived some place, and it was not until later I discovered her full wrath. It turned out the car was a BMW something or other. It looked like an off-roader, but wasn't. It was a fake 4x4, a modern, trendy imitation of the real thing, just like she was.

I later discovered the seat was honed from the finest Connolly leather. It looked and felt like plastic to me, but what did I know?

Still bound, I was carried to another cell, which they called 'my room', not my bedroom. My bonds were released and I lashed out, but missed. Those people were good. The door slammed shut, and I heard the lock click over three times before a deadbolt was slammed across, from the outside.

I had ended up in prison again. A care home, and the room was bare. I had a metal bed with a hard mattress. There was a metal sink, and that was it. There was nothing else except sheets for the bed. I was let out for meals, but under strict guard. All the other girls seemed to do what they pleased, and several were smoking. I knew they were trouble and only glanced at them from my side vision.

The second day I was woken at 6 a.m. for breakfast. I was still asleep on my feet, and the only one in the canteen. The food was rancid, precooked, and even the fried eggs were already cold and undercooked. I was led away before anyone else came into the large dining hall. Lunchtime food was similar, but there were other people about; all of them a lot bigger and older than I was.

I was one of the last allowed down for dinner, and was handed a plate that had been left out for me. I was told the matron (bitch) had discovered what I had done to her driver's seat. The food was inedible, all gristle and no meat. It looked like somebody had already eaten all the good bits, and spat out the bad. I wanted to puke.

The gang leader waltzed over nonchalantly, and flicked her cigarette ash in my food. Half a dozen other girls, all heathens, surrounded me. She shoved her boot on the table, and in doing so, knocked my dinner into my lap, where it slid and crashed onto the floor. The plate shattered and they tried to make me lick the soles of her Dr Martens, before ramming my face into the remains of my meal. She said, "Bitch, this is part-payment for wrecking matron's car."

I fought back, despite them being twice my age. I freed one arm and landed a very good punch. The bully hit me back. The blow, a 'boy punch', landed full on my chin. I don't know what happened next.

I came to sometime later. I do not know when, but it felt like a while. I was back in my cell, alone. My body hurt everywhere, and I was covered in blood and vomit. I cried.

As soon as I did, knocks came battering my door, and the bullies called me names much worse than 'Sissy', and 'Mummy's Girl'. Some of the words I had never heard of before. I had no idea, at that time, what they meant. I knew they did not sound very nice, especially the way they said them. Yet again, I was suffering extreme physical, mental, and emotional abuse. This was directly due to the actions of the SS, and Family Court. I realised they didn't care a thing about me. But why? I tried to work out their angle, but gave up, it was too adult for me to understand.

I smelled dry sick, and realised I had been thrown on my bed as I was. My pillow wreaked where my face had been, and touching my cheek, I felt the crusted remains of my own vomit. Gross. I tried to get up, but everything hurt. I felt queasy, and a little giddy. I guessed they put the boot in after I passed out.

I hobbled shakily to the sink in great pain, but nothing was broken. My eye hurt and was puffy. I stripped off and saw boot marks on my skin, knowing the deep red welts would later turn a nasty purple. There weren't as many bruises as I imagined. Presumably they gave up once they realised I was out cold, and not aware of what they were doing.

I washed myself as best as I could, using the sink. The single tap had only cold water. It was freezing cold. It was difficult, as I was only just taller than the bowl. Eventually I clambered up onto it, and sort of had a bath. This was my life as fact, not notional SS fiction.

The exercise helped get my muscles working again, and while the pain remained, it was much less by the time I had washed my hair. There was no soap, no shampoo, and my hair was frizzy when it eventually dried the next morning. I washed out my top, plus anything that looked or smelled of sick, including the pillow case.

I needed to poo, and I had to do it. I banged the door and called for the guards, which only encouraged the female thugs outside. There was only the hand basin. I lowered my panties and did it in the sink. It was gross. Afterwards, I had to clean myself, plus ponderously at first, wash my pooh away with my own prodding fingers: Gross.

Something within me died that day. I was no longer a little eight-year old girl. I was changing into something else. I was becoming me!

I went to bed, but the banging and chants got worse, so I stuck my figures in my ears, and stopped crying aloud. I still sobbed, and tears rolled down my cheeks. I knew I had to escape from that living hellhole. The next morning I was one of the last released for breakfast. I put on my damp clothes, and nobody noticed. The guard let me out of the cell, and I immediately tried to get back in.

The gang was waiting for me, and the ringleader asked me to be a part of their gang. I was still learning, so said, "OK."

She was nice to me, that is, until she chose my breakfast for me. The cooks turned away and would not look at me, they had seen it all before. I knew something was seriously wrong.

I walked back to their table with my tray. I was looking for any way to escape, but I was surrounded. I reasoned that if the gang wanted me to join them, they would protect me from others. Huh!

I learned I was their target. I was not allowed to eat, but had to sit with my hands inside the top of my thighs. They wanted me to frig myself, but I had no idea what they meant. It seemed to involve me moving my hands up and down the crack of my jeans.

At the end of it, I was none the wiser, but they shot video on their mobiles all the same. I was slapped every time I tried to move away. My cheeks stung, but there were no lasting marks, except for my black eye

[Isabella: "Bilty, I find it strange that the gang was not arrested and sent to prison for causing my black eye. After all, my father was imprisoned for the same crime, except he never hit me. My head hit a kerbstone. There were witnesses. Those things were ruled inadmissible by Family Court. My parents were imprisoned for the same offence, so why aren't those guardians of the SS prosecuted exactly the same? Am I missing something here?"

"No, Isabella. Your are entirely correct. You have been abused repeatedly, and I fear the worst is yet to come. Please go on."]

They all ate, in-between making fun of me. I resigned myself to fighting them off making me lick the bitch's soles again, but it never happened. That was the only good thing about breakfast.

Once they finished eating, everyone was offered a cigarette, except me. I hated the things anyway. They blew smoke in my face, and I tried to get away to the toilets. Hands held me down. They were much older and cleverer than I was, but that would change over time. It did not change that day.

They flicked their ash in my breakfast, and knowing what was coming, I heaved. I was hit hard on my ear, and was deaf for several minutes afterwards. With a nod, the gang extinguished their cigarettes, two landing in my orange juice. They stirred it for a long time before forcing me to drink. I spat out the filter tips, but I was made to lick them up off the floor, and swallow them. Gross does not come into it.

It got worse, not better. I thought I could take two of the girls, one on one, but the rest were far too big and strong. My cold dish of bacon and eggs was placed on the floor. The Leader flicked her ash again, and I sniggered as she missed the egg, but it dusted the bacon. She put the cigarette out in the middle of the egg, toying and stirring the runny yolk to make her mark.

The egg burst all over the plate. I was made to eat it all like a dog. Sometimes, especially where there was runny egg, boots held may face down and pressed it into the mess. Someone got up on my behind and made rapid thrusting movements. She said, "I'm riding my latest bitch," but it made no sense to me.

One time I could hardly breathe, and sucked up runny-egg into my nostrils. Nobody came to my rescue. The guards laughed, and the cooks pretended to be doing something important. The only person that could rescue me was me, and I was too small to deal with it. I endured until the bullies got bored, and guards came to lock me up again.

For the first time, I was happy to get back to my prison cell, as at least I was free from the constant persecution on the other side of the door. I was not pestered at lunchtime, but I noticed some girls were going to reception, and followed. I watched and learned. I waited until the receptionist got back into the card-game on her computer, and stole a moment on her. Arriving quickly and silently at the door I said what the others had said, "I'm going out for tampons."

The door buzzed before she looked up, but I was already gone. I didn't know what a tampon was, but it seemed to be something big girls needed. That word puzzled me for ages, but I never got to ask anyone before I understood. That did not last long either. Nothing seemed to last for long in my life.

I ran out of the door, afraid for my life. I headed left, and ducked left again down an alley. I hurried away, and threw a V sign at the back of the building. I didn't know there was a back way out until I saw the outline of the main bully. I turned around and walked away as quickly as I could, keeping well out of sight. Her day would come.

I wandered the streets for hours. I had learnt to keep to the side streets, and tried to mix with the street life. It was just so Martian.

I made it to a railway station, I think it was called Marylebone, but I'm not sure. I met a nice man in a suit who bought me a cola. He asked me, "How much for a blowjob?"

I knew he meant something I did not understand, but what?

He went to the toilet, telling me to follow. I ran away and hid, taking the cola with me. I was still puzzling about what the man said several hours later. I was by then, south of the river and heading for any place that sounded friendly. I saw an ad for the London Eye, and followed because I wanted to learn the city. The next big junction was all-wrong for pedestrians, and I was very tired. There was a sign that said Waterloo, and the setting sun echoed my emotions. I had my 'Waterloo Sunset'. I shouted out loud, "I want to meet my Waterloo."

"This was my life. Live it with me Bilty, even though I loathe it. I'm done for this afternoon. You will stay, until evening, or come again?"

"Yes Isabella, thank you. It has been a harrowing telling, even for the listener. Let's break for now, as I have some errands to run. I'd like to pick this up later this evening, it suits my schedule well. That will be about 'The Streets of London'. OK?"

"OK Bilty. Is that your real name? It's a bit weird."

"It's my pseudonym as an investigative journalist, but almost my birth name. Here's one of my favourite quotations, and most applicable in your case. 'They say that we are all haunted by a Spiritual Presence, of whose existence we are only fitfully and sometimes never conscious'."

"Hmm. That may be true. I also know of the poem you relate to, thanks for being honest ... it's a rare commodity nowadays."

Isabella's eyes seemed to lose focus for a moment, until she said, "I realised years later, presiding Judge Selwyn Lewis, Manchester, was a close friend of both Judge St. John-Smythe and Mohammed, who will be introduced, if later. He had already selected me for child prostitution.

"Tens of thousands of other girls, who through no fault of their own, and mostly at Social Services behest, and Family Court bidding, ended up as unpaid child prostitutes to Muslim rape gangs. It ain't a pretty story. Domicile; lack of any form of care.

"Huh! Tell me about it? But you cannot. I can, because I, we, lived through the hell of it."

"I now know the only reason I was ripped away from my family, was because Social Services could make a lot of money out of me, as state payments [Ref: R 7.3, Ref: R 7.4] for my care home placement and, their targets would also be met. But there is more, stick around and learn.

"Regards my life of that moment, I had escaped, but I was not free. The only place in the whole world I was not allowed to go, was *home*. Kinda sucks, don't it. I could go anywhere else.

"Until later, Bilty. And make it eight o'clock, as I have something to do beforehand. *Sayonara*."

Bilty:
Personal Journal:
I remain astounded by the avalanche of emotional abuse IW was subjected to by Social Services. This appears to be only exceeded, by the physical abuse she repeatedly endured. There appears to be zero support except, perhaps, for ticking administrative boxes.

Point:
What would her daily life have amounted to, had she still been at home. Much better, I am certain.

Notes:
1. People who are not happy react.
2. The 'Care Home' appears to be anything but. There was zero induction, no counselling, just exposure to the inhabitants bully-culture, that seemed to be overly excessive.
3. After each meeting, or segment concludes, I note the subject needs a break. I have some experience of psychiatry, and know this to be emotional release. Isabella is putting herself through the wringer to tell me this. Much respect.

Chapter 8 – The Streets of London

Project Domicile
Interview: 04
Location: Fiddlers Court, The Oval, Holborn, Central London.
Time: 20:27 hours, Thursday, 12th October.
Subject: Isabella Waites.
Others Present:
> Melanie, Zoë, and later, Vikki.

Observations:
> IW is happy, but comes straight to her armchair, and regales her past immediately. I was not expecting that. Something else may have entered the equation, but what, or whom? I found myself playing catch-up immediately.

Isabella
> Waterloo station has a smell and an underclass all of its own. It is unique. I had hoped I would meet my Prince Charming, but I found out he doesn't go there.

> Instead, I met Ratney, a slum-infesting sewer-rat who provided personal services for gentlemen. I did not know what he meant exactly, so presumed he carried bags and ran errands. He seemed OK.

> He behaved like an adult, but turned out to be fourteen, and very street-wise. We hung around, and he offered me to stay for one night. His hovel was one room, and I made it good for us. He had a boyfriend who lived with us, and I took an instant dislike to. I'm not sure why, but he was bullish, and he became a fact of my life.

> Ratney and I were often alone together. We talked, and I discovered he did blowjobs for a living, and seemed to enjoy his work. I asked him to explain what he was saying, and when he did, I wanted to be sick. I thought the whole idea was vile. I was learning about real life in the city.

> We sort-of made a deal, without ever talking about it properly. I had a roof over my head, as long as I kept the bedsit tidy, and cleaned up the mess they made. It was more fun than the dysfunctional school, safer than the care home, and I was learning a lot. I was free. I liked freedom. But what I really liked, was being in control of my own life.

> I was no longer treated like a little girl, but as an equal. The pain of being kidnapped from my family was gradually replaced by a feeling of belonging. However, that viscid scar in the depths of my heart would never heal. Meanwhile, I got on with my daily life. I learnt how the local streets and the inhabitants operated, and began to make sense of the strange world that was my new home.

Ratney was very kind to me, and I will never forget him. He taught me many things, like how to make money to survive. At first, we tried begging, which worked well until the wrong sort of people targeted me.

I learned to spot them before they saw me. He tried to show me how to steal a wallet or purse, but he was useless at it, and I didn't believe it was the right thing to do. We did not argue about it, we knew we were better at other things.

Ratney said he was very good at having sex with men he did not know. I didn't really understand sex much, but over time he tried to explain it to me. I concluded he did not know much about love.

I did not like his boyfriend. But then, I had never imagined in real life, that a man and a man could ever be partners. I had only known about a woman and a man being partners, so at first I was shocked by what he told me. I knew from the TV, that men could live together, but that wasn't real, was it. It was TV.

I also believed a boy and girl, if they were in love, might have sex. I still didn't know what all the fuss was about. For me, marriage for life to the man I adored was the only thing a girl should need.

His words bothered me. How can a man, and another man have sex? I puzzled about that for ages, and until Ratney asked me how a woman and a man could have sex together. I replied, "This is how the Good Lord God made us. Only a woman and a man can make a baby."

He laughed at me, not insensitively I should add, as we were already firm friends. He told me I was naïve. In time he taught me about sex, mainly how a man does a man, if only because he did not know how to have sex with a woman. He either did it, or was done in the mouth or bum. I thought that disgusting.

One day we were chatting, and drinking wine. He had made a lot of money that day. He told me how to give a good blowjob, even though I didn't want to hear it. I still thought that was awfully weird. I felt safe with him, but his partner always made me feel insecure.

My suspicions were confirmed one day when the other guy tried to make me do something with him. I think he would have forced me to, if Ratney hadn't come home just at that moment to protect me. I may have done Ratney, because he looked out for me, so as to practice my technique. Apparently, he thought of it as a very high skill. Much later I was to learn he was essentially correct, if sexually misguided.

I stayed for more than two weeks, but felt the need to move-on. His partner was a danger to me. I left while they were both out. I lived on the streets, begged, and took things left unattended to trade on. Like other street life, I found places to live, and moved on before anyone got wise to me. Most people I met were only interested in themselves, but some offered tips and sound advice.

The streets I walked were different, if similar. I had found a good place to go begging, but moved around as bigger people bullied me off their turf. I also avoided the police scoping for kids not at school. Some Americans stopped and talked to me. I told them a little about myself and they said they wanted to adopt me. They asked for my name and address, but I didn't tell them the real ones. I lived in cardboard city. They gave me ten quid, which was a lot of money, and promised to call.

I did not know at the time, but Ratney had been searching for me. He had been worried about me. He found me and insisted I went back with him. He told me he split up with his partner. Later that night we talked, and we both knew it would be one of our last sharing's.

Ratney explained things I needed to know about life on the street. He warned me of the dangers, like HIV. He told me to always use a condom, unless I knew the guy was clean. Even then, he said I should always use one because otherwise I might end up with a baby. I laughed and said, "Don't be silly. I am much too young to be a mummy."

I stopped laughing when he said very seriously, "My big sister got pregnant when she was just eleven years old. Always use a condom."

He was quiet for a while and I could see the hurt in his eyes. I hugged him and said nothing. It was up to him if he wanted to talk about it, to share. He never did.

A while later, he told me other things, like how much he charged, and the types of people to be wary of. During those few hours, he did his best to complete my education as a street-wise kid.

I stayed for the night, and he left early the next morning. He did not return that evening, nor the next. I tried to find out where he was, but it was useless. A week passed and I knew something bad had happened to him. I did not know what to do, but I had a roof over my head, and I was living on my own.

A few days' later, a knock came to the door and I opened it on the chain. There was a big man outside who looked mean and grubby. He asked me why I had not paid the rent on time. I said, "Ratney must have forgotten. How much do we owe you?"

"One-hundred and twenty quid, cash." He was looking at me all wrong. He told me to unchain the door so we could chat about it.

I was about to let him in, when I saw his leery smirk. From the internet, I already knew people could pretend to be whoever they wanted to be. This was exactly the same, only real-life. I asked him for his ID, but he said he was not carrying it with him. I let him believe it didn't matter, and that I would remove the chain so we could sit down and have a natter. As the door closed, I slammed it shut, my shoulder pressed into the wood, as I deadlocked the bolt.

He battered the door with his fists and boots for ten minutes or more, and I learnt a lot of new swear words in the process. Eventually he seemed to leave, but I did not trust the creep. I had a think, and laid-low, waiting for the hands of the clock to catch up with my intention. I crept out of there just before daybreak.

I cleaned Ratney out of cash and anything useful, and snuck down the fire escape a few minutes later. I left with a rucksack full of stuff I needed for survival on the streets. I kept the important stuff in my jeans, and just as well because a gang of thugs robbed me a few days later.

I met many people during those months I spent out on the streets of London, and quickly learned which ones to avoid. I worked out it was usually safer to hang out with gays, because they weren't interested in sexing me. After a few gropes and close escapes, I got to tell at once if somebody wanted me. There was a look in their eyes, or not looking at me. Sometimes just the way they held themselves around me.

I got on well with some straights. Rich was a great guy, and his mate Danno. We'd hang out sometimes, but they were from monied families, and into making a killing in their own right. They badmouthed their parent, and the establishment. I found them good fun.

Summer is a good time to be on the streets. The police aren't looking for kids not at school, and sleeping rough is not too cold most nights. I didn't realise I was nine-years old until the following week. I was in a derelict building hanging round with some kids when I saw a newspaper and read the date. I couldn't believe it. I'd missed the biggest day of my year. Mummy and daddy always made it feel so special, but out on the streets of London, it was just another day.

I had no money and wanted to buy a cake to celebrate. I went out begging, but it was useless in that neighbourhood, and I tried not to rob anyone unless I was starving. I was no good at it anyway. I gave up and was hiding out in a derelict office block, when three older kids came in bringing some cheap vodka with them. I knew two of them and was offered a swig by Rich. I coughed the first time, but the second slug went down nicely. It made my tummy feel all warm inside.

They moved through to a different room, and I went with them. I usually preferred the company of the older kids because they were more streetwise and I learned things. Danno, the other one I knew, pulled out a tin and started to roll-up. Loady, the new guy said, "She cool?"

Everyone looked at me. Rich said, "Who Bella? She's co-dee breh."

Loady took the tin and rolled a spliff. He pulled out a small bag of finely chopped, vivid green leaves and sprinkled a pinch over the tobacco. The joint was passed round and I watched how they smoked it. They did not take a drag like with a normal fag. They took a large draw and held the smoke inside for a long time. It looked well-cool.

They took three hits each before passing it on. Rich was last, and after his turn he looked at me, and offered it. I looked at the toke before reaching out and taking it from him. I tried to act cool just like them, but the smoke seared my lungs and I had to cough. All three were still looking at me, but I ignored them and took another hit. That time I managed to do it properly. I had one more drag before passing it on.

We sat around and chilled; that was my birthday party. Somehow, the vodka got me talking, but it was all gone too soon. Danno went to get another one. He was only gone for a second, or so it seemed. He came back with a load of munchies, and a birthday cake. We lit the candles, and I blew them out. We shared the feast, and shared — what I cannot remember, but it was my best Birthday Party ever. I was trashed.

Loady rolled several more spliff's and a little later somebody said something. It was so funny I burst out laughing, and that triggered everybody else. We spent hours laughing.

It was well past daylight by the time we fell asleep. I woke up in Rich's arms. My head was pounding as I tried to move. I managed to check his jeans were still on and his zip done up. I relaxed in the knowledge that nothing had happened. The effort was way too much, so I snuggled into the boy's warmth and drifted.

Rich woke up and slowly came to his senses. In spite of the loud drumming in my head, he made me giggle by telling me how bad he felt. We all slumbered, half awake, and half asleep.

The guys were good fun, and most evenings we ended up drinking and smoking spliff's. Loady was a small-time pusher and he did quite well. We got on swell together. He only sold genuine drugs, but the price was higher. He was making a name for himself all the same.

On the fifth day, I started carrying for him, and I watched how he made deals out on the street. There was a secret language used, and some special gestures as well. Three nights later, we were in a spot near a club and business was brisk. I ended up making some sales on my own, just so we could keep up with demand.

Loady left me to get some more drugs, telling me to hide until he got back. I carried on selling regardless. Fortunately, he was not gone for long, as I felt quite frightened on a couple of occasions. It was hours after midnight before we were done, and we left. I gave him all the unsold drugs, and the money I had collected. He looked at it and said, "There's a lot here Sis, you sure some ain't your own money?"

I looked up at him, shrugged my shoulders. I stated, "I don't have any money of my own."

He gave me a searching look and I turned away. He reached into his pocket and said, "Here."

I looked at his hand and saw a rolled up note. I told him "No," but he insisted. He said, "I had one of my best nights ever, and that's because of you. You earned this money tonight Sis, take it."

I took the roll and thanked him. He turned away and walked off. I'm glad he didn't see the tears in my eyes. I followed him as he went to an Underground station and made for the lockers. I was told to wait nearby, and not look. I did as instructed, but later asked him to explain.

"It's dangerous to carry drugs unless it's selling time. I usually keep a little for personal use each night, but am otherwise clean. The cops won't slam me in jail for carrying a small pack of leaves or resin."

I already knew about the Stop and Search, although being a small girl the Bussies had never searched me. He added, "I keep my money in these lockers. I was once robbed at knifepoint by a couple of thugs. I have lockers in several stations, just in case I'm caught. Always use the free ones, or the ones that return your coins."

"Why?"

"Because they check the pay ones, and have to open them to get the cash. Also, never use ones where there are cameras."

We went for a burger, and chatted. I almost felt like a normal kid for a short while. I couldn't believe it when I went to the bogs, and discovered Loady had given me twenty-five quid. I was stunned. That was more money than I had ever possessed in my life, excepting what I stole to get home that one time. My tummy felt funny and hot. This was my own money. I liked him a lot. We left when I got back to him, and he stopped to get some bottles of cheap vodka on the way back to the gang.

The next day I got my own locker and put twenty quid in it, keeping a fiver for a treat. That was my first bank account. I worked with Loady for several weeks, and made a lot of money. He taught me how to roll a normal fag, and how to make spliff's of different sizes, strengths, and types.

I also learned a lot about different drugs, and how they were cut. He warned me about dodgy stuff and what to look out for. He also made me promise never to do the hard drugs, because that was for idiots and ruined your life. I had heard that before at school, and thought it stupid. Out on the streets, I saw the results of what happened to addicts. Some were a total mess, and it shocked me to the core. I knew I would never end-up like they were.

I was pretty settled for those weeks and felt happier than I had done for ages. Nevertheless, life was always changing...

One evening Brad arrived, and Rich told me that he had just got out of Juvie [Juvenile prison]. He was older, and at first, he seemed nice. Later I saw him looking at me all wrong, and once he tried to kiss me. I went to the toilet when he was skinning-up, and never returned.

I missed those days a lot. I felt like a little girl lost and all-alone in the big city. I guess I was.

I no longer felt frightened of London's streets, but I did feel vulnerable when not with others I trusted. I had decided to go back to Marylebone, an area I wanted to know and intimately understand – at street level.

I was also headed towards Shepherds Bush, given time. My first contact with London. I would avoid Ken and Fred, they were paedophiles, and by then I understood what they wanted from me. Headed northeast, I plotted my revenge against them, and survived from one day to the next.

"I'll take five here Bilty, there are some calls I need to make; the business and all. Anyone fancy pizza? It'll keep us sober if nothing else. I will say a lot this evening, if you have time, Bilty?"

"Yes, that's ideal, but I will need to make some calls as well. A late night?"

"No, but maybe a few more hours. This is the easy part. Zoë?"

"I'll order the pizzas, but tell me what you want before you leave."

Bilty:
Personal Journal:
This evening IW seems much more relaxed, and enjoying the retelling. I can only conclude this is because accepted authorities are not involved with her story.

Point:
Isabella has shown repeatedly, even at so young an age, a rebellious and independent nature. She was happy with life and living with the lads, Loady and all, until Brad showed up. She left at the first sign of trouble for her. She has some spunk. I believe this became a part of her nature, and the why of who she is today.

Notes:
1. Watch for a change in her psyche when authorities reappear.

Ah. IW returns with Vikki, and they chat aside, before kissing on the lips. I found that a little embarrassing. Boxes of pizza are served, as are fresh drinks, and we will begin again after a short break.

As the break concluded, Isabella said, "Bilty, this is the same Vikki as in my story. You may talk to her—but later if you wish. First, let me tell of how we met.

"Vikki, don't interrupt. Pin back your lugholes, and I'll begin."

Chapter 9 – Vikki

Isabella

My plans went awry when I met Vikki and Sarah, who took me under their wings and treated me real fine. I was soon living with them. Although they were gay, they often talked about finding a guy with money. Sometimes it would be a woman, but usually a man. That puzzled me. It seemed to be the only thing they were interested in.

I told them a little bit about Ken and Fred, and they both said at once, "They're old fogey pedo's, don't go near them."

They were both very kind to me. I liked Vikki best. It turned out they did 'Tricks' to earn money. It sounded like fun. They giggled, and asked me if I had ever done tricks, and I admitted I wasn't sure what they meant. That's when my real education began, and I learned what sex was. They explained it in words I sort of understood, but I was left a bit confused.

In time, Vikki found a way to explain the difference between a man and a woman, one that I did understand. I knew I was right about the Maths teacher, when she explained a bit about what she called his 'trouser-snake'. She held me close as I told her all that had happened, and her grip on me became fierce, clingy. I wanted to escape, but saw her as my latest protectoress, my substitute mother.

Vikki never did become a substitute mother. She did become my closest confidant and advisor, teacher as well. Her enlightenment was similar too, but obliquely at odds with Ratney's view of this world. Sarah was often outspoken, and butch. I think she liked me, but she was more intense than Vikki.

One day Vikki came back home dishevelled, stating she had been raped. I did not understand how a prostitute could be raped, but apparently, it happened sometimes. Despite her bedraggled looks, she held me tight and told me a secret; "Nowadays, love has been replaced by lust, and we girls are just meat on the platter of male lust.

"Promise me, you Bella, will get the hell out of here, and make a good life for yourself. Get a good education and a University degree. Never become a pawn in this man's' game."

I heard her, and promised with the whole of my heart. I did not know much about life, a girls' life, the truth be known — in those days.

She said, "Bella, I agree to have sex for money, and that is my decision. I make a good living, but it is dangerous sometimes. My deal is the man can have sex with me, if he pays me what I ask. If we have sex and he does not pay me, that is rape. My agreement to have sex is conditional upon being paid. Nowadays I always get the money first.

"Tonight, I got separated from the girls and was on my own. A guy asked me how much and I told him, 'fifty quid for a fuck with condom'."

He laughed and belittling me, told me I was not worth that much. He was trouble. I screamed for help, and ran for the main street. But he was faster and incredibly strong. He rugby tackled me to the ground from behind, and I could not fight him off.

"Bella, do you know he was refusing to wear a condom, that was until I told him I had HIV. I do not by the way, at least I think I don't..."

Her words trailed off, and I waited while her thoughts drifted like clouds upon a merciless sea. Finally, she looked at me, before giving me advice, "He was strong. He would have taken me bareback, that's without using protection, a condom. I told him I had HIV, but he did not believe me. I said, 'Fuck you arsehole, welcome to the AIDS club'.

"He stalled. I reached into my bag and showed my appointment card for the VD clinic. I took out some packs of tablets. He took the free condom I offered. He used it as he pleasured himself at my expense."

A potential smile played around her face, finally catching the corners of her mouth as her inner strength slowly returned. She revealed a secret, "Those tablets were nothing special, headache and birth control pills. I'll explain about that another time. What he did not know, is that I get checked out at the clinic every month for STD's, that's sexually transmitted diseases. What I showed him was my appointment card, but it had the right words on it."

"Tonight, I decided to keep myself safe and let the guy have his way with me. I said to myself, 'Vikki, this is just another client', and waited for him to get it over with. As soon as he was done, I got the hell out of there and came home. He had sex with me, without my consent, and that, Bella, is rape."

"Why didn't you report it to the police?"

Vikki laughed disdainfully, "The police are not interested in us. If a prostitute reports being raped, they snigger at you. Usually when I cross paths with them, they ask me for a free go. A few of them even tried to blackmail me into having sex when I first started, threatening to arrest me if I did not. I got wise, and nowadays I retort, 'For what, I'm doing nothing wrong'.

"Being blackmailed into having sex with somebody is also rape."

With that she hugged me and finished, "Be clever Hon, use your wiles, and don't let the bastards get to you."

Vikki sort of laughed, and her indomitable spirit reappeared, shaken and stirred-up. I helped her into the bathroom where she purified herself with water and lots of bath scents. I washed her body, until she topped up with hot water and said she wanted to soak.

I left her alone, and thought about her words. Vikki seemed to imply there were degrees of rape. I wondered if the courts allowed rape victims to give evidence in their defence, or say anything at all. After my own harrowing experiences, I thought it most unlikely.

I concluded that, had she gone to the Bussies, she would have been interrogated, just like I was; being found guilty – of being born female. The man that raped her would most likely be venerated as a saint [R 9.1].

[Bilty: "Isabella, that does not make sense. The entire case is built upon what the rape victim says, and it is usually considered to be the truth. The defendant has to disprove the lie, or he is convicted."

Vikki answered, "Really? Many college girls are 'Crying Rape', just to get back at boys they willingly had sex with."

Bilty replied, "The system is skewed in favour of the girl. Proof of penetration is the standard for conviction."

"If the girl is telling the truth, Bilty. Otherwise, it's a woman's word against a man's, and most times, she is believed."

Isabella said, "We will come to this later. If I may?"]

Vikki and I went to bed together that night, and snuggled into each other in the emotions of sharing secrets. Vikki and I never did have sex together, not back then. I think she wanted to, but I am not sure. She did let me nurture her bosom sometimes, but she knew I was seeking childish caring, and not sexual release. Her bosom reminded me of my mother, and I felt safe.

Feelings are like that, and judge me not. Even now, many years later, whenever I spy an attractive or motherly female, I always check out her rack first.

That is not a sexualised statement. I am still, to this very day, missing my own mother's personal sanctuary; the one the authorities that be, denied me. They ripped me away from a loving home, on the pretext of possible physical or emotional abuse. Had I been at home, my ninth birthday party would have been a burger treat, kids party, and presents. I would have been safe.

As it was, I was living rough. I was drunk and high. That was the direct result of the Family Court and SS interference in my life. They had physically and emotionally abused me, repeatedly. And they got away with it. A dark cancer of embittered hatred was growing inside of me.

Meanwhile, Vikki gave my life purpose. In the weeks that followed, we talked about higher things in life. Sometimes our thoughts fled upon the wings of dreams, and we would lie awake talking all night. We'd mumble our heart's deepest wishes, unto the enfolding darkness. The thing I liked best about those times, was coming half-awake and snuggling into her sleepy warmth. There's no other feeling I've had since, that has been so profound a statement of unconditional love.

I stayed with them for a month, and during that time, I learned that both Ken and Fred had been planning to fuck me. The taxi driver must have called the Bussies, and because of her, I was saved from being raped. Vikki told me the first time usually hurts and the girl bleeds a bit, but after that, you make loads of money.

Like Ratney, Sarah said, "Always use a condom, and never do anyone who injects drugs. Only do something with a boy if you want to, and are happy with doing that particular thing with him. I do not have sex with men for any other reason, other than to make money. Sometimes it feels like rape to me, kiddo."

Vikki explained, "My first boyfriend wanted us to have sex, and became increasingly insistent. He showed me porno clips off the web, and kept telling me what he wanted me to do, sexting and stuff I could not do. I believed I loved him, but I just wasn't ready for sex. So rather than do what he said, I dumped him. Back then, having sex for the first time was still a dream gift for my husband on our wedding night."

She cried, because we both knew that dream was long dead and buried. I held her close and in time she rallied. In the days that followed, she taught me a lot more about sex, how to do it, different ways of doing it, and all that stuff. I found it interesting, but was not yet ready to try it myself. I understood how she had felt. I sometimes wondered who my first lover would be. Would he take me on our wedding night?

I found out what they charged, and that they got almost double for not using a condom, but that was extremely rare. She explained, "People who used prostitutes have a far higher risk of carrying VD, or HIV."

We talked about it for a long time and I learned so much from her. I told her she should teach Sex Ed in schools, but she laughed. I was dead serious, because she really explained things properly, and in ways and words I could understand.

I realised I was falling in love with her. One night, as I lay in her arms, she mentioned that she and Sarah had talked about getting married. I felt torn and jealous immediately. I thought about my feelings for her, and realised two people could never become three, and my love for her wilted as it blossomed.

A few days passed, and it was time for me to leave. I had to go before my feelings for Vikki became a problem. Vikki wanted me to stay, and forced me to tell her why I was so determined to go. The moment of truth came and I blurted out, "I'm falling in love with you, yet there is no place for me in your life."

I did not cry. I waited, and she said she loved me, but she loved Sarah more. She was kind and held me close. We exchanged small words until finally she broke away and said, "Perhaps you're right."

She gave me a long kiss as we said goodbye. She made me promise to excel at school, and return to see her one day.

I was heartbroken, but in a new way. I left quickly, and never looked back. My heart hurt a lot, but I also knew I had made the right decision.

That feeling was well-weird. With nowhere to go, I, unintentionally at first, started heading back towards Shepherds Bush.

I became sidetracked, and made new friends in Marylebone. The police kidnapped several days later. They just happened to be raiding the place I was staying in, and although well hidden, they found me.

I made the mistake of talking to them at first, telling them my real name and stuff. I felt their interest rise, and I stopped talking. I was learning. That time I did not bow to their bullshit and empty threats, but demanded a lawyer before I spoke another word to them. They always said that on TV, so I knew it was true.

I learned that only applies to adults, and on television.

They informed me I needed a responsible adult. I laughed, telling them, "I only know two responsible adults, and they are my real mother and father. The rest of you are all scum, Bussies in particular."

I remembered Vikki, and Ratney was probably OK. I was about to add their names, but clammed up. Never reveal your true friends in times of distress, especially to the law. I realised if they knew I had friends, they would be kidnapped and imprisoned also, just because they knew me. That's what the police do to the people I love.

Instead of a lawyer, I got Social Services. I still wanted a lawyer, but time had moved on. What could have been, had already come to pass.

I later learned, the Bussies kidnapped me late on Friday evening — after sitting on the case since Wednesday.

I had to suffer their cells all weekend before being transferred back to Hammersmith nick on Monday. Several cops recognised me and greeted me with a smile, "Hello Wildcat, you back again. What mischief did you get up to this time?" One even remembered my real name.

During the hours locked in my cell, I figured out that I was now becoming a part of the system. I was starting to feel a lot more grown up. I was let out for ten-minutes in the rear yard for 'exercise'. Many inmates were there, and everyone was older than me, but some were older kids. One guy asked the policeman for his cigarettes, and the co-dee gave out, offering a light. I joined the queue, and like the rest, asked him for a fag. He looked at me and asked if I was sure. I said, "I need the buzz," and he gave me one.

I was not a smoker, as I still hated it, especially the smell and taste. Yuck. Virtually everyone on the streets did it, if and when they could afford roll-ups, or a real pack. It was a kind of bonding to show that you were co-dee, an Outlaw just like them — Unwanted, forgotten. The drag was OK, and offered me acceptance by the others in the pig's sty.

The same happened later, and again the next day. I was smoking with my new friends. We chatted and some co-dees gave me tips about the Bussies, interview strategy, and street life in general.

Life in lock-up was mega-boring as usual. On Tuesday, I had to go to Family Court again. I knew they were not happy that I had escaped from them. That time I was not allowed to speak at all. I looked around for my parents, but they were not there. Otherwise, most of the people were the same. All of them, even my lawyer, worked for the other side. My Responsible Adult worked for Social Services, come-on! That is the other camp, the ones who kidnapped me in the first place.

I felt doomed, that was until Wednesday morning, when I met two 'nice' ladies, who took me through to talk to me in a luxury cell. The only difference between us, as far as I could see, was that they could leave, and I could not. They told me as soon as we sat down, that the room had cameras. I could not see any, except the ancient one pointing at the door. I knew there was at least one more.

That puzzled me, and as they droned on, I looked around for the other cameras. I had looked at the two fire alarm sensors on the ceiling, but they seemed normal. We only had one in our entire home.

The word 'home' almost floored me as it came into my mind; such a brief reflection. As I began to cry, I spotted the back of the laptop opposite me. I saw a small, round, shiny piece of plastic in the middle at the top, and knew at once that was a camera. I started to try and pay attention to their words, because the meeting might be important.

I was dreading yet another interrogation, but they were both overly nice to me. The strange thing was, the main woman spent a lot of time asking me why I ran away from the care home, but never once mentioned my mother. I did, and was told not to speak about her, or any of my family, as we would come to that later. We never did.

They asked a series of questions next, about religion and coloured people, and stuff. They even asked me if I had a boyfriend, and I told them, "No." Silly people. The younger one told me in confidence that her boyfriend was from Pakistan, and asked me what I thought.

"There isn't much to think nowadays." I told her, "If you are in love and he loves you, it's fine with me."

She asked, "When you grow up, will you have a Pakistani boyfriend like I do?"

I wasn't actually sure I liked the idea, but I knew they wanted me to say 'Yes'. "Maybe."

They laughed and made a joke I didn't understand, before whispering briefly. The younger woman came to sit next to me. She seemed to be most concerned about me. She asked me about my interests and I told her I liked music, going for a fast food, and being with my friends. Sadness welled up inside me, knowing everyone I loved was so far away.

Before I could mention my mother again, she asked me incredibly quickly, which pop music I liked. She coaxed at first, but I soon discovered I knew a lot more about it than she did. She encouraged me to tell her what I knew, and I was soon singing the latest hit by Rihanna.

She stopped me, and asked if I knew one of Rihanna's top songs. Stupid woman. I told her so as well, "Of course I do silly. I know all the words, and the dance steps."

She asked me to show her, and cleared the chairs away so I had a small stage to perform on. I know I was good, and it had to be on camera. I was going to ask them for a copy, but she clapped as soon as I finished, and asked me if I knew another of her songs.

Again, she chose the track, one of Rihanna's best. My dad banned me from dancing to it, but I knew all the moves by heart. I had practiced it when my parents thought I was doing homework. I bowed to my audience first, before bringing my hand to the side of my face, and past outstretched fingers, conspiratorially whispered a secret, "This won't be half as good without the backing track, and my sex clothes."

I giggled, but got my mind right to perform. I felt sooo Naughty!

The main woman, the boss that had been working intently at her laptop, looked up at that moment and said, "Isabella, we'll get you some great clothes, just as long as you do what we say."

I felt a bit happier, and thanked her. At the time, I thought she was quite nice. The clothes never came. They lied to me. Sometimes what big people really mean, is opposite from the words they actually say.

I performed, as the younger girl encouraged me, and she even took backing vocal as we danced on stage. The older one worked at her computer. I thought nothing of it at the time. I was away with the music in my head. Her mobile rang as I got into the main dance routine – that's the really sexy bit, and I wasn't paying attention to what she said.

That is, until I heard her say, "Yes, that's her now."

I wasn't quite sure if she was talking about my performance, but I thought she was. I went into automatic and tried to listen to what she said. "Beautiful, simply perfect … two, three-years tops … Sophie Anderson, Wow! … She'll fit right in, trust me. Look, I must go, miam [more in a minute]. Ciao."

I finished my dance routine with a flourish, and the younger one put my chair back exactly as it had been before. I noticed she put each leg on top of small marks on the floor. I thought to move the chair just to annoy them, but they asked me some more questions and I forgot. The boss tapped her assistant on the arm, and she sent a text message. It must have been a saved one, because it was sent far too quickly for an old person. Well, she was twenty-five, and that was ancient to me.

I had almost finished answering the next question, when another woman knocked the door and entered. She stated, "You are needed urgently on a serious case, Ma'am."

The oldster in charge told me I ticked all the right boxes. She closed quickly and we all had to sign a form. I was asked to read it, but there was no way I could even spell some of the words they used, never mind pronounce them.

The younger girl said, "I'm your Responsible Adult, and I checked this form myself. It is fine, so please sign it. OK. I had never signed my name before, but I had been practicing for when I was older. At last I had signed something myself. I felt so proud and old.

I was also thinking to myself that mine was not a serious case, as the boss was being called away from dealing with me, to attend to one. I was led away by the younger woman and asked to wait in a sort of cell, but it was not like the police ones. It had TV and a games machine. I asked for a burger and chips, as I was hungry. The woman squatted down to face me, saying, "You poor child. Don't tell me the police never gave you any breakfast. I'll have a word with them."

She cursed and spoke a rude word. I laughed, because it was a word I was not allowed to say at home. She said, "A lovely lady called Sophie will be here in a few minutes to pick you up. I will ask if she will take you for a burger treat."

I felt very happy. Later, after I had time to think about what happened properly, I decided there was something dreadfully wrong about all of them. I just couldn't figure out what?

Vikki called a break and said, "Bilty, this is hard for me. Look, I'll speak to you about this later, maybe another time. I don't have much to add except, I never realised she loved me so much. Nor what I feel for her. She's very special."

Isabella was confident in her denial, "I'm not gay you know, or bi. It's just that sometimes I sleep with women. That's not sexual desire or release, but emotional nurture. Can you understand?

"The SS and Family Courts denied me familial love, so I made do. And I do love Vikki, but as a best friend. She became the nearest thing I knew of as a mother. Until Sophie.

"I'm ready to go on, so finish your notes Bilty. I need this done and dusted. The really bad stuff is yet to come."

"I'm about done Isabella, so resume when you are ready."

Chapter 10 – Foster Care

Sophie was extremely 'nice'. She was bright, chatty, and full of fun. She took me for a mega burger treat as soon as we left the police yard. The kids at her home were happy and not aggressive. I found that very strange. I began fighting my fighting instincts, so as to fit in. It almost worked, except for lapses of my tongue.

I was street-wise, and I needed to hide it. I needed to return to being the girl I was just a few months before. She was long-gone. Somebody new was awakening to take her place.

The house was fine, and similar to the type of home I used to live in. It was much bigger, and had four floors, as ours had only two, and three bedrooms. There were twelve bedrooms in the new home, one for the owners, and eleven for foster kids. On the ground floor were a living room, dining room, and a playroom, plus kitchen and small WC. My room was on the third floor, and looked like a proper bedroom. I knew it could never be like my real home, but it was good and felt nice.

Unlike the first foster home, there were few rules, but those they had, were listed on the dining room wall. The good thing was, we were free within reason, as long as we all behaved. There was a roster of daily chores, which changed each week for each of us, until the eleven-week cycle completed, and started again. We all had to help cook, clean, and wash-up. At first it sounded strict, but it was just like helping mum at home, with more of us to share the work.

I soon realised it was a safe place to live, and although I made mistakes, I tried my best to fit in and be good. After my previous experiences, this was my best chance to live a decent life.

I found the school was pretty good, and again I went into the top classes and did well. They were actually teaching, unlike the other school. I was to realise this was because it was an independent Academy, not a typical state run school. Most of us went there, so from the beginning they looked out for me until the new-girl tag was dropped, and other fresh meat arrived.

There was one girl a year older than me in the house, but she was extremely timid. I was tempted to pick on her, but her eyes had a haunted, defeated look in them. Instead, I was nice, even if I knew we could never become best friends. Later she told me that her mother's boyfriend had raped her repeatedly. I knew what that was, and she did not want to talk about it. What happened to her did not sound nice.

I was hanging around with our clique after lunch one day, near the end of that first week at the new school. The timid girl went to the toilets, and was gone a long time for a pee. I also needed to go, so went to check on her. I found her being hassled by a couple of older boys. One was poking her chest and shoving her back against a wall. The other was trying to feel the top of her legs, inside like. A third boy stood behind telling the other two what to do. I ran up to the controller and hit him hard on the chin with my best ever boy punch. I was so mad, but very in control of myself.

He ran away crying, as I turned on the other two. They backed away and also made a run for it, shouting threats behind their backs.

The girl, Belinda, fell into my arms and tried to thank me through her tears. I watched over her after that. The great thing was, I never got detention either. Word soon spread, and apart from a couple of challenges out of school, which I won, all eight of us from the foster home were left completely alone after that incident.

The other three in the house were in secondary school, and working hard. They spent most evenings during the week on homework. At first I thought they were stupid, but later I realised I had missed some things the other kids in my class had already learned.

I surprised several teachers by asking for extra homework in order to catch up. I had wanted to ask my parents about it, but that was impossible. I made that decision myself, and in doing so, kept part of the promise I had made to Vikki; my aim was University.

The teachers were delighted, and soon I was back near the top of my classes. My interest spurred them to teach me more than those that did not pay attention. It also made me feel like one of the older children at home, even though I was the youngest.

One day I was told I was in trouble, and was sent to see Sophie. I was petrified I would be sent back to the care home. That's an in-joke for those of us who know how the system really works—the only 'care' ever practiced, was that of the managers for their work targets and personal bank balances. They didn't give a shit about us.

I didn't know what I'd done wrong. I was close to tears and trembled slightly, before finding my courage to knock the door of her office. I waited and planted my feet firmly, to counter my mind that was doing somersaults. She said, "Enter." Sophie had a stern face, which I later learned was an act.

I was shaking, and was allowed to sit down opposite her desk, as I waited for my fate to be determined. She said, "The council told me the rubbish was not sorted properly, and would not be accepted. Have you ever done the recycling before?"

I said, "Yes I have. Well, I have been shown what to do, but it's very complicated. This week is the first time I did it myself."

I heaved as I finished, and my chest bucked somehow. I stifled a sob, as big girls don't cry. I turned away and brushed my face with my arm, so she wouldn't see the tear running down my cheek. I did not even have time to sniffle before her arms engulfed me, holding me tight. They were not my mother's arms, but they were exactly so close to the caring I needed. She renewed my belief in myself.

Somehow, her soft words made me tell her that I knew she was going to send me back to the awful care home. I remember she smelled nice, but cannot remember what she said. She was also warm and felt soft in all the right places. I liked that. When my heart settled she told me, "Isabella, you made a small mistake. We all make mistakes, even me."

I looked at her properly for the first time. "All you did was muddle some of the things for recycling, but you will learn over time. Even I find it difficult sometimes. Now don't worry, because all I wanted to do was to try and help you get it right next time. That's all. How about I help you sort out the rubbish tomorrow?"

I nodded my head and said, "I'd like that a lot."

Sophie led me over to a settee, which had a couple of armchairs and a table nearby. She sat with me and held my hand. She was needily comforting in my moment of dire distress, and we talked for a long time. Afterwards I felt a lot more secure, and it was definitely the closest feeling I ever got to being like home.

What I liked most about those years was the fact that everything was almost normal. We lived like a large family, we had a lot of fun, and laughing was definitely encouraged. We all did well at school, even Belinda, who did become my close friend, but not my best one-ever. There was always this shadow in her life, and mine — like we should not even be there, but at home with our real parents.

I was watching TV one evening, and saw my own mother being found guilty of kidnapping … me!

The police, Social Services, and the Crown Prosecution Service made the charges stick. I fell against the arm of a chair, aghast. I cried, because the real truth was nothing like that — she, my mother, rescued me when all others' failed to look after me. The SS didn't give a damn about me. It was they that had kidnapped me. My mother rescued me when I was is extreme danger. The SS were nowhere to be seen. For saving me, she was to be sent to prison for 3-years.

The judge's final words were, "Sabrina Waits, you disgust me. What were you thinking, kidnapping a minor. One you are expressly forbidden by law, to have contact with. You will be sent to prison for three years. Parole was expressly forbidden."

That was Criminal Court. Lackeys supporting the distorted views of their misbegotten brethren in Family Court. There was zero justice.

My tears dried when the following report focused upon a serial female bully, who had already served time for serious GBH charges. She attacked one man with a broken bottle, after she had broken [R 10.1] the champagne bottle over the head of his friend, who was still on life-support, and in a coma. She got a 12-months suspended sentence—fill your boots with British law enforcement and judiciary, they only ever support the people in the system, wherever they crawl out from.

My mother was the only person that night in Manchester, to be there for me. Social Services, the police, were nowhere to be seen. They did not even know I was missing: 'Duty of care'. Spit!

My mother did nothing wrong, and tried her best to make everything right. On first offence, she got three-years in prison. The charge of Kidnapping was totally ludicrous. My tally of people I would one-day get even with was increasing exponentially. They ripped my life away from me, so they would pay with their own.

I became moody and blamed myself. If I had not run away, none of it would have happened. During the days that followed, Sophie asked me several times, what was wrong, but I said, "Nothing."

That week I was doing the drying up after meals. There in my hand was a shiny Cook's knife about six-inches long. It was extremely sharp. I ran my finger along the blade and easily cut myself. I wondered if I had the courage to slit my wrist.

The big girl washing up, scolded me, "Hurry up Issy, I'm running out of places to put washed dishes. Stop daydreaming. Why is your finger bleeding? Come, I'll run the cold tap."

"I'm sorry, the knife slipped in my soapy fingers."

"Then why were you looking at your wrist? Give it up Issy. That's one bad idea."

That broke the spell, for the moment. Similar thoughts returned to me when I went to bed that night. I knew I could creep down to the kitchen when everybody was asleep, and do it before anyone could stop me. I resigned myself to my self-inflicted fate, and fell asleep on my bed.

I woke in the morning and was almost late for breakfast. I had forgotten all about my plans with the knife until later, when I was alone in my room. I decided I didn't want to die, I wanted to get even.

I was playing a game with Belinda, later that Saturday afternoon, when Sophie called for me. I went to her office and she asked me to close the door. She said, "I have to run an errand in a minute. Would you like to come with me? My husband Jeff is head honcho today, so we can take our time. I know, I'll take you for a burger treat afterwards. Don't breathe a word to the others, or they'll all want to come."

I felt special and delighted. I had to change quickly, and met her waiting in the car outside. She went to the nearby town and bought some stamps and stationary. Afterwards, we went to a fast food place, and she was very chatty. Being with her, and away from the normal routine, cheered me up a lot.

The afternoon was warm and sunny. Sophie took the long way home, and stopped on the edge of town, where there was a small shop near a popular beauty spot. She bought us both a large 99 ice cream, and we ambled through the short grass to where there was a bench seat. The view over the lake, river, and nearby forest was stunning. The sun was milky warm, and insects buzzed with the exuberance of late spring. The air hung heavy with the intoxicating fragrance of youthful milieu, as we coalesced unto nature's commune.

There were a lot of people in Richmond Park that day. Most of them were down by the lake, and none of them anywhere near us. Sophie told me a little about the area, "I grew up nearby, and used to come here quite often when I was about your age."

Subsequently a memory surfaced and she told me a funny story that made me laugh. I learned that when she was young she was always getting into trouble with her parents.

We finished eating our cones as she completed the story. She was silent a moment and gazed out across the park. Turning to me, she took my hand and spoke quietly, "I know something is seriously wrong in your life. I know you have been thinking about taking your own life, and that is never the answer. Trust me, I tried it once, and it hurts like hell. Bullies picked up on it, making my life not worth living, I thought at the time. But not now."

She showed me a scar on her wrist. It was old and difficult to see, unless you knew where to look. "I did that because my first boyfriend ditched me for my best friend. He was a rat. Life can be like that. I can never believe I was so stupid back in those days. I know you are not stupid, so please Issy, tell me what is so dreadfully wrong?"

I sat still, and somehow my face balled up, like I was about to cry. There was this big lump at the back of my throat. It made my voice sound all funny, and turned my words into unrecognisable squeaks. I was determined not to cry, and I didn't. However, that did not stop the tears from forming in my eyes. In time, some rolled down my cheeks. I did not care. I felt innately bereft.

Sophie handed me a clean handkerchief, one that smelled slightly of perfume. I nodded distractedly in thanks, and wiped away the tears. Later, I blew my nose. I thought to offer it back, but she wafted her hand and let me keep it. She had not said anything at all. She held me close, and waited for me to get control of myself and tell her.

I began clumsily, "Mum was sent to prison, and it is all my fault."

Tears returned and that time I was about to cry forlornly. I managed to add, "But it was not my fault, it was all their fault."

I could say nothing else. I heaved and shook, the pain too intense for me to bear. My eyes flooded and I became a sobbing wreck. Sophie held me closer. She cooed gently and let me cry myself out. Several times, I almost settled. I tried to get a grip of myself. Each time I thought about what I was going to say, frozen emotions thawed to overwhelm me once more.

The first chill of evening breeze touched us, before I was finally able to speak. The early evening shivers fixed my mind in focus, and I told her my story, right from the very beginning. What had happened at home to split our happy family apart, and the first foster home. I moved on to running away and heading home to my mother. I told her everything honestly, although sometimes she stopped me to clarify a point. I don't know if she believed me, but it was the whole truth.

I told her how I was bullied at the care home, and she was visibly shocked. I confirmed I was only eight-years old at the time. She squeezed my hand and had to pull out a hankie herself to dry her eyes. Nonetheless, she encouraged me to continue.

I told her all that had happened, and about my months living on the streets. She could not believe that I survived, and was still a virgin, but I was. She was taken aback about how much I knew about sex, alcohol, and drugs. In time, I came to the present, and thanked Sophie for giving me such a lovely home.

I told her of my promise to Vikki, and my dream of going to University. I stopped speaking then, because there was nothing left to say. We sat and cuddled for a while in silence. I was still held securely against her breast after I finished the tale. Her warmth and compassion helped me get through it.

When I was done I wanted to cry, but all my tears were gone, all dried up, desiccated like I was. I struggled with my inner turmoil, while she thought deeply. In time she spoke, "There is no way that you are to blame. The whole thing is absolutely ridiculous. You should never have been taken from your parents in the first place.

"As for what your mother did when she arrived to collect you in Manchester, I would have done exactly the same. You and your family are the victim's, never forget that. There is a conspiracy here Issy, and it is one I cannot challenge. I would lose everything I have in the world and hold so very dear. I would inevitably lose."

She brought the hankie to her eyes again, and this time I knew that she believed in me. At last, there was one adult on my side and her love made me strong. We stayed a long while, talking quietly. She treated me as a grown-up, and we grew much closer together.

Sophie did not focus on what had happened to me in the past, unless it was important to the present—like when I ran away the last time. She said that showed I had a will to survive against all odds. She praised me for living for months on the streets, and not getting into any serious trouble, avoiding the usual snares. She explained what rape was, and at last I understood why Belinda was the way she was. She told me off about Ken and Fred though, "But for the taxi driver, you would have been raped, and possibly murdered. You were very lucky."

She hugged me again, as we had broken apart some time before. "Issy, I understand your thinking, but it is misguided, trust me. You will discover this yourself when you get older. But what I want to say is this, by challenging their thinking, you have shown a unique ability to think for yourself. You have taken decisions yourself, like asking for extra homework. I believe you are a very special person, and I wish you were my own daughter, honestly I do."

Those words hit home hard. I kissed her cheek just like I would have done with mum. Afterwards their impact hit deeper inside me, and I hid my face in her breast. Again my mind reeled, but for all the right reasons. That time I did not cry. I had a second mother, and that was all that mattered.

After that day, Sophie insisted on coming with me when I had to attend Family Court or the SS. I had already been a couple of times right at the beginning. I was watching when she challenged Social Services, asking to take the role of Responsible Adult, as she was my foster mother. They had an argument about who was my legal guardian. I did not understand all of what they were saying. But it seemed to be, that Sophie was responsible for me at all times, except in Family Court.

Sophie lost, and had to watch from the gallery. She was charming to the SS. At first, I thought she had sold me out, like all the others. She said nothing about it until we were in the car and on the way home. I didn't even have to ask her, she came right out with it. "I'm so sorry Issy. I tried to be there for you, but they would not let me. The words I spoke with the social workers had many double entendres, two meanings Issy, some of which you may have guessed.

What I really said was, "I should be Isabella's Responsible Adult, as technically the Court have appointed me to be her lawful Guardian."

The girl from Social Services rebuked me, "That is not so. I was originally appointed to act as Isabella's Responsible Adult."

We disagreed. I was told I could challenge her and lose — not only the issue, but also my 'Preferred Status as foster care Provider'.

"This is my life's work sweetheart. Please, don't think unkindly of me. They would close me down if I went against them. I need the money, but I worry more about losing the other ten children I care for, because you know where they would end up don't you?"

Her words hung in the air. I said, "A care home."

I pretended to spit, and she did not pull me up about it. Sophie knew how deeply I resented my past experiences.

She was going to say more, but I turned to her for a cuddle, mumbling that I understood. Sophie was driving, but hastily pulled over to the kerb and held me tight. Once I recovered, she detoured, and we went to a pub for lunch. It was great. It was my first time to be in a proper bar, not a pub restaurant on Sunday lunchtime. It opened my eyes to a new and surreal world. I liked it a lot.

Somehow, Sophie always found a way to turn my bad times and rejection, into the best of experiences, like that time on Richmond Park. She became my new mother, but never quite replaced my real one, although I know she tried so hard.

One day, almost two-years later she called me to go out with her on an errand. By then I knew this was her way to get me alone for a serious talk about something. I had no idea what she had to say to me, but I enjoyed the treat. This time we went to a Wimpy kiosk for Saturday lunch, and I preferred it to the others.

I know she had planned to take us for a walk, but the heavens opened and hail lashed the car, making a deafening din on the tin roof. We ate and tried to chat, but it was difficult. As the storm passed, I opened the window and stuck out my hand. I caught a hailstone and marvelled as it melted in my hand. My palm hurt where it had landed, but not too much.

I was drying my hand when Sophie said, "Next term you will go to a new school, and I think you should go to Newbury High. You are bright, advanced for your age, quick-witted, and clever with it. You need the right teachers and ambience to excel. Newbury teaches higher qualifications than State Schools. I went there myself some years ago.

"Would you like to visit the place? Tell me if you like it?"

"Yes please!"

Bilty:

1. I note that while IW was reliving her life, she was much more relaxed, almost playing for the camera. There is a steely depth to her character; yet frailty. Ah, emotional frailty. The only time she was tense, was when recounting her thoughts of suicide, and the emotional wreck she became when speaking with Sophie.

2. The undeniable point of this revelation, is that the young Isabella was settled, and she accepted Sophie as her new mother. That woman offered her the first familial care since her departure from home. I do not understand, as of this moment, what could have gone so awry.

Ah. Here she comes again, a fresh drink in hand. Time to hear the next instalment of her life.

Chapter 11 – Newbury Academy

Isabella

We went the next Wednesday afternoon, after filling in forms for me to miss afternoon class, which was only crappy art and sports.

Newbury Academy was holding an open day, and the school was very old. It was an all-girls school. The people talked all posh and funny, like the Queen's English. Sophie said, "Go off and make friends." She winked at me, and I knew it was my chance to really check out what went on there.

They wore uniforms, and there were dozens of rules. However, I was allowed to ask a lot of questions, and decided I liked the place. They taught real things that mattered, and not the dumbed-down basic stuff of normal British schools.

I talked to many of the students. I considered they were not like ordinary pupils. Some opened up to me, especially the groups, and they moaned about how strict the teachers were. They talked openly as they showed me around the school. They spoke with disgust about having to do things I accepted as being normal. I knew this was the place to learn for the future, and change my life.

The school also had lots of trophies for sports, some going back centuries. There were hundreds of them. My current school, built a decade ago, bragged about coming third in the local inter-schools football three-years ago.

I noted that in the last few years, Newbury High had won cups for: Hockey, Badminton, and Tennis. I had never even tried any of those games. Last year they had won the Volleyball Cup for the whole of UK, and that was a game I liked, and was good at—except we played a class game only twice a year. Crap. I knew my world was quite small, and I needed it bigger, much bigger and large.

I was told by an older girl to report back, and shortly I met the House Mistress from Σος, that's Latin for Sigma House. She turned out to be a senior teacher who was in charge of one-quarter of the pupils. It sounded like a game within a game, and they were competitive with the three other Houses in the academy.

After getting to know me, the House Mistress insisted I should be on their Volleyball team. I really liked her idea, and said, "Yes please."

Interrupting, Sophie asked me how it went outside, and I said I loved the place. Well, I didn't actually, I absolutely adored it. I left with Sophie a short time later, and I started talking as we left the office. I was still telling her how good the school was twenty minutes later.

We stopped for tea and scones at a wayside café. The place was deserted, so we could talk openly, if quietly.

Sophie stated, "I would have to pay an awful lot of money to send you there, but I think you are worth it. I have never offered this to any child before, but there is a fire within your heart that cannot be quenched. I admire that in a girl, just don't let me down. All I ask, is that one day in the far future, you pay me back. That will be my pension, of sorts. How about it?"

"Yes. I won't let you down."

"Good. Legally, my position is a bit iffy, unless you were to become my adopted daughter. That would mean I become your mother, whom I can never replace, God forbid. It's all that stuff with lawyers, you understand."

I nodded my head, although I didn't really understand. It sounded about right, and I trusted Sophie with all my heart. I knew she would never sell me out, and had my best interests at heart. I really missed my real mom all the same. It seemed to me, Sophie was the best thing that had happened to me for years. I hugged her so tight.

To her credit, Sophie applied to adopt me, and was rejected. We talked about it for a long time, and there appeared to be no valid reason. She appealed the decision, and lost. She found the money to send me to the good school, and later, whenever I felt I could not cope in that new world, I remembered her kindness, and strove to improve myself.

[Bilty: "Sorry Isabella, but I'm not getting this. Surely Social Services are always looking for new foster carers and especially adoptive parents. Why on earth were you turned down?"

"Ah, Bilty. There was a lot more going on than is apparent so far. In a normal situation, this would have been welcomed, and quickly approved. But you see, mine was not a normal Domicile. I'll come to the why of it later, but the SS were up to their necks in the scam of it all.

"Meanwhile, ask yourself why the SS would want to retain full control of me. And no, it was not in my best interests.

"I'll join the dots for you as we progress, but think about the larger implications, Bilty.

"Oh. And for homework, look up the word DOMICILE. You'll soon need to understand all its insidious leverages and constrictions. That is the life I, and others, were forced to endure."]

Time moved on to late July. Blood came out of my Fairy one day, but it wasn't much, followed by nothing for a few months. I was worried, and wondered if I had been raped, but that answer didn't feel, or seem right. Surely, a girl would know if she had been raped?

Months passed, and I thought I was cured. I didn't say anything to anyone. I remember so clearly, it was the day after my eleventh birthday party. That was a grand day and we had a great party.

Soon after, I started at my new school. I discovered they were all way ahead of me. I was used to being at the top of the class, but there I was usually bottom. They knew much more than I did. I spoke to Sophie when my tests neared, and she asked me, "What did you do last time?"

I was confused, but she would not tell, and left me to work it out for myself. The answer, when it came to me, was so obvious, because I had done it before. Once I understood the problem, I singled out the most important subjects I was weak in, and tarried behind when class finished to speak to the teachers.

"What do you want?" said Iron Britches, our name for the English teacher. She taught us both English Literature and Language.

I said, "I know you think I'm stupid, but I haven't been taught as much as the other girls. I am clever, and I want to show you I am as intelligent as everybody else. I do not have the knowledge they do. Can you please give me extra homework so I can fill in the gaps? Ma'am."

She looked at me quite stunned, as if she actually did consider me stupid. I think she had never considered that I had not been taught stuff the others knew. She shook her head, held it in her hands, losing her shield of invincibility in the process.

I said, "Ma'am, I need to catch up with the others. Can you help me. Please, I want to learn."

I am sure she indulged me, because she ruminated before replying, "Show me by what you do. I do not believe a word you are saying child. You will come to my detention every Wednesday afternoon. You will have Sixth form library access, and you will also come here every Saturday morning. Do we have a deal?"

Saturday mornings had become quite special. Sophie usually took only me to help her shopping. I loved those times we spent together. Wednesday afternoons, Oh My God!

Wednesday afternoon was sports, and I was on the junior Volleyball team. I also liked Badminton a lot, which I was getting good at. We celebrated winning or losing afterwards, and that meant I got in with the bigger girls in our House. I needed the acceptance to survive in the new environment.

Take the chance, or lose it forever? I already knew life moved-on too fast, and said, "OK."

The English teacher started to say, "I knew you wouldn't…"

She stopped in mid-sentence, and looked at me properly for the first time. "You are a feisty one. I admire that in a young girl. Prove to me I am wrong about you, and I will give you One-on-One teaching until you are as good as the other girls."

"That sounds great, Ma'am." The upshot was, I got my homework, and a lot of extra tuition. Later, the one-to-one coaching helped me tremendously. My grades improved considerably, but my life centred on school. That got harder as I tried my best to take on other important subjects from the list I had made weeks earlier. Reactions were muted at first, but when they found out I was serious, and compromising my life in the quest for knowledge, I became accepted.

I also started moving up the leader board. I knew I could never be Number one — too much education already lost. But I was in the top ten sometimes, and that was a great achievement, even if I say so myself. I knew stuff even the eldest in our home did not know about, and that said it all, and they were years older than me.

The next semester, as they called school terms, my remedial studies schedule altered, and I was able to resume sports. Again I was in the volleyball and badminton teams. That year we began playing at inter-schools level, and our teams went all over the country.

My academic grades continued to improve, and I was doing really well. Flourishing at both greatly increased my confidence, and I began to see a bigger picture of life, to experience much larger world.

One evening the Maths teacher came in to take prep. It was a Thursday, although don't ask me which one. We all knew he liked a tipple now and then, and sometimes we knew he did it in class. We forgave him, because he was one of only three Male teachers in the school. The other had a large, bushy moustache, maintained a military bearing, and taught history. We called him Colonel Blücher because his favourite phrase was, "Forwards!" I'll come to the art master later.

That Thursday he asked me to stay behind, as he wanted to help me, and show me something interesting. That took up a lot of time as he probed me for the correct response. Eventually I learned a new way of approaching maths, wishing I was one of the boarder's at the school, as they only had to go to their dorm to sleep. I was faced with a one-hour journey, and ran for the last bus. I saw it pulling out as I got to the main road. I ran and waved, but the driver did not see me.

London is not a big city, unless you are eleven years old, and have to walk ten miles to get home. At ten o'clock at night, I knew instinctively I was in the wrong place at the wrong time. I repeatedly tried to call Sophie, followed by Belinda, but the network was down.

My street urges came back. I needed to survive, one night more, just one more time. I ducked down a road I thought looked promising, only to walk a mile sideways and end up with nothing, except a place I did not know at all. I had been in similar situations before.

I headed for the brightest lights, looking for the alleyways: shelter. There were none. Instead, I was entering Kingston Town, a place where the rich live, and was looking for a sign for the Underground. I heard a car pull up, and immediately turned to look in a shop window.

There was no way I could wear, never even afford, what was on display. I didn't even want to buy any of the stuff, but I needed to see the driver in the window reflection. I waited hoping he would go away. He pulled off, and I remembered Sufdar.

The taxi came back round. The 'Asian' driver said he was worried about me. I turned around to look at him. He seemed OK. He was Pakistani, the taxi was legit, and the hire sign was off. I needed to con him for a lift home, so spoke to him.

I didn't have any money for the fare, but he waved at the sign and affirmed he was off duty. He leaned towards me, and I backed away in response. "Young Lady, my last work of every day is to take a very wealthy man back to Kingston. It has been this way for ten years now.

"I am finished work, and am going home to Shepherd's Bush. I offer you a ride, for free, but you do not like me because of my religion. I know it. It is always the same with the white people."

He wound up the cab window and started to pull away. On impulse, I ran a few steps and banged the boot. He stopped, and I got in his cab. At first, I opened the rear door, but worried about child-locks, so closed the door and got into the passenger seat in front.

I knew nothing was ever for free, but looked at him from the corner of one eye, watching where he put hands, whilst checking where the taxi was heading with the other. It was going in the right direction, and by the quickest route. I had clamped my legs tight together, and was ready to jump out at his slightest move towards me, car in motion or not. I took a photo of his name and details just in case. He turned out to be chatty, and a gentleman. He pulled over as soon as I asked him to stop.

I opened the door ready to run, but he smiled and thanked me for making the long and boring journey a pleasure.

I had not picked up anything untoward in what he did or said, and stayed to thank him. I was expecting him to lunge and try to rape me. Instead, he gave me his business card, and told me to call him if I were ever stuck for a ride home again. His name was Asif. He turned away and put both hands on the steering wheel. I was not expecting that.

I got out and walked in the wrong direction, even crossing to the other side of the main road, away from my destination. I waited until I saw him drive out of sight. When his cab disappeared from view, I hid and watched for his return. He did not come back. My mind went its own way. I was once again thinking street-wise, and knew what to look out for. I wanted to throw the card away, but kept it with me until I was in a back alley. I ripped it up there, tossed the bits away, and walked on.

He had not looked at me the wrong way, even once, so I relaxed. I admonished myself for being stupid. Regardless, I walked a figure of eight, watching for the cab to return, but there was nothing. I took a connecting alley, walked several streets, and made it home to safety. I was a little late, but not too much. I picked up a late-night snack, and went to bed.

As long as I stayed with Sophie I knew I was safe. I spent almost three years living with her. It was a home in the real sense of the word, but it was never my real home, no matter how hard Sophie tried.

One Sunday afternoon, I was in the common room watching TV, when my stomach started to feel weird. I felt the need to pee, but that wasn't what my body wanted to do. I got to the toilet, but there was only a dribble. I knew something was wrong with me. My stomach felt heavy, but I returned and tried to get into the TV again. I was cramping down below and felt bloated, somehow. It was odd.

It felt like I had a headache, except my mind was clear. At that moment, something lurched deep inside my womanhood, and made me feel sick. I felt something trickle deep inside me, and ran to the toilet. I took down my knickers. They were full of blood.

I thought I was dying. I screamed. I felt weak, as if something had been ripped from my most intimate self, something essential. Those long-buried feelings of being hunted resurfaced, and I probed the blood tentatively with my outstretched finger, wishing it would go away. Another load dropped into the toilet instead. I was disintegrating. I knew I was cursed.

I cleaned up as best I could, but the blood would not come out of my panties. I panicked, put them on wet from washing and wringing, and stuffed wads of toilet tissue inside. It was soaked before the next blob arrived, but I was already running for my sanity. I was bleeding to death. I didn't know why.

I wanted to call my mother, but she was still in prison In my panic, I ran to find Sophie. She was not in her office, so I went upstairs and banged loudly on her bedroom door, the only place in the house that was sacrosanct and always out of bounds.

Sophie threw the door open, and I thought she was going to hit me, something she had never done. Nevertheless, I was doing the worst thing ever. Her face was angry-red, and I shouted, "I don't care if you beat me. There's blood everywhere. It won't stop. I'm dying."

Her face changed to one of concern. She enfolded me in her arms, and asked where the blood was leaking from. I told her. She said to me, "Poor child, your first step to becoming a woman. We women do this every month, every woman. That's what makes us so special."

I muttered, "I'm cursed."

"You are correct, because we do call it 'The Curse'. However, a bigger curse often follows if this does not happen. Come with me Issy, there is nothing to fear, you are growing up." She kissed me on the cheek. In the bathroom she explained about my first period.

I had done the Sex-Ed classes, but it's so very different when it happens to you, personally. Sophie was so kind, so motherly. She gave me some 'Towels' as they are called, and told me never, ever, to use tampons, like put anything inside me. She told me using them caused cancer. I still didn't know what a tampon was, but they sounded pretty scary. I discovered years later her true intention was to protect my hymen, but I did not know that at the time. Was that an SS directive? I do not believe it was, but she was protecting my hymen.

Some weeks later, the SS arrived to do their six-monthly check. It was just routine. During the interview, they ticked boxes, and discovered I had had my first proper period. They check that stuff for some strange reason. I was nearby when they left, and they were introduced to me. I thought that was a bit odd.

One month later, I had another period, and that time I knew what to expect. Sophie provided me with towels for the duration, and although I didn't feel like doing anything at all, I went to school and got through it all that week.

The next week a social worker dropped by, using the pretext of being nearby. They sometimes did that, and I was at school. Sophie told me the woman in charge asked inconsequentially about my period, and she confirmed I had had a second real one. Neither of us thought anything more of it.

Bilty

"It seems to me your life was turned around, you were happy and settled. I don't understand what could have gone wrong."

"Yes, that was a very happy period of my life. But never underestimate the evil that is the SS and Family Courts. So far you have three clues: my kidnapping by SS, my hymen check, and now this, my definable puberty. I'll tell the next part after a break, maybe tomorrow?"

"Is this related to what is yet to be told?"

"Most definitely. I wanted to provide a coherent background for later on. Some of this is of paramount importance. Much is linking background information, that has a place in what became of me. Shortly you will understand.

"Please excuse me. Yes, Zoë, what is it?"

"Sorry, but you need a word with Genie, she's…"

Bilty:

Personal Journal:

IW is in good spirits, and seemed to enjoy the retelling, even if parts of it were painful at the time.

She also has an indefatigable belief in herself, her commitment to her education is more than any youngster I have ever met, especially at so young an age.

Point:

Isabella has much more to tell, but joining the dots so far, has eluded me, except for some far-flung impossibilities.

Notes:

1. There was no real change in her psyche during this part of her recollections, again. I'll continue to monitor for the next instalment.

2. I am beginning to worry IW is too relaxed, an indication of deep-seated denial, or dominance, but which? Both?

3. The latter: Dominance. She is highly educated, and has the seat on the board of an international company.

I welcomed the natural break and said, "Isabella, it is getting late, and I should be going. I'll come again tomorrow afternoon, two o'clock?"

"Yes, admirable Bilty. That should be a short session. I still have to plot the entire course of these revelations. And anyway, we need to get ready for clients."

"Yes. Your business. It's a Ladies Club? It operates from this building I presume."

"More of a Gentleman's Club actually, Bilty. It's mainly off-premises, but we do offer the most exclusive services in town, on-site, as it were. Why don't you stay a while?"

Her words were cut off as the other girls giggled: 'give him a free go, it's no big deal'. 'Yes, why don't we. He is kinda cute'... They threw lascivious glances in my direction, like 'vamps' from a long-gone, glittering Hollywood era.

It was then I realised the style, the elegance of the whole building, was of a bygone age recreated. I knew this was Isabella's doing, and my respect for her rose.

So did my libido, and for the first time, I felt unsettled, vulnerable to the wiles of the female. I quickly made my escape.

Chapter 12 – Returned to Care

Project Domicile
Interview: 05
Location: Fiddlers Court, The Oval, Holborn, Central London.
Time: 12:12 hours, Friday, 13th October.
Subject: Isabella Waites (IW).
Others Present:
    Melanie, Zoë, and Vikki.
Observations:
    IW is relaxed, and again, straight into her delivery as soon as we
have all settled.

Isabella

At the time of my next period, Social Services came back to make an
Emergency Reassessment. Unusually, they took over Sophie's office, and
she seemed to be crying when she came and took me to her personal lair.
I had been kept off school that day at the social worker's request. Sophie
knelt down outside the door and pecked me on the cheek. She said she
loved me, and opened the door to her domain. I turned around to look for
her, but she was already shambling away.

I went in and found the young girl from three-years before, was now
the boss, and another younger girl was to be my playmate. They were
both charming, but this time I knew they were liars.

I endured ages of boredom as they battered my senses numb with
dumb, and dumber questions. Meanwhile, my stomach was cramping
and I was still losing too much blood. I felt tired, drained, and just wanted
to curl up in a ball. They played on this, I knew it instinctively. My first-
ever really heavy period, and they wanted me to sign a release form. I
refused. Once again, I locked my arms around my sides, and stared into
the distance.

Sophie was summoned back, and they threatened her with arrest on
suspicion of committing an offence — sending me to Public [Private]
school. It was not on their list of approved state schools, and I knew they
were using this as a pretext to get to me.

Sophie's home was threatened with closure, and they used
intimidation, like threatening to revoke her licence and being withdrawn
from the foster care system. I remembered her words from Richmond
Park, and thought about the other children she was protecting, and
offering the chance of an almost normal life to. My heartstrings were
wrung-out before them.

The sentiments of an old film came to haunt me, Gene Roddenberry
in his excellence: Which is more important? "The needs of the many
outweigh the needs of the one." It was simple to figure out.

With undue catharsis, I spoke up, "If you drop all charges and black marks against Sophie, destroy the file on her, and allow me to continue at Newbury High, then I will sign your form."

Sophie screamed, "No!" But nobody heard her, except me.

I looked at her and stated, "I know what I am doing. Protecting the other kids, Mum."

She visibly wilted, and accepted my decision. She knew that many more vulnerable children, were depending upon her, and I had just made myself expendable to protect them. I looked at the form and it read, 'Release From Foster Care'. I voluntarily signed my life away.

Sophie begrudgingly signed the release form also, as did the other two in the room. They commended Sophie on running an excellent foster home and said she was a central pillar in their child support network. Meanwhile, I was led away. Sophie grasped my shoulder as I passed, as if to say, "Sorry." I could hear her sobbing when the door slammed shut, as if a herald's call, separating my past, from my future.

I waited a few hours in the SS lair, before being taken for a medical. It was like the last time, and I got it over with as quickly as possible. Again, they inspected my Fairy, 'A-okay'.

A little later, I was brought before the same Judge as last time in Family Court. I felt his eyes probing me, as if he was visually inspecting me, appraising me in some way. It was a very strange feeling.

Sophie was true to her word, and she was in Court to support me. Again, she asked if she could adopt me, but it was never even considered. I shouted out, "You have already ripped my happy family away from me. Now I am settled, and you want to take Sophie from me as well. I hate you. Every single one of you are kidnappers!"

[Bilty: "I do not understand this turn of events, Isabella. Why? Why take you away. You were settled and happy."

"Ah, Bilty. Now we began to unravel the real reason I was removed from my parents. Allow me to explain."]

I wish I had been allowed to stay with Sophie, but like everything else in my young life, mean, mealy-mouthed Social Services, wrecked all budding aspirations of a normal life at source.

We shouted out the truth in court. After that 'smash mouth' outburst, neither Sophie nor I were allowed to say anything the Court did not want to hear, and to cut the malaise short, I was sentenced to go back to the care home. My heart quailed, but by then I was bigger, stronger, and much more streetwise. I was allowed a few parting words with Sophie.

I learnt my first big word that afternoon: **Domicile**.

Sophie took time to explain it to me, "Virtually every person in this world has what is termed a Domicile. It is where they legally live. For instance, my domicile is as a British subject. I can live where I wish, but I cannot change my passport, my citizenship. That stays with me for life.

"As a minor, your Domicile is with your parents, at least until you are eighteen years old. But, in your case, your parents have been discharged of their Domicile duty to you by Social Services. It is they, as directed by Family Court, who now define your Domicile. Or, where you must live. However, you remain a British subject and citizen. Do you understand? I can use simple language if you prefer."

"No Sophie. Thanks. I understood it all perfectly. I am well educated, if thanks to you. We use big words like these at school, but I will research Domicile [R 12.1] in full, just for complete understanding of my personal situation.

"This is so unfair. Why couldn't they just leave me be?"

"Whatever their reasons, they are known only to the SS and Court."

"Yeah, sure. But I understand so much more about my life and current situation. Put simply, Domicile means that this is the place people, other than my parents—incredibly big, self-important people, have decided I have got to live. In law, there is no choice for me. I was never allowed to express my feeling, or preferences in Court, neither were you. Nobody was at all interested in what I wanted."

I hugged Sophie, and she whispered, "You are always welcome to come back, anytime, as my daughter."

We shared tears of parting, and I kissed her hard on the lips. It was a needy kiss. I told her I loved her, and she replied in kind. We were interrupted. Urgently I was ushered away to greet my fate. I glanced back, and Sophie was holding a handkerchief to her eyes.

I thought about Sophie's words, until I understood what I was up against. The word "Domicile" is forever burned deep within my heart, like a red-hot, searing, brand that can never be healed. Instead, this was destined to fester like canker, seeking retribution, for years to come.

I left with the two bitches from the SS, because now I knew what they were. I was taken to a different care home and was told it was only opened last year. There were around fifty inmates, and they were all girls. I didn't get to meet the boss as she was away on holiday. The deputy matron was officious, but tried to be as pleasant as she was able. She asked me if I was settled at school, and I said I was.

The matter was left there, which surprised me. She went on to tell me the rules, and had me sign a form of residency. One of the rules was rather odd. There were several shops nearby, but we could only use the one at the end of the road. She covered by stating, "A friend of the matron's owns it. We have inspected it, and it is cheap. The owner is extremely nice, and called Mr. Vijay Hussein."

I was escorted to my room and it looked a lot better than the last care home. It was still a prison cell. But the mattress was a little soft and the bedding vaguely reasonable. The bedclothes smelled as if they had bothered to wash them fairly recently. There were pictures on the wall, and drawers to put stuff in. The vanity unit and toilet without a seat, sat in one corner, shattered the ambience. I'd get a screen to hide them.

I did not have much to put in the drawers. I had the rucksack I had packed hurriedly, and the clothes I stood up in. Past experience had led me to leave most of my valuables with Sophie. I was back in gaol, but it seemed OK at first, and this time I knew the ropes.

I was starving, but had to wait a couple of hours for dinner. Nearer the time, I checked out the building, headed for the dining hall, which was like a school one. Other girls came into the room. I could see them checking me out, but I tensed my body in fight mode, took stance, and nobody came near me.

I was the first to be served, and the portions were decent. I sat down at a table in the middle of one side of the room, my back to the wall, so I could see everybody, and where no one could take me by surprise from behind. Some older girls came in and went to the front of the queue, forcing others to wait. I knew they were trouble.

They headed to the back of the room and sat together. A short time later, one of them noticed me. The gang leader sent three of them to greet me. They swaggered over, acting as if they owned the place. As they neared, I got up and stood to face them. The lieutenant said, "This is our table, you better move."

I was a lot wiser by then, and had taken Personal Defence classes at Newbury. Before she had time to poke her finger in my eye, I knee'd her as hard as I could in the crotch. She fell, and I swung a punch at the next girl, hitting her hard on the jaw with a good boy punch. The other girl backed away as I advanced on her, and she turned to run. I kicked her up the arse and she started crying. I turned and found the lieutenant clutching herself and bent over. I kicked her in the face and told her to fuck off. I looked up at the main bully, and our eyes met with menace. I knew I couldn't take her out, and for some strange reason, bowed my head to her out of respect.

[Bilty: "Wow! That was some reaction. Weren't you scared?"

"Scared shitless Bilty. But I knew I had to attack immediately, otherwise they would bully me. You have to stand up to bullies. I wish I had known how to stand up to the SS bullies, but they played by rules I did not know. This is all prelude. If I may?"]

They called me Wildcat (again) after that, and I quite liked their appraisal of me, plus I played on it. This time I was ready to fight. I did not cry, although I missed Sophie, the old house, and most of the guests. Now I knew in my heart, "Big Girls Don't Cry — they get even." I was making up my own rules, based upon my personal experiences of life.

Isaac Newton was half right, but for me his theory read, "For every action against me, there will be a greater and opposing reaction."

I was becoming a new person, and a force to be reckoned with.

I cruised for a few days, and was not bothered by anyone. The gang advanced on me sometimes, but I knew their shit and was ahead of them, snuffing out whatever they had planned, before they had a chance to implement it. Attack-first worked for me.

I was left alone most of the time, and this time I could almost handle it. I still cried at nights, but nobody heard me. My heart had been broken a second time, but this time I covered it with my fist and boot. Needy aggression was my only salve. My heartache manifested as anger, and nobody got near me. I was all-alone, and I liked it that way.

[Bilty: "Isabella, we are straight back to where you were years before, except that this time you could handle it. At least, appeared to. This still conflicts with all SS and Family Court statements: 'The needs of the child remain paramount', and especially regards, 'possible future physical, mental, and emotional abuse'."

"Huh. Tell me about it. To me, those words enshrine the unholy grail of Domicile, as practiced by officiously empowered wrongdoers in modern UK."

"I'm going to have a field day with this, but first, tell me the all of it. Were you able to continue at the Academy?"

"Yes, but it became surreal. I was living two distinctly separate lives, with zero overlap. I'll pick up again there."]

I woke up at six on Monday morning, and was the first down for breakfast. I was gone before seven, and headed for school. The trip took a bit longer than before, until I worked out a different way to get there. I left early, and got back late. None of the staff [R 12.2] were bothered about me. No surprises there then, this was supposedly a 'care home'.

Saturday was my first problem. I didn't see the sense in going back to the home at lunchtime, because I had nothing to do there. I went to the school library and did some homework for a few hours.

A teacher came in and placed a sign on the wall. He was the art teacher and his advert read "Model Required..." He was the third male at the school, and Italian. I approached him as he left the room. He took one look at me and I was hired, if I could begin at once. He was cute and harmless.

I was a little worried, but he did not touch me, or even make a single suggestive remark, even though I was posing semi-nude. I asked the teacher if he had a wife or girlfriend. He said, "No, neither."

I followed by cheekily enquiring if he had a boyfriend. He threw a tantrum, extolling the Holy Mother, and said many Italian words I did not understand. Unexpectedly his eyes fixed me like a demon. He drew the sign of the cross on his chest, and grabbed his palate, quickly becoming lost within his own world of rapid brushstrokes.

He looked up at me, and I pouted provocatively. He immediately spouted a lot more Italian words, which sounded a bit religious. He looked up at the ceiling, and his mind left me again. His work was excellent. He tried to explain it to me, but switched to Italian, and I felt I had done my bit. He requested me to sit for his next work, "Mary and Cherished Babe." I posed some weeks later, and he was very crazy. We got on well and had some good laughs. I learned a lot of Italian swearwords, but not much else.

Afterwards, I had no reason to return to gaol, so wandered around, and the only thing happening that I could join in was a Latin class. I sat in the first week, and registered the next. I knew instinctively what the art teacher had spoken was intimately related to this archaic language.

I cruised to my routine the following week, until Saturday morning. The bullies were waiting for me as I left, and took me by surprise. The leader, looked pissed off, her henchgirls surrounded me.

"I need vodka and orange. You will steal it for me."

"No, never!"

I tried to run, and hit one girl real good, but was easily overpowered by the rest of her gang. They punched and kicked me, and it really hurt. I couldn't fight them off. After the barrage I was held secure as Psycho smoked rapidly on a cigarette, before looking at me intently. She brought the hot tip to my eye. I could feel the heat on my eyeball, but I couldn't move my head away. I was held firm.

"You either do this, or I blind you for life. First one eye, then the other. Your choice."

She grinned, and I said, "I'll do it." I pleaded, which made them laugh. I was frogmarched to Vijay's Hussein's store, and shoved inside. They watched and waited outside. One of them followed me inside.

I grabbed some food, and went to pay. I whispered, "Vijay, sorry, but they want me to steal vodka and orange from you. I cannot fight them, but I'll pay you. I need it to look like theft. I don't know what to do. They'll kill me."

"You should get out of here. They are not good people."

"I can't. I am forced by law to live here."

"I understand, but regardless, you should go. Ah, the Candy Monster. I understand. Pay me now, and I'll ring the other in after you leave. That brat likes Absolute, and orange with bits in it."

Vijay winked, took my money, and as I turned to leave, so did he. I followed his instructions, and escaped as quickly as I could.

I was running late and hobbled for the bus stop, but I was too late, the bus had gone. I waited for the next one, another hour away. A taxi stopped abruptly, and I heard a horn pip. I looked, and found Asif had pulled over nearby. He beckoned me, and I went to his taxi. He said, "I'm on my way to Kingston, the big Boss. You need a ride?"

How could I refuse? That time I didn't fear him, I thought he was looking out for me. I was at best, naïve. The journey was fun, and we had a good laugh. I needed that to rid myself of the morning robbery. It was also much quicker than the round-about bus route. I arrived early at school. He offered to pick me up at seven o'clock, and I accepted. I now wish I hadn't. But 'Asi es la vida'.

[Bilty: "This is where it changes. Why was Asif there?"

"Why do you think? He was grooming me, if lightly. I fell for it. Who wouldn't. Now, ask yourself why I missed the bus. Come on."

"Because of the Bully. Oh my God! It was a set-up."

"Now you're beginning to get it. 'Slowly, slowly, catchy monkey'. *Comprendre*?"

"So, if I understand this correctly. You were deliberately delayed by the bully gang, so you would miss your bus to school."

"Yes. But they also made me rob, and that is coercion. Keep up, Bilty. This is how they work. They recorded me robbing Vijay, and later threatened me with reporting it to the Bussies. But I called them out on that one. That was my first clue to how to fight back. But that's for later. Let's move on.

"So why did Asif show up just then. Hmmm?"

"Because he knew in advance. I don't believe it, but it makes sense. I think I'm getting a handle on this now. Saints preserve us."

"Are you, Bilty? Mohammed, who enters the story next, probably ordered Asif to get Psycho to delay me. It had never happened before, nor since. Yes, time to meet Mohammed."]

Asif was a little late, but it was OK with me. I saw his taxi and waved before his car pulled to a stop beside me. I moved to get in the front with him, but he told me through the opening window, "Please Isabella, this is a very big boss, and he is a gentleman like me. No harm will come to you. I promise. Please sit in the back and talk to him.

I was about to object, but the window went up as he pressed the button. The rear door swung open, and I had a choice to make. I knew that the rear doors might have active child-locks, and there would be no way I could get out. The man could rape me for all I knew. I reasoned that as Asif said he was a nice man, so it should be OK.

The thought of making my own way home worried me. It was a long way, and would probably put me in far greater danger. I got in the back of his cab. It was quite risky, but at that time I trusted Asif.

Mohammed put his phone down, and greeted me with a great big smile. He was a young man, in his early thirties. He looked like an executive, and was very well dressed. He took my hand as I entered and kissed the back of it in a most non-sexual way. He proved to be the perfect gentleman. We chatted as Asif drove. His English was excellent, and he made me laugh, a lot. I remember he smelled awfully nice and I complimented him on his after-shave. He said, "This cologne is made especially for me, and is very expensive. Their perfumes are also exquisite, I'll order a bottle for you, for next time."

He discovered I had to go to school early in the mornings, and gave Asif a good telling-off. I don't actually know what he said, because it was all spoken in 'Muslim', or whatever language they used. But it was quite clear Asif was being bawled-out. Asif had always been nice to me, and I tried to object. Mohammed told me I would be collected and returned to my home every day. I quieted a bit, but Mohammed continued speaking for a while in their foreign tongue.

When they finished talking, I again said it wasn't necessary, but Mohammed insisted that Asif take me to school, and bring me back at night. He said, "I am the owner of this taxi service, and they do as I tell them."

Reluctantly, I agreed. Anyway, it gave me forty more minutes in bed every morning, and that was an excellent result.

As we neared Hammersmith, I became a bit wary, but I was dropped off where I wanted to be, and knew I had a new lifeline for schooling. Mohammed kissed the back of my hand as I left, complimenting me on my delightful company and wonderful skin texture. An emotion I had never experienced before exploded within me. It was scary-nice, and overwhelming.

I only just focused on his words of parting, as he said, "I look forward to the pleasure of your company next Saturday. Miss you."

I left, knowing he would kiss my hand again next time. I know I blushed. I thought Mohammed was well-cool.

I got out of the cab at the end of my street thinking that at last something was going my way. Many of my thoughts centred upon Mohammed. I did not wash where he kissed my hand for several days.

Bilty

"Now then Bilty, you wanted to know how this all works. I did not understand the all of it until many years later. I also discovered that Mohammed actually said to Asif as they pulled off, 'Slowly, slowly, catchy monkey.' Now my earlier remark will make sense.

"Neither did I know at the time, that Mohammed had possession of a report, stating that I was still a virgin, although my God may know why it—my virginity, managed to survive on the Streets of London. I don't?

"So there are a couple more clues for you to dwell upon. The answer when it comes, is very simple. But then, normal people do not think that way. Enjoy my enigma."

"I have a very good idea what comes next, pardon the pun."

Isabella smiled sumptuously, her hand waving aside, "In that case, a quick refresh, and I'll introduce Zoë to the story."

Bilty:

Personal Journal:

IW remains in good spirits, and I am becoming increasingly worried about where this tale is going. I do know how it ended, and that is not really helping me with the present of the story.

Notes:

1. IW's psyche remains stable, and growing in comfiture, despite what I know is to come. She is one remarkable woman.

Ah. She is having a word with Zoë, before refreshing her drink, and coming back to interview.

Isabella

"OK Bilty. I'm ready and will plough ahead with the next. You'll soon begin to put the pieces together, just as I did in real life. Nevertheless, you'll have to wait for some time before the all of it is resolved.

"Let's resume."

Chapter 13 – Romancing Isabella

On Sunday, I was late down for breakfast, and sat in the middle of my table as usual, facing the bullies. No one ever sat with me, or tried to befriend me.

A new girl wandered past and asked if she could sit. I waved my hand without looking at her, and ignored her. Another new fish added to this stagnating cesspool of human debasement and indifference.

She sat opposite me and said, "Hi, I'm Zoë, and I hate this place already."

She offered me a high-five, and I hit her palm with mine. She was about my age and chatty. I ignored her as best I could, but there was something unusual about her. In time, we talked, and I found I quite liked the young bitch. I realised as I mentally spoke the thought, that my mind was warped. By habit, I expected the worst of everyone I met.

Later that day, I went back to see Sophie. I didn't tell anyone. She lived several miles away, and I walked much of the way there. She was delighted to see me, and so were the other kids. She took me to her office and held me tightly in her arms. I cried with relief.

We talked and I told her I was settling in OK, not being bullied, and was making friends. I told her I didn't really spend much time there apart from eating and sleeping, elaborating about my extended hours at school. She was cheered by my progress and heartened by my dedication. She told me the boarders had sports and remedial classes on Sundays, and I told her I would check it out.

Later I cleared out my room, which did not yet have a new occupant, although she had been offered one in a few days time. I asked her how she knew, and her eyes clouded, before she looked away. There was no need for words between us, we both understood the implication—another young child was about to be kidnapped from a loving family by Social Services.

I left the most important stuff with Sophie in her room, but took most of my own things with me when I left. That was, after I was invited to stay for dinner. Subsequently she drove me back to the gaol. She parked a good distance down the road so she would not be seen.

I watched her leave and waving, waited until her car was out of sight. I stood on the pavement with mixed emotions. I loved being back with her and could still feel her arms holding me so tightly, lovingly. At the same time, there was renewed sadness in my heart, knowing I was not allowed to live with her. Too much heartache. That drove me not to see her again for a long time.

Domicile!

Domicile is not a made-up word. It is a physical means of child abuse, that people you don't know, and who have only their own best interests at heart, employ to try and control you. I was allowed no say in my current, or future situation of life. In reality, they use it to make money for themselves, and create enforcement empires, irrespective of the needs of the child.

I was mad as hell when I returned to gaol, and everybody avoided me, even the bullies. Only one person came to stand at my side, and helped carry my things, Zoë.

Later that evening, Zoë joined me in my room and we got a lot closer to each other. We talked about music, boys, clothes, and sex. She left me quite late, but too soon, fond memories of Sophie resurfaced.

Asif, or Big Daddy as he liked to be called, was waiting for me on Monday morning, and I arrived early for school. Over the days and weeks that followed, my grades continued to improve, and I was becoming a lot more confident in my abilities. I checked out what was available on Sunday. Most of it was sport, with a few prep classes in the morning, plus arts and social deportment.

I asked to see the Deputy Head, and she told me that officially my status was only as a weekday student. The House Mistress was called to attend, and she was aware of my voluntary Saturday attendance, and saw no reason I could not come on Sunday's also, just as long as I did not sleepover, and paid for my weekend school meals. I was delighted, because it also let me use the library and spend proper time on my homework in the right environment. The deputy Head agreed, and sanctioned my endeavours.

I mentioned this to Asif as he took me home, but he said it would be difficult and I had better mention it to Mohammed. By prior arrangement, I was collected one hour later than normal on Saturday evening. It suited, allowing me to get on with homework in the Library.

Mohammed was charming and again kissed my hand when I got in the back with him. He held it for a short while, and ran his thumb over the back. Once again, he complimented me on my beautifully smooth skin, and I blushed once more. He was charming, almost saintly.

We talked about my life, and we laughed a lot. He seemed genuinely interested in what I was doing, often dropping suitable compliments into his banter. He asked me if I had a boyfriend, and I said, "No, don't be silly."

He replied, "I would love to be your boyfriend, but I am sure a beautiful young lady, such as yourself, finds me far too old and boring."

I said, "No, not at all. I think you are a wonderful man. It's just that I don't know if I'm ready for a boyfriend yet."

I was actually thinking about it, but he broke the spell, "So, you mean you would consider being my girlfriend?"

"Er... Maybe?" I said without thinking. I was so caught up in the moment my brain went dead, but my heart was so alive. He kept me laughing all the way back. As we got near the home, my gaol, I said that I hoped they still had the canteen open, as I was starving. He looked genuinely shocked, and insisted I join him for dinner. He made a short phone call, barked a command at Asif, who changed direction at once.

Mohammed took me to a posh restaurant and we went inside. It was very swish. I was presented with a menu without prices, but I got to look at his when he pointed out a dish to me. His menu did have prices, and the food was incredibly expensive. He appeared unconcerned, and after checking what I liked to eat, ordered for me.

The waiters were most courteous and professional. One came to ask what we would like to drink, and Mohammed ordered a bottle of wine. The waiter came back with the bottle in an ice bucket, and two glasses on a tray. He presented a small taste for Mohammed's consideration, and enquired most politely, "I presume the young lady is old enough to drink, Sir?"

Mohammed replied casually, "Of course, I am sure my niece would love a glass of wine, wouldn't you my dear?"

I was acting all grown up and behaving like one of the older girls at school. I said, "I would love a glass of wine, it goes so well with lobster thermidor, don't you think?"

I chose the moment and told him about the offer of extra schooling on Sunday. A cloud passed his face and he said, "That will be difficult, but leave it with me and I will try to arrange something. It won't be for several weeks I'm afraid. But I will get something sorted for you."

Apart from that one minor disappointment, the dinner was terrific and we really enjoyed ourselves. I was deeply thrilled and I had a great time. I was sad when the evening came to an end. Another of his taxis came to collect us, this time driven by a big man called Khan. When we neared my home Mohammed asked me, "What is wrong Isabella? You seem sad. Have I offended you in any way?"

I looked up in astonishment and replied, "No, I had the most amazing time tonight. It was fantastic and the best night of my life. You are such a wonderful man. Thank you for spoiling me. I'm just a little sad that the evening is over, that's all."

He leaned closer to me and I could smell his cologne. He said, "I also had a wonderful night, because you are such a beautiful and entertaining young lady. I do hope you will allow me to become your boyfriend?"

I slowly nodded my head, but I did not know how to reply. He distracted my thoughts by bringing out his mobile phone and asking, "Please, allow me to take a picture of you. You are so very beautiful. It will help me remember our happy times together, until we meet again."

Mohammed appeared so taken with me I could not refuse. He took several pictures, before adding that my skirt was a little too long, and that instead of tights I should wear white ankle socks. Soon we pulled up at the gaol, and he kissed my hand again, this time flicking the back of it with his tongue. He asked me if we had a date for next Saturday, and I said, "Yes, of course." He made me giggle and I was extremely happy.

On Sunday, after breakfast, I was summoned to the matron's office. I could have dropped dead when I entered the sacrosanct, because the woman greeting me eagerly was the same one who put me into care. It turned out she had taken redundancy, and was now offering her services by running a care home. I knew instinctively she was running a scam, I just couldn't figure out what it was at the time.

She gave me a load of bullshit and informed me that she had taken a special interest in my case, which is why she had requested me brought to her care home. She did ask about my schooling, and I told her everything was going extremely well.

Somehow, she knew about the taxi rides I was getting, but I reasoned people would have seen me using them, and probably mentioned the fact to her. Matron said, "They are my preferred firm, and are extremely honest and reliable. I know the owner personally. Mohammed is such a lovely man. Many a girl would dream of marrying him."

That morning I was haunted by Mohammed's words. He had asked me to be his girlfriend. There was absolutely no mistake. I could not believe it. He was serious as well. Matron had all but confirmed he was single. I felt grown-up. I started adding up everything I liked about him, and it was a long list. I tried to think of anything I did not like about him, and drew a blank, until I remembered Sunday taxi service.

My thoughts turned to what it would be like to have a proper boyfriend. I knew I was falling for him. I realised I had agreed to a 'date' with him for next Saturday. I wondered if that meant he was already my boyfriend. I wasn't sure. In time, I wondered if last night already counted as a date, and I became even more confused.

I decided to take up the hem of my school skirt and buy some ankle socks. I found some Wonder Web for the hem, and a pack of white ankle socks at Vijay Hussein's store. I was on my way to pay when I saw the make-up display, and stopped to look at things I was not sure how to use properly.

I spent ages using the free samples, trying to get the right shades before the owner's daughter joined me. Siroun was a nice girl about sixteen years old. She asked me if I wanted make-up for a date. I said yes, and she asked me what look I wanted.

Siroun laughed as we made friends. She said the makeup depended upon if my boyfriend was black, Asian, or white. I said he was from Pakistan, and she enthused. She told me men from her country didn't like a lot of make-up, and chose for me, matching what she offered to my skin colour and tone.

The bill was more than I expected, but I knew Mohammed was worth it. Vijay was very chatty, and we were becoming good friends.

I got back and took up the hem of both my school skirts. Zoë was there to help me, and soon it was done. One ended up being three inches higher than before, and the other almost as short. I tried them on when I got back to my room, and they looked and felt dead short to me. Zoë told me they were perfect.

We spent the rest of the day together, going out after lunch and hanging out. I checked buses for Sunday, but there was nothing suitable. I would have to rely on Mohammed and hope he could sort something out. I thought about him and wondered if he was missing me? Was he looking at my pictures right at that moment? The thought was such a turn on. Zoë interrupted my wandering wishes, and we moved on, me telling her about Mohammed, all over again. He was the only thing on my mind.

We were ambling towards the high street, knowing most of the shops would be closed. We were close to a Balti house when Zoë saw the main gang leader from the home. We were about to turn round when the bully called us over and asked what we were doing. I was ready to punch her, but she seemed chilled and said, "Here, have some candy."

We both took sweets from her. I wondered why she talked American. But they tasted good, and we took several. Years later, I was to discover they were laced with a small amount of drugs. Hence her name: Candy Monster. Well, she either did that, or used her fists. Either way, her prey always submitted to her whims. But, she was toying with us, and we both fell into her trap. She was very clever, at least in some ways––Using and abusing people.

Sometime later, she offered us both a cigarette. I took one and she lit it for me. Zoë was undecided, but wanted to look big, so took one also. By then I was feeling good; she had already mildly drugged us.

The girl seemed to be OK on her own, and we chatted about music for a while. A short time later, two of her henchgirls arrived, but to our surprise, she kept talking to us. She asked us if we had boyfriends, and Zoë said no. She asked me a second time, and feeling under pressure, I said, "Yes I think so, but we haven't had our second date yet, so I'm not quite sure."

To change the subject away from me, I asked her if she had one. "What? Just one? I have several."

She laughed at our astonishment, before adding, "I'm waiting for one of them right now, and he'll have some free booze and smokes."

95

A Pakistani woman left the shop just then, and minutes later the bully was beckoned inside. She turned to leave us as her girls joined her, but looked back before they disappeared inside, and asked us if we wanted to join her. I looked at Zoë feeling a bit unsure. Candy Monster shrugged, "Up to you," and went inside. We followed her, not wanting to miss out, and also wanting to get in with her.

We went straight through to the back room where there were a couple of young Pakistani men. They were dressed quite well and made us feel welcome. Immediately we were offered drinks, and I chose vodka and orange. Zoë did the same and we all drank a toast of friendship. One of the guys got out his tin and started rolling. I knew it was skunk and told them I liked the stuff. He asked me if I could make a spliff, and I said, "Sure, no problem."

We all smoked the joint and passed it around. Before it was finished the guy handed me the tin and asked me to make a couple more. It had been a few years, but I remembered, and soon had three more lined up on the table. I felt in complete control, showing off my expert skills.

That afternoon was a great blast, and we drank a lot. The joints were good and soon we were all laughing our heads off at the slightest thing. Everything was so funny.

I came up wise when a line of white powder was laid on the table. They wanted us to take it, but I refused point blank, and stopped Zoë also. Loady's words of wisdom came back to me, and I remembered what I had seen on the streets of London. For the first time I felt uneasy, and knew we needed to get out of there while we still could.

They tried many male tricks to stop us leaving, but I was determined. A couple of girls I did not know arrived just then, and they did the drink and drugs at once. They also had a pizza, but I declined — I worried it was laced with something. Eventually we were let out the back way, with a nod from the bully.

They said, "Come back next Sunday, and have some fun."

I said, "On condition I don't do hard drugs, we have a deal."

It was dark outside and we were still laughing our heads off when we got back to my room. I have no idea what we talked about. Zoë slept in my bed that night, and in the morning, we both felt awful. I didn't want to move, but knew I had to get ready for school. I forced myself to eat breakfast and drank a lot of water. I left early and got chocolate bars and a bottle of isotonic Lucozade from Vijay's.

Asif was waiting for me outside to pick me up. He said he had seen me enter the shop as he arrived. I thought nothing of it. I ate all the chocolate and drank some Lucozade. He told me to sleep on the back seat, and I did. I was still feeling rough when Asif shook me awake and told me it was time for school. I gathered he had stopped and waited until just before class began. He was so kind to me. Somehow, my new, short skirt

had ridden up much higher as I slept, but again I thought nothing of it —
at the time.

Asif had been checking something on his mobile phone, but he put it
away as I came awake, and he dropped me at the school gate.

> [Bilty: "This is sick, Isabella. Mohammed, Asif as well, they
> were grooming you. That's if I read the situation correctly."
> "Yes you do. But let's not get ahead of the story. And don't
> interrupt, or I lose the flow. Now where was I? Oh yes."]

The day started badly. I was pulled up about the length of my skirt.
Nothing was done, and in time, the school seemed to accept and forget
about it. It was no shorter, comparatively, than most of the older girls to
be fair. I got through the first couple of classes feeling like shit, but
brightened as the day wore on.

That evening, Asif was pleased to see me rejoin the human race, and
was chatty. We had great fun on the way home. Somehow, I ended up
telling him where we were on Sunday, and he was pleased, saying, "The
manager is close family. You should go there again next Sunday.

"They guys are my good friends and relations. You have nothing to
fear from them. They like to have a good time on their one day off each
week." It seemed reasonable, and he encouraged me to attend next time.

I made it back in time for dinner, Zoë was waiting for me at our
table, and it looked as though she had had a rough day. I asked her if
anything was wrong, but she shook her head.

We went up to my room, and I had to do some homework before I
could spend proper time with her. We talked about yesterday, and she
wanted to know why I didn't try the white powder. I told her straight,
realising I sounded like one of the boring drugs-ed teachers.

I stopped, began again, this time telling her a little about my life on
the streets, of Loady, and followed with what I had seen. I described the
addicts, and told her about the sick on their clothes, their shaking, fevers,
loss of memory and identity. I told her most of them smelled bad because
they never washed.

She was shocked when I went into detail about Tina. "That's what
we call Crystal, or crystal meth. Loady told me that at first it's great
because it makes sex feel much better. Months later, addicts can only have
sex when they are high, and soon after, they can't get it up at all. You can
tell them easily because they lose all their teeth, and scratch at imaginary
bugs under their skin. One guy I saw had large wounds on his arms, the
centre was a sickly yellow, but the sore was outlined with a black ring.
They get angry and cannot sleep for days, weeks even."

With the passing of my words, she thanked me, but did not seem to be any happier. I asked her what was wrong, and this time I forced the truth out of her. She asked, "We didn't do it last night, did we?"

"No, don't be stupid." She sighed with relief, we cuddled and fell asleep in each other's arms. It was vaguely like being held by a mother, except we were growing into adulthood. We had nowhere else we were allowed to go, and no one else to turn to, except towards each other.

The next evening Zoë seemed more settled and was a lot surer of herself. Again, we went back to my room after dinner. She ran her hands over my body, not sexually, but inquisitively. I told her I liked it, sort of.

That made her cry, and later she told me a little of her life. It was not pretty. Social services had made an absurd case against her parents, and made it stick. Her father was arrested for assault, neglect, and ill treatment of a minor. Her mother lasted longer, but eventually they got her to on similar charges. Both ended up in criminal Court.

Her sad tale reminded me of my own life. How my own family and I were treated — Social Services fabricated a case that was all lies, and Family Court never allowed us to give evidence in our defence. Zoë and I wound up in a 'care home': gaol.

I held her for a long time, and tried to imagine the anguish she had endured. So many years of being abused by the system that was supposed to protect her, us, from people like Child Services. The mere reminder of it turned my stomach, and festered in the deepest recesses of my mind like a callow, scabrous wen.

Our emotional wounds were still raw and rankling. Our shared and bitter resentment was turning gangrenous — the only balm being the close and physical proximity of each other. In that small haven of warmth, we shared understanding, and mutual absolution.

On Wednesday Zoë came up after dinner, and she was back to being her usual chirpy self. I wish she hadn't, because she was determined to find out everything about my boyfriend. By snippets and tugs, she dragged the truth out of me.

Once she had the full story we became more serious, and I asked her if she thought I should have Mohammed as my boyfriend.

"He's a bit old, isn't he?"

"No. He's fun. And he makes me laugh. He seems devoted to me, and if the age difference doesn't matter to him, it doesn't matter to me."

"He sounds nice. I'll need to meet him before I can advise you. But, if he's as wonderful as you say, I'll take him away from you."

We howled with laughter and laid bets on which of us would be his girlfriend. I knew I would win, but loved teasing her.

I now wish I'd never done that, but time reveals all. I did have a boyfriend, well almost, but I felt I was not ready to have sex with him, just then. I remembered Vikki's words, and pondered her deeper meanings, ones I by then understood better. I thought about having sex most of the time, but I still didn't understand it.

Zoë and I became close that day, and closer still in the days that followed. During that time, Zoë became my first, true, best friend.

We did everything together, well apart from school, and at first, seeing my boyfriend. She helped me get my new make-up just right, and I worked on hers as we experimented. That was such a blast. I knew *he* would ask me to become his girlfriend again on Saturday, and I thought I would accept.

Bilty:
Personal Journal:

Comment:
This is beginning to become insidious. What the hell is a man thrice her age, doing with Isabella? I cannot ignore the sexual component, but that beggars belief, doesn't it?

She was still a child, for God's sake.

Point:
What is beginning to puzzle me, is how in fact, these secretive agencies and Courts work. Obviously, they have a jealously guarded secret agenda, but I would need to know the way it should work in theory. Research required.

Notes:
1. Isabella's mother shielded her daughter from much of what went on. The SS processes' I also need to understand. Those of the Family Court also.

2. I am resigned to spending hours on research, unless there is a short-cut to deeper understanding. There's no harm in asking.

Bitly
"Isabella, do you, or anyone, have the full documented process, as used by the SS, the Courts?"

"I don't Bilty, although I can tell you the legal points, because I studied them as a vocational course."

Mel said, "Nope. I just did what I had to."

Vikki was delighted, "I never went there, thank God!"

Zoë said, "I do. I wrote it all down. But it won't make sense unless I tell it, like how it was for me and Mom. Like, back then. Issy, do I have to?"

"No Zō, you do not. But I think you should."

"Humph. Okay then, I guess. I'm not happy with this, so get me something 'nice' to help me through it ... iced Eccles cakes, and Tequila shots on the side. That should do it.

"I'll be ready tomorrow midday, Bilty."

"Zoë, Isabella, I really need this information. But, well my wife and I, we usually unwind at the end of the week, go out for a meal and relax, share. Can we pick this up on Monday afternoon? No wait, I am in Oxford. Tuesday perhaps?"

"Why not come tomorrow or Sunday. Bring your wife, but she only listens and takes notes."

"Yes, she mentioned the same, actually. The video is great, but it does not tell of the greater atmosphere and emotion within the room. I'll put it to her, and call. I guess mornings are out?"

"Completely. Luncheon is breakfast, and we begin. Let me know. I need to break the back of it, the all of this emotional abyss."

Note:

And there it was again. A throwaway remark, but so full of deeper meaning. 'emotional abyss'.

Chapter 14 – Zoë's Story: The Accident

Project Domicile
Interview: 06
Location: Fiddlers Court, The Oval, Holborn, Central London.
Time: 12:52 hours, Sunday, 15th October.
Subject: Zoë
Others Present:
   IW, Melanie, Vikki, and Candice my wife.
Note:
This is scheduled to be a long telling, but my wife and I need to hear it.
Observations:
   Zoë is not happy. She is wringing her hands, and even grasping a stiff vodka sees her hands shaking. I am inclined to stop proceedings before they start.
   But then, IW whispers something to her, and they high five. I was not expecting that.
   Zoë's eyes are downcast, but her body language changes, becomes resolute, a strange combination. She begins speaking immediately. The words are mumbled, until we reposition the mic.

Zoë: Take 1

   Issy has told most of this story, but I want to tell my story, myself. I worked on this for a long time, writing down each thing the SS did to us. What they said versus what they did. They way they use words to mean something else: opposite. Scumballs.
   This is the SS process. I'll begin at the beginning.

Bilty

   Silence.
   Zoë stood and gulped her drink like a dart's player, down in one, one-hundred and eighty. Immediately she was walking for a refill, her palm out, held up against protestation."Just one more. I feel ragged."
   She was way too stretched emotionally, and again, I wondered if we should quit. The poor girl.
   But then, she had the info we needed. To this day, I'm not sure if it was the pills or the spliff that calmed her. The drink was her crutch, let's be clear. After all those intervening years, she appeared to be as strung out as ever, except for Isabella, and her true friends calming influence.
   Candice whispered, "Relax Bilty, this is going to be great. Wait for it. There's so much emotion about to escape this girl. Think of it as being an inner cleansing."
   When she returned, her fabulistic demeanour I had glimpsed before, was displayed in full colour.

This was going to get interesting. We began again.

Zoë: Take II

Issy has told most of this story, but I want to tell my story, myself. I worked on this for a long time, writing down each process the SS go through, what they say versus what they do. They way they use words and phrases with two meanings.

This is the SS process. I'll begin at the beginning.

We were not a rich family. My father was a labourer on a building site, but work was drying up as the development completed. My mother worked part-time at the local Co-op, but money was very tight. Despite this, we were well cared for, and I was the eldest of three children. Our parents made sure we were well fed, clean, and properly dressed. I did not have expensive designer gear like most of the kids at school, so learned early how to fight the rich-boy and bitch bullies. But at home, we were a close and loving family.

I lived in Bradford in those days, and was nine years old at the time Social Services became interested in us. Like I said, money was tight, so, one-day mummy was upstairs giving the younger kids a bath together. They loved it, but I, being older, knew the real reason was to save on water, and water heating bills.

I had been hoping to go to the hair salon, but dad could not afford it. My hair was kept short in those days, and it needed cutting. Dad had done this several times before and was quite good at hairdressing, so we went into the kitchen that Friday evening, where I perched on a stool.

He was about finished, and just tidying up around my right ear, when there was an extremely loud bag outside. It sounded like a gun going off, but we later realised it was an old motorbike backfiring. Unfortunately, this happened just as dad was making a snip, and as we both reacted instinctively to the noise, the outcome was he inadvertently cut my ear. The noise was very loud.

It wasn't a bad wound and didn't hurt too much, but there was quite a bit of blood to begin with. Dad was ever so sorry and concerned, but we knew, both of us had moved slightly at precisely the wrong moment. It was a natural human reaction. As it was, the cut stopped bleeding a few minutes later, and dad put a plaster on it. We thought no more about it. It was just one of those things, an accident [R 14.1].

At school the following Monday, I had forgotten all about it, and although clearly visible, the wound was healing well. When I arrived for class, one of the teachers I did not like a lot, because she always had it in for me, noticed the cut and asked me about it. I told her the full story.

A few hours later, I was called out of class and sent to see the Headmaster. I had no idea what I had done wrong, so was at bit confused. Two women were in his office when I entered, and he asked me about the cut to my ear. I repeated my story truthfully, wondering why he, and these mystery women were so interested in it.

I was told to wait outside, and a couple of minutes later, the Head came out and told me I would have to leave with the two women, as my case had been referred. It was only after that, I discovered they were from Social Services. I was taken to their offices, where they 'tut-tutted', exchanging knowing looks. I knew they were up to no good.

Once I was trapped in their den, I was left for a while, before they interrogated me. Like Issy, they asked a lot of questions, and one seemed to be helping me answer the stranger ones. One of those was, "How often does your father abuse you?"

I think I knew what she meant by 'abuse', but wasn't too sure. The other woman explained, "It is when your father cuts your ear."

I understood, so said "Once. It was an accident. We both moved because of the backfire, it sounded like a gun going off."

They didn't like my answer. I knew something else was going on, I just couldn't figure out what. I was a little scared. The place was strange and smelled horrible. All I wanted to do was go home. The next question was, "How often does your father cut your hair?"

I replied, "Almost every week. Why?"

The older one smiled and said, "So, your father abuses you at least once each week. What was your mother doing at the time?"

I tried to tell them the 'abuse' only happened one time. They told me to shut up and answer the question about my mother. I was confused. She had to repeat the question for me. I now realise they were distracting and manipulating me, like lawyers do, but at that time, I was young and trusting. I am not anymore.

When they were done, I had to wait ages, before I was told, "You'll be staying with a lovely couple tonight, for your own protection."

I screamed, "I want my parents. You've no right to do this to me!"

The older woman scolded me and said, "Child, we have every right to do whatever we like with you. If you ever want to see your parents again, you had better do as I say."

That is emotional blackmail.

I was gob-smacked and burst into tears. I now know that was emotional abuse. The younger one tried to be nice. She comforted and confided in me, "Zoë, it will be a lot better for everybody, especially your parents, if you go along with the situation for now. This is a misunderstanding, that's all. Stay with these nice people tonight, and we will sort it all out tomorrow."

I was forced to stay with strangers that night. They treated me OK, but I was very unhappy. They spent a lot of time trying to soothe my fears, and eventually I came to trust them enough to tell them bits of my story, and a little about my home life.

They were eager to share and support me, so I suppose I ended up telling them quite a lot. I also talked because it helped me remember my family, and it soothed my heart. Their questions were always positive, but became a little intense, and I started to feel uneasy. They were clever with words, like the time they asked me, "Zoë, it is clear your mother and father look after you all extremely well. You seem well fed, but was there ever a time when you were hungry?"

I didn't need to think and said, "No." I thought them done, but one said, "You said your father takes work whenever he can get it. What happened when school was closed for the afternoon two weeks ago?"

I now know they were fishing, but I was naïve back then. I had to think quite hard before I remembered, "Dad knew I would be home early, and he said he would make some tuna sandwiches for us when I got back from school, he does them real special. Mum was working afternoon shift, only four hours, but that was when I would arrive home early. She timed her job so that she could collect us from school.

"That day dad had a couple of hours work and was due home at his breakfast break-time, which is ten o'clock on a building site. That's a pretty odd time for breakfast, don't you think? Anyway, he was offered work with another contractor, if he stayed and worked until eight that evening. It was good money, his first job for them. He later told us they were pleased, and would offer him a lot of extra work in the future.

We were delighted. It was enough money to pay the electricity bill that month, and take us for a burger treat. But that was the future.

"He called home and left a message on the answer machine, telling me he had work, and told me to nuke a pizza. I was really happy, and the pizza was great. I ate it all myself."

I smiled at the couple, feeling quite proud of how we, as a family, pulled together to survive. I noticed the man made some notes, but his wife distracted me by asking more about our home life. Not long after I said I felt tired, so went up to bed — not because I was actually tired, I was tired of their questions.

The next day I was allowed to return to my home. My mother was delighted to see me, but she was extremely touchy, like clingy, which was not like her. She jumped every time the phone rang, but always looked disappointed when the caller was revealed. "Where's dad?"

She looked away, before saying; "He has a lot of work, and may be gone for a few days with the new contractor." I enthused it was great, and although she tried to appear happy, I knew she was anything but.

I put up with dad's absence until the weekend, and was worried about him. He had not returned, or even called. That was so unlike him, and I knew something was wrong. Mother sat me down and talked to me like she would an adult. She said that dad had to go away for some time, and told me everything would be all right.

I accepted it at face value, but she was holding something back. She had never done that before, and I knew she was trying to protect me, and the family. The days passed into weeks, and I worried more and more. I did not know at the time, mum met the SS again.

The following day, mum told me what the SS said. "We are most pleased with the way things are going. Everything should be resolved over the coming few weeks. We are working on a Child Protection Plan. You need to complete a core assessment, and a couple of core meetings."

Mum agreed, even though she did not fully understand some of the jargon they used, because they did not use words ordinary people understood. We later discovered their words were full of deception and secret meanings. Issy, what did you say it was?

"Jargon disguising culpable, deliberate deception."

That's it, thanks. It was a month later when she was ordered to attend another meeting with the SS. Like last time, she had to go to the local authority den, and although she asked for a morning appointment, she was given one midway through her regular afternoon shift at work.

The night before, she talked to me after my younger brothers had gone to bed. She seemed bright and cheerful, although she did add that her boss at work had given her, her first ever official warning for taking too much time off work. She had completed the core assessment and related meetings, and seemed confident everything would be fine.

She did mention that these meetings had always been scheduled for afternoons, hence her warning at work. However, she was certain that everything would be resolved after the next meeting.

The next day the Outline Child Protection Plan was agreed, and mum was assured that after a couple of weeks, and a few police checks, we would be fine. I was happy and we had a lovely evening, just the four of us. I missed dad, but knew he was doing his best for us.

Then, something strange happened. The police had never been to our house before. After that day, they started coming to see us every day. This was because mum had agreed we three kids should be put on the Child Protection Plan. I looked at her, and she explained it was only for a couple of weeks. The aim was to have us taken off the plan after we had been checked out. She added that once they were happy, everything would return to normal, and the police were simply doing their job.

Mother was led to believe this meant we would be free of them, and once more a happy family. Having since heard the stories of many girls who endured something similar, I now realise their words actually meant, "Until they can get us adopted or into care." They are liars! There were two ways to get us off the plan, what we understood as the end of it, and their intention to kidnap us.

At first, the police called once each day. But after a few weeks, when we presumed the visits would stop, the police started to drop by several times each day, including late evenings. I tried to find out what was really going on, but mum was frightened, jittery. She was becoming confused and elusive. I had never known her in such a state. I knew she was scared. One evening, after my younger brothers had gone to bed, I decided to get the truth out of her. She said, "Everything will be OK."

She looked away, and I knew instinctively, everything would not be OK. I plagued her with questions until she finally admitted dad had been arrested, and charged with "Assault, neglect, and ill-treatment."

"What? How? Who? It doesn't make any sense."

"They say he assaulted, neglected, and ill-treated you. It's all lies."

I could not believe it. It was ridiculous, twisted. I was still trying to puzzle everything out when she said, "Because of this, he is on bail from criminal court, and is not allowed to come home."

I cried and she held me close, rocking me, as was always her way. I felt her tears drop onto my shaking shoulders, and we cried together. We were both extremely upset, trying to reason why dad was being treated that way. We were interrupted when a heavy hand knocked the door; "This is the police, open up."

The police picked-up on our emotional distress, and compounded it by asking us a lot of needless questions; "Why are you both upset?"

"I was explaining why her father cannot come home. Why are you still pestering us. You were supposed to check us for only two weeks."

"We will check for as long as we wish, until we are satisfied."

"Satisfied of what?"

"That your children are not being abused. It seems your daughter has been. You appear to be an incompetent mother."

"Just what the hell is going on here..."

We had an argument, and we both explained why we were upset. But they were aggressive bullies. They were dismissive of our feelings and concerns. At one point, a policeman pulled me by the arm into a different room. The policewoman wasn't there.

He was bending over to intimidate me, shouting at me, and jabbing his finger in my face. He never quite touched me, but he was fearsome. I backed away. I have no idea what he said. I was scared stiff.

Mother hauled me away and put me behind her legs. She said, "Get out of our home. Stop harassing us!"

I now know that is what the police, the Bussies as Issy justly calls them, had been angling for all along. They were doing legwork for the SS. I have no doubt they got a backhander for terrorising us. Shame they weren't chasing real criminals, instead of wasting their time on us, eh?

The nasty policeman said, "Mrs. Rendell, you are refusing to co-operate, and are preventing safety checks. I note you appear to be mentally and emotionally unstable, and unable to cope. Your daughter is clearly suffering from emotional abuse. Good evening, Madam."

We had been upset before the Bussies arrived, by then we were distraught. We clung together, and my brothers joined us, because they had been woken by the commotion. We were all frightened. Mum was drowning in her rage and becoming enfeebled by the onslaught of powers previously unknown to her. I got up and made us all hot chocolate drinks. That broke the spell, if only until the next morning.

I had already left for school, when Social Services arrived with a police escort, to arrest mother and my brothers. Mum was the only one charged. Her crime was allegedly causing me emotional abuse, and having failed to protect me from 'assault'. This referred to when dad was cutting my hair, and accidentally cut my ear when the motorbike backfired. She was upstairs bathing the kids at the time, so I don't see how she had anything to do with it, but that's the Bussies for you.

The two women from the SS were waiting for me when school finished, and I was taken to another foster home for a couple of nights. No one would tell me what was going on, I mean they all appeared sympathetic and caring, but they would never tell me the whole truth. Adults with power, using and misusing that power, and the meanings of words to kidnap me. I began to believe it that night.

This time, when the temporary foster caregivers tried to befriend me, I did not believe them, and kept mum. They wanted to keep me off school the next day, but I insisted upon going, even though I hated the place. I hated them more. I made sure I got detention that day, which gave me another hour away from them. I was reacting to the way I had previously been treated and misled.

They were pissed-off when I finally straggled out of the school gate, but they tried to hide their animosity towards me. I made their lives worse by playing-up as much as I could. They were probably quite nice people, but they were not my own parents. It was as simple as that.

I was there for two days and two nights, before I was allowed to go home. In the meantime, mother had been charged and released on bail, her trial being set for several months in the future. That night we all slept in her bed. I think she needed us just as much as we needed her.

Bilty

"This is horrific treatment, a nightmare you had to live through. I am appalled at the way you were mistreated by the police. They picked up on your distress, and compounded it. They also broke the law by physically moving you, and with intimidation. I will be calling for an investigation into their conduct. One male officer took you aside and physically threatened you. There can be no mistake. Can you remember anything else about him, Zoë? His name?"

"Er? He was big, nasty, a bully. Oh, and he had three stripes on his upper arms."

"That means he was a sergeant. That narrows down the field. It also means he should have known better. But then again, perhaps he thought he did, and could get away with it. So far, he has.

"The charges against both of your parents appear to be fictitious. I am most concerned criminal court was supportive of these cases, and did not throw them out immediately. I will investigate.

"Candice, do you have anything to add?"

"No love, not at present. And I won't labour points already raised. I will say this, that being here is helping me a lot. I am getting the emotion, which I will relate in the book.

"I've also logged the process for you, which order things usually occur in, although Emergency Care Orders can be issued at any time.

"Zoë, thank you. This does you great credit, and your memory is excellent. This is thirsty work, may I possibly ask for a Gin and Tonic?"

Isabella was attentive immediately, "I'm so sorry Candice. We all know to help ourselves here, apologies. Vikki, you are the Go-for today. I'll replenish glasses before we continue. Zoë, what do you need?"

"Same again, and to be done with this. But I'm feeling OK so far. Just don't interrupt me, OK?"

Bilty:

Personal Journal:

This is going better than I expected. Zoë is obviously stressed, but is telling it how it was for her and her family.

Notes:

1. There is clear deception here by the SS. They lead a family through a process, letting them think the next hurdle would see the return of the child. It does not. Each step makes it harder for the child to return home.

2. Discover all I can about the police involvement in this case.

3. Similar with the actions of criminal court, which should only rely on certifiable evidence, not that as supplied by Family Court.

Zoë

"OK Bilty. Let's get this done with. There's still a lot more to get through, so keep up."

Chapter 15 – Zoë's Story: The SS Scam

The next day I skipped school, we needed each other in a close and family way. Being the eldest child, mother began to turn to me for support. She had always been a strong woman, with things she understood. She was clueless regards the evil schemes of Social Services, and their buddies within the police force. I turned my feelings inwards, and stepped up to support the greater well-being of our family.

During the kid's afternoon nap, mum told me about her horrendous experience. I learned never to trust the police. She had to sign many forms while she was incarcerated. The Bussies or SS put them in front of her and told her to sign. She did as she was told, and was not allowed to read them.

She did not realise one form was unique. It was a Section 20 Order under The Children's Act, by which parents may voluntarily put their children into care. Mum still has no recollection of signing that form, but the SS have many means to distract you from their true intentions, as do the Bussies. To me that is lying to your face. It is dishonest, and trickery. Mother never gave her knowing consent, so that is illegal.

Mother was not arrested the next day. Instead, the police arrived at dawn the day after, with several social workers. We children were taken into care, for our own protection. Mum, to her credit, tried to stop them taking all of us, but was again arrested, this time for causing emotional abuse to all of us, and assaulting a police officer.

I ended up in another foster home, and it must have been planned days ahead. I know my younger brothers were taken to separate foster homes that night, and we were not allowed to go home for days.

Sometime later, we had to attend our first court hearing. Family Court did not allow us to say much at all, and without our own testimony being allowed as evidence in our defence, the Judge believed the SS. I repeat, we were not, ever, allowed to speak in our defence! I was never once asked what I wanted.

It was a Kangaroo Court [R 15.1] [and: Case Scenarios R 15.2], and it was clear we had all been proven guilty before we even set a foot inside the building. We worked out they were already planning behind our backs, and the Family Court appearances were only to rubber stamp what they had already decided behind closed doors — what the fate of our once happy family would be.

During the hearing, mother was forced to sign a Consent Order, as part of the now all-pervading Child Protection Plan. They told her that if she did not, the judge would make an Interim Care Order. They added to the pressure by stating she would not get us, her children back that day if she did not. She was bullied, in closed court, into signing the form. Her legal representation was supplied by the SS, and surprise, surprise, he urged her to sign the form. It was court approved blackmail.

[Bilty: "Surely that is illegal. The court sanctioned this? Unbelievable! I will be pursuing this travesty of justice. It was coercion inflicted on the defendant in full knowledge of the Judge."
"You're starting to get how they work now Bilty. That's why everything is kept secret, so no outsiders can challenge them."]

They also told Mum, she must undergo a psychological assessment, because the police that checked on us had reported her as being mentally unstable. That would be 'opinion', as I'm sure the sergeant had no mental health qualifications.

It was also made clear to her, that if she did not, they would immediately apply for an Interim Care Order. That would mean we were collected from school and kindergarten, and would, after the following hearing, be taken to stay indefinitely with foster parents.

Mother had no choice but to sign the Consent Order as means to preserve our family unit. As it was, we kids still had to stay with strangers a couple of nights each week, so that she could get some 'respite'. The only *respite* we needed, was for the SS and Bussies to leave us alone. Fuckwits! Mum reassured us it was only temporary, until everything was sorted out officially. I was not so sure, but kept mum.

However, the Consent Order gave those child-snatchers permission to check out every small detail about our family, without us knowing.

Mum had to produce a lot of certificates, and most at her own expense, provide Social Services with things such as criminal record checks, bank statements, and similar personal records. These had been entirely clean, until the series of events the SS began, caused undue and pre-planned strain upon our family. Of course, this view of our happy family was never admissible in court, nor echoed in their highly biased files and reports.

Our family's medical records were also open to scrutiny, even though mum was never allowed to look at them. Later we realised they had spoken to our neighbours, seeking only anything bad, and neglecting all the good and charitable work both of my parents did within the neighbourhood. Several stated they were perturbed because the police were always round at our house.

Mother shouted out, "The Police had never been to our house, once before, until the SS began their hate campaign against us."

"You will only address the court when invited to, Misses Rendell. Your remarks will be overruled as inappropriate."

The same went for mother's place of work, dad's workmates, some of whom were jealous he was given work during harder times. They took statements from the school, kindergarten, and even from sales assistants in local shops, that may have seen any of us, once before, for a fleeting moment.

Social Services systematically dismantled everything positive about our family, all things good, and focused entirely upon the slightest thing they could infer, we did wrong. They created an avalanche of wrongdoing, upon the slopes of the mountain of all the good we did. It was extremely unfair, and so biased as to be beyond belief.

We had all suffered enough, but a couple of days later we were hauled back into court. Social Services made a preliminary case for a Care Order, by stating we were at risk, and needed to be removed from our family, for our own protection.

This was also rubber-stamped by the Judge. No one bothered to listen to us, and if we dared speak in defence of our family, we were told to be quiet or face being charged with Contempt of Court, and an inferred automatic six-months imprisonment.

Mother and I shouted out. She was removed from court. I was physically subdued, and hauled out after her. No one bothered to listen to what either of us said--they treated our words as being irrelevant. So much for Article 12 [R 15.3] of the UN Convention on the Rights of the Child.

["Thanks, Mel for looking that up for me. Issy, taa."]

At the time, none of us realised these were only threats. We believed it was what would happen to us if we told the truth.

They did that deliberately to silence us, and to stop us protecting ourselves. Social Services had arranged for a defence lawyer, but he was acting for them, and not representing our family's best interests. Mother had tried to appoint one that would act in our own defence.

We thought we had a kind heart on our side, but he took our money first, and when the SS legal people stated he was not on an approved list, he aborted the case. The money was gone, and his bill covered it exactly. He did nothing for us. What a scammer! That's lawyers for you. Only in it for how much they can con, for the least amount of work. Mum had borrowed most of that money, as we were living well below the breadline, my father not being there.

Mother had been networking. I was not quite sure what that meant at that time, but she got new help from another lawyer.

The female lawyer was very good, and she assembled a defence case for the first time [R 15.4]. As soon as the Court, the prosecution, and the SS learned about her new defence council, she was denied the opportunity to represent us.

It seems to me, the only legal representation allowed within Family Court, are those approved by the prosecution--lawyers acting for them, and never the defence. Isn't that illegal? If not, it should be.

Chapter 15

After that second so-called hearing, my brothers officially disappeared into the system, even though they were not present in court. I have never been allowed to know anything about them since, except different foster parents adopted them. In British Law, I have no legal right to contact them, and my parents are expressly forbidden to.

I was taken to a different foster home, which was in Leeds. I saw mother a few times after that, but we were never allowed to show our true emotions, mother had to go along with whatever they said.

Time passed and I endured living with strangers as best I could. There was no love, no bond of family in the world the SS forced me to inhabit. It was a drab, sad place.

I was suffering extreme emotional abuse because of the SS.

I was put in a new school, and it really sucked being the new kid. Everyone tried to pick on me, until I learned how to fight back. I was never much good with words, but I became very good with my fists.

At the foster home, the other kids also tried it on with me, and I learned another lesson, the caregivers never see what is done to you, but they are always there to witness your response. In my frustration, I started hitting out at them. After that, I was sent to several foster homes, never settling in any one for long. There was a deep and bitter loathing inside me, one that got bigger and worse as I got older.

I was classified as being disruptive, but I was only standing up for myself, and our family. I started cutting myself, and got a tattoo done on the inside of my forearm. It was real cool, look, a preying eagle. Beneath the 'V' of the wings, the bird's talons clutch a scroll that reads, "Fuck You." I liked to show it off when anyone tried to tell me what to do. In reality, all I wanted to do was go back home to mum and dad, my brothers, and live a normal life. Was that too much to ask?

Apparently, it was.

The next hearing was some months later. The SS had been busy, secretively preparing the Local Authority Statement to support a Care Order. Mum was informed about it the week before, and told she would be given a copy of the Statement before things came to Family Court.

I used to tell my guards, as I called my foster parents, I was going to the shops, but in reality I was making reverse charge calls to my mother, and had been doing so virtually every night. We met in secret a few times, so we could talk properly, and cuddle. She had a sense of belief, that this would finally be over and done with.

In one phone call she told me of the 'psychological assessment', and I was mad by the time she finished — not at her, but at the system that treated us like dog-poo on new shoes. This is what she said: "I had to take the afternoon off work again to go see the man, and got a second official warning for time-keeping in the process. I attended the psychologist appointment, but he had been called away on an urgent matter, and had cancelled the meeting. They said they had tried to call me, but there was no message on my mobile, or the answer phone, even after I got home, so I knew they were lying.

"I was getting incredibly fed up with everybody's treatment of me, and ranted at the girl in reception. I knew it was probably not her fault, but she was the one who eventually admitted she had tried to call me. Once she said that, I called her a liar, and many other words. I stormed out of there vowing never to go back.

"Once I got home I had calmed down, and rang to apologise. The girl said she understood, but told me my attendance was no longer necessary, and the psychological assessment was now being completed without my needing to attend for consultation. I started yelling at her again, and she put the phone down. I guess my number was displayed, because I rang back several times, and the calls went unanswered."

We worked out mother had been manipulated to act in entirely unnatural way, by forces outside of her control. We agreed it was a set-up, but knew that without seeing her personally, the report he made would be without any substance. How can you judge somebody's sanity without ever meeting them in person? I wandered back to the stranger's house I was forced to live in, lost in my own thoughts.

Social services came to see me several times, asking me leading questions and trying to turn my innocent words into proof of neglect and emotional abuse. I was already telling them nothing, when they mentioned the weekly abuse by my father. This was what the first social workers had tried to make me say, and I knew everybody was out to get me. I screamed, "My father never abused me! You do every time you crawl out from the cesspit you live in. I hate you!"

I stopped talking completely, except to answer every question with, "You are all liars. I hate you."

I folded my arms, because they were twisting everything I said. I looked at the floor in front of me and totally ignored them. One of them came over to try to gentle information out of me. I lost it in that moment and lashed out. I wanted to rip the bitch open with my nails, and tried to kick her. I would have got her real good as well, but the other one manhandled me so I could hardly move. They left me with raw cuts and new bruises, and were gone a few minutes later. They never came back, but they did hit me. That is physical abuse, and I reported the fact. But nothing was ever done about it. Apparently, I was being restrained.

I snuck out when nobody was looking, and went to the hospital. I complained that the two bitches from Social Services had attacked me. I had expected the police to arrive and arrest them. Instead, they arrested me and took me back to the foster home in handcuffs. No charges were ever brought against them, the ones that did physically abuse me.

Once I returned, the man told me to help my mother in the kitchen. I quipped, "She's not my mother. You are not my father. Fuck Off."

I ran up to my room and locked the door. Soon he and his wife were banging on the door. I ignored them and cried silently, knowing I was destined to go to hell. When I quieted, I thought about my parents, my mother especially. I wished I had her faith in the system [R .15.5]. One that actually did abuse me, personally, far beyond any form of justification.

I guess the physical abuse was my ruse, because I was attacking them. What has zero excuse, is the horrendous mental and emotional abuse Social Services forced me to endure.

I still deeply resent what they did to us — our once happy family. In Law and Family Court, they maintain, "The needs of the child [R 15.6] are paramount." If you ask me, that is just a sick joke. Some made up phrase that is never applied in real life.

I was told I was not allowed to go to the Contested Hearing that followed. How can they call it a Contested Hearing, when they denied me the right to attend?

Apparently, this was for my own protection, again. I had already worked out this was a ruse to prevent me from speaking out. To prevent me from stating what I wanted. I snuck out of the house on Thursday evening when my captors were not looking.

I spoke to mum, and knew right away she was upset. This is what she said. "Zoë, I am still waiting for the report to arrive. They promised it would arrive on Friday, but it's still not here. Believe me when I say that I had no idea what they were trying to do to us. At the time I believed whatever they said, and did whatever they asked of me. After all, they are supposed to be the experts, aren't they?

"Can you ever forgive me?

"Remember I love you, and I always will, despite whatever happens on Monday. I will never stop loving you and your brothers. These people are evil. Never trust a single word their mealy-mouths utter, because they will twist each and every single word to suit their own demonic purpose. Promise me."

I promised her, and I knew she was telling the truth. It was clear she was distracted, so it was a short call, but I promised her I would call again after the hearing on Monday.

The guards caught me when I returned to their house, and we had another row about my conduct, and especially me sneaking out of the house. They demanded to know what I had been doing, and I refused to tell them. The result: I was grounded.

That time I was locked in my room. I was only allowed out for meals and to go to school. I finally managed to call mother on Tuesday lunchtime, skipping school. I was using a public phone where no one would find me. It was just as well, because the school contacted my guards, who went out looking for me. They never found me.

Mum told me everything that day, and before she was done, I learned to hate. She said, "They told me this was just a formality, and my chance to put our side of the story. I half-believed them.

"I was told the report would be sent to me before the hearing, and I would have sufficient time to read it, seek legal advice, and ensure everything was factual. As you know, I was expecting their report to arrive a week before, which is what their words implied. The hearing was scheduled for Monday, and eventually a courier service delivered their information to me on Friday afternoon. Supposedly, there had been delivery problems—Sure. I was out at work, so had to go down on Saturday morning to collect it from their depot. It was there I found out it had been delivered for despatch, to the courier at Friday lunchtime. It was one Friday later than they had promised. But then, they never specified which Friday it would arrive. See how they lie.

"When I got home I tried to read it all, but it was a very long and complicated document. When I got to the part relating to their findings, I was utterly dismayed. They made out I was a useless parent. I cried. They had twisted everything, every fact, and inference against me.

"I did not know a lot of things they stated as fact in the statement. Most of it was distorted and untrue. Hearsay statements they had obtained from people I had never met before, stating how our family were cheats, we owed money—which we do not, and how we regularly mistreated you three children.

"You remember when Little Tim came home from kindergarten with head lice. We could not afford the expensive medications, so I cut off all his hair and washed his head regularly using TCP. Joey's also. Well, they had a statement from the head of the school saying she considered this to be both physical and emotional abuse. They even got a statement from Tim, saying how he cried after I cut off his hair. That is correct, but he was crying because of the itching from the head lice, and not because his hair was gone. See how they twist everything. Omit the actual fact."

Mum cried for a bit, before realising I was still on the phone. I said things to try and comfort her. I was also thinking about how I could get back at our real abusers, the SS. She rallied enough to continue, "Zoë, you know I love you and your brothers more than anything in the world. Never doubt that. This has been so hard for me.

"That Saturday afternoon, I tried every solicitor in town, but nobody was available. I decided to write a statement myself, and poured my heart out to try to protect you all. I thought I was doing the right thing, but once admitted as evidence, they used it to support the psychologist's report [R 15.7] that I was both mentally and emotionally unstable, and a risk to your safety.

"I have absolutely no idea how they could have come to that conclusion. Later, I thought about what had actually happened, and I knew I had been manipulated. The supposed psychologist [R 15.8] was in fact, a part of the system. He had based some of his assumptions on the receptionist's statement. She noted my abusive language, hysterical nature, and my refusal to accept her phone calls in relation to rescheduling the appointment. I remain certain that was a deliberate ploy. She never called me, not once.

"I was unable to find an independent solicitor, so had to accept one of theirs' on Monday morning. I was provided with a court appointed lawyer, but he never challenged any of the lies told against us, so I did, and dismissed the waste of space. In due course, I was forced to represent myself, us, alone. I was given a few minutes to review the case before I was back in Court. I leafed through the few remaining files, because the solicitor had taken virtually everything relating to the case away with him.

"At first, I was allowed to speak, but the SS twisted my words. The Judge warned me, because I did not raise my objections in the correct manner. Eventually, I shouted when I contested what they were alleging, and after that outburst, I was not allowed to speak at all.

"Before I knew what was happening, the Judge granted an Interim Care Order. I was told I could oppose it every twenty-eight days, and that is what I intend to do, although how I can afford it is another matter entirely."

I could feel there was something else going on, something she was not telling me. I knew she had fought gallantly in court, but she wasn't a trained solicitor. I admired her for doing her best. I congratulated her for standing up for us. We talked about the hearing a bit longer, but there was little to add. I also knew this was only one of the things that worried her.

We said our farewells, and just before I hung-up the phone, I told her I would call her tomorrow. She did not reply straight away, as would be normal. Instead, she tried a couple of times to say something, but her words never came.

I had to find out, "Mum, what's going on?"

She finally admitted, "Zoë, with your father gone, it has been very difficult to pay the bills. Just before you called, I opened a letter from the telephone company. It stated that unless I pay the bill immediately, they will cut off the telephone. I cannot afford to pay it in time. If we get disconnected, I will have to pay an additional charge for reconnection, after I have settled the outstanding bill.

"I am going to try and borrow the money, but it may cost us more than the loan is worth from pay-day loan sharks. Zoë, whatever happens, remember that I love you. I do love you with all my heart."

The phone went silent, and we were done. I knew mother was drowning in circumstances she did not comprehend and were beyond her control. I was too young to understand properly, but I could fight back in my own way.

I was so belligerent when I finally returned to the house. It was after midnight, and I was evil. I started smashing the place up, and in doing so woke my captors. The next day I was placed with another family. They didn't last long either, but that's another story.

Bilty

"Thank you Zoe, I now have a pretty clear idea of how the SS process works. I'll update my notes as you refresh glasses."

Bilty:

Personal Journal:

This is going better than I expected. Zoë is obviously stressed, but is putting on a brave face, and telling it how it was for her and her family.

Notes:

1. The means by which the Section 20 Order was obtained are illegal. This is a major move towards removing the child from the family home. And yet the mother has no recollection of signing the form. She should have been made very aware of the consequences.

2. I also take task with the fact she was not allowed to read the forms, but ordered to sign them. That was done under duress, and would be inadmissible to any normal court.

3. Again, as is becoming all too familiar, the children are not allowed to speak in Family Court. This goes against the cornerstone principle: 'The needs of the child remain paramount'.

4. This also flouts EU and UN law, which I have an understanding of, but will read in depth. Mel seems to have the resources at her fingertips.

5. Zoë raised a serious question regarding legal representation. I had not heard of this approved list of lawyers for Family Court before, so more to check out.

6. The mother was bullied and blackmailed in court, by the SS, with support from the judge, into signing the Consent Order. I'll see if there is a case to bring against the judge for perverting the course of justice. I believe there is a case to answer.

Comment:
What is most striking, is the SS and Family Court, the police also, do not consider the sometimes extreme emotional, mental, and even physical abuse they cause to the child, the parents, as being at all relevant.

I do believe in all sincerity, that this abuse is of primary importance, and should be weighed most heavily against any 'possible' future abuse they suspect the family may use. The harm being done by Social Services is incalculable.

Zoë

"OK Zoë, I think we are close to being done here, let's finish up."

"Uh. Nope. There's still a fair bit I have to tell you. You see, the SS and Family Courts true objective, is to forbid any contact between parents and children, and between the children themselves. They are not happy until the family is completely destroyed."

"You cannot be serious!"

"Deadly serious. Listen up."

Isabella added an unsettling observation. "You may want to ask yourself, why? Why do they feel the need to totally destroy the family. There is a most insidious reason for it, but we'll come to that later.

"Zoë, you OK?"

"Yes. I just want this done with. I'd rather slit my wrists — You gotta razor knife?"

"No! Just tell it Zō and have done."

"Back to it I guess."

Chapter 16 – Zoë's Story: The Outcome

I tried calling mummy many times after that, but there was always a long tone, which meant the number was disconnected. However, I was not too upset, as the court order allowed her to visit for six hours each week, which was far more contact than we had been allowed before.

Hmmm.

The first meeting was on a Wednesday, and I was looking forward to seeing mum again, as well as my brothers of course. The appointment was for the afternoon, deliberately to clash with her work I suspect. She would have several hours travelling, so I expected her to be a bit tired.

I was due to leave at 2 o'clock, but we got a call at 1:20 telling us the meeting was cancelled because there wasn't a supervisor available. Surely, they must have known that at the beginning of the day, if not the day before? I immediately knew the SS were up to their usual tricks again. I headed back to school for the afternoon in a bad mood, and got detention for beating up some other kids. I had no excuse. I bullied them because I felt so frustrated with everything else in my life.

I later discovered mother had attended the meeting, only to be told it had been cancelled. The SS said they had no way to contact her because her landline had been cut off. She was upset, and asked them why they had not called her on her new mobile number. They agreed to add her mobile number to her contact information, only to discover they already had it. Mother tried to file a complaint, but they had mysteriously run out of forms.

Another meeting was scheduled for Friday, and this time I did get to meet mother. However, the SS said my brothers had a cold, so could not attend. We were both extremely disappointed, and went to cuddle each other. The supervisor stepped in and told us we were only allowed limited and specific physical contact.

What would any normal family want to talk about in similar circumstances to ours? How we were coping, how the case was progressing of course. It was the biggest thing in our lives. Mother started telling me about her plans for appealing the Interim Care Order on the twenty-eighth day. The supervisor stepped in again, forbidding us to mention the case in any way. Mother gave me a ponderous and fleeting look of dismay. She was clearly very unhappy, as was I.

To break the spell she asked me how I was doing at school, and I told her I was doing OK and making friends. She knew I was lying, because life at school was hell. However, we found things to talk about. I told her that a dozen families had fostered me, and they were all…

The supervisor barked at me before I could finish, and gave us both a lecture on what we were, and were not allowed to talk about. Clearly, talking about my current home life was not permitted. I knew mother wanted to hug me, but we had already been warned that we were not allowed to do that. I desperately needed that hug: Forbidden.

I asked her how dad was doing, and she became emotional. She started to say something, but she became upset. The supervisor again came between us and took her to the corner for a private chat. I could just about hear what was being said, "Misses Rendell, please remember you are not allowed to discuss any adult issues, or show any emotion during these child visitation dispensations. You must remain happy and unemotional at all times, otherwise the session is over, and I will have to make a report about your unruly conduct."

We were both learning a new set of rules, ones that were turning valuable family contact, into meaningless words one would say, like the weather to a stranger at a bus stop. But, we knew each other extremely well, and via eye contact and body language, managed to work out a code that the supervisor often missed, or could not react against.

That meeting was very strange, and left us both feeling extremely frustrated. When the time was up, we were allowed a brief hug and kiss, but it was extremely short. Mum told me she loved me and everything would be all right. The supervisor cut her off again, telling her she was not allowed to tell me she loved me. The meeting was abruptly terminated and we were led away in different directions.

That is what I call emotional abuse, and it was inflicted deliberately, by social workers, against both of us.

Seeing as both my mother and father had been charged with emotional abuse, I went down to the cop-shop that night and made a complaint. At first they were sympathetic, until they realised I was complaining about Social Services. After that we argued, and as a result, I had to spend the night in police cells. The next day I was given a Police Caution, and returned to foster care. Apparently, I had wasted police time. I thought the police had wasted my time, and I knew they were in the pocket of the SS, but what could I, their victim, do?

I wasn't allowed to go to meetings the next week, because I had tests at school. The following week I saw mother, but as before, my brothers were not there. It is difficult to talk only about inanities, when your family is being deliberately torn apart. During our parting hug, mum whispered to me to wear something with big pockets next time.

The social worker ended the session instantly, and later I could hear mum being bawled out for whispering. I heard the threat just before the door close, "Misses Rendell, pay attention. If we ever catch you whispering to any of your children again, all visitation rights will be immediately cancelled. You will never see any of your children again. Do I make myself clear?"

I was looking forward to seeing her again, even though we were not allowed to say anything important to each other by the British SS – a supposed protection force so similar in many extreme ways to the Nazi "Schutzstaffel [R 16.1]."

Just being in the same room with mum brightened my drab existence considerably. I was bitterly disappointed when the next meeting was cancelled, and I played up worse than ever as a result.

I was transferred to another foster home, that time one that specialised in 'Problem children'. I would have been good as gold, if adult strangers would stop lying to me, and I were at home with my real family around me.

The new place was run more like a prison. It had strict rules about what we could and could not do. I reacted badly and was always in trouble. They put up with me for two days before hitting me. It was not a gentle smack, it was a punch to my stomach that winded me badly.

I reported the incident to the school, the police, and finally Social Services. I learnt that if anyone hits a child, they face serious charges, and probably a prison sentence. Both the school and the police informed me that any action must be accepted as a creditable accusation by Social Services, before any criminal charges could even be considered [R 16.2].

I guess there may be a few honourable social workers in UK? But I doubt it. This is my personal experience of the way they treat children, supposedly in their care.

When I reported the incident to them, I was informed that they did not believe me. Instead of being protective, proactive, they buried my complaint and told me no further action would be taken against my foster parents. After that, I learnt to push my 'caregivers' whenever I could, but never cross the line. I also learnt never to trust any person in authority, because they were all in this sick plot together.

To me, something is either Right, or it is Wrong. An act is either done for Good or Evil. The macabre world I was domiciled to inhabit every single fucking day of my life, was Satanic!

[Zoë: "Sorry Bilty, I need a short breather, and a top up, strong this time. You got any skunk Issy? I need to feel happy. Very happy. This hurts me real deep inside. And we haven't even got to the Paki's scumbags yet.

"Bilty, if you want a bottom line to the all of this, not just my story, but what is to come, then know this. Young, white girls are at the back of the cue when it comes to justice in Blighty."

Isabella responded, "'Queue' Zō. But you are correct. Bilty, Candice, know the system victimises pubescent Christian girls. They, we, are all Caucasian. White. I call that institutionalised misogynism. Rape of our emotions, and later, our bodies.

"Here Zoë, the best skunk we got. This joint is only for you. Anyone else want a spliff while I'm rolling?"

Zoë took a deep draw and said, "Ah, that's better. I'll get back to it, and this time, be done with the all of it. Mel, Bilty."]

My life continued without hope. Sometimes I got it wrong, and got a good beating. It seemed, my foster care-providers knew the law also, and revelled in their power and control over me.

In retaliation, I poisoned their beloved cat. I deeply regret doing that, but I needed to find some way, any way, to get back at them. I'm sure they knew I was responsible, but they could never prove it. Just like my frequent beatings, the ones I was never allowed to charge them with in any Court of Law: Spit! All I had been left with was rough justice.

I had blood on my hands, and after my disgust mellowed, I felt much stronger. I know it was wrong, but what else could I do?

Later I discovered contact sessions with mother had been reduced to three-hours each week. This was because my younger brothers had become extremely upset when they met mum the week before. She ignored the social worker, held and comforted her sons. What else would any mother do? She also committed the cardinal sin of telling them she loved them. The session was terminated instantly. She was informed she would only be allowed special visitation rights in future.

I was allowed to see mum, but only once more. It was an uneasy meeting, but it remains my last memory of her. When we were allowed to cuddle before parting, she twisted our hug sideways, away from observing eyes, and slipped an envelope into one of my large pockets. I coveted it, knowing finally we had made true contact. I have always respected her for planning ahead, and finding a way to do that.

I still have that letter here. I think she had finally worked out what the SS and their lackeys had done to us. In it was her new mobile number. She offered me advice, and told me her view of the way our family was torn apart.

It was a Dear John letter, because she admitted the chances of us officially meeting again were virtually zero. I was in floods of tears as I read it, and every time I have read it since. The SS inflicted extreme and unwarranted emotional abuse on all of us—They remain: Unforgiven!

[Bilty: Zoë stands aggressively and hits the wall in frustration, before downing her drink, and drawing heavily on the joint. Even now, one decade later, she is visibly upset. I wonder she can carry on, but she continues, determined to tell the all of it.

Returning with a fresh glass, she thrust a tattered envelope at me. "Here Bilty. Scan it, but I need it back, like in seconds.

"It is all that remains of my family."]

In the letter, mum explained how she could hardly ever get a case to court to oppose the Interim Care Order, because at first, there was not enough time. Later she succeeded, only to be dismissed by the Judge, because her circumstances had not changed. Her appeal was dismissed and the next time she was able to get before the Judge, she had made changes to her life.

My heart bled for her, as this admission only reinforced the original verdict, that there was something wrong with her life, and the way she cared for us previously. Mother wrote about having to meet a 'Threshold', one that was always just out of her reach. This is total bollocks, and a travesty of justice. This is how the system works on you, grinds you down, because they are always several steps ahead, and leading you into traps of their own design.

I read her despair in the words she wrote. Any, and every allegation made by a social worker was a fact, unless she had evidence to prove it was not fact. How can you offer evidence to prove your child 'Will never suffer from Future Emotional Harm'?

Every single day, Social Services inflicted severe emotional harm on me. But it seems that does not count, at least in the eyes of the law.

Mother went on to tell me dad was in prison, and that she was preparing her defence to similar charges, plus assaulting the obnoxious policeman, and a public order offence. That happened when a special appointment with my brothers was cancelled, and she only found out after she arrived in the SS building in Leeds, again.

Understandably, mum was livid. It was a long and relatively expensive trip for her, and also meant she had to take more time off work. She and the receptionist at Social Services got into a heated argument, and security were called to escort mother from the building. I'm sure they did it deliberately. It was a set-up used to goad her.

I discovered that this led to another hearing. They applied for an S34.4 Order because mum could not behave appropriately. They condemned her on a dodgy report from a corrupt psychologist, who Mel later discovered had no proper qualifications. His report stated implacably, "The mother is incapable of caring for her children."

[Mel: "I checked. He was paid Thirty-five Grand for writing that load of bollocks. Oh, and appearing for a few seconds in court.]

Testimony from the SS supported his allegations, when they alleged that after her last meeting with the boys, they were left crying because she pinched them—something she had never done, and could never conceive of doing. She had attempted to tickle Joey, that's all. He loves that, but the SS bitch had butted in.

The truth of the matter was, like me, they missed their parents. Nevertheless, the social worker supervising the meeting reported that she saw the mother pinch the child, and she was believed, without the slightest corroborative evidence. That's what I call abuse of power, and lying. Child abuse at its worst, delivered with impunity by the SS.

I, we, her children, were not allowed to give evidence because this was considered to be emotionally abusing us. Mum was forbidden to see us because she had told us she loved us and missed us. Apparently, we children and mother cried and showed emotion during the contact sessions. Well of course we did: Morons!

This was considered by the inquisition, to be emotionally harmful, neglectful abuse of her children, us. They dutifully arrived at the conclusion that due to mother's elements of anger at the social workers, her tone of voice, and for unproven lying, and proven abusive nature, she was shown to be of an unstable mental state [R 16.3]. The SS concluded her children were therefore at risk. So, from that moment, she was prevented from seeing us at all by the S34.4.

I remain adamant, there cannot exist a law that is applied arbitrarily against parents, resulting in criminal conviction and a prison term. One that is readily discounted when a child victim of emotional abuse, tries to apply the same law to social workers and caregivers, the local authority, the police, and Family Courts, that do cause undue and excessive emotional abuse to the child: Me!

I called mum a couple of times, and we updated. Mother did not have a car, but kept her job by working mornings, and not telling the SS. She was alone, and didn't have us to look after. By then she had a criminal record. Although charges were within due process of law, they still showed up somehow on the police computer, as pending convictions. How can that be? The case hadn't even been heard in court.

Without dad's income, she fell behind with the rent, and services were aggressively cut off. Eventually she was evicted, and placed on a council housing list. Her bank account was frozen, and the bank lied to her, in order to get her to return her cash card and chequebook. The deal they had made over the telephone, at her premium talk expense, was later rescinded, and she was left without a bank account. She could not get another one, as she was in default and her credit rating was trashed. She was deemed to be a bad payer.

To put all this right, the answer is very simple. Return our family to how it was, before the SS mounted their determined hate campaign against us. We would all be much happier, safer, and meeting our obligations. Instead, the evil SS monsters deliberately destroyed us.

I now understand, from Issy and Melanie, this was because they could make a lot of money out of us, and fulfil their targets. I am not as clever as they are. I want to murder each, and every single one of those lying, backstabbing bitches!

They took it upon themselves to destroy my family, and my life. So, I will do the same for them. Done-deal. They just don't know it yet.

In her letter, mum told me she wandered around our home, abstractly picking up our toys, smelling our clothes, and wishing we were there. Inside her grew a deep bitterness, a resentment that could never be put right. I was still able to call her infrequently on her mobile. Then her number would not work. I don't know if the phone was stolen, or what. It rang out the first time I called, but was out of service afterwards. I guess someone changed the sim card. I was left all alone in the world. I had nobody to turn to.

One year later, I absconded and went home. Mother was gone, and our happy home was a derelict wreck. A neighbour, one who had supplied damning evidence against us, found me crying. She tried to comfort me, and I hit her, hard. I told her exactly what I thought of her. I left before anyone could find me. I no longer trusted anybody at all.

I hated the Bussies at first, but hated the SS even more. In time, I hated my ever changing foster parents. But most of all, they all taught me how to hate anyone in a position of authority. Nobody would listen to me, or even pay me any mind, until that fateful day I met Issy.

In the meantime, I managed to blow up the cooker of my latest domicile, by placing the wrong ingredients in a pressure cooker, and turning all the other gas rings on without lighting them. I had hoped the house would catch fire, but although I did set the kitchen alight, my dreams of retribution were scuppered before they materialised.

Later, they discovered I had put salt in the sugar, and sugar in the salt. I did many more things to upset them, and although I never managed to run away, successfully, they got so tired of my antics, they gave up. That was my intention all along. I thought I had escaped hell and celebrated, but the worst was yet to come.

I was sent to another foster home. This time it was run by a couple of gay men, and they were charming on the one hand, and exceedingly nasty on the other. They liked young boys, and I mean, very young boys. I think I confused them because I was a girl.

To my young mind, they were not men, they were perverts. I called them both by female names, homosexual references, and bad-mouthed them whenever we came into contact. I thought I was doing real well, until we had a fight. It started with words, before they had taken enough of my insults, and overpowered me.

They raped me in my bum first, and it hurt like hell. I understood why all the young boys in the house lived in fear of these men. They did it several times before they plucked up the courage to delve their maleness into my exclusive, female sexuality. I did not know it existed, until their first proper rape. Afterwards, I was no longer a virgin.

I was quite frightened when I reported what had happened to the police, but yet again, they stated I had to report the matter first to my social workers. I did, and I wasn't even sure back then what to call what they had done to me, but I knew it was very wrong. Instead of comfort and sympathy, I was chastised for making-up ridiculous accusations.

I still don't know if it was Cedric or Eldritch that took my womanhood first. Regardless, I now know it was rape. Rape of a seriously underage child, and one in their care. One the SS had responsibility for, and to protect. Huh!

I remember crying and lashing out, as they berated me for being an evil child. Nevertheless, he did tell the SS. "Zoë is a troubled child. I hate to admit this, but she is always telling fibs and causing trouble. Do not worry, we know how to handle her."

After that, they had free licence to rape me whenever they felt like it, mostly, anally. Sometimes they both did me at the same time. Nobody followed up my complaint, and I was sure the SS were deliberately stopping it at source. I felt utterly alone and completely betrayed. The care system was responsible. My foster parents were free to repeatedly rape me, and it seemed to me they knew they were above the law.

I was their prisoner, and they proved to be extremely good at keeping captives. However, I persevered, and eventually made it to the police station to complain about my multiple rapes, a second time. As soon as they discovered these were my official foster parents, they told me I was not allowed to make any allegations against them. I was booted out on the street and they laughed at my distress.

What does it take, for a child in care to get justice? I don't know.

Remember, foster parents can do whatever they like to you, and will always remain above the law, unless Social Services accept and report the accusation. Trust me, to cover themselves and their money earning, target orientated scams, they never do. They never did for me.

The gays sexual abuse of me continued for several years, and until they started selling my body to their 'friends'. After the third gang-rape, I was losing my mind. I had to escape. One night I crept into the kitchen, and worked the supply to the gas hob until it was broken. I wiped my prints, and went up to my room. My life was no longer worth living.

The explosion took a long time in coming. When it eventually happened, I was asleep. The place became a fireball, and we only just got out in time. Idiot firemen said it was fatigue to the pipe, but blamed the cause on someone smoking. Their report suggested foster carers and visitors to their home, be banned from smoking cigarettes.

The SS did not believe me, but they could prove zero. Zilch. I had hit them back, and hard. I had become a liability, so they sent me off to a care home, just to be rid of me. I walked in, and the place was crowded, but one girl sat alone at a large table. I thought she was only real person there. I'd picked her out straight away. I walked over and said, "Hi, I'm Zoë, and I hate this place already"

After we high-fived she ignored me, but I knew at once, she was not like anybody else in that gaol, except me. She was openly dismissive of everybody around her. I sat down and waited. I instinctively knew we were destined to become the best of best friends. I laid my tray on her table, and I never once regretted that instinctive action—even though knowing Isabella changed my life in so many ways. We were two peas in a pod.

There's little more to say. I have no idea what happened to my brothers, and given my current life, I have no need to search for them.

Father was a real man, and once released from prison, he went round to the SS offices and started killing everyone concerned with our case, with a shotgun and machete. He refused to surrender until he was reunited with his family. He was shot dead by a police sniper. I admire and respect him immensely. He killed all of them. I also miss him.

It was years before I learned how mother reacted. I think she loved my father more than I did. A short time after dad died, she went to Leeds, and waited outside the SS offices at lunchtime. When the leader came out, she rugby tackled her into the traffic. Mother was run over and killed by a truck, the SS official suffered a broken torso. She hung on for several days in critical care, but died on the third day. Good!

Mum and dad gave their lives for us, and that's what I admire most about them. It appears our family address our grievances personally, and physically. Neither death was reported in the press. Why not?

Issy has told most of the story, but I wanted to tell my story, myself. How Social Services and the police, the cynical Family Courts of injustice, deliberately destroyed my family.

Somehow, Issy kept me sane throughout those years of gang rape by Muslim, Paki bastards. Those with double standards and tongues of cobra snakes. They raped us, and afterwards they'd double-pray to Allah in the belief they would be granted forever-life in Allah's heaven.

To me, they also remain The Unforgivable! So does the system that put me there in the first place, calculatingly deliberate, and without the slightest regard for my best interests as a child.

Without her, Issy, I would never have survived. I asked her to kill me one time. She refused, but she did give me the strength to endure, the guts to get through the hell of it all, and live to see another day.

I believe the truth will eventually out. For me, it's the way you use that knowledge that really counts:

So, when Issy came to me one day with a plan to get even, I didn't even think, I immediately said, "Yes!"

Isabella

By the time Zoë had finished telling us her story I was seething with anger, and also deeply unsettled. The treatment of both her father and mother made no sense, as did the sentencing. I could not get my head around the fact she could not report her foster parents for grossly raping her. Pimping her. We already knew the court's ideas about justice were completely skewed, but that was impossible, wasn't it?

No it wasn't. It reminded me of my family, what the SS had done to my own, hundreds, probably <u>thousands</u> [R 16.4] of other families: Domicile.

Domicile!

Bilty

Zoë repeated, "Twice I was not allowed to prosecute, or even report my rapists. I learned that crimes such as rape, extreme physical abuse, and mental, emotional abuse, cannot be reported as crimes to the police, unless sanctioned by the SS."

Bilty replied, "Three times in fact. So let me get this straight. You are saying that you were repeatedly raped by the foster carers, and others, but the police took no action because you were in care?"

"Yes. The SS have to approve a complaint, such as repeated rape, and they never do. They are all in this scam together--along with the local authority, the police, and the judges.

Bilty said, "Thank you Zoë. You look strung out, please take a break. Yours is the first full account I have recorded. It details exactly the ways and means Social Services kidnap children from loving families."

"If you need me again, I'll be at the bar. I did not need that, and you owe me for putting me through that hell once more. Issy?"

"I'll join you. Bitly, we're done for today. We'll pick this up next time. This is all highly sensitive, emotional stuff, and we need a break. Our friendship deepened in the process, of surviving those atrocities."

"I accept that, and thank you both for the revelations. I can take this a very long way. Next time I need to return to your story, Isabella."

Bilty:

Personal Journal:

I thought this would be a short session, but Zoë knew what she was about to say. It was equally enlightening, and extremely worrying. That Social Services behaved in this way I find absolutely appalling.

Notes:

1. For the SS to claim they could not contact Misses Rendell, and then find they had the number, amounts to deliberate harassment. Not having complaint forms was evasion, self-protection, and probably a lie.

2. The SS went through the motions, just as Zoë called it. The rules of contact appear medieval, and unrelated to modern culture. Kissing, cuddling, saying 'I love you' are all natural, as is wanting to talk about the family, and the case. That these were expressly forbidden is a point of uttermost concern. Why? The SS protecting themselves, again.

3. I found that Zoë being unable to report her first physical assault to the police, was untenable. I will check the law concerned, but fear it will be corroborated.

4. But, the serial rape of Zoë by her last foster parents beggars belief. Then she was pimped out. That these were not actioned in criminal court, as the serious crimes they were, leaves me shocked to the core. I have a lot of questions to ask about this. She was ten and eleven years old during that period. It beggars belief.

5. I find Social Services complicit as accomplices in the continual rape of Zoë. They were supposed to be her legal guardians, with her best interests at heart. By knowingly permitting her to be raped (daily?), demands the SS personnel responsible receive long prison sentences.

6. I add the offence of sexual abuse, to the crimes of emotional, mental, and physical abuse already committed by Social Services.

7. None of these crimes were ever committed by her parents.

8. Check why Zoë's parent's deaths were not reported. Was there a gagging order in place?

Comment:

What is most striking, is the SS and Family Court, the police also, all appear to sanction the repeated rape of seriously underage girls and boys. I know of a campaigning newspaper that may be interested in pursuing this point. The police should never need the approval of Social Services to investigate serious crimes, such as rape.

I fear the law may need to be changed to support this.

Bilty Steadman

"OK, I'm done. Are you finished, love?"

Candice replied, "Yes, just about. I'm making some notes while the feelings are fresh in my mind, but one minute will suffice. That was an awesome telling, and I'd like to come again, get to know Isabella. She's the one with the education, and I'll need to show that."

Mel had stayed as chaperone and said, "She's highly educated, the only one of us. But we are all best friends here. I've copied today's video for you, here.

"Do we have a minute? Bilty, explain your personal angle."

"I work freelance with good press connections. I take commissions to investigate specific things, say for a campaign the paper is mounting. The Range is large, but usually of national interest and public concern.

"And now, yourselves. You are the only children, now adults, to have done anything constructive about it. I am proud to know you.

"Thank you Melanie. We'll be back, but my early week is hectic. Deadlines you know."

"Issy needs to spend time at work as well. The Jewellery that is. I'd call it for Friday, but Sir Richard is back. You'll learn about him later. Swap emails with me, and we'll fix it up between us. Issy is far too busy most of the time. What about next weekend? I can set a room aside for you. Friday will be out, knowing her. But Saturday and overnight?"

"Thanks. We'll see. Candice?"

"All a go for me. Until next time, and thank you, thank you all."

Chapter 17 – Isabella's First Boyfriend

Project Domicile
Interview: 07
Location: Fiddlers Court, The Oval, Holborn, Central London.
Time: 13:50 hours, Saturday, 21st October.
Subject: Isabella
Others Present:
    Zoë, Melanie, Vikki, Genie her friend, and Candice.

Note:

1. We return to Isabella's life, and her first proper date with Mohammed. I reread my notes before we began.

2. We are staying for the weekend, the idea to cover as much ground as possible, before our ordinary lives catch up with us.

Observations:

Isabella seems to be extremely relaxed today. Genie serves her a drink first, which she ignores. I watch the pecking order, which at times is complex. There is only one leader in the room, and she is about to begin. Cue cameras, and action.

Isabella

I readied for my first proper date with Mohammed. I had butterflies in my tummy all day on Saturday. I did my make-up after class, and fixed my face just like Siroun had taught me. I looked so cool and seductive. I only hoped Mohammed would like it. That was an awfully big worry.

I was still not sure I would be his girlfriend by the end of the evening, but I thought I would accept. In shock, I worried he would not ask me again. That made me curse and reprimand myself, I should have accepted last time. My mind was pretty scattered as I waited for Big Daddy Asif to arrive, but he did not. The waiting made the torturing butterflies in my stomach worse.

A large car pulled up and I turned away, ready to bolt for the safety of security on the school gate. I heard the electric window wind down, and Mohammed said, "Care for a lift sweetheart?"

I turned in amazement, and it really was him. Mohammed had called me his 'sweetheart'.

I rushed over and got into the passenger seat all a'fluster. He kissed the back of my hand, flicking it with his tongue. He complimented me on my skirt and ankle socks and said they were perfect. He put his hand on my knee and squeezed it gently, running his fingers inside my knees at the bottom of my thighs. He traced delicate circles on my skin, and I longed for more of his touch. The hand was gone too soon, and he asked to look at my face. He studied my efforts and asked if I had made myself up especially for him.

I said, "Yes," and looked below, downcast. I knew he hated it.

I found the strength to mumble, "I'll remove it if you don't like it."

My heart bulged with the contrite damnation of self-loathing. I was prepared to be bawled-out. His smile was large, his eyes alive, and he chuckled to charm me; "You look radiant, like a dream come true."

I was stunned. This man wanted me. Mine was not some silly schoolgirl crush of fantasy. This was real love.

He said, "You look absolutely stunning tonight my dear. I have looked at your photographs many times each day, dying to be with you once more. This week has passed so slowly without you by my side. Please let me take some more pictures of you."

I posed and pouted at his direction, as he snapped half a dozen shots. He showed me the results, and he told me he was an excellent photographer. I was leaning over to see properly when his face came incredibly close to mine. I could feel his hot breath on my neck and it gave me goose pimples. I could smell his cologne, as his finger came up to my chin and tilted my head upwards, and towards his.

He was so close, and I watched in stricken wonder, as he slowly moved his face closer and closer still. His lips met mine for the first time. I almost swooned and my tummy did somersaults. I could sense every fibre of my body, and unexpectedly my nose was completely clear. I tingled all over, as I became confounded by the moment, and lost within the man's immediate proximity.

He pulled away and apologised at once, "I am so sorry. I did not mean to kiss you, but you are looking so ravishing tonight. Irresistible! I could not help myself. Please, accept my sincere apologies. That is unless you liked kissing me, and would like to do it again?"

Even with my make-up on, I am sure he knew my cheeks were bright red. I felt thrilled and in a dream world. My boyfriend had kissed me for the first time, and I wanted more. I stuttered to say, "You are wonderful. I like kissing you."

He leaned over to me again, pursing his lips. I moved my head towards his and we kissed again. That time I kissed him, and we were even. I was so hot for this man. I think I would have given myself to him right at that moment, except he asked, "Does this mean you will be my girlfriend?"

I had no hesitation and said, "Yes," right away. He punched the air in delight, and kissed me again, full on the lips. It was a sexual kiss. He broke away before I was ready, and asked me where I would like to eat.

I had no idea. My mind was blank. I could only remember the feel of his lips on mine.

He thought for a moment and decided we would eat at the best Tandoori restaurant in town. He made a quick phone call, but I did not understand what he said. I had never had curry in a restaurant before, and told him as soon as he had finished the call. He smoothed my hand and my worries, by saying, "I'll order a mild curry for you. Oh, and you will be able to drink there as well." He winked at me, and we moved off.

He explained all the tricks his massive car could do. It was a Mercedes, and the most expensive executive model. He told me how much it cost, and I couldn't believe it. He added he changed it for the latest model every year. The car had gadgets an executive house would envy. It was fantastic.

We were laughing again and he asked me to open the glove compartment. Inside was a tin. He looked at me cheekily and said, "I know you are very good at rolling-up, so make us something nice."

I opened the tin and there were the makings of a spliff inside. I set to work before asking him how he knew. He smiled at me and said, "I'm the owner of the Balti House you were in on Sunday."

I am sure my mouth dropped open. This was one serious guy, and he wanted me. I rolled a cracking joint, we smoked it on the way. I think I had most of it, because he kept asking me to hold it, as he was driving.

The end of it was wet and I knew we were swapping spit. Normally I would have found that repulsive, but the thought pulsed my desire for him. The buzz hit and I wanted him badly.

It never happened. All too soon, we arrived at a posh restaurant, and were led to the best table in the house. He must have booked it in advance, so that would explain the phone call he made.

We enjoyed the most wonderful meal, although I could not eat the hottest dishes. Most were flavoursome and delicious. We shared several glasses of wine, and I ordered a sweet before we left.

It was raining outside and a door attendant offered to see us to the car with an oversized umbrella. Mohammed raised his jacket over both our heads, and we ran for it together. The rain was driving into me and I knew my school blouse was soaked through. We got in his car and he reached over to kiss me, thanking me for the most wonderful evening.

Our tongues collided. I had my first ever French kiss. It was breathtaking. My heart was pounding as my remaining resistance turned to needy aggression, and I became lost within the new sensation. I have no idea how long the kiss lasted, but I wanted it to last forever, I wanted him so very much that night. In time, we broke apart and he started the car. When we came to the exit, he stopped, turned to look at me, and asked, "Sweetheart, do you want me to take you home right now, or would you prefer we go somewhere quiet for another spliff?"

There was no question about my answer. I said, "Spliff please."

He grinned and asked me to make two. I rolled, as he drove a short way. I think we were behind a disused bowls club, but I wasn't paying attention. We were somewhere nobody else was, and that was all that mattered to me. He parked the car in a secluded corner, and invited me into the back for another drink. How could I refuse?

He pulled out a bar when we were inside the back, and asked me what I wanted to drink. "Vodka and orange please."

Mohammed handed me a large glass and I hit his glass at with mine, "Here's to us." He smiled and replied in kind, as he wound his arm through mine and guided my response. We drank with arms entwined. That was so romantic, and Wow! Was the drink strong!

I lit the spliff and we shared as we kissed and cuddled on the back seat. He took a deep draw and kissed me, gently breathing the smoke into me. That was so adoring and it seemed so right to me. The minutes fled, and soon he poured another drink and asked me to light the second spliff, complimenting me on how good I had made them.

He was worried I would catch a cold, so my blouse was removed, and we started making out. I loved the way he touched me, and I felt like putty in his hands.

He kissed me all over my chest and shoulders, my stomach, everywhere there wasn't any fabric. His fingers worked in tandem with his kisses and tongue, his touch—electric. My body grew to need those new sensations more, and increasingly.

All of a sudden his lips were gone and he said, "Here, let's have another drink and something to smoke."

I panicked. I was becoming so lost in his dreamy, fairytale world, that I felt a great emptiness. He never stopped talking, telling me how beautiful and sexy I was, and making me laugh. His compliments battered my senses to overload. He reached forward and refreshed my drink. He rolled another joint. lit it, purposefully wetted the end with his mouth, and handed it to me.

He said, "You look stunning my love. I must take another photograph of you."

I nodded and played for his camera. My mind had crashed when he said, "My love."

He was in love with me? I hardly heard what else he said, as I concentrated on those two words he had spoken. Finally, he got the perfect shot, and it looked brilliant. He encouraged me to celebrate with him, and we toasted with a shout of "Bottom's up!"

He looked at his watch, and said, "It is time I took you home. I apologise if we did anything tonight you did not like?"

What?

That's it?

I was devastated. My bodily sensations were on fire. All I wanted to do was give myself to this utterly adorable man. Instead, he was still being a gentleman. I felt frustrated, and I wanted, I needed him to make love to me, to drive me senseless within my desire for him, but it was not to be.

Disappointment washed over me as I got back into the front seat, and he drove me home. I determined that on our next date I would make love with him, even if he objected.

Naïve didn't come into it. I did not understand back then, adults' could be so extremely deceptive. Mohammed was a master manipulator, with the gift of the gab--a 'Smooth Operator' regards women, never mind children.

Mohammed pulled over a few streets before the home and parked. He looked at me with longing and said, "Issy, I can't wait one whole week until I see you again. I am falling in love with you. You are the most wonderful person I have ever met in my entire life.

"Please, can you be free on Wednesday afternoon, so we can date?"

I was thrilled and promised to meet him. He gave me his private number and asked me to call him to confirm. He said he would collect me just after midday. He gave me ten pounds and said, "Top up your phone so we can talk."

Minutes later I ran back to my room, and jumped on my bed. My hands replicated what he had done not long before. I was imagining his hands on me, and his maleness surrounding me, driving me senseless with desire.

I continued to run my fingers around my body, needing, searching for fulfilment. Zoë rapped my door and I dragged her inside. I was so horny I almost raped her. Instead, she wanted to know all about my date. I had so much to tell her, and rattled on for ages.

I woke with her in my arms. It was early and she was fast asleep. Images of Mohammed and what we would do flooded my brain, and I had a serious problem. I would have to wait for him until Wednesday, and that seemed like æons away. Mohammed had become the focal point of my entire life.

On Sunday, Zoë and I hung around trying to act cool. We ended up at the Balti House, but the woman was late leaving and we had to wait. That time there were four guys in the back room. We were welcomed and drinks flowed. I rolled joints and we laughed. The bully started making out with some guy, but after he slipped her some serious notes.

The next time I looked up they were having sex. I reasoned that was her business. Soon Zoë was making out with two guys. Later, someone came in with pizza. I was fine, until someone drew lines of white powder on the table, cut them with a razor blade, and offered me a rolled note as a straw. I knew it was time we left, and rose to leave.

The guy with the straw changed from being nice, to hitting me hard. He kept hitting me, and twisting my arm until I did as instructed. I felt nauseous, and wanted to throw up. I tried to stop myself puking, and was hustled out the back door. I realised my last drink had a funny aftertaste, and that the pizza was probably doctored.

I made a run for it when nobody was watching me, and escaped. Zoë stayed. I wanted to rescue her, but there was no way; I'd only be trapped again.

I ran home alone, and wondered why nobody found me attractive. My scattered brain eventually worked out that none of the men had tried it on with me. I did not understand why. Anyway, my heart belonged to Mohammed, and I fell asleep thinking of him. I used my own hands to simulate his imagined touch of my skin. I started floating, and at first it was cool. Later I felt sick, but couldn't spew up. I was dizzy, woozy, and slept badly.

I was still well laced on Monday morning. I was late and awfully thirsty, plus horny as hell. Asif took one look at me and drove us up the road to Vijay's store. He bought some stuff and I was made to swallow and drink, before he moved off with me already asleep on the back seat. Monday was a blur, but I got through it somehow.

That evening Asif knew I was still not right and took me to a back street Balti house. He ordered for me and waited while I ate. He gave me some pills and told me to drink a lot of water. Afterwards he dropped me back to the gaol and said, "Look after your friend." I went to my room and lay down. I drifted for a while, and came round some hours later. Finally, I began to feel human once more. By that time, I knew some of the joints and drinks had been laced with hard drugs. I was still thirsty and horny, so concluded it must have been Tina.

I got up and went to look for Zoë. I found her blanked out in her room. She was still high and didn't know what she had done. Her words made no sense, and I knew she had done some hard drugs after I left. I made her drink some water, and left her to get over it.

She was not my problem. Waiting interminably until the next time I could see my boyfriend was, and I needed him. I imagined becoming his Queen … Within the harsh glare of hindsight, reality is not like that, although it can appear to be similar at times.

Tuesday was a long haul. I was trying to decide whether to let my boyfriend make love to me. I was offering him my virginity, and would become his in return. We were so right for each other. I believed that with all my heart. I was just not sure I was ready.

I called him on Wednesday morning. I was in a stress of worries, and a bit mad he had not called me at all. I was expecting a long, loving chat full of romance. He was preoccupied and said he was in the middle of some extremely important business, and that I would have to wait until later. He told me he would be late, would ring, and cut the call short. I passed the time in the library, but could not focus on homework.

I was everything but patient, knowing he would eventually come for me. He called to say, "I'm on my way. Sorry, something came up."

It was almost one o'clock before I spotted his car, and he was most apologetic and as charming as ever. I was to learn later, just like the SS, he was very good with words.

He kissed my hand and seemed relaxed. He asked me to skin up as soon as he drove off. He had skunk, resin, and some white powder. I asked him which he preferred, and he said, "Whatever turns you on."

I knew what he was insinuating, so rolled skunk. I liked feeling happy. I wasn't most times, well, since the SS ripped our family apart.

If I had still been at home, my parents would have advised me about the romance and drugs, but they'd been taken out of the equation. The SS supposed 'Duty of Car', apparently applied only to themselves.

Meanwhile, Mohammed and I shared the joint, but I had most of it. Soon we parked up in some remote spot and were in the back seat. He offered me a glass of vodka and orange, and it was dreadfully strong. Soon we were making out, and his kisses combined with his delicate touch, soon had me all dreamy. I was in heaven. If he wanted to take me, I was already very willing, and my Fairy agreed.

He asked me if I was wearing matching bra and panties, but I would not tell him. I was playing hard to get. He asked me to sit on his lap and began kissing and teasing my neck and ear with his mouth. Tingles of anticipation ran through me. He spoke, gentling me, "Can I undo you blouse, my love?"

He had said those magic words again: 'My love'.

Meanwhile his hand was circling up my thighs, which parted naturally at his invasion. My breath caught and became laboured. He reached for his camera and had me pose for pictures, then a short movie. He said, "You are such a perfect model. I'm already in love with you. We should marry at once, except our ages are wrong."

He seemed to wilt for the very first time. He was faced with something impossible. I eased his fears, and we talked quite seriously about eloping together, just the two of us. He said, "Isabella, I will give up everything in this world, just to spend the rest of my life loving you."

There could be no doubt this time. He had called me, "My Love" for the second time that day. I nodded acceptance, and I felt the neediness to pull his head up to kiss him urgently on the lips. He placed the camera on the back shelf, as his arms enfolded me.

His hands returned to stroke my body, but never, quite, where I needed his touch most. I started moaning as my passion for this great lover mounted. His scents, his soft words, delicate touch, were all driving me crazy. I felt I was rising higher into heaven itself.

My mind was in another universe. I tried to sit up as he poured another drink. My arms and legs were too shaky and he stopped what he was doing to help me. Once I was sitting properly, he kissed me and said, "Thank you. You are wonderful."

I had no words to express what I felt. I replied, "So are you, my love."

There, I had said it to him back. He looked at me as if shocked, and said, "Don't play with my feelings. I am sure you do not love me. You are just toying with me, like all the other girls."

His eyes looked wounded. I held his head in my hands, inches from my own, and looked deep into his dark eyes. "I do love you Mohammed. That is the truth."

A great smile split his face and he kissed me hard. But before our passions rekindled, he broke away and finished getting our drinks. I tried to roll another spliff, but was still shaky, so he took over from me. We reclined with his arm around my shoulders and I cuddled into his chest. He was so much man I felt safe and secure in his arms.

We talked of small things for a while, before his car phone rang. He said, "Speaker on. Answer."

A speaker came to life and a Pakistani voice was talking urgently. Mohammed replied at once. He leaned forward and paid full attention. The conversation was short, and I have no idea what was said. My lover turned to me and said, "Apologies my love, I want you so badly, but there is a crisis I must attend to immediately. We must leave at once."

I reached for my blouse and quickly did up a couple of buttons, pulled on my skirt, and grabbed my school cravat from the floor. We finished our drinks and he took his camera with him as we got in the front. He started the engine, but stopped and turned to look at me.

"I want you so much. Next time, we will make love."

"I want that so much, and I'm ready for you."

"Prove you love me." I was puzzled, thinking about what to do.

He shocked me by saying, "Will you give me your panties?"

I was a little taken aback, but he played on the fact of me proving my devotion to him. I sat straight and eased my hands up my sides, and hooked my thumbs into the waistband. It was a bit tricky at first, but after I got them down to my thighs, they came off quite easily.

He held out his hand and I gave them to him. He brought them to his nose and inhaled deeply. A look of total bliss enlightened his face and he complimented my gorgeous aroma. I blushed. I worried I was now completely vulnerable, but we were not in the back anymore and within moments he was driving me home.

We made plans to meet again on Saturday for our next date. I skipped into the house, and up to my room. I was still a virgin, but he had said we would do it on Saturday. Anyway, I had just given up my heart to him. My mind went over all that had happened between us, and I slowly began to understand how fantastic love could be.

I was lost in my dream world and almost forgot about dinner. I went down but there was no sign of Zoë. I went for dinner on Thursday, only to find her already eating. She looked awful. I wanted to know what was wrong, but she would not say. I was bursting to tell her all about my date, but she was remote and preoccupied.

I wondered whether to take her for a walk, like Sophie had done with me. I was about to suggest it when I noticed the bully, and her gang sauntering over to us. I stood at once to challenge them. Zoë looked up and said, "Oh no, not again."

She looked at me with defeated eyes. I asked, "What's going on?"

She shook her head and said, "Get out while you still can." She rose to leave with them, her dinner remaining half eaten on her plate.

I went up to my room and thought about Zoë. I had not known her long, but we were already very best friends. Something was dreadfully wrong in her life. I needed to find out what it was and save her. We had hardly spent any time together since Sunday. She was fine then, right up until I left her making out with the two lads. I wondered if she had had sex with them. That would explain part of it, but not what happened tonight. Why did she go with that awful girl? I had only questions and no answers.

Bilty

"That's some story Isabella. You are totally blameless. He appears to be a charmer of women, never mind vulnerable young girls. That such men exist makes my blood boil."

"Yes, I know that now. It took me a while to admit to myself that I had been completely conned by him. But I was lucky in some ways. He charmed me. Most girls are threatened, beaten, and raped.

"Once you are in their clutches, there's no way out.

"But there's more to this, as regard me. I was not the only virgin I'm sure. What I relate next, is the beginning of my hatred, and my understanding of what the whole thing was really about. It took years to fully understand, but we got the proof."

Bilty:

Personal Journal:

And now we get to it, what really happened to all these young, white, Christian girls.

Notes:

1. Isabella exposed the grooming, as it applied to her.

2. That she was considered special, because she was a virgin, is of deepest concern.

3. Of greatest concern is the fact that she was eleven years old.

4. Others would have been threatened, beaten, and I know those tales are yet to be told.

Bilty said, "Did he ever hit you?"

"Huh. No. Many others did. But he was the worst. He charmed me with words, manipulated my emotions, like a harpist, an orchestra that stole my heart. He's a monster and serial rapist."

"Yes, I agree. Oh, one last thing. Why does Mohammed always make a phone call before taking you somewhere?"

"It took me a long while to realise he always did it that. It was to check on the whereabouts of his wife. Obviously, he didn't want to bump into her with me in tow.

"If that's all, we better get on with the story."

Isabella reached for her glass for the first time, said "Cheers!" She downed the brackish liquid in one, clearly distressed. We recommenced once Genie had topped it up.

Chapter 18 – Raped and Pimped

Isabella

They say that girls remember everything. Well, that's not entirely true. The biggest event in a girl's life is losing her virginity, or perhaps having her first baby. For me that would always remain pretty blurry.

Most women reflect on the moment with fondness. It is a rite of passage, changing from being a girl, and turning into a woman.

I cannot remember my first time.

I don't even know who was the first man to fuck me. Love. Making love, had no place in what happened to me. I think it was Mohammed, but that answer never felt right. Don't ask me if it hurt, because I don't know. All I know was that I was no longer a virgin.

It was Monday morning, and I was still trying to put the pieces of that night back together. I desperately wanted to know what had happened on Saturday. I had a flash backs, but everything was a muddled mush of misplaced memory. I know there were at least two men, and one was old and white. I have no idea how he could have come into my memory of that night, but he was definitely there.

I remember everything until we were in the hotel room, before it all became fuzzy. Mohammed must have drugged me, but why? I was ready for him to make me a woman. After that it all goes hazy.

On Saturday evening Mohammed was early and waiting for me when I got out of school. Some older girls were standing at the bus stop, and they couldn't believe I got into such a flash car. I felt proud, exclusive, even by their standards. Mohammed kissed me on the lips, saying, "Tonight's the night."

He squeezed my hand as he said it, and I repeated his words with great enthusiasm. I kissed him back before the car moved off. I rolled a spliff without being told, and asked him, "What are we doing first?

A smile lit up his face and his eyes twinkled as he looked at me before asking, "Before we do what?"

I said, "You know."

He said, "I don't know. What is it we are going to do tonight?"

It was a good laugh as he pretended he had no idea. He made me say, "Before we make love."

He acted surprised, "Oh that. I had completely forgotten about it."

"Oh no you haven't, you've been thinking about it all week."

We continued our banter, and I was giggling constantly, his eyes alive with sexual innuendo and absurd innocence. We had been hedging around the subject of sex without talking openly about it. I was still laughing when he said, "Do you still love me?"

I said, "Of course I do, lover boy."

He looked at me and said, "Prove it."

I had no idea what he meant until his eyes looked between my legs. I knew instantly, but acted stupid like he had done. Eventually, I forced him to say the magic words, "Please take off your panties, my love."

I had been waiting for the cue. I did as he asked and put them in his outstretched hand. It felt naughty and nice. I loved the sense of power over my man. I took as much of his wit as I could bear, and was saved when we pulled up at a Balti house. I asked him for my panties and he replied, "I thought you loved me?"

I said in all truth, "I do love you, Mohammed."

He smirked and said, "Then you know you will not be needing to wear your panties again, on this, such a special night for us, my lover."

His cheeky grin reappeared and I was giggling again. He made everything so much fun, that I guess he was correct about my knickers. Not wearing any made me feel extremely daring, and sexy, although I was petrified everyone would know, or the wind would catch my skirt.

We went inside and he asked me to wait at the counter. He went into the back and was gone about five minutes. I spent time looking at the menu. The guy behind the counter was friendly and made me laugh.

I was extremely self-conscious that I was not wearing my panties, and I thought he must know. But there again, how could he? It was a sin. Nevertheless, it seemed no one noticed, and I was getting away with it. That changed my mindset, and I was not worried anymore. Instead, I was horny as hell. Don't ask me how that works, because I have no idea.

When Mohammed came back and closed the door behind him, I'm sure I heard Zoë shout "No! I'll do it," followed by a door slamming. I was puzzled. A man came through and gave Mohammed a package. I heard the TV and reasoned what I had heard was on a program.

We left quickly, and Mohammed asked me if I wanted to try some real food from his family village. I gathered he was inviting me to become part of his inner circle, his family. I was on a journey of discovery that night so agreed. He made a short call.

The place he took me to turned out to be a low-class Balti restaurant. We walked in past shelves with all sorts of sweet things on display. I had never seen anything like the food before. Mohammed asked if I wanted to try. I said, "Yes, but I don't know what anything is."

He chose two delicacies for me, and the woman behind the counter put them in a bag. I said, "Thank you."

She gave me a disdainful look, and I decided I did not like her.

The tablecloths were printed oilcloth, and there was a sink on the back wall so people could wash their hands. Most of the patrons were using strips of roti or chapatti to eat a bowl of stew with their fingers. It was all very strange. We went through to the back room where there was a dining table, and a three-piece suite with coffee table at one end of the room. We made out on the settee when nobody was about, and I had to remember to keep my legs together, but I kept forgetting. I don't think anybody saw anything. It was such a turn-on. It was our secret.

A friend of Mohammed's came in with some vodka and a bottle of cold orange. He poured for me and we all drank. It was fun, and despite the dingy surroundings, I felt relaxed. We had several drinks before the food arrived. It was fantastic. I enjoyed it, but felt quite full afterwards.

The bottle of vodka was empty somehow, so I was offered Bacardi and cola instead. I had never tried that before, but it went down a treat. I preferred it to the other. We smoked a spliff, and sometime later, were parked outside a good hotel. I was told to wait outside for one minute, before going straight to the stairs, and I make my way to room 101.

Mohammed was opening the door when I arrived in the corridor. I was slightly out of breath, which suited my emotions perfectly. I saw him go inside. I rushed to be with him, and he held the door open for me. He gave me a peck on the lips as soon as I was inside, before ducking his head outside to check the corridor. He put the 'Do Not Disturb' sign on the outside of the door, and locked it behind us.

At last, we were alone. I was about to lose my virginity.

I had expected to feel butterflies in my stomach, but instead my mind was floating. My lover-to-be picked me up in his strong, masculine arms, and kissed me. My feet were dangling off the ground as he carried me in our passionate embrace, before he threw me on the bed. The mattress bounced and Mohammed jumped on top of me like an animal, he was so manly.

He rolled to my side and looked deep into my eyes, as he deftly unbuttoned my school blouse. He kissed everything but the fabric of my bra. He licked and kissed his way down my tummy, before jumping back and opening the bag he had brought with him from the Balti.

He fixed me Bacardi and coke, poured whiskey for himself, and rolled a joint. He came over and handed me my drink, and over time, we shared the spliff. That was one of the few occasions he took as much of it as me. It was even stronger than the ones we had before.

We continued to make out, and I was dripping with anticipation, when he got up and said, "You don't mind do you?"

I had no idea what he meant, but gave permission. He got his camera out and took a few photographs, before setting it to record on the low cabinet opposite the bed. He checked the shot and adjusted the angle, before he went to fix another drink. He asked me to remove my skirt. I did as requested, and was handed the glass of booze as reward.

We leaned against the headboard and he played with my bra. Eventually it fell to his desire for me, and I was left naked apart from my pumps and socks. He continued to treasure my young body, before asking me if I loved him. I looked up and said, "Of course I love you Mohammed," and I meant it.

He took off his shoes, but not his socks, and stood up to undo his belt. That's when his mobile rang. I had turned my phone off, and wondered why he had not done the same.

He walked away from me and talked quietly in the farthest corner of the room. He didn't say much, but spoke English. I didn't think much of it at the time, because my mind was focused on what I was about to do — become a woman in my own right.

I heard him say "Yes," before he said, "That soon, admirable."

The call complete, he said, "Sorry, I meant to turn it off."

He made a joke, before removing something else from the package he had been given at the takeaway. He took my glass for a refill. I thought I had had enough to drink. I wanted to get to the action, but one more wouldn't hurt, would it?

He rolled another spliff after he made the drinks, and wandered over with a glass in each hand, and something large inside his trousers. I stared at the latter with longing, wondering what it looked like, felt like, what it would feel like inside me.

My mind overly preoccupied by loves' imagining's, I took the drink and had a gulp. It was a lot stronger than the last one. It tasted good, but had an odd tang. We touched glasses and he said, "Bottom's up." He drank his glass of whiskey in one go, and I did likewise. He refilled them, before we lay on the bed and shared the spliff.

Time skipped a bit, it could have been seconds, but then skipped some more. Then everything went a bit skewed. Like fast-forward, impossible, shuttering, unrelated scenes, as if seen from one railway carriage passing another in a tunnel. Time hurtled forwards, like a roaming stroboscopic light. Randomly empowered highlights disappeared before I could focus on them properly, in an evanescent cacophony of bewildering, half-glimpsed imagery.

Was there a knock at the door? Did I see a white man? I do not know. Within the whirling constellations of my personal perception, I lost the essence of who I was. My senses became all mixed up.

What little I retain, is all muddled into a grotesque pastiche of illogical confusion. Time passed. Moments came unbidden, and flowed into the darkness without conscious reason.

I know I lost something essential, someone important to my life. Some one's body, and for one night only, my mind.

I know I lost my virginity. The most important event of my life, and all that remains are the briefest snatches of utter uncertainty. Mere scattered frames, remnants of an epic journey into adulthood. That was the sum-total of what my disorientated mind retained.

It was daylight outside when I came round. Mohammed was thrusting inside me. I reached up to bring his lips to mine, but he did not bow his head. I wrapped my small legs around him as best I could, and grabbed his buttocks with my outstretched hands, urging him on.

He was hitting me deep inside, and it hurt a little, then a lot. Soon he tensed and thrust himself to the depths of my womb. He became lodged so deep inside me, that his whole body shook in pleasure. I felt my heart go out to him, as at last our love was consummated. I swooned as he withdrew. He could do nothing wrong. I was now a 'Woman'.

I became the woman he created.

Mohammed kissed me hard on the lips and said he had to leave on urgent business. He got dressed at once, collected his camera, and picked a fat envelope up off the table. He checked the contents, and it contained a lot of money. He blew me a kiss and left.

I didn't expect that. I had imagined meaningful moments, shared treasures of our united beings. Instead, I was dumped. I reasoned he was a successful executive, and had a lot of important work to do. I fell into a half-sleep, wondering if I was carrying his baby.

I woke again when housekeeping knocked the door, and was told to vacate the room. I felt disorientated. "Gimme five minutes."

I am sure it was nearer fifteen minutes by the time I managed to get dressed and leave. I was bewildered and wobbly. Everything I looked at seemed to move. There was a spliff and a five-Pound note lying on the table, so I took both. I looked over at the bed, at the deep red stain so evident, and waved goodbye to my virginity. I was now a woman. The cleaners didn't celebrate, they seemed pleased to see the back of me.

I called Asif as I had been instructed, went out the back way, and a taxi was waiting for me. I got back to gaol, had the spliff, and collapsed on my bed. I was feeling like shit when I woke up. I drank orange juice and tried to remember what had happened. It was a useless pursuit.

I sat up to get out of bed, and fell over. I landed heavily on the floor, and realised I was still in big trouble. I must have slept again, because I came awake and was cold. I crawled back into my bed. Next time I woke up properly, my mind awash with scattering images. I tried to connect them together, but I had to give up—they were disparate, unconnected flashes of the uncertainty of fact. Instead of blissful memories, the orange juice came back to haunt me, and I vomited, trying vainly to reach the bog in time.

I was still wearing my clothes, so after wiping myself down and rinsing my face, I staggered up to Vijay's shop and collected some food from the shelves, intending to nuke it in his microwave. I went to pay, forgetting I did not have any money. Vijay raised a finger before me and asked me to follow it with my eyes. I did OK at first, but somehow I was on the floor again. I felt strong hands grab me and I was somewhere else. I didn't know where. I realised the spliff had been doctored.

I woke in a daze. I had no idea what day it was, where I was, and I was lying on someone's sofa. My head hurt, my jaw ached, and I needed to be sick, urgently. I blundered through the darkness, knocking several things over, and crashed into a door that was locked, before I found some tiles on the floor. I did it there. I was still heaving when the light came on and I recognised Vijay's voice. I puked again, and asked him, "Where am I?"

He said, "You are in my kitchen."

I tried to look up at him, but instead, I lost my balance and crashed headfirst into my own sick, my stomach heaving once more. I heard commotion all around, but opening my eyes was beyond me. Vijay said to his daughter, "Give her a bath, and do not come out until she is completely cleansed, and her clothes are washed."

He shouted orders to his wife, as my mind went blank once more. I was in a hot bath. I was clean, but knew I had to clean the inside of my womanhood myself. Siroun turned away.

There had always been something inside the entrance to my sex before, but now it was gone.

I put my own finger inside myself for the very first time, and cried. I kept repeating to myself, "It's gone, it's gone." But they could have been words' spoken inside my head.

Siroun comforted me as best she could, but I knew instinctively she was still unmolested, a virgin. My virginity was gone. It didn't matter anymore. I had been fucked. My life was already fucked. What of it?

I tried to pull the fragmenting epicycles of my shattered psyche together, as Siroun offered me a sari to wear. It didn't fit, but felt right in that household. Vijay smiled when I appeared, and I was able to walk on my own. He bade me sit down at his table, where his wife gave me a bowl filled with thick soup, and several chapattis on the side. The woman said many things in a totally incomprehensible language. All I remember, is that she was most kind to me, and I thanked her.

Vijay told me, "This is a special soup, and it is only for young girls. Eat your fill and sleep. Tomorrow you will be restored."

They all left and went back to bed, or to the shop. I don't know, because it was open twenty-four seven. Vijay came back with a condiment set. I did need to add salt, and experimented with the other substances, some good, some hot or sour, and some quite odd.

The soup had made me hungry, and I went to check the pot left simmering on the cooker. I took two more full bowls from it, adding salt each time, and sometimes other spices. Replete, I walked away, but in my hindsight, I saw the low flame. I went back to turn the cooker off.

I tried to sleep, but it was somebody's sofa, not my own bed. I suffered for a while and managed a few hours fitful slumber. I was waking-up to my post-coital world, and it didn't look that nice for a first-timer. I had imagined my heart would be fulfilled, and I, deeply in love. Instead, I hurt below, and felt empty.

In place of fulfilling love my virginal gift bestowed, my heart was rendered empty: drain'd. My emotions ripped, like I had been excoriated of some essential essence. My self-esteem was an empty husk of nothingness. I felt numb, used, and discarded—Like a worthless cigarette butt tossed uncaring into the gutter.

At last, I was awake properly and beginning to function. I wanted to cry, but it seemed pointless. I found my clothes in the dryer and changed as the remains of the soup reheated. I wandered out into the shop and picked up a pack of white panties. They were not sexy, but neither was I. Vijay let me pay for them next time and took my hand as he gave me the bag, "You must get away from here. I tell you for the second time, they are not good men. Please say nothing to my wife and daughter, for they know nothing of this world I, and now you, inhabit."

I thanked him for everything he had done, and said I would make it up to him. Asif was waiting outside to take me to school. There was a big box on the front seat, so I had to get in the back. I was still floating in and out of reality on occasions.

I was asleep again when the taxi came to a stop. The first thing I was conscious of was Asif ripping off my panties and throwing them on the floor, "You no longer need these bitch," he leered.

I protested, and he hit me very hard. He had entered me before I knew what was going on, and he was many years older than my father. I asked him to use a condom. He goaded me and hit me for my impertinence, just before he emptied his balls into me. He sneered at me and stated, "I have worked through weeks of hell to fuck you bitch. Now it is payback time. You are mine."

He stated he would fuck me again when I finished school, and he did. After Asif dropped me off that evening, I spoke to Vijay while paying him back, and upon his recommendation, found a doctor's surgery, and went in. I had to fill in forms, but made up my name and address. I was told to come back for my appointment in three day's time. I was stunned, as we always got in that same surgery at home.

I had to choose a doctor, so asked for a female one. She looked at my form and said, "I see you are fourteen years old. Is this about sex?"

I nodded my head and blushed. "I see. You had better see Doctor Wright in that case. He's extremely good with young girls."

I lied about my age. A doctor may prescribe The Pill to a <u>fourteen</u> [R 18.1] year-old. I was sure he wouldn't give them to an eleven year-old.

I went back and saw Doctor Wright on Thursday evening. He asked me what I wanted, so I said "The pill." He was not surprised, but wanted to know about my sex life. I mean, he wanted to know a great deal about my sex life. I couldn't tell him what was actually happening, so I made up a story.

I don't think he fell for it because he gave me a lecture on underage sex. He used words like 'Chastity' and 'Maidenhead', as if they mattered a damn to me anymore.

What he said was really boring, but he seemed to enjoy talking to himself — Most adult's do, especially if they have a tied and needy audience seeking assistance and assurance.

I told him I would think deeply, and even offered to change my ways and act upon his advice. The doctor liked that, and after due consideration, he agreed to keep me safe. I came out with an implant in my arm. He said it would keep me from having a baby for three years.

I was working out what it meant to be a girl in a world full of men. I wanted to wind-back the hands of my personal 'Clock of Life', but it was already far too late. Instead, I peered into the future, if only because that was something I knew I could change. It didn't look too bright. I dismissed it all that night, with a bottle of Bacardi.

I now knew exactly what Vikki said to me all those years ago, because her life was never the one she wanted, nor wished for. It was the one Fate dealt to her. I also remembered the promise I made to her, that I would do something with my life. I decided, I would not end up like her, cast adrift upon the streets of London. I would make something of my life, no-matter what.

Asif used my young sex every morning and evening that week. I got my period on the Tuesday, but that did not stop him. It seemed to delight him because he said, "I see you are a virgin again, just for me."

There was no room for love on the back seat of his taxi. I have no idea why I didn't try for the bus, except he was always there for me, and I still trusted him. Some might consider that strange?

OK, so he was raping me twice each day, but other than that, he was actually looking out for me. By the end of the week, I knew to open my legs for him, or get another beating until I did. I got in the back, removed my panties, and waited until his urgency subsided inside me. That was all there was to it. Later in the week, he did it in my mouth, and my bum, and that really hurt.

I took to wearing panty towels, not because of my periods, which were light, due to the alcohol and drugs, bordering on being nothing. I used them to mop up the seemingly never-ending, sticky male deposits.

["Bilty, I'm going to carry on, as I'm in the groove, so ask your questions later. One minute, and I'll resume.]

Chapter 19 – Neighbourhood Girls

I did not see Zoë at all that week and worried about her. I knocked her door every evening, but there was no response. I woke up on Saturday morning and noticed a note pushed under my door. It was virtually illegible, but the scrawl read, "Get out while you can."

I was certain it was from Zoë, so went and banged repeatedly on her door. I was sure she was inside her room, but she didn't answer. I went down for breakfast that morning, worried about my friend, but soon I was headed for school. That time it was not Asif who collected me, but Anwar, a driver I had never seen before. He said little on our journey, and drove quickly towards our destination. I presumed he was in a hurry, and it turned out he was.

He pulled over where Asif usually fucked me, and I tried to get out of the rear. The child locks were on and he laughed at me, rubbing his crotch with menace. I tried to fight him off, but he was far too big and strong for me. He slapped my face and punched me hard in the stomach. He made me remove my panties and beg him to fuck me. He hit me very hard until I said the words to his liking. It was rape. It was also one degree worse than the way Asif had taken me.

I hoped Mohammed would collect me that evening and take me out for dinner. Deep within my broken heart I knew he would not—he had used me. I knew it from the lowest depths of my being, which was now a shattered mess of haunted dreams.

Mohammed did not collect me, but another driver did. Khan pulled over in the rape place, and took me. Again, I thought to fight him off, but it was useless. He thought his words were funny, and laughed, "I'm giving you a free ride, so you will do the same for me."

I asked him to use a condom. Instead he slapped my face so hard, I could not hear properly until I got back to gaol.

There were not many girls at dinner that evening, so I was allowed seconds. I went up to my room and tried to work out what I was becoming mixed up in. At least I still had taxi service for school, even if the cost was a free fuck. I guessed that might be OK, because the fare was way beyond my means.

I desperately wanted to continue at school and make Sophie proud of me, and keep my promise to Vikki. But, was that worth the price of being raped twice a day, six days a week? If I stopped going to school, what would happen? I would be sent to a plebs school and learn nout. There was the bus, but that cost too much time. My mind wrestled with the dilemma as I sought any agreeable answer. There wasn't one.

I spent a lot of time thinking, unable to understand what had become of me. My emotions mourned, but I drew comfort by remembering what Vikki had told me about the man that had raped her. She essentially said that she was his victim, until she thought of him as just another client. She purposefully overlooked the fact that he was not paying her, and in the process, regained control of her emotions, and in due course, of her life.

From out of nowhere, I remembered another from the past. I never knew the guy well—his name was Nick. He had a habit of arriving, looking enquiringly at people, and asking, "Is your mind right?"

He always moved off after he had said it, and it was quite funny, although I never understood what he really meant. I realised that what Vikki did was get her mind right, so she could survive, and move quickly on from the situation. She wrote off her rape as one of life's occupational hazards, and being a prostitute helped her, I am sure.

I know she never forgave the man, but that is a different thing entirely. She did not let her feelings fester like a feted sore. She accepted what had happened, and got her life back into gear. However, that never precluded the fact that she would take revenge upon the moron, given half a chance. Street-life can be like that.

This led me to examine accepting my daily rapes, and get on with my own life, and in every other way that mattered, on my terms. I imagined adopting that thought, and it suited me. Meanwhile, the other voice inside my head was screaming at me, that I was only eleven years old, and something was very, very wrong about the whole thing. I ignored it and "Got my mind right."

I stopped thinking about meeting Prince Charming, a fairytale wedding, and married bliss ever after. Instead, I rescued myself from a potentially life-debilitating abyss. That did not happen overnight--these things take time, but the new outlook settled comfortably within my mind. In time, it gave me the strength to endure, and the ability to rise above my past, and my persistent daily rapes.

This does not mean I did not deeply resent each rape, nor did I ever stop hating the bastard's that inflicted their selfish male desires upon my body. My new attitude allowed me to build impenetrable armour, to shield my emotions and be my own person, not somebody else's victim.

My new mindset did not imply forgiveness. I added each new crime against my humanity, to an exponentially growing list, vowing that one day I would take complete and utter revenge upon my abusers. I started keeping a diary of who raped me, and when. The exercise also distanced me from the horrific events my life had become. I used the info to build a security wall; one day, I would use it against them.

[Bilty: "Do you still have the diary, Isabella?"

"Yes I do. Mel, give Bilty a digital copy please."]

Some may wonder why I never went to the police. The answer is simple. The SS have to sanction a complaint, such as rape. I knew they would not. As far as I am concerned, they were complicit [R 19.1] in my daily rapes. I would not have been in that situation, but for them. Their 'Duty of Care' was a dereliction of sworn oath. I hated them all.

By Sunday, I knew I was making the correct choice, and felt much stronger. Nevertheless, the shift in attitude did not come without a cost. It robbed me of my innocence, and made me much tougher.

I finally saw Zoë at lunchtime. She was sitting with the bully and her gang, and that surprised me at first, but I realised I was hardly ever there. Except for Sunday's, I lived an insular life away from the rest of the inmates. I was pleased when she finished eating and came over to talk to me. What was not good was that she was in company with the bully, Candy Monster, or Psycho as we called her behind her back. She was flanked by two of her minders. Zoë still looked miserable but said, "Hi, long time no see. How about we go hang out sarvo?"

I was almost finished eating, so said, "I'll meet you out front."

She did not look all that happy about it. I was excited. It had been too long between us and I looked forward to doing nothing with Zoë, just like old times. I made plans to treat her to a burger, and afterwards take her for a walk and find out what was wrong with her.

I found her out on the street loitering aimlessly with the Psycho and the same two girls. The five of us walked up the street, and it seemed OK. I didn't trust anyone but Zoë. However, they were being pleasant to me and inclusive. We walked a mile, until we turned a corner and crossed the road. I was still trying to speak to Zoë, but she wouldn't say anything of significance with the other girls nearby.

We came to a Balti house and I recognised it at once. I said, "Isn't this the one Mohammed owns?"

Psycho laughed, "His uncle owns it actually. Mohammed is a good liar, as you now know, my little ex-virgin. Come, let's have some fun."

There was menace in her voice, and something about the way she said, 'come' that should have warned me. Instead, I was focused on my broken heart. We went straight into the back room, and I saw the guy I met before. He seemed nice and we settled into easy chairs. There was drink on the table, and spliffs already rolled. Perfect!

There were four men and five girls in the room, and everybody seemed happy, even Zoë. I had a vodka and orange, and lit one of the spliff's. I took four hits before passing it on. I told whoever made it that it was excellent. That turned out to be the man I had met before. He came over and somehow we both ended up sitting in one armchair, with me perched on his lap. I wished I were on Mohammed's lap, but I ended-up making out with the guy just to spite my first love.

Soon we were kissing and touching each other up. He left with Zoë's guy to get pizza, and me Bacardi and cola. She came over and squatted beside me, "I told you to leave before they got to you, stupid."

A minder called her name. Zoë went back to her seat, and I thought about what she said. When my guy came back he offered me a large glass of brackish liquid, and a slice of pizza. I sniffed the drink and took a sip. It tasted just right. I ate and took the joint he offered. I checked out the pill that followed. It was stamped with an 'E' that looked like a crown. It appeared kosher, so I popped it in my mouth. I washed down with Bacardi, and finished the glass. After it was refilled, my beau wasted no time in kissing me.

I was drifting within kisses and fumbles, searching for love anywhere I could find it, when an argument broke out. One of the men had been cooking something in a foil wrap, and had drawn a liquid into a syringe. I tried to escape, but I was pinned down and helpless.

Zoë demanded a hit, and her look askance to me was one of protection. I got the remainder from the same needle. I tried to fight them off, but it was useless. The guys were too strong, and experienced.

I knew the hit as soon as it entered my bloodstream. It was what Mohammed had given me the night he raped me—I could just snatch that memory back from the ghosts of time past. It was Heroine—I must have either smoked or drunk it that night.

I remember we had one last joint, before a man looked deeply into my eyes and said, "It is time. You will go upstairs with me."

I said, "Yes," without any reason.

I had known for some time that this was all about, rape. Instead of running, or letting my mind fry, I went with the flow and accepted what was to be, as already being my choice. Doing so gave me confidence. There was no option, and my compliance would save a beating.

The room was bare except for an old mattress on the floor. There wasn't even a sheet on the bed. I think there was a table and a few chairs, but that was about it. I was on the mattress kissing him, and he was inside me. I remember seeing the black flag of Allah on the wall, and I stared at it as the man thrust inside me. I realised he was close because his pace changed, and he was awfully deep inside me.

I kissed him as he thrust inside me again, but when I looked back from the flag, he turned out to be somebody else. I heard that voice again in my head, the one that was ringing alarm bells. I tried to respond, but by that time, somebody else was fucking me. I would have told the fourth guy to stop, but I was so close to a powerful orgasm my brain shut down in utter confusion.

I came to back to sanity in my room. Psycho was hammering on my door. I staggered out of bed and she said I had to get dressed. I looked for my bra, but she told me, "Don't bother with bra or panties. You won't be needing them."

I took her advice, put on my shortest school skirt and a boob tube.

She walked out into the night. I was staggering and disorientated. Zoë supported my attempts to walk. Her steps were no better than my own, but together we made it out onto the street. A taxi was waiting for us and we got in the back. In my mind, I thought I was going to school. Instead, we pulled up at a house and were given drinks and spliff's. I still hadn't come down from last time, so it hit me hard.

That time there were five men, and just we two girls. I was handed another joint and took just one drag. There was something utterly wrong about it. My mouth had instantly gone dry and I knew instinctively it was Tina, so I passed it on.

The guy who made it was offended, and asked me why I did not enjoy it. I told him it was not right, and that I didn't need it. He came close and kissed me on the lips, before looking into my eyes and stating, "You will smoke it or I will beat you. Do you understand?"

His eyes turned ugly as he drew his arm back, and I said, "OK."

Just like last time, was that only last night? It was hard to remember. Anyway, just like before, time jumped. I was on a bed, but this time I still had all my clothes on. OK, so what if my boob tube was holding the folds of my school skirt around my waist, I was still dressed, wasn't I? I was also feeling horny, and despite trying to appear to smoke the joint, I knew some crystal meth had entered my system.

He fucked me for ages before finishing inside me. I had to go to the toilet and wash it out. When I got back the next guy was waiting for me. I refused, and was beaten with his fists until he grabbed a hammer and hit [R 19.2] me several times with it. It really hurt, and I agreed. He fucked me. I washed his cum out, and afterwards the next guy hit me, and fucked me. All five took me that night, and then pissed on us.

I was just a piece of meat to those sick bastards. The next night was virtually the same, except it was a different house with different men. I wised up and did not draw deeply on the tokes that tasted funny. I learned not to fight, and came to accept my beatings in prelude to my rapes, as an unpleasant fact of my daily existence.

So much for us, supposedly, being in 'local authority care'. We would never have been in that predicament in the first place, had it not been for Social Services, and the Bussies. We would still be at home with our loving families, and I would still be a virgin. Kinda sucks, don't it?

On Wednesday, I managed to eat for the first time in days. Well, I had eaten at the houses, but it was my first proper food without additives. Zoë came in and sat with me at dinnertime. She was morose and said, "I hoped you'd be spared this, but it is a fact of my life now. Our lives. The sooner you accept it, the sooner it gets better, I suppose?"

I looked up at her and said, "Let's go to the police."

Zoë replied, "I'm not stupid you know. After the first gang rape, I tried that. I went Tuesday morning, following the Sunday when you left early. I wish I'd left with you, but I guess they would have stopped me somehow. Unlike you, I wasn't a virgin.

"I went to the police. I told them I had just been raped by four guys, and handed over my cum-stained panties. I believed British justice would come to the rescue and stop it, as this time I did not tell them I was in care. The police and hospital staff humiliated me. They promised to take action, and nothing happened.

Chapter 19

"Sure, they swabbed the inside of my 'precious', and sent samples of Pakistani sperm for processing, but you understand, right? This ain't a straight issue. The police are shit scared because these are 'Asian', as they insist on calling them. No, they are not!

"They are Pakistani Muslim paedophiles, and the police are afraid of the race issue, never mind the religious one. Therefore, in the meantime, I continue to get gang raped every fucking day, by a never-ending succession of Paki's I have never seen before, nor since. The authorities, nobody wants to know about it. I am almost twelve years old, and I deserve a better future than being some Paki-gangs fuck-toy.

"Once they discovered my situation, the police were nasty, and interrogated me for hours. They tried to make me admit I was a whore, so they could prosecute me. They threatened to charge me with underage sex unless I admitted my crimes. I stopped speaking to them, and sat there stone-faced with my arms across my chest. They gave up and released me with a police caution.

"I am the victim here, yet I get a criminal record, and my rapists get off Scot-free. Don't talk to me about care, because that is just some made-up word, and I no longer want to know, or give a shit."

She looked up hesitantly, a vapid smile playing upon her face for the first time in weeks. Tears rolled down her cheeks. "If I gave you everything I own, would you — would you kill me? Please! Could you? Would you make this stop? End it all. Make it go away, like forever?"

[Bilty turned to stare at Zoë. She said, "I meant it with the whole of my heart, and still do even now. It was the only way I could escape the life I had. But Issy found another way. Run it again, and I would still choose death over that shite of life I had. Nobody understands how bad it was, 'cept us. The fallout was…"

"Stop Zoë. I'll get to that part soon. Let's get on with this."]

I was on my feet before she finished speaking. I held her so close in my arms and told her she was wrong, and that one-day we would find a way to fight them. I don't think she believed me, but we kissed and it was a deep kiss of love and shared sisterhood.

The voice came behind us, "So what've we got here. A couple of Gays, two lesbo's. 'Lesbos R Us'. Here kitty-kitty."

Psycho and her gang laughed at us, mocked us in our time of great neediness. I broke our kiss and swung my arm round to hit her in the stomach. I missed because my chair was thrown over onto its back by one of her trusties. My head hit the floor hard and started throbbing. The bully lowered herself onto my face, squatting to thrust the rub of her jeans between her crotch and my lips.

I was still on the chair, sitting, perpendicular like. I turned my lips inside my mouth. There was nothing I could do except endure the stench and humiliation. I tried to hit my persecutor, but my arm was easily parried and fell away. My hand outstretched, landed on Zoë's, who was beside me on the floor. It reminded me of how we held each other during last night's rapes. I held her hand as they had their fun with us, but luckily, the bullies soon got bored.

We escaped, after Psycho had demonstrated to all she was the Alpha Female. After that, we got used to being called lesbian names. We were actually taking more man-meat than anyone else in that God-forsaken 'care home'. We were the youngest you see.

Psycho came to my room some hours later, accompanied by her minders. We were given five minutes to change: boob tube, short skirt, white socks and pumps. No bra, no knickers. This time the taxi took us to the Balti house. We both got high, smoked spliff's and ended up together on the mattress upstairs. Again we were being taken by a gang of Paki men we had never seen before, nor see again. I made sure I was not too high, and noticed my next fucker handing over a purple note to the man guarding the door. He had just paid fifty pounds to fuck me. I didn't see one penny of it, nor a penny from any other man who took me, or Zoë, that night. Some paid even more.

I put my hand out and found Zoë's. I clenched it as the guy came in my cunt, my Fairy was long gone. Zoë gripped me back, and hard. Together we endured the seemingly never-ending abuse.

Thursday was a mess. We both did six men each that night, but Zoë insists it was seven — but then, she's not that good at maths. They took us more than twice each, you see. We were hit hard until we did it just right. I mean, we had to fuck them, all proactive like, on top. Zoë almost lost a tooth in the process, and I thought my ribs were cracked. They abused any orifice that they wanted, often two or more together. My rectum was bleeding, and my throat sore. Then it was over.

As it was, we came round to Psycho knocking our door the next evening, and repeat. During those days, Zoë and I drew closer together, both eleven years old, and both in local council care, courtesy of Social Services. The police knew what we were being forced to endure, against our will, yet took no action. That means they were colluding in our abuse. There can, and never could be, any other logical conclusion.

We went out together virtually every night after that. We did five or more men each time, and they all came inside both of us at least once. They never used condoms. Sometimes we reached orgasm with our rapists, and that just made them horny enough to take us again. It screwed with our minds, and we drew ever closer together as a result. Fortunately, most of them were only good for banging us once, each. They also shot video, and had us pose having sex, or just naked, sometimes with semen dripping out of us. That's one way they sold us.

The week wore on and I probably fucked thirty-odd guys. They were evil, because after raping us, they would sometimes make this big show of double praying to Allah. I didn't get that. I mean, the guy has just fucked a girl that he knows to be eleven years old. He has a wife and children of his own, and afterwards he prays thanks to his god?

If I were Allah, I would never forgive the perverts, but of course, I had no way out. My despair became unhinged, as another unknown cock entered my cunt. Some preferred to fuck my mouth, or even my bum. There was no place for love where I lay.

There was never any love, nor foreplay. My body became a vessel, a receptacle, a dump for Paki cum. Could any normal person endure my life? Zoë's? And where were Social Services, the Police? Nowhere.

I made the sign of the cross, and endured the Devil's design of purgatory. Zoë and I suffered the abuse, we had no choice in the matter. I was already a Paki whore, only I never got any money for fucking the bastards, the lieutenants kept it all.

That is not quite true. Sometimes they would give us a fiver between us as a special treat. That's fifty pence each, per man, per fuck. That is way beyond humiliation. By doing so, they belittled us, made us believe we were completely worthless, lower in value than an animal.

Such derisory payment for what should be our unique gift of new life, turned our minds inside out, threatening our sanity. Our only defence was to endure and wait for our chance to abjure the torment.

I never doubted for one instant, that I was far more worthy of any God's Heaven than they were. My innate inner strength gave Zoë hope. However, she never could alter her thinking the way I had done, and I continued to evolve in doing so. She relied upon my strength to see us both through the habitual, daily anguish. The next day, it would repeat, like a vinyl record stuck in a groove, the groove of my womanhood.

Bilty

"This is monstrous treatment of children. I am aghast. Speechless and angry. Not only regards the rapists, the violence they used, but also the police and SS. How could they knowingly permit this to happen?"

Candice interrupted, "And to keep reoccurring. I feel sick. I need a break, but we'll continue. I need to hear the all of it."

Isabella smirked. "Thank you. The worst is perhaps yet to come, but the telling will be relatively short. I also need to get through this. So we will finish this part today. Take a drink downstairs, or a walk in the park opposite. I'm, ready when you are, but then I know what's coming. Please excuse the pun."

"You are OK with the sexual abuse?"

"No, never. But it is the emotional abuse that really gets to me. Us."

Chapter 20 – Living Life in Hell

Isabella

Friday is the Muslim un-holy day. That afternoon was a washout, and I ended up with Zoë, in her bed. For the first time since the daily fucking began, we were not high on something. We talked and kissed. It seemed natural. She nurtured my small budding breasts, but it was not sex. Others may not understand that—how we were drawn so close together. We shared a deep sense of emotional betrayal, by and because of our carers, mixed up within a needy craving for maternal nurture.

We had been gang-raped so many times we needed a mother's comfort. We only had each other. Zoë was losing her mind, while I battled to keep her sane. We felt ashamed of what we were doing, what we had become. No one else loved us. All we had were each other.

That night, like many others, I blamed myself for allowing this to happen. I knew rationally, that none of it was my fault, but another voice inside me insisted, "You should never have gone to that Balti house." My thoughts drifted to Mohammed, the voice in my head daring me to admit that he conned me; "You shouldn't have sat on his lap," and, "How did you allow that to happen?"

There is a lot of humiliation and stigma attached to sexual abuse, so I've never told anyone until now, except Zoë and later, my friends here. I wanted to excoriate myself, and would have fallen into a black hole of self-loathing, were it not for Zoë's bodily warmth and comforting arms that prevailed, and anchored me firmly in the present.

I thought about my mother, and later Sophie. I wanted to be with them, both of them. I imagined us together, me between them in bed at night, draped with sumptuous quilts that kept us warm and safe, protected, and secure. That was perfect. As far as I knew my mother was still in prison, for coming to my rescue. And Sophie, well Sophie needed to play the system. I missed my father equally.

Love. That word embodied maternal comfiture and total security. Zoë was suckling my pubescent boobs. I drew her mouth away, so I could suckle hers. We were needy of anything remotely normal. Nurturing, any sanity of our own craven device. I too sought succour.

We shared emotional sanctuary, a place where men, and their apparent obsession with raping us, held no quarter. It became a psychological release, allowing our reason for living to endure and flower again the next morning.

The following day, Zoë told me she would not be with me that night, because she had a special job. I asked her what it was, but she was reticent. "It's a favour I owe Mohammed."

"Why?"

"I'll tell you another time. I'm the 'entertainment' at a party being held in his offices."

"That sucks."

"Yeah. I'll probably be doing most of that."

Somehow we broke out laughing. It was surreal. To deflect me probing further, she said, "I've not been to school for almost three weeks, and the matron, with Social Services approval, wrote it off."

I knew there were laws about that and education, but she replied, "Apparently I am now doing 'Home Schooling'."

She added distractedly, "It seems that I have Special Needs."

We broke out in fits of laughter, and it was so good to see her happy again. I had missed her true self far more than I expected.

She rallied and added, "And so do many other girls here. So, they use that as an excuse to get us out of the regulated educational system, and it allows us to do our 'work'."

Her eyes were rheumy, but she did not cry, or seek a hug. She lifted her shoulders, as if to bear the yoke of her destiny. Zoë stared at a spot on the wall, as if using it for focus, and added, "Maybe my home life wasn't so bad after all. Well, it was great, and at least they loved me."

I thought about what she had said for some time, before I realised the full implications of those words.

Later, we planned all sorts of spiteful things we would revenge upon our rapists – the slowest of exquisite tortures so they would die knowing how deeply we utterly loathed them. They had defiled us, despoiled our burgeoning womanhood, and deserved to die.

On Saturday, Zoë left for her 'Special Assignment'. I shared the cab. She entered an office block called Hussein Brothers. There was a large Mercedes parked by the main door, one I recognised instantly. Finally, I had tracked Mohammed to his lair. I left Zoë to her fate, and was dropped off near town. It was my ruse to discover Mohammed's lair.

A few weeks before, I was a typical eleven-year-old virgin. That day, I could not remember how many men had fucked me, but it was a big number. More than seventy I was sure. I knew the names of a few of them, the rest were cocks that fucked me. They came inside me without ever using protection. None of them had my consent to sex. Does anyone know what it feels like to be raped?

Imagine being gang-raped, every fucking day of your young life. This had been Zoë's life, and now it was my own. I had to laugh, because some of the inmates were put into 'care' to stop their father, or uncle perhaps, making love to them occasionally.

Now they were taking five unknown Paki cocks every night. Sure, tell me about how great, Britain's care system malfunctions. Our carers had to know what was going on. I was becoming certain they did, but how could I ever prove it?

I did learn that if I played along with the Paki rapist's, it did not usually hurt as much. I do not mean the sex, by that time it was presumed in advance, already accepted, and written-off in my mind.

They loved to hit me, to treat me like a sex slave. After they finished, some would have me open my lower lips wide and spit into them. A few even pissed on me [R 20.1], or into my sex and mouth. Urinating [R 20.2] on, or into the raped girl is gross. It is utterly demeaning. Sometimes they'd do it as a group, before praying to Allah. The national papers never reported that. Why not?

They treated me worse than an animal. But instead of being cowed like everyone else, my unrequited rage smouldered deep within me. Over times yet to come, those emotions were to coalesce into a bitter shard of malice, one that demanded full redress and redemption.

My young life had moved well beyond gross. There are no words to describe how utterly humiliated I felt, how debased I had become. I hated all of them. I vowed to kill every last one of those monsters.

My hatred kept me sane. Others' cast adrift in life's ivory towers of a normal existence will probably condemn me. I don't care what others think. Remember, I once had a normal life. Social services ripped that away from me, deliberately, and made me into who I was—A white, eleven year old, Christian, Paki-Muslim cum-dump. I began to wonder if this was actually some distorted sort of religious revenge.

On Sunday, I made it down for breakfast, determined to get my life back together again. At ten o'clock that morning, I entered the same building Zoë had not long left. The Merc was parked outside. I was mad as hell. I demanded to see Mohammed. I was refused, at least until I started smashing up the place, and dialled the police emergency line to report my rapes. That did the trick. Instead of my first ever boyfriend, I found a Muslim snake hissing the back of my hand. I snapped it away from his grasp, and slapped his face as hard as I could.

I don't think anyone had ever done that to him before. I saw his face redden, but not with blushes like I had naïvely done some weeks before. His face was filled with frenzied wrath, and I knew he was going to hit me, very hard. I stood my ground. His arm swung back to empower his strike against me. Instead of running away, I stepped boldly forward, locked his eyes with mine, and called him out as a man. I knew he could kill me with one blow, and I didn't care.

The blow never came, if only because his wife came storming towards us, her own rage upon her. However, he and I both knew it was because he could never break my spirit.

They got into an argument. I did not understand most of the words they used, but I'm sure I understood what she was saying. Neither was I surprised to discover he was married. It seemed to fit the low-life scumbag. Any remaining love for him died within that instant. But within the broken mess of my heart, I found shards of my former self, and clung to each, and every one, like scattered, irreplaceable treasures.

My plan worked perfectly, because it was plainly evident, Mohammed needed me gone, and quickly. I said, "I will do your tricks, but you will re-instate my school taxi service. I will not do hard drugs. Do you understand?"

"I'll see you end up in the canal, face down, first."

"No way! Zoë and I are the favourites. We are also the youngest. We pull more tricks than any other girls. Your rape business can't afford to lose me, and that's a fact."

His wife rejoined the fray, "What is this 'rape business' Inzamam?"

"Nothing. The wild imaginings of a child."

I began to reply, and to get rid of me, he agreed. I felt elated and strong. I was not like all the other girls. I had finally clawed a little of my own life back from those monsters.

I now wish I had never done that, but back then, I didn't understand how evil they were.

I realised I was free and walked the streets with a little bit of cash in my pocket. I spent most of it on a burger treat, and tried my best to feel like a normal kid. That sentiment never came, how could it? Nevertheless, I revelled in the pretence.

Somewhere in between, I regained a zest for life. I did not realise it at the time of course. Nonetheless, humanity is not made only of black nor white, but of myriad colours, and associated depths of grey, which we may sometimes realise as outpourings of human emotions.

It was late afternoon and I was meandering back towards gaol, lost deep within my freedom and heartening thoughts. A taxi screeched to a halt beside me, and I was told to get in. It was one of Mohammed's Uncle's taxis, well, they had driven most other taxi firms out of the area. The driver bawled me out for being late. I apologised and said, "I got lost, thanks for rescuing me."

I know he instinctively wanted to hit me, but I got away with it. Zoë was high and down to her panties when I was dropped off at a different take-away. I waltzed in and said, "Hi. I'm sorry for being late."

The guys on the sofa looked pissed-off, so I headed for them at once and sat between them, kissing each of them quickly, before asking them if they wanted a drink.

I had worked out in the taxi, there was no use fighting. I decided to take the lead, and make a performance out of the malaise.

They were so used to grooming young, white girls for sex, that they were not prepared when I took the initiative. Wimps. That time it was I topping up their drinks and rolling spliff's. I let them remove my clothes, albeit with a slight, but expected, female coyness of encouragement, as I tried to catch-up. As it was, I was pretty sober and sane when we went upstairs to fuck. That was a drag.

Asif was waiting for me on Monday morning, and I went to school for the first time in ages. I sat in the passenger seat, and when he pulled into lover's lane, I got in the back and let him fuck me. I had paid my fare, and it was cool by me. I felt a new resilience growing deep within, one that would never be denied, whatever they did to my body. *Quid pro quo* became *do ut des*, and in time: *lex talionis*, as each transgression against me would, in time, be repaid as part of my revenge.

The deputy head gave me the third degree about my missing time, but what could I tell her? I said, "I had an awfully bad fever."

She didn't buy it. "Isabella, you missed two weeks. What has been going on, and I want the truth this time."

"I can't tell you. You wouldn't believe me, nobody does. I have sorted the problem, and am back for good. There will not be a repeat. That's all I can say, except I need extra homework so as I can catch up."

"Is this to do with your care home, or that taxi service you use? I have no idea how you manage to afford that."

"Yes Ma'am, but with all due respect, I cannot tell you. Please drop the subject, and never mention it again. It is sorted."

"I still need to know, so spill the beans."

"Sorry, but no can do. I repeat, it is sorted, Ma'am."

"And the cost? Never mind, I have a shrewd idea. But when you feel ready to talk, know my door is always open to your confession. Now, be gone with you, and don't let me down."

After that, my life settled into a new rhythm. During the daytime, I went to school. Almost every journey I was fucked by the taxi driver. Almost every evening, Zoë and I took on a gang of Paki's and fucked them dry. I also got to pass on the hard drugs. This was not any sort of life I could ever have imagined, let alone have chosen, but we got by.

We endured and got used to doing five men both, each night. Within a short time we were considered regulars, so they dropped to cheaper drugs and we knew what was happening to us most of the time. Neither did they want us to become addicted to the worst ones, especially Tina and H. I warned Zoë off both several times.

We were doing thirty or more new faces each week, and they were all different. After fucking us, they would break for prayers, and double-pray to Allah for his dispensation. I wondered once more at this supposed god's double standards? In all honesty, I could only relate to Islam as a misogynistic ruse men used to enslave their women.

If I could have moved, I would have kicked their shite-holes as they bent over in His worship, but that was never within me. The softer drugs and alcohol took it all away. Neither of us wanted to do it, fuck those guys, but we had zero choice.

Care workers and police [R 20.3] were not to be seen, except for running away in denial of our existence, and how they had allowed, encouraged us to become preteen sex slaves. These authorities supposed 'Duty of Care', seemed to only extend to their burgeoning business we empowered as underage sex slaves. Otherwise, we remained the forgotten children, the rape-fodder that made them their money.

I missed another birthday while being used as a Paki-fuck-toy [R 20.4] , and it was several weeks before I realised I was twelve.

We screwed our brains down, and got used to being fucked every day. I never saw my boyfriend, Mohammed for a long time. I knew he was running the scam, and I swore an oath that one day I would kill him—flashy cars don't mean much when some ancient Pakistani grandfather is shooting his load inside you.

I wondered if all Muslim men were paedophiles?

Or was it only the Paki's?

They were certainly all misogynists.

There were thousands of them wanting to fuck us. Well Vijay wasn't, but every other one I had ever met in my life appeared to be a serial paedophile. How can that be? Even in Native societies, the age to have sex is arbitrarily twelve years old, or first proper menstruation.

I said to Zoë, "Do you know the age of consent is nine in Yemen, although girls are often married when they are younger."

"What do you expect, they have small cocks, so need a tight hole to get off. That's why they stitch the women up so they can't pee properly, leaving only a small entrance hole to the vagina. They also remove their clit so they can never enjoy sex. That to me is 'miss-oggy-nism'!"

"Misogynism, Zoë. You know, I'd never thought about it that way, but I'll be damned if you haven't hit the nail on the head. It makes perfect sense, and answers the question of why they do it to their women. Brilliant Zoë.

"You challenge them when they are not feeling horny, and they quote Islam at you. They tell you how it is wrong to smoke, do drugs, and drink alcohol. They make you learn sutras, and repeat them. When they want sex, they do the lot. They encourage us to drink, smoke, and do drugs, just like they do. Then they rape us."

Bilty

"Do you want me to tell you about debasement and degrees of rape. Bilty? Do 'YOU', or your wife, your children, want to take my place, or Zoë's? For the first time in my short life, nothing ever changed. Before my thirteenth birthday, I had fucked thousands of different men. They were all Paki's. Not one of them did it with my consent.

"11 Years Old—Imagine…"

Candice spoke into the quiet, "No, I cannot."

Isabella replied, "Then let me try. Candice, imagine that tonight, five ethnically and religiously different men from you, are going to gang rape you. They will use any orifice, and hit you until you do it just right. Then they will piss on you. Tomorrow night it will repeat, and the next night, and the next. If you report events, the police will ignore you, and the Muslims will threaten your family. You will be drenched in petrol, and to save your life, that of those you love, you promise to be there the next evening. Now do you understand? Walk in our shoes.

'*In nomine Patris, et Filii, et Spiritus Sancti*'.

"So, no place for the Mother, the Daughter, or Female Creator then?

"The females' unique ability to impart the spark of new life.

Candice quailed, and Bilty rose protectively. "Thank you Isabella, that was some telling. I need to speak to you, but can I go somewhere else to chill for a moment. I found this extremely unsettling. Candice?"

"Yes, me too. The papers never reported the extremes of violence, or the … urination. That is debased. Maybe a quiet corner in the lounge.

"Thanks. There's a little that's worse to come. But that's how we all felt, hundreds of us. Let me show you the way. Vikki, see we have somewhere more comfortable to sit, The Churchill, or Raffles Corner perhaps. Come, a short chill. Apologies Candice, but I had to do that."

"Turning it on myself has deeply unsettled me. Now it's personal."

Mel added, "I'm transferring cameras now, just in case talk continues. Plus I could do with a stiff drink. We're still going warts and all, right? My turn will be up soon, and I'd rather play the video from before; it was of the moment. I can't do your memories as happening now. My life has moved on. Thank you all. And Issy.

Bitly felt glum but energized, two emotions at conflict with one another. Candice reached out her hand for succour. They shared strong liquor healing, before Bilty updated in his log.

Bilty:

Personal Journal:

I had never imagined the depths of abuse, mostly physical, these very young girls endured. That no responsible authority was interested in their plight demands the most serious investigation. I am expecting to witness: police, social services, and local authority to be imprisoned for a very long time. They all had a responsibility of 'CARE', which was at best, nonexistent.

Notes:

1. Isabella was considered special because she was a virgin. But that alone does not make sense. There were other virgins surely. She stated as much. So what else was going on? This is of deepest concern.

2. Isabella's rape is most unusual. She says she was a willing participant, so why did Mohamed need to drug her senseless?

3. She has vague recollections of an old, white guy. Why? Her memory, splintered as it may be, appears sure upon this point. This appears to be much more than a simple rape, when her virginity is taken into consideration.

4. Then there was the money Mohammed collected before he left. A lot of money. Was her virginity sold? And if so, to whom?

5. Moving On: What these very young girls endured was sexual slavery. Yes, Human Trafficking also. They were prostituted by thugs of an alien culture, who used them as a means to make money.

6. Both had been urinated upon. This happened elsewhere, but was largely not mentioned in the news reports. This shows the rapists' deep-seated loathing of the girls.

7. The 'home schooling' is a new issue to me, and one that warrants full exploration. Not only does it prove the Care Home bosses were aware of what was happening to the girls, but it facilitated their ongoing abuse. That the girls' education was badly compromised is an obvious outcome. It is not commensurate with the actions of a place of care.

Comment.

I remain amazed at Isabella's resilience, and the fact she fought Mohammed for reintroduction of her taxi service. That she considered the cost worth it, is her decision. By doing so, she ensured she got the very best of education. She is indeed, a remarkable young woman.

During the repose we lost Genie to a man in the saloon, and Vikki to manage the business. We were ready to resume when Isabella said, "It will begin to get busy in here before we are through. Let's go back upstairs and I'll go straight through to dinnertime."

Candice asked, "What is this place. A brothel?"

"A secret. It's the most exclusive bordello in town. With our backgrounds and education, what else could these girls achieve in life. I keep them safe and well found for. It's better than life on the streets. Were it legal, we'd pay taxes, be licensed. But the politicians, some of whom are our best clients, are too dumb to see it. Police, the elite of British society all come here, and I have videos––I call it insurance.

"But no more of this place. I'll come to it much later. I need to be done with my past life, the hell of it all. We all do. Come."

Chapter 21 – Innocence Lost

Isabella

I remembered being taken from my family, and later taken from my mother after she rescued me. I also remembered my first proper period, and boy did that suck. I have the best memories of Sophie, and a few of the people I met on the streets of London. Sophie was still paying for my education. I loved her truly, and not just because of that. I was considering going to see her, but something always came up.

I think I could have endured that life forever, except things did change eventually. I was thirteen, Zoë going on fourteen, and by that time, we had fucked thousands of men. If you think I exaggerate, do the maths: 5 men x 6 days per week x 52 weeks per year x 2 years = 3,120. Zoë and I usually did them as a double act. We learned to play their games, and seldom got a beating. My diary has names and addresses.

The only place we were always beaten was number 119 Filbert Street, where they believed in physically casting out the devil from within, in our case: Christianity. Fortunately, we seldom went there.

We were virtually free to drink and drug as much as we pleased. Zoë usually did a lot to blot it out. I on the other hand, did as little as I could, because I needed to stay sharp for school.

Big Daddy Asif was Mohammed's main lieutenant. He had told Psycho they needed new and younger girls, more fresh virgin blood to spill. We all knew about it, and talked about it when not supervised. We wondered if that would free us, at least in part, from the daily grind.

It seemed, the age of the girl mattered to the Pakistani clients; the younger the better. At thirteen, we were becoming too old for some the client's needs. Originally, we had been the youngest, our services in great demand.

As we got older, we worked out of the area quite often, usually still in London. Mohammed's uncle's taxis took us to our clients, and usually brought us back to gaol afterwards, but not always. Sometimes we had to make our own way home. With no money in our pockets, how do you think we paid for the fare? That's when we learned white men are usually bigger down there.

One Sunday morning I looked for Zoë, and found her in her room. She was in floods of tears. It took me a long time to get the truth out of her. Eventually she showed me her secret papers. The CPS had decided not to proceed in prosecution of her rape, because they considered Zoë to be an unreliable witness—so the creeps got away with raping her, and nothing was going to be done about it. Typical.

She was on the verge of telling all, when Psycho banged hard on the door. "Here Kitty-Kitty." Once inside she said, "One of the new girls needs introducing to the Balti house after lunch. You will take her there and not leave until they fuck her. Do you understand?"

I was aghast. I blurted out, "No, never."

When I refused, she had her gang strip me, and hold me so I could not move. She boiled a kettle [R 21.1] full of water and sauntered over to me, spilling the odd drop with menace. Sometimes she had an evil look in her eyes, and this was the worst I had ever seen. She said languidly, "I usually get two hundred pounds for every new girl I recruit. You get ten percent, or I scar you for life, and you will still do it anyway."

She moved close as her henchgirls held me fast. I felt the heat from the kettle as it neared my skin. The steam caressed my face with an evil embrace. She lowered the weapon, held the spout between my breasts and slowly started to pour. I knew she had done it to a couple of girls before. I was horror-struck, and shouted, "I'll do it."

Psycho was not convinced. She loved to hurt people, just for the sake of it. She pressed the kettle into my boobs, my nipples, and it was bloody hot, even for a cool-wall kettle.

I panicked and promised to do it, begging her before she believed me. You have no idea how much relief I felt when she finally put the kettle down. There was no scar, but I hurt for several days afterwards.

I did as requested, and felt little as the eleven year old was plied with drink and drugs, as was Zoë. I had seen it all before, far too many times. The young girl was out of her tree some hours later, and the first guy I met there years before, came to me and said, "It is time."

I had been told what to do. I called Mohammed and told him, "The new girl is ready for you. Come over now."

"Thank you Isabella, I've been so looking forward to fucking this bitch. Congratulations on your first time in charge."

I smirked with disdain, "Thanks lover-boy, you can call me Kitty."

He started laughing and hung up. I looked at the guy beside me and said, "He'll be here in twenty minutes."

They took the young girl upstairs to meet her fate fifteen minutes later, and I had to show Mohammed upstairs to take his latest conquest [sic]. I acted blasé, but deep inside of me grew my utmost hatred of him. I was smouldering with abhorrent revulsion as he fucked her. I could not believe I once thought I was in love with the monster. He was the embodiment of Satan, pure evil.

I stayed to watch him take her, and it was just another short fuck to him. He finished quickly, and left as soon as he came inside her. I doubted he would remember her, or even knew her name, and I was certain she would not remember him at all. Her virginity was gone.

I helped the girl to wash herself out, showing her the ropes. She was pretty, and pretty much out of her head, but there was still some fight left in her. She told me she wanted her mummy.

I stood guard and watched through the open door, as she went to the toilet and used the sink, to cleanse all Mohammed's seed out of her. I took her back, and Asif was waiting. He had bullied his way to the front of the queue and was shouting, "I want a go, I want a go."

I made sure she cleaned herself in between, as all the men took her once only, it being her first time. She did six of them that day. Welcome to the real world of underage Paki-rape [R21.2].

I went to the toilet when they started praying to Allah, thanking him for his wondrous gift that day. I spat in disgust, and instinctively drew the Sign of The Cross on my chest. The new girl followed me and cleansed herself for the last time that day. I knew all too well, the stain against her humanity could never be removed. I discovered her name was Alice, although no land of wonder awaited her.

She was sore, bleeding, and had difficulty walking. We went downstairs together and I gave her a strong drink and a spliff.

When the Pakis finished praying, they came down for another fuck. Zoë did one and I another. I took the last, to save the youngster from more rape. I allowed myself to drink properly and get high. I needed to blot out what I had just done to this innocent young girl, but it would never go away. Some stains remain for all eternity, deeply embedded within the human soul. Regardless, it would have happened anyway.

The next evening, after I got back from school, I found Zoë in her room. She stared at the wall, and tears rolled down her cheeks, but otherwise her face was made of stone. I could not imagine what was going on in her dissembling mind.

She paused to look at me, and burst into tears, not trickles as before, but wracking sobs that came from deep inside her. I held her so tight until she stopped shaking. She kept repeating, like a mantra of wordy balm, "I'm sorry. I am so, very sorry."

She urgently kissed me on the lips, and breaking from me, added, "Can you ever forgive me?"

Her tears erupted once more, and I had no idea what on earth she was talking about. I gentled and comforted her, and told her I loved her. She crashed into my bosom and asked, "Do you really mean that, despite what I have done to you?"

I shushed and cooed her raven mind, telling her everything was all right. I persuaded her to get it all off her chest. I found out in-between her blubbers. She was talking about our second visit to the Balti.

["You want to tell it Zoë?"
"No. You're better at it than me."
"No, I'm not. Just a short piece, this scene that's all. Promise."
"OK then."]

167

Zoë

That day after you left, well, I made out with some guys and got completely out of my tree. That was the first time I did H. Heroin. Unexpectedly your prince charming was there, and he led me upstairs. He was the first to rape me that day, and he left as soon as he had finished. After that Asif, and all the others did me.

I wanted to tell you, but how could I? I knew you were in love with him. The only difference between us was, you were a virgin, and could prove it. That made you special. Why do you think they let you go that day? They were under orders not to do anything to you. Not to touch you, not even one finger in the wrong place.

[Isabella: "I was shocked, but perhaps I could accept it, as by then I knew what a snake Mohammed was. I expected Zoë to be relieved, but she was hiding something else. I caressed her, both physically and emotionally until she blurted out a little more.
"Go on Zō, You're doing great."]

Do you remember those first dates with him? I was with Asif and he had just discovered I had gone to the police. I thought he was going to kill me. I truly believed that. He hit me so hard I passed out.

When I came round I was in a room naked, lying with my back on a cold floor. Mohammed was there with Asif. Candy Monster beat me within an inch of my life. Mohammed laughed as she and her girls punched and kicked me. Psycho doused me with petrol. She lit a cigarette, and toyed with the match. It went out. The intent was clear. I pleaded for my life. Thank God it worked.

I think they were playing with me. They all pissed on me, including Candy Monster. They laughed. I was scared to death.

Anyway, I was only fucking, extended family in those days, so Mohammed still took me sometimes. He was big down there, and most of them are quite small. I was quite tight in those days. Do you want to know why he was late that Wednesday?

"Carry on Issy. I hate this bit."

Isabella

My eyes opened wide and I said, "He said 'Something came up'."

Zoë almost smiled, but her fearful eyes returned to drench the embryonic flicker of normality. She took a deep breath and said, "Sure, his something came up inside of my something."

She breathed in deeply and held her breath. A weird sort of mewing sound came from the depths of her being. I was mad, but not at her. Mohammed was the target of my loathing. I encouraged her to tell me all of the story, because we both needed closure, or otherwise it would fester like an abscess between us.

I coaxed her, and warily, she continued.

[Isabella looked at Zoë, and nodded her head upwards with a sideways flick, as if to say, 'get on with it'.]

Zoë

OK. After the beating, Mohammed raped me right there on the floor. As soon as he was done, Asif took me, as everybody present cheered him on, and mocked me.

I guess they had been enjoying my distress so much that Mohammed became lost in the moment. One of the girls asked what the time was, and Mohammed glanced at his wristwatch. He said, 'Shit, I am going to be late'. I knew he was leaving to see you that Wednesday afternoon. I am so very sorry Issy, but there was nothing I could do.

"Then Khan appeared, laughing. I hurt real bad. He took a cigarette, and drew deeply. I could not understand why he kept drawing on it, because the red end grew more vivid and hotter.

"That was before I realised his true intentions. He smiled and said something nice to me. I knew that meant big trouble. I was held down and he brought the tip to just above my clitoris, and pressed it home, drawing on the tobacco until the stench of burning flesh filled the room. He laughed in my face as my mind flipped in searing pain.

"I remember he said something like he had marked me for life, and I belonged to him. I don't remember very much, except the pain. I agreed to do whatever he wanted, and he hit me with a hammer. He stood and looked back to admire his work on me with manic eyes.

He said some words, and someone disappeared. He came back with a red hot poker. I was still pinned down on the floor. Khan laughed as he branded my small, budding breast with his name.

I fainted from the pain. And I still bear that scar, even though I killed him years later. I must have it removed … sometime. But knowing it's there keeps me sane. Does that make any sense?

The man was pure evil. He branded me, pissed on me, before he, and a load of other perverts fucked me. I hardly remember it.

Later, Asif took me to somebody's house and the bully gang got me drunk and high. Some hours later, I went to the toilet and heard Asif shouting on the phone. He cursed the police and made a second telephone call. As I squeezed past him I overheard him speaking to Mohammed, and I heard you giggle in the background, Issy. The police wanted to interview him about my accusations.

Mohammed understood the seriousness of what I had done, and came back urgently to deal with me. He made me call the police and withdraw my statement. And that's why CPS consider me an unreliable witness. He was fucking me with the blade of a small, sharp knife at the time of the call. My Fairy still bears the scars to prove it.

That was not the worst of it. As he held the phone to my right ear, he was whispering into my left, telling me all the gory details about the various types of Muslim, underline female circumcision [R 21.3]. He embellished how much I would enjoy the release, and how I would come into my femininity before Allah. He emphasised his point by using his knife to draw along my lower lips, and pressed the blade under my clitoris. The whole concept was just gross. His intention, crystal clear.

The next day, under that heinous threat, I went down to the Plods House, and officially withdrew my statement. They did not check that a Paki always accompanied me, a man I had already accused of raping me. His photograph was on one of their fucking boards for Christ's sake! But they didn't recognise him at all. The Bussies are so stupid.

> [Zoë: "Issy, I'm done. I need a drink. I'll be in the bar. Finish this. I never want to have to remember that, ever again!"
> "Go Zō. I'm as frazzled as you are. I'll see you in a minute.
> " Bilty, Candice, now you know the depths of their depravity.]

Isabella

I knew those men could be mean and dangerous, but this took everything to a more intense level of evil. I cosseted Zoë and held her tighter, because I knew she had more to repent. She was in her shell and only I could ease this blot within her soul. I could never expunge it. I could only offer her my unconditional love as salve.

I was also mad as hell, and thought of how I would get my revenge upon the lying bastards. These were false thoughts of communal bravado, as I was much too young and entrapped, too estranged to lift a single finger to stop it.

She looked up at me for the first time in ages, and interrupting my thoughts said, "Why don't you hate me?"

I replied soothingly, "Because I love you."

I had never really thought about whether I loved Zoë or not, but we were more than best friends, so I guess I meant it. This saw a chink of a smile crease the corner of her mouth, her eyes, and she asked, "Do you want to hear the rest?"

"Yes. Tell Me." Zoë is a most private person. I asked, then pleaded with her, before she give up. I don't know if I believe any that astrology shit, but this was her character to a tee, Scorpio, so private and so proud.

She began the final revelation, "I avoided you. I knew you wanted to tell me how much in love you were with Mohammed. He always fucks the new ones first, unless they are a virgin with a hymen."

She stopped and looked at me, as if she were done. However, she could not hide the truth from me. I knew her far too well, and there was a little more for her to tell. I came back to the topic and encouraged her to release the last of it.

I needed a ruse to open her up, and there was always one question that bothered me; "Zoë, the night I lost my virginity, where were you?"

"Misbaq's Tandoori Takeaway, why?"

"So you were there when Mohammed went in the back. I had to wait at the counter. I heard you scream before we left. What happened?"

"Nothing much. That was my first airtight sex--you know? They do all three holes at the same time. It really hurt, and I bled for days afterwards. I must have been trying to fight them off, as Khan lit a cigarette, and started drawing deeply on it. I shouted, "No! I'll do it." The other guys ushered Khan away. He stormed out of the door, slamming it behind him. Why do you ask?"

"Because I knew it was you there. I just needed confirmation, that's all. You were OK?"

"Yep. I know something about that night. Can you remember it?"

"No. Nothing after we got into the hotel room. What you got?"

She took a deep breath and said, "Everybody knew you were special, select. Nobody was ever allowed to touch you. Mohammed was not the first man to fuck you. I do not know who it was, but it was somebody very rich and powerful. Don't ask, because that's all I know. I only found that out by accident as well, I overheard it and scarpered."

I smothered her. I kissed her hard, "I knew it!"

My anger rose as I said, "He gave me a <u>date-rape drug</u> [R 21.4], and heroin. Even now, I remember almost nothing, except an old, fat, white guy, and in the morning Mohammed fucking me. Before he left, he picked up a large wad of cash off the table. The cretin sold my virginity to the highest bidder. I am so going to kill both of those bastards."

Zoë was shocked at the vehement malice in my voice. To allay her concern, I pulled her forcefully down onto the bed, pinning her down on her back. She was shaking and terrified. I kissed her mouth fiercely, and subsequently by stages, more gently. I felt her relax slightly, and whispered into her ear, "I love you Zoë. Thank you. I knew it all along."

Abruptly, I was taken by surprise. A veil had been torn asunder between us, and she took me with dynamic urgency. Our lovemaking was ferocious. Our mutual needs too long tempered and restrained by our mundane lives of sexual servitude. We girls did it for ourselves.

We both came together and blacked out. It was breathtaking. Together, between us, we had created a small place were the harsh realities of life, and men, could never touch us.

From that smallest beginning, we slowly began putting the pieces of our lives back together. Later, we cuddled and slept.

Bilty

Isabella rose immediately to depart, but said, "We're not done. But that was perhaps the worst of it. I, Zoë, need a while. Let's pick this up again after dinner. Anyway, I have work to do. See you later, alligator."

She left, and I doubt she heard my standard rely. "In a while, crocodile." Then I wondered what exactly she needed me, an investigative journalist, to sink my teeth into.

Bilty:
Personal Journal:
And now we get to it, what really happened to all these young, white, Christian girls.

Notes:
1. Both girls are extremely upset, and these events happened years ago. The mental abuse is vividly displayed by their reactions to retelling the despicable tale.
2. The rape of Isabella is strange. That Zoë confirmed Mohammed was not the one who took her virginity is most troublesome. I have an idea who the old, white man may have been, but surely, that is absurd?
3. Another point, is that during prosecution, of those rare cases that have so far come to court, no one has been charged with possession or administering A Class drugs to minors, never mind supplying them alcohol. It seems our justice system is not worthy of the name.
4. I have a major problem that Zoë was branded, just like cattle. That they urinated on her tells of subhuman treatment. Of subhuman thinking. After they had been grossly raped.
5. To date, no prosecutions have been brought against the people in authority. I include: Police, CPS, Child Services, and the Local Council Authority. Out of respect for these girls, I guarantee that will change.

"Candice, we should leave this for today. It has been––harrowing."
"I would agree Bilty. You are such a love. But no. I need this done and done with, as much as they do. I need to know how the hell they survived. Let's have another drink downstairs, then eat. Melanie?"
"Yes. Count me in. You don't know the half of it, yet. But thank you for trying to help us. In some ways, that is the worst of it over with. But then, the real story has yet to begin.
"Isabella made a difference to our lives, where tens of thousands of other girls in our same, or similar situation could not. Follow me."

Chapter 22 – Young Blood

Isabella

We were chilling on Monday evening in Zoë's room, when the door was pounded, followed by the usual jibes, "Here kitty-kitty."

I shouted, "Fuck off Candy Monster."

The bully laughed and retorted, "Hello Kitty Lover. Tell Box Licker you are both on for some man-lurve in five."

Candy Monster was normally charming, persuasive, and so manipulative, but also clever with it. However, if you did not comply with her suggestions, she was extremely cruel. Everybody called her 'Psycho' behind her back, but if she heard you, she would prove it with an impromptu demonstration. She almost scalded me, remember.

We did our tricks that night, again with Alice, and that time she seemed to accept her fate. She drank and smoked as much as she could before the inevitable happened. Later, they took her twice each. Nobody else was fucked until Anwar turned up to collect us. He came with several 'friends'. We were instantly busy satisfying their male libidos. It was rape, but what the fuck, that's seemed to be our only duty in life.

We did the same on Tuesday and Wednesday, well, different houses and different men, but the rest was all the same. I looked into the new girl's eyes at dinner on Thursday, and knew something essential within her had died. She was empty, forlorn. She was in 'Care': Spit!

Later, when we had fucked all the men dry that night, Asif said, "Kitty, Zoë. You will be the stars of a special event on Saturday. I need you in school uniforms, white ankle socks, pumps, and tight blouses. No underwear. I'll give you the pickup time on Saturday. It will be late afternoon. Be ready."

The great thing was, we had all of Friday off, excepting Alice. After dinner that day, I watched the young girl shamble lackadaisically away towards the waiting taxi. I wanted to run to her side and comfort her, but my heart was already drowning in order to keep Zoë afloat. I could not succour any other, or my own crusade would flounder.

It was Saturday night, party night at a local Paki function room. We were the only girls. There were an awful lot of men. I counted twenty-seven, twice. Zoë got twenty-five and twenty-eight. I already said her maths weren't much good.

It was supposedly a meal for us all, but we spent most of our time refreshing the glasses of devout Muslim men with alcohol. Everybody groped us. The mood changed from inquisitive to over-friendly, and I knew it was going to be bad. I drank as much as I could, whenever I could, and inhaled every spliff that came my way. Like Zoë, I had to find a way of not being there. The only way I could leave was by getting out of my head — the only thing they could never control.

The sweet course was served, but we were led away by Candy Monster to prepare for our act. I don't know when she arrived, but she was sober and meaner than ever. I stopped walking when we passed the bar, turned, and kissed her full on the lips. She was a little stunned, which was all the time I needed. I grabbed a litre bottle of Bacardi and a large bottle of coke, plus a large tumbler. Zoë got vodka and orange. Psycho also grabbed a glass before leading us through.

The dressing room turned out to be the female bogs, and we tarted ourselves up as the bully explained the plot. She was the Headmistress, and we were two naughty schoolgirls. Zoë and I chinked our glasses and emptied them in one. I made the mistake of saying, "Bottoms up."

Psycho looked at me, and smiled like a cat teasing its prey. She said, "Kitty, that's one excellent idea. I better go find us a stout cane. It's been such a long time since I last punished anyone."

She came back with a pool cue, and some balls.

I could tell you what we did that night, but that is for perverts.

I could tell you we enjoyed ourselves, and mean it, occasionally.

I could tell you we came, and we did.

I could also tell you that neither of us, never, ever, want to do anything remotely similar again, nor not quite mean it.

After the show, we were used and abused as cum-dumps. Once the guest's lust was sated, they left us to the wiles of the staff. Anwar took their money before they fucked us, and when they were satisfied, he took us back to gaol. In the meantime, we got out of our heads.

My first recollection was of being fucked, again. I did not even want to know who it was. I reached out my hand and touched something cold and clammy. It was another body. Zoë fastened her sweaty fingers between mine, and interlocked our hands as one. I died once more within her indefatigable grip.

Somehow, we were in a taxi and Zoë was hallucinating. We arrived somewhere, and moments later, my mind skewed sideways — forsaken by all those charged with a public duty to care for us, and paid good money to do their job.

We surfaced in my bed at the gaol. I saw a bottle of Bacardi and a bottle of vodka lying on the floor. There was little left in either of them. I reached for the vodka and held it to Zoë's lips. One of us said, "The hair of the dog that bit you."

I slugged the neat Bacardi until it was gone, and threw the bottle away. In that moment, I felt that something deeply important was missing from my life. I looked at the empty bottle and needed a full one. I collapsed on top of Zoë. But you know, some memories always survive, no matter how hard you try to blank them out forever.

We woke up properly, with a lot of new bruises, and total zero recall. I think some of my ribs were fractured, again. They hurt like hell every time I tried to breathe, never mind move my torso. Zoë was in a worse state than I was, and was still incapable of speech. We both had loose teeth

We didn't have any new clients on Monday. As it was, our rapes, passed into history before we even became aware of them. We were sore and puffy down below for days afterwards. Zoë was virtually fourteen by that time, and the men were beginning to lose interest in us, because we were getting too old.

Much younger girls, like Alice, were starting to take our places. It seemed we were being gradually steered towards out of town gigs, and more extreme forms of sex, and we were both afraid for the future.

Autumn was upon us, and the weather had aggravated our disconsolate mood. One Tuesday morning the sun was bright and warming. I told Zoë, "They call this an Indian Summer."

She gawped and said, "You better make that a Pakistani Summer."

We laughed, and it was good between us. It was also half term, and I had the week off. I hoped to revise using the library at school for a couple of days. It would be open because of the boarders. I planned to take the bus, as the less Mohammed knew about me, the better.

Zoë needed some new clothes, so we decided to spend the day shopping. We headed out just after breakfast was finished, and checked out Vijay's shop first. We knew he would not have everything we needed, but he would much of it, including the bulky stuff, and he really was the cheapest place in town.

We bought more than we expected, so headed back to gaol to drop off our bags. We were almost outside when I saw Mohammed's car pull into the street. It parked nearby as we went up to the main door. He called to us, so we waited. We knew never to upset him.

He greeted us both in his charming manner, "Isabella, how lovely to see you. I do hope everything is going well at school. Shouldn't you be there today?"

I am sure he knew it was half term, so that's what I told him. He turned to Zoë, "You are looking more beautiful than ever my dear, your new look suits you.

"Oh. And you are both invited to a special party this weekend. Please get some extremely short school skirts. I prefer the pleated ones that rise up when you twirl around. I also think it is time to drop the white socks. You had better get some black hold up leggings that leave a gap of a few inches between the hem and the top. That small glimpse of

175

thigh is extremely sexy you know. The last thing is you must wear short sleeved, white blouses that are a size too tight, and absolutely no body hair. I recently got complaints that you both had a little stubble down below, so use a proprietary brand hair remover."

I smiled demurely and said, "Kind Sir, we know this is a problem, but we cannot afford the creams, and have to use a disposable razor instead. You know how little pay we get for our work, I am sure."

Fortunately, he was in a good mood, or otherwise he would have hit me for my impudence, right there in the street. Instead of a public beating, he opened his wallet and gave me ten pounds. I took it. Zoë's hand replaced my own. His eyes glazed as he stared at her palm, but cleared before his rage settled, and he handed her a note of equal value.

He squinted as he replaced his wallet, and said, "Make sure you are perfectly bald down there. Saturday is a very important night."

We looked at each other a bit stunned, dismayed at what the weekend was likely to bring. Mohammed said, "Please excuse me, ladies, I am in a hurry."

He held the door open for us and we went inside. We continued walking as he stopped to check his pockets. Zoë thought nothing of it, but I knew his ways better, he was waiting for us to leave. We turned the corner and headed up the main stairs. I stopped when out of sight of reception and waited. Zoë gave me a funny look and came back to me. I held a finger to my lips.

Mohammed walked up to the receptionist and she greeted him pleasantly, saying, "Matron is expecting you and will see you in a moment. Please take a seat."

The receptionist had hardly finished announcing his arrival before he was shown into her office. We crept away and were back in our rooms minutes later. Zoë came through to mine, as it was nearer the way out. We talked about his arrival for a few minutes, and later about the weekend. Both of us were dreading it. I could not understand why Mohammed was there, so we talked some more, before going to a window on the main stairs and waited for him to leave.

I looked at my mobile when he finally appeared outside, and said, "He was here for twenty–five minutes."

Confused, we made our way onto the street, stopping at the end of the road to light a cigarette, and plan where we were going.

We went to my locker bank and made a withdrawal of funds. We got a burger, and for the first time, I heaved at the smell of cola. Zoë pushed her orange juice across the table, and drank my drink instead. We were still hung-over, but burst out laughing. Sometimes, what you use to get high can be the obverse of what you cling to, to reverse the low. That set the tone for the rest of our day.

We did most of our shopping on the high street, but were getting nowhere with the school skirts. We even tried a sex shop, but although they had the right gear, everything was too large for us. The manager, Ben, came over when the shop was empty; "If you need to look like sexy schoolgirls, call this woman. She makes them order, but it costs a bit."

He gave us her number, and we called from the shop, Ben making the introductions. We had an appointment for early afternoon, and thanked him. He said, "I have a feeling you two are already very sexy schoolgirls, without needing to dress up. What's going on?"

He was hitting on us, and we flirted back. Neither of us were much good at flirting—we seemed to have skipped that stage. We ended up doing the guy, with a condom. OK, it was the same condom, but we got paid a lot of money. Afterwards he said, "You pair could earn a lot more money you know. I have a list of clients with special needs; schoolgirl needs—perhaps £500 per night. Each."

He gave us both a card and we were in shock. I said, "We'll think about it, seriously."

He replied, "Don't leave it too long, because the price goes down the older you are, well, except for super-escorts of course."

We left with serious considerations, and a means to a new life, could we ever escape the one we had? The words, 'super-escort' plagued my mind for a while, but were destined to lodge deep inside my memory for many years.

Later, we got measured for our new skirts. The Seamstress worked out what we needed for blouses, girlie bow type school ties, and thick, black stockings. She did our outfits. It cost us virtually all the money that Ben gave us, but we knew we would look exceptionally irresistible.

We did a houseful of men that night, and again on Thursday. We had Friday off to prepare for the big night. Asif took me to school Thursday and Friday, and my presence during the half-term break was noticed and praised by the deputy Head. She got me alone and tried to pursue why I sometimes skipped classes. What could I tell her that she could possibly believe? I thought I had stopped her asking last time.

I told her, "It's all stuff to do with the SS and Family Court, plus my emotional reactions. It is most complicated, and the less you know, the better. Ma'am."

She took my hands in her own and said, "Dearest child, if you ever have nobody to turn to, know I am here for you. Tell me now. Nothing leaves this room--you have my word of honour. I yours?"

"I keep a diary of everything that has happened to me. I update it regularly. One day I may show it to you, but not today. Please, I need to sort this out my way. It is nothing like you think, or can even imagine."

Her sprig of olive branch tore me apart. "I was raped as a child you know. My uncle Den. Of course, I didn't know what to call it back then, and I enjoyed the most of it, to be truthful. Our relationship, of which I was a willing partner no less, repeated in spasms, until my younger sister reached puberty.

"I saw him recently you know, and he apologised for having sex with me. I told him, 'I liked it, everything we did, except the drinking'."

"He said, 'Know I cannot trust an older woman anymore. All they want to do is emasculate me, take my money, and fuck around behind my back. That's why I like young girls. This is not an excuse, but it explains why I am the way I am. I am only like this because of the mean ways women have treated me. I was looking for love, marriage for a lifetime. I wanted to create a family: I got shite-all. Your Aunt now lives in the house we shared, and I alone paid for. A building I have no rights over. The court gave our home to her. The home I worked my whole life to pay for. So now I live in a rented flat. Go figure.'

"Isabella. I very much doubt there is anything you could say to me, that I would find offensive, nor not understand. Try me sometime."

I cried you know. She hugged me so tight, and when I was released from her grasp. I knew she had, more or less, worked me out. As I made for the door she said, "How do you pay the taxi fare?"

I stopped, and turning, pierced her eyes with my own. "I have no money, so how do you think?"

I lingered to add, "Yes. My education is that important to me."

Her head drooped, shook, before dropping into her palms. I left to resume my own life. She needed to deal with her own demons, herself.

Zoë got our new uniforms on Friday, and that night we tried them on. We looked damn hot. The skirts fanned out when we twirled around, exposing everything we had to offer. We used the special cream on our mounds and beneath. There was not much hair there, or under our arms, but we had our orders. We did our legs just to make sure.

We had been expecting another gross gang-bang involving twenty or thirty men. Instead, there were one dozen men and two white women in attendance at Mohammed's executive dining room. One of those was Psycho, and the other was 'the co-ordinator', or bully, from another care home. Three of the men were white, although English they were not. We arrived after a big meeting, and learned that business was good and growing. There was talk of girls being swapped between regions, as in racial gangs, to help keep up with the demand for fresh faces.

Zoë and I listened to every word, but acted dumb. We were groped, and topped up glasses for all the guests. Psycho had a really good feel of me below, as I was pouring the guy beside her a drink. I couldn't believe it. That was her revenge for me kissing her.

Later we moved to an adjacent room and danced, encouraging the men and women to enjoy themselves. Our whirling skirts were applauded, something Mohammed complimented us upon.

Note: we had to source the skirts and pay for them ourselves. Low-life scammer.

Half the guests left while it was relatively early. We got fucked, but only by half a dozen each, and not all by the same men either. We also got nicely drunk and high. It was a great bash, even if we did have to double-team the Albanians.

I was forced to do them on the boardroom table. It was not pleasurable, but I endured. I switched off, and stared at the only thing in my range of vision; the smoke alarm on the ceiling. I even made out the make and model. Remember, because later, that is important.

Bilty

"That last meeting is a big clue to the bigger picture, Bilty. What do you think was going down?"

"Supply and demand. They were growing their network, and selling or swapping girls with other sex traders. These would be local gangs of different ethnicity, you mentioned Albanians, but there would have been others."

"Not bad. The thing is, what the Paki's ... no, that's not truly inclusive. It was only the Muslims that were into really young girls, preteens. Look up Aisha sometime, Muhammad's third wife, and you'll get your first glimmer of understanding.

"What Mohammed had, were a lot of older teens, much older than us. They didn't command a high price. So he traded them with a growing number of other Muslim cells, mainly Pakistani, but not always. We knew because every so often some would disappear. That must have been with SS, and Family Court connivance. Or, I heard reference to older girls who had left the system, but were still held under Muslim sexual thrall.

"Bitly, please understand this was not a local issue. It had spread all over London, and the main players were the Muslims, Albanians, and Romanians. The latter preferred late teens. There were other nationalities, too many to list. All of them wanted white, British, Christian girls.

"To me, that is an act of war. Raping and cross-breeding the women. They see it as such, be under no illusion."

"Thank you. I had not realised that, nor the extent of the bullying. This gives me much corroborative research to compile, but now I have a foot in the door, as it were. I understand their thinking. Candice?"

"Illuminating, and you are so strong, Isabella. Bilty will need a moment for his notes, so could we have a large pot of coffee? This is bound to be a long evening."

Bilty:
Personal Journal:

Notes:

1. The paedophile plot is far bigger than any have imagined. That these gangs collaborated across the all of UK, has never been envisaged, but Isabella says trading between them was common.

2. This is Human Trafficking.

3. Isabella never followed up on the offer from the sex shop owner, Ben. I wonder if they lost contact, or is that a story yet to come. She plays her cards close to her chest, which may be what saw her through the hell of her life, one no child should have knowledge of.

Ah. We are about to pick up where we left off. But first, refreshments are available, and new girls are entering the room.

Isabella

"Time to resume. I would like to introduce three dear friends, who also suffered as we did: Billie, Ellie, and Felicity, known as Frog. How they came to join us is different. Like Mel, they do not wish to speak of their experiences personally, but will be on hand to answer questions. They will all be working later, so best we get on with the telling.

"I will continue our sordid tale, and speak of when they told us of what happened to them, the three sisters that is. I'll follow with Mel's tape. Melanie: Camera, Computer link, Action!"

Chapter 23 – Billie and Melanie

Some months later, we were at dinner when the news broke, Candy Monster had started her <u>Pathway Plan</u> [23.1], and matron had already signed off on her deal. I spluttered, shocked! "She's leaving?"

It had never occurred to us, that eventually we would be old enough to leave. To be out in the real world, have a flat and a job, and finally be rid of the malign, preteen, Paki prostitution racket. By then I was fourteen, meaning that in two years, I could be leaving.

One of Psycho's minders was taking over, I had already bested her one on one. The big change was that, when Candy Monster left, I could drink, smoke, and fuck who and when I wanted. It was almost the same for Zoë, but she needed the release, and I abhorred it, most of the time.

Occasionally I partook, but I was still escaping Paki clutches and personal demons, albeit slowly. After what we had endured for the past few years, that was a perverse kind of heaven, perhaps it was Allah's?

Zoë came back to the real world during that period and weaned herself off the harder drugs. We were a pair, and she was outwardly harder than I. What nobody understood was that Zoë could never forgive a system that deliberately drove her mother and father to commit suicide. To her, it was institutionalised murder.

Zoë and I often talked about what was going on. We deduced that Asif, Mohammed, matron, the local authority, and Social Services, were all in it together. I did not know how they all fitted together, but it was impossible for them not to know what was going on.

The next couple of years were strange. Zoë and I stood apart from the others, both the bullies and the victims. We turned our tricks when required, but the local demand was for the younger, more pliable fish.

Our dinner table began to fill with others seeking revenge. Not just on the Paki's, but the local authorities, Social Services, courts, and police. The first to join us was Billie. A few months later, her younger sisters, Ellie, and Felicity nicknamed Frog, joined us. It was obvious the Muslims and Social Services had done a job on the family.

One Friday evening we all got trashed in Billie's room, and she told us her story, Ellie and Frog chipping in with their parts. That night Zoë and I learned that the Muslims had groomed Billie directly, away from the care system, and out on the streets.

Billie's Story
As shown on the video recording. Billie is speaking, Isabella narrating.

"The Muslims seemed nice at first, and I guess I was flattered with the attention of one guy in particular. On our third date, I was falling in love with him, and would do anything he asked of me. That night he took me to a different Balti House across town, where I was plied with drink and drugs — but it seemed like fun at the time. They treated me to burgers, and topped up my mobile phone.

"I lost all track of time, and vaguely remember staying all night. They must have given me Rohypnol, and took me upstairs to a bed, where two or three Paki's raped me. I don't remember the rapes. I sometimes get an image, but it is gone. I know I was a virgin when I went there, and I wasn't when I was eventually released.

"They dropped me somewhere afterwards, and all I know is that I was walking the streets. Later, some guy was really bothered about me. I told him to 'Fuck Off!' Some woman joined him. She asked me where I got my love bites, and I had no idea, it was none of her business.

"I was cramping badly, and I had severe pains in my abdomen. They took me to A & E. I was waiting to see somebody, when a coloured guy in a white coat said, 'I am a doctor. Please come with me.'

"Instead of being examined, he led me outside, where two accomplices put me in a taxi. Later, they half-carried me into a hotel. I have no idea where it was, but a Paki porter opened a door at the back. I was offered drink and drugs. I was forced to wear a sari, and gang-raped by many Paki's over a couple of days. I'm pretty sure it was a Muslim hotel, as the room had a device pointing to Mecca. Then, somehow, it was morning, and I was in my normal clothes again. The bastards even dropped me at the gates of my school.

"I waited until they left, and went home. My mum was working, so I lay on the sofa and went to sleep. When she came home I told her what had happened. She was deeply upset and swore a lot, which was most unlike her. At first she was angry with me, but she worked out I was so out of my skull, I had no idea what had happened. Then, she got angry at the Paki men, and we went to the police station.

"My panties were handed over as evidence, and they had cum stains from several men in them. I distinctly remember there was a health worker, who called in Social Services. I was too young for Nightstop [16-25], but they took me for one night. The next day I ended up in a foster home. I needed to be with my mother.

"The following day I was taken home, and we had some kind of quasi-official meeting. Mum and I both signed some forms, but neither of us knew what they were. The SS told us they were necessary to get me returned home. They left soon afterwards, and I was alone with mother. She was heartbroken. Can you imagine being the mother of a twelve-year old girl, only to discover one dozen Paki's had raped her?"

Billie cried as the dam within her burst. Her sisters held her tight. It was not long before she asked for a strong drink, and spliff. I knew she was trying to plaster-over the cracks in her fractured mind — except these were not mere fractures — they were raw, livid, viscid chasms.

Billie's mother believed the police would act immediately, and put the perverts behind bars for life. Instead, the investigation stalled, before it was archived. There were no prosecutions, and she came to believe the police [R 23.2] were active in promoting child prostitution.

Social Services played their tricks, as Billie was slowly edged towards foster care, via the compliant Family Court circus. Billie told us, "I believe they could have done that a lot quicker, but needed me to remain in the community at large, until Social Services, at Mohammed's behest, completed the destruction of our, once happy family.

"The Paki's continued to rape me most days. They would be waiting when I finished school, and many nights I was fucked so often, I never made it home. I knew I smelled, but I hated the fleabites more. I felt disgusted with myself, but what could I do? I told the school, the police, Social Services, and every single one ignored my plight.

"I couldn't imagine ever escaping their vile treatment. I tried to kill myself, and cut myself a lot. I endured because I believed it could not get any worse, but then both my sister's fell prey to the same gang."

[Isabella: "Billie, the truth this time. The real reason."

"Damn you! But you are right Issy. OK. I was threatened, and I mean with a gun held to my head. The next time they had a can of petrol, and when I refused, they splashed the petrol on me, and one produced a lighter; 'Say nothing, or you will be burned alive.'

"When they got Ellie, I was told to behave or they would set fire to our home, behead my father, and gang-rape my mother.

"I believed them, so I did what they said. They are evil."

Bilty said, "These are sick, selfish savages."

Isabella moved things along. "Time to tell the all of it, Billie."]

"One day some months later, Ellie was walking to school, and a taxi stopped for her. The driver mistook her for me, until she got in his cab. It was Asif. He made her laugh and she ended up at the Balti House. She drank and smoked something. They asked what she wanted to eat, and pizza was delivered, her favourite. They dropped her near the shops close to home, giving her a couple of quid to buy some sweets.

"The next day, Ellie clambered willingly into Asif's cab, and by the third evening, she was well fucked. Again, she told our mother, and the panties went down to the police. They did squat all.

"Mother determined Frog would not fall prey to this paedophile ring [R 23.3]. She spoke to the SS, but they were too busy to see her. Her complaint was logged, but never actioned.

"Desperate for help, she called the school, who were evasive, and then the police again, and finally the local paper. They were the only ones interested to take her story, which was never published.

"Then they got Frog as well. Mother was past her senses when she found out. She did not usually drink, and had a low alcohol tolerance. I know she was heartbroken, and deeply upset because of what was happening to us. She needed Social Services to help, and rang them up again to ask for their assistance. That was her biggest mistake.

Frog spoke for the first time. "That evening mother allowed herself a glass of wine. Later that night, I got home with Ellie, after being raped by a load more Paki's. We found mother asleep on the sofa, something she would never normally do. The bottle was still half full, and she was in fitful sleep. We covered her with a blanket when she did not rouse. We bathed the Paki cum out of ourselves, and went to bed.

"Mother was in a bad way the next morning, but still managed to make us breakfast as usual, and prepare us for school. We all knew she was worried about something, but exactly what, she would not share with us. Khan was waiting for us when we left for school. You know he loves to hit you hard. He's an animal who gets off on beating up young girls. He doesn't deserve the title: 'man' as far as we were concerned."

[We all knew Khan was one of the worst, and spent a few minutes bitching about how violent the man was, with all of us. Our cursing ceased, if only to allow Billie to finish the story.]

"That morning, Khan knocked on the front door, and mother answered. Seeing him she tried to slam the door closed. He hit it hard, and it flew back with his power, breaking her nose. Mother fell back, losing her balance, and her blood splattered the walls. After she fell, I saw it spurt all over the carpet.

"You know how evil he is, right. He kicked her in the stomach, and told us to get in his taxi. We were afraid, and with looks, decided to run for it. That may have worked, if he had not placed his large hands, one to either side of Ellie and Frog's necks. Remember how he can press something at the side of your neck, and it makes you pass out. He says he could kill you. He cuts off all blood to your head.

"His fingers pressed on those arteries of my sisters, and he held them extremely close, and securely. What could I do? I collected our school bags, and we got into the back of his taxi. The child-locks were on of course. We had no way to escape.

"Mother watched all three of us being kidnapped, and ran outside to try to stop the car. She almost had her hand on the rear door, when Khan hit her hard on the jaw. The punch knocked her out.

"Now here's the thing I don't understand. How did the SS know to arrive at our house, that particular morning, a few seconds later?

"Nobody has ever explained that to me satisfactorily. I believe they were either, watching and waiting, or Khan gave them a signal. They had to be close by to arrive so quickly after we left.

"Apparently, mother was hauling herself up from the muddy front lawn when Social Services arrived with a gang of armed, police bully-boys to interrogate her. They could smell alcohol on her breath, and as any drinker knows, it always smells a lot worse the next morning, when you are in fact sober, just hung-over.

"The front door was open, so the cops needed no pretext to go inside. They did not take her to hospital. Instead, they took her to Family Court, where she was already listed to attend. How can that be?

"It can't, unless it was premeditated.

"We were officially taken from her later that day, as she was obviously an unfit mother. She does not remember signing the forms, but there it was—her signature condemning us, her children, to a life in care on the Consent Order. The Interim Care Order was a mere formality, and actioned before the sun set."

Ellie said, "Frog and I went to a different care home miles away, and we hardly saw the Muslims. They had their own scam going on there, still underage sex, but mainly they used us to rob people. I guess Asif complained, and after a review hearing, we were sent here."

Isabella

During the weeks that followed, talk between us turned to doing something about our predicament. I caught up mainly at weekends. Billie was the driving force, and slowly at first, we began to recover evidence of what was going on.

Ellie and Frog were best at getting the girls to talk about what had happened to them, and over time the girls recounted their stories. We started keeping a log, and I added brief notes about each girl. It was the best we could think of at the time, and gave us a simple record.

One day Zoë ushered Melanie into our confession room. She was clever, frightened, rebellious, and all alone. She had arrived a few days before, one of the first to be transferred from a care home far away. We presumed this was to ease the demand for fresh meat. She was already, mentally and emotionally, well passed the wringer.

Melanie's Story
As shown on the video recording. Melanie is speaking, Isabella narrating.

We listened to Melanie's tale. "My Uncle raped me when I was seven-years old. In the years that followed, he and the other uncle took me regularly. I loved the times with my Uncle. The cousins found out somehow, and began to bully me for sex. They raped and bullied me.

"I fell pregnant not long after my twelfth birthday, and had an abortion. My parents knew nothing, and had never touched me. It was a great shock to them, and they disowned my uncles. But I was soon in the clutches of the SS who said I remained at risk. I sent to a care home near Bristol.

"I was insubordinate and a loner. Male family members living nearby continued to stalk me, aggravating the situation. Between them, Social Services and the Court connived to transfer me out of the district.

"I spent one year in a care home in east London, before ending up here. I've been Paki-raped thousands of times, and I'm pregnant again. I tried to kill myself, but was rushed to hospital. The SS acted quickly and as soon as I recovered, I was sent here."

I looked at the thirteen-year old sitting before me, her fourteenth birthday was but weeks away. I recoiled in disbelief, knowing that she was already too old for some of our 'clients'.

I used to think that was sick. Now it was just a normal part of our lives. It was also becoming the norm that around ten percent of the young girls in the home were pregnant. Melanie was five months gone, and I was surprised to learn the SS forbade her to have an abortion.

Finally, the girl opened up and began talking freely. It may have been the drink, or the drugs, but I like to think it was the prospect of salvaging her personal dignity that made her say; "You know that when they fuck you, you have to wash it out before the next one does you.

"Most of them don't like doing us when we get our period. It offends Allah or something. Then they do your mouth or bum. Anyway, they say this is one reason why they need the younger girls. Huh! They are paedophiles. I'm not stupid you know. Frog said, 'I was a typical, innocent ten-year old when I was first raped'. Sure, too young to bleed.

"I wanted to kill them all, but what could I do except hold her hand as we were Paki-raped together, side by side on the same bed last night. I knew she was holding Ellie's hand tight on the other side.

"So Kitty, you tell me what you're going to do about it, to stop this happening again, and again, and yet fucking again?"

I thought she was about to cry, but her steely resolve showed through as she demanded, "Please. Make it all go away!"

"Melanie, what will happen to your baby?"

I swear her eyes clouded. I mean, deep inside her eyes, like a cataract, before she turned away and tried to hide her tears. There was a tsunami ravaging deep within her soul. She wailed and rocked back and forth for several moments, unconsciously wringing her hands, her mind awry. I let her be. These things hurt, deep inside.

I judged the moment and sat by her side, putting my arm around her shoulders. She began speaking, as if it was a confessional in some church, one no God would ever visit. "I want to hold my baby in my arms and suckle her to my breast. Is that a crime?

"Instead, I already know she will be taken away from me before I ever see her [R 23.4]. Issy, do you know, that if you are a young mother within this so-called 'System of Care', you are automatically regarded as unfit to parent [R 23.5]your offspring. I want to hold my own child in my arms. I don't care if she is the product of gang rape. I want to be her mother. I gave her my essential essence, and I want to protect her from what happened to me. Nobody understands this."

I laid my free hand upon her arm to encourage her, but she shook my sisterly advance away. Instead, she stated belligerently, "It is my idea, she will be groomed by SS from birth, to take my place in this paedophilic circus one day. How can I, her mother, prevent that from happening?" She stopped speaking. Her words, her emotions: drain'd.

That time, I held Melanie closer than close. As she heaved into my enfolding arms, my mind was working, and from their looks, so were Zoë's and Billie's. I almost broke, because they, 'The System', had almost taken my own sanity away from me.

Melanie distractedly added, "You want to know why I tried to kill myself, and failed. The only reason is, I want to murder every single sick bastard involved in this evil scam, before I die!"

Melanie did not have to say anything else, she had become dearth, all dried up inside. Like a desiccated flower, picked in bloom from the fields of youthful forthcoming, like gathering a rosebud. But she had been pressed between the crushing pages of a system, filed, and forgotten. She was like a favourite, childhood scrapbook memory, nobody could be bothered to open, nary look at anymore. I knew from that very moment, there was something unique about Melanie.

We all knew of, and embraced her pain. We all felt the same, the shame. It was etched forever deeply into our own psyches, and that special place where the true spirit of every person resides.

Isabella

"That's great Mel? Anything you want to add or contest?

"No. Thanks Issy. Strange, but rummaging through old, and best forgotten memories, gave me strength. As it is, they'll probably plague my dreams tonight.

"Fuck! I'm done, and done with this. I'll leave the camera rolling, but I need to get torpedoed, and right now."

"Bang!" That was the sound of the door slamming behind Melanie, her departure abrupt.

Chapter 23

Bilty:
Personal Journal:

Notes:
1. Ouch. Melanie has gone, and she has left more questions unanswered, than told. I find it difficult to understand why she was taken from her parents, who never mistreated her. They had broken all family ties, so there was no risk, surely.

2. My second thought is to applaud Billie's courage, to speak most of her story herself. What surprised me at a psychological level, was the volume of hard spirit she and her sisters needed to finish the tale. This indicates extreme stress, even now, years later.

3. What these grooming gangs were doing was not just rape, but something far more sinister: Subversion.

I observed, even though Melanie hardly spoke during Isabella's narration of her video confession, it clearly hurt her. Very deeply.

It can be quite easy to write off these incidents as immature, or simplistic psychological responses, but that is not what is going on here. This is quite complex, both regards individuals, and the group as a whole. Isabella rushed to accompany Mel out of the door, followed immediately by Frog and Ellie.

Zoë remained, stalwart as ever. "It should be OK, given some time. I need to be with Melanie, so let's return to the saloon. You'll be well cared for, and later, perhaps, we can resume.

"You are now witness to the emotional toll this forever rape, took on us. Do you understand why Mel needs her space? Why we will all gather to protect her—I wonder if you do?"

Bilty's mind jumped through hoops: 'Uncle rape, no. Nephew rape, no. Abortion, yes. Next: Pregnant again. Accepted. Ah!'
"She needs to suckle her child. Be a Mother. Instead, she will never see her baby, courtesy of social services child-snatching."
"Correct. Good. Come with me, or go home. I suggest you stay."

That was the first time I was confronted by Zoë's mettle. She left us at once, another girl coming to attend to our needs.

I was shaken and disturbed. Candice said, "Love, these girls have given us so much of their time: emotions. I'm staying, and woe betide you if you do not. Listen, they have a band playing downstairs. But, I believe we are done for today. Come, dance with me, enjoy life."

Chapter 24 – Matron's Office

Project Domicile
Interview: 08
Location: Fiddlers Court, The Oval, Holborn, Central London.
Time: 11:54 hours, Sunday, 22nd October.
Subject: Isabella
Others Present:
     Zoë, Melanie, Vikki, Genie, Candice.

Note:
1. After the trauma of the previous evening, all seems relaxed and people are once more at ease.
Melanie said, "Sorry, about yesterday. It just got to me. Today I'm fine. Amazing what a good sleep, and new day can do."
"Yes, and a terrific breakfast also. Are you all ready to go on?"
Isabella took the lead, "Yes Bilty. I'm ready when you are."

Isabella
It took me a while to work out what the system was doing. They always kept us in fear, individuals lost within the maelstrom of a life that was being imposed upon us. Melanie said something at dinner one evening. I forget her exact words, but it meant "Divide and Conquer."
I was still going to school six-days each week, but had given up with Latin—it was an extremely crazy language. The next day I went up to see the Latin teacher, and she said she would explain the words Melanie had spoken, on condition I started taking her class again. Once I rejoined her lessons, the teacher not only explained the words in Latin and English, but the thoughts that were curried behind them.
She explained the maxims: *divide et impera*, and *divide ut regnes*, were utilised by the Roman ruler Caesar, and the French emperor Napoleon. My teacher followed by expounding upon the example of Gabinius. I came away with 'Divide and Rule', and I knew instinctively that was what was being done to us poor girls, by ripping us away from our families. I felt I needed to change that.
I decided that Napoleon, and especially Julius Caesar, were probably quite good at what they did within their lifetimes—as at least, centuries, or millennia later, everybody knew their names. After that, Latin became central to my understanding of the modern world I lived in, but of course, mine was no ordinary school, and neither was my life.
I reasoned it was time to start turning the tables on our oppressors, and while it did not amount to very much at a casual glance, it gave us all a unique identity, a sense of all being in this together. Before, there had only existed individual girls, separate, living in fear and repression. We

developed a fledgling, if fragile unanimity of shared suffering, and a growing unity of purpose.

I used the ubiquitously obvious "Hello Kitty" branded device, and every girl in the home wanted to wear the clothes, bags, watches, and mobile phone wristbands. That included the bully and her gang. I encouraged them to choose their own designs. This acceptance gave us a bonding, a sisterhood. Kitty was also my nickname, you remember.

There were probably sixty percent more girls out in the community than directly controlled by the care homes. They still lived with parents, well, one parent at least. We met some of them from time to time, and we kept in contact. Later, most came into the 'care system'.

Melanie took over co-ordination and filing. She was extremely good at computer stuff, and she logged and cross-referenced everything.

Billie took over the physical part of the operation, and with Ellie's help, expanded the collecting of semen-stained panties and other evidence the girls gave us. Names of rapists were added when remembered, plus pictures or short video, but that was dangerous. Ellie set up a network of locker deposit boxes, all items sealed in plastic bags, catalogued, and off premises. Girl by girl, we were slowly increasing our evidence and dominion within the extant, and greater hegemony.

I watched as little by little, slight changes overtook every girl's life. It was a slow and subtle process. We would be crushed like insects, if our enemies discovered us, before our revolution blossomed.

Sometimes Ellie was down, and feeling so low it was hard to cheer her up. This was because some of the girls talked to her about their lives, things she was too young to fully understand. We talked about the girls cases, and I saw a deeper plot emerging, one run by the SS as a means to get hold of young girls for underage prostitution, without pay.

After one harrowing story, we were all left emotionally disturbed and subdued. I needed to calm my emotions, so began to write the tale down. Ellie supported me as best she could, but it wasn't fluid like when she spoke originally. Zoë interrupted and said, "You cannot recreate the feelings. We need to record these admissions for posterity."

Melanie enthused, "Yes, why don't we? I can set up cameras in a spare room in the loft, and we can invite girls up to talk about their lives in full privacy. I can save the footage so their stories are never lost."

I beamed at her, the first smile I had offered since hearing the distressing tale. "I agree, let's set it up now. And of course, we can add this to our database and use it to get back at the system. With dozens of testimonies, the police can't ignore us forever, can they?"

The pragmatic Billie said, "I wouldn't be so sure. You'll need the press if anything is going to be done about this mafia."

We acted immediately, and over the weeks that passed, videoed the girls' confessions. We opened a new locker deposit box, which was soon filled with factual confessions of the depravity of humanity. We had lockers all over the city, and still the evidence never slowed.

Being the most literate, I added a short description of what the ordeal amounted to, and Melanie saved everything in a computer folder, sub-folders being dedicated to each girl. Ellie was asked to add more correlating descriptions to her growing collection of panties, and these were cross-referenced with our information database.

In doing so, we moved from being victims, to the beginnings of fighting back against the system. We had no idea what we would actually do with all the information, but it was a big step in the right direction. Most of all, it confirmed our unity of sisterhood.

Out on the streets of real peoples' lives, nothing ever changed. Yet, one day, something did change. I discovered my mother had been released from prison. I still have no idea why I ended up in the park with a neat bottle of Bacardi. I needed to drink away recently resurgent memories of my father, my mother, and what could have been my life, should have been my birthright—clear out of my mind.

And yet, thoughts of them would never leave me. Zoë was the first to find me, secreted within our favourite haunt. By that time, I was lost deep within the never-never land of alcoholic nightmares. She caught me within the last visages of sanity. We moved somewhere, and much too soon, many people I knew were with me. My mind was blown.

A sea of woes was drowning me. I was stretched too far, too much, for far too long a time. Embracing the hurt of everybody else's lives had taken its toll. I needed to retreat, and look after myself first, on my own.

From somewhere distant, clarity came to me. I asked myself a question, albeit just before I keeled over, "Issy. Is your mind right?"

I answered my own question, "No, but by tomorrow it will be."

I woke up clutching John. Not a man, but the cold ceramic of Mister Thomas Crapper's design. It felt mighty accommodating and peaceful to me. Oh how I did abuse his loving creation. I had been in far worse states, but that time it was personal. Zoë cleaned me up, and we went to her room. I did as I was told, if only because my mind was still too wracked to define itself. Billie came in with a large wrap of bacon sandwiches. Mel followed and set up the camera.

Zoë and I held each other close, as if in union. The mere presence of a warm, forgiving body was enough to give me strength. It felt like the familiar, needful embrace of my own mother, or Sophie. I needed the succour and I guess my subconscious took this as a cue, as by dribs and drabs, I started to tell her my story.

I was a little incoherent at first, feeling my way deep inside locked emotions that were secreted deep within my mind. I had been there the previous evening, so my barriers were already breeched. It was only a matter of time before I let the heartfelt stains tumble from my lips.

I had tapped the source and knew it would all flood out of me. Zoë read me well and gave me a drink. I downed it in one, and she brought the bottle over with a second glass and some mixer. It was vodka and orange, but I didn't realise at the time. I drank the strong liquor, until my courage rose, and pretence unravelled.

My mind was shook-up as I relived the horror once more – an attempt to find salve for my sanity, but my emotional distress was overpowering. Tears rolled down my cheeks as the memories unwound, unbidden. With the third drink, I found focus.

I've have already stated what happened, and there is little to add in hindsight, although the future was to turn out more perverse than imaginable. Remember, I was domiciled to prevent possible future emotional harm. Huh! No one in authority gave a damn about me. I was subjected to extreme mental, emotional, sexual, and physical abuse, because of them.

What is important, in the greater context, is that word soon got out that I had shared––told my story. This encouraged others to do the same, and I gained prestige in the process.

After our confessions to one another, I made it a rule that no girl should be forced to tell us her story, and if they decided to tell us about their lives they could. By offering the token of trying to trace their family, we were mostly successful.

Over time, Billie became the one who tried to trace families, with Melanie's supportive computer skills and nous. The mountain of misinformation was massive, and matches proved elusive, but Billie did manage to trace many parents and siblings.

Unlike everybody else in this child un-care system, we kept our word and tried to make things better for the victims: the children, lest we forget. Our team earned the empathy of many inmates, and by subtle changes, we became regarded as caring, compassionate friends.

Time passed and Melanie came to term. She had been away in hospital, her baby being removed at birth and before she could see her offspring, never-mind hold or suckle her child. She didn't even know if her baby was male or female.

Melanie was bereft, an emotional wreck when she returned. A new bitterness and needy compulsion for revenge festering within her. She scoured the internet for support, and showed us a report of the SS illegal [R 24.1] baby-snatching, followed by another webpage [R 24.2]. She said, "Now these child-snatchers don't even wait for the mother to give birth. Look."

We read with astonishment, how a pregnant Italian woman visited UK for a fortnight's job training. During her first evening she became stressed; she was bipolar and off her meds due to the foetus. The police did not take her for treatment. Instead, she was sectioned and put in a mental asylum. There she was drugged unconscious, and later, woke up in a different hospital, only to discover her baby had been removed against her wishes, by C section, and she was returned to Italy.

Social Services ensured she never saw her baby, or was allowed to find out what became of the child, except to be notified it was to be adopted in UK.

Zoë said, "You couldn't make this up. These bitches are evil!"

Melanie added with venom, "Yeah. The SS up to their old tricks as usual, in cahoots with the Bussies, doctors, and judges. The baby wasn't even born for Christ's sake! If the woman were here for training, then she certainly wasn't anywhere near full term either. I hate them all."

Melanie was losing it fast, and I had to turn her thinking around. "Girls, think! This cannot possibly be about the child, like you say, it wasn't even ready to be born. There are many legal ruses to have kept the mother in this country until she came to term, so that rules out meeting government foster and adoption targets.

"This is clearly about something else. Money?

"Yes. The legalised kidnapping of children, so the perpetrators get rich. Mark my words, that is all this scam is about. Now, what are we going to do to prove it, to stop it?"

I think we may have lost her, had we not spoken those words that day. It seemed to give Melanie a reason for living. Not long after, we managed to copy the deputy matron's office keys. From that point on, it became simple. Melanie threw herself into our new project: Revenge. She taught Ellie about entering details of all our inmates into a computer, and how it was backed up off site.

Let me tell you how mad I felt!

I had to copy the matron's spare set of keys in the deputy matron's key press, to get to the juicy information. It was difficult, but we did it. I finally found out why I was taken away from my parents, and I howled with despair. At eight years old, matron had flagged me as being pretty enough for Mohammed to be interested in me. She was still the boss of her SS unit back then.

All that bullshit about what went on was a smokescreen. She singled me out because I looked cute enough for a paedophile to want to fuck. I repeat: I was 8-years-old.

I was snatched from my parents because of her paperwork, a trail of outstanding malfeasance, and the Family Court Judge signed off on it. I copied a CD, and discovered the Rihanna dance I did all those years ago was faithfully preserved, as were cute and sexy pictures of my younger self, all used as advertising to sell me. Zoë and Billie were too engrossed within their own personal files to think it through. I knew there was something more, but I couldn't identify what it was at the time.

Over several weeks, we returned when we could, and copied all the personal files. We got through the bulk when the Deputy was on holiday. It was a large undertaking. Mel added them to our computer, and we sifted through the data, finding recurring patterns. The victims of their scam were pretty, naïve, and easily manipulated.

I had been expecting our lives to change upon the crest of some momentous event. Instead, my own life was about to lurch sideways. Frog was eleven years old, but still at Primary school. She was taken out of school one day to have her hymen replicated.

Alarm bells rang within me. I needed to prove, or disprove, something. We put a twenty-four seven watch on her, but knew how it would go down. We had all seen it before. Mohammed was so very predictable, and that was what we were counting upon.

I do not know the technical stuff, but somehow Frog was able to transmit her geo-location data back to Mel, and we tracked her in real time. The feed died just south of Kingston, but came alive as she headed out of the city. It stopped at a hotel near Reigate. Melanie brought in a camera feed; she had put a camera inside Frog's bag, and Frog place it appropriately so as to capture events. We watched as Mohammed did the same shit to her, as he must have done to me. I spat at the screen. My first love? Huh!

He opened a package similar to one I remembered, and added some of the contents to Frog's drink. We all knew it was Rohypnol. The smarmy bastard even made her ask him for the drink.

Mohammed got her ready, sexing the girl before her mind became lost. He dribbled some of his drink into her nose, and she was well out of it. A knock came to the door. I knew the man at once, and I hated him intensely. He was the same man that destroyed my family.

There was a short disagreement over money, before Mohammed was paid £10, 000 in cash. He counted his money, as Family Court Judge: Ferdinand Aloysius St. John-Smythe QC & Bar, took Frog's virginity [sic], before he left in a hurry. He appeared chastened, but the why of it is for sexual miscreants and psychiatrists to unravel.

Those fleeting images from years before now made sense. The same fat, old man had raped me. The bastard! The Judge that sentenced me to Domicile, to a life in care, did so, so he could fuck me. So he could take my virginity.

I was sick. I mean, I ran and heaved into the bog in the corner of the room. I was gagging-up everything that was left within my stomach, my heart, my soul, and my sanity.

Somebody fed tissues into my hand as I rose with my anger afire. I vowed aloud, "I am so going to kill that bastard!"

Mel said, "I have it all on video." But I stormed out of the room, and went to my own. I knew my team would look after Frog. At last, I knew who had taken my virginity, and he was not a pretty sight. I also understood why I felt so reviled when he looked at me so intensely in court. He had been mentally undressing me.

Zoë tried to stop me drinking and doing drugs that night, but in the end, she stayed to keep me company and limit the damage. I felt morally raped, and I needed out of my mind.

For the very first time in my life, I wanted to kill somebody, and in all seriousness, wanted to eviscerate the scumbag from the face of the planet. I now knew his name. We began plotting the child-rapist's execution that night. All I needed to make it so, was Girl Power.

I thought about Right versus Wrong, knowing in time the manifest reality of our miserable and sordid lives would surely be revealed. The basic right of every woman, denied to us, to me. To be at liberty to choose my own preferred sexual partner, my mate, and create my own family. In time, I fell asleep, my dreams a litany of retribution.

That explained to me, precisely why Family Courts always hide behind a cloak of secrecy, and non-reporting. They have things to hide.

Bilty:
Personal Journal:

Notes:

1. I have no words to describe how much this changes things. This has now turned into a plot. The Judge concerned, ensured Isabella was taken from home, and placed under supervision. His plan, to take her virginity when she was old enough.

2. Now her being removed from Sophie makes sense. She was a pubescent young woman, and ripe for the judge to deflower.

3. The most worrying aspect is the support he received from Mohammed, and the total miscarriage of justice by both the Social Services and police. No doubt others in the system, lawyers perhaps, were aware of what was really going on.

4. With Felicity, it seems Mohammed made an easy killing.

5. One thing stands out from earlier in this telling. Isabella created an identity for the girls to share, and over time, they appear to have become a unit. The confessions of these girls will be damning evidence.

6. The girls managed to get images and videos of their rapists. That is phenomenal. That should aid police enquiries greatly. I'll ask Melanie for a copy.

7. Then there remains Matron's office. The first proof of any kind, that social services were acting illegally, and that the matrons knew what was going on. I will need to spend time on the related files, but so far, I have found no reason to doubt Isabella's testimony.

Isabella

"Isabella, you cannot be serious. The judge that sentenced you to domicile, later raped you when you came to age?"

"Yes."

"But surely that's preposterous, isn't it? Candice?"

"Listen to what she is saying, and then research it. You are the best at this. I also need confirmation. Isabella, you are certain it was him."

"Positive. Later I will prove it to both of you, so best you just accept it as fact for now. I also got him real good, you should remember that, Bilty."

"Huh. Yes I do, sorry. This came out of the blue."

"So how do you think I felt at the time? Best you complete your notes. I need to make a phone call. I'll be back soon."

Isabella returned, and enquired, "Are you ready to go on, Bilty? That is just the tip of the iceberg, so to say. But before we get to the rest of it, I want to follow the real-life chronology. It is a slight diversion, but one that would eventually lead to this place. After the last, you'll be pleased to know, it is rather light."

"Candice, the next part highlights one aspect not yet covered. Consent. The topic of sex is far reaching. When is it rape, and when is it not? I believe, that only the particular girl, herself, can decide. It concerns her feelings of the time, taken from her point of view.

Also, the intentions of the man and woman involved, need to be ascertained. In British courts, they are never considered as being of any worth. They are vitally important.

"I'll recommence, and I entitle this new adventure, 'Role Model'. Keep up."

Chapter 25 – Role Model

One Saturday morning, Zoë and I were out shopping, and we wandered the streets looking to kill time. We were taking a detour to avoid the crowded main streets and visit the more unusual shops. Lost within our own conversation of girlie intrigues, we were surprised when a man called out to us and hurried over, it was Ben. He asked us if we were hungry, and in due course he treated us to a pub lunch.

With all the changes back at gaol, we had forgotten about his offer, until he pressed us again. He explained, "Girls, I have an extremely important client who would like your company this evening. He will pay you £500, each, in cash. All you have to do is turn up in his hotel room at ten o'clock tonight, and stay with him until morning. After breakfast, his chauffer will take you home. How about it?"

His eyes were alive, flicking between us, and waiting expectantly. I looked at Zoë. We knew we were free that night, and had nothing to do until tomorrow afternoon. At Zoë's nod I said, "Condom's, straight sex, no hitting us, and we have a deal."

Ben stated, "This guy is a really nice man. You will have the time of your lives, but he won't wear a condom."

I weighed the odds without considering Zoë, and looked up to reply, "OK. We could wear our new school uniforms, do you think he would like that?"

Ben asked if we had pictures, and I smirked, almost coyly, but perhaps more seductively. I sent him only one photograph, and he drooled instantly. His jaw dropped open, and he had to readjust his trousers for some curious reason. We laughed at his obvious discomfiture. "Damn, but you two chicks are so fucking hot! Send the rest of these pictures to my mobile and I'll get you a ton of work."

He pleaded with us, as we milked our charàde. When we were laughing our heads off and could take no more, we took pity on him. I forwarded our photographs, and he remained agog. We were coming into our own sexual power, and it felt real good.

That night we both had butterflies and fits of giggles. We were in a top West End hotel and couldn't believe how rich and extravagant the place was. We were ten minutes early and took a seat to one corner of the massive foyer, trying to keep a low profile. It was impossible. It was also exceedingly public. Staff had begun to notice us, so we moved quickly to avoid them, by heading towards the lifts.

There was a bellboy controlling the lift door, and he asked us which floor. Zoë answered before I did, selecting two floors below the one we were headed for. It made sense to cover our tracks. We waited outside the lift until the corridor was clear, before using the stairs and finding the room, it was called The Ambassador Suite.

Chapter 25

I knocked the door and immediately a butler opened it. He ushered us inside and asked, "Are you the expected guests of Mr. Goldblum?"

I told him we were, and he showed us through to an elegant lounge. We were offered drinks, and I asked for our favourites. The glasses were small and the contents not strong enough, but apart from that, everything was going well. I mentioned that we needed to change, and the butler showed us to a vacant bedroom.

We donned our school uniforms and returned to wait. Zoë made the next set of drinks to our liking. The butler watched us intently, especially when he thought we weren't looking, but he never spoke. We ignored him, giggling like the innocent schoolgirls we should have been.

Zoë had just finished fixing us both a third drink when a tall and elegant man entered the room. He strode straight towards us proffering his hand enthusiastically, apologising for keeping us waiting. He wore an aura of power, yet was a true gentleman; the first one we had ever met. He bowed and kissed the back of our hands in turn, before standing back to admire us. He said, "My, my. Aren't you two just perfect? How old are you?"

I put on my coy little-girl voice and replied, "I'm fourteen years old, Sir, and my friend here is almost fifteen."

He sat down in a leather armchair and leaned forward, looking at us intently. We both knew we had his undivided attention, which became manifest when he asked us both to turn around. We turned slowly the first time, but spun quickly a second time so our school skirts rose up. He muttered aloud, "Oh My God!"

His eyes were still fastened on the tops of our legs, where our panties should have been. He spoke absentmindedly, "Jenson, Whiskey on the rocks, and make it extra large."

The drink was brought and the butler was dismissed. He disappeared into another room within the suite. We made friends. The man was cultured and charming. He was in his early sixties with a full head of silvery hair. He was lean, slightly muscular, and quick-witted. He made us laugh and we played up to his fantasy.

He wanted to talk first, get to know us, which we had not been expecting. We made up some half-arsed story part-based in fact, one that included both of us attending my school. Zoë replenished his drink and he reached out to take a purple pill. I took the packet from him and offered the tablet to his tongue. Zoë brought the glass to his lips to wash it down. We were dotting on his male ego, which was about to explode. Minutes later his trousers were as well. We played him like it was second nature to us. He needed to get off, and that was our job.

We moved to the bedroom, where he made slow, gentle love to, and with us. Zoë and I made out a little bit, occasionally, which only seemed to excite him more. When his urgency took over, he took us both by turn, and we both received his offerings. He proved to have staying power, and we all had a brilliant time. I mean that.

We slept in his bed, one to either side of him. He awoke with us nestled into his chest, his arms around our shoulders, and we did it again. He kept repeating, "I am lost and gone to Heaven."

That made us feel awfully proud, and encouraged us both to try even harder to please him more. It was not a chore. It was not rape. It was a consensual pleasure. The first time either of us had agreed to have coital union with a man. Later he admitted that it was his first ever time with two girls, and he was overjoyed.

Finally, he was sated, and we ordered breakfast in his suite. Jenson dealt with room service before knocking discreetly to say, "Breakfast is served in the anteroom Sir, Mademoiselles."

Breaking fast, our talk was light and cheery. We were all in a great mood, and I knew the butler was dead jealous. Our host asked if he could take our photographs, and we played and coyed for his camera.

I am sure he would have done us both again, if his office phone had not started ringing. Jenson fielded his calls for several minutes, but it was clear it was time for us to depart. Sir Richard asked if next time he could book us directly, and I said, "Yes of course. We would love to meet you again, kind Sir."

We exchanged personal mobile numbers before he added, "Plans in my line of business change rapidly, but at the moment I am scheduled back in London in two weeks time. I hope you can be free that Friday evening for dinner, and stay with me until Sunday lunchtime. You will need dress clothes of course. I will ask Miss Constance to action it at once.

"Please excuse me, as I must attend my desk urgently. The gold market is quite unpredictable just now, although gemstones are my main business. I will set some aside for you in due course. The chauffer will collect you in five minutes. Please forgive me for a moment. I will see you before you leave."

He hurried away, and we casually wandered back to change into our everyday clothes. Zoë kept saying, "He hasn't paid us," but I assured her there was no need to worry. Soon we were talking about what was our first consensual sexual experience with a man — and it felt mighty fine. Well, I guess Ben was actually the first, but he didn't count. We were both extremely happy, and feeling drifty in an emotional sense. We were already looking forward to the next encounter avidly.

The chauffer knocked the door and asked us to follow him. I hesitated, but Jenson told him to wait and went to the office. Mister Goldblum rushed through apologising, "The Bank of Milan on the telephone, sorry. We have a gold deal going down right now. This is what we agreed I believe, and this is your tip. I do so look forward to enjoying the pleasure of your most exquisite company again, in the near future."

Chapter 25

He bowed and kissed the back of our hands most graciously, before hastening back to his office.

We were both dying to see what was in the envelopes. It felt like a lot of money. Instead, the chauffer led us out the back way, and we were ushered into the rear of the longest car I had ever seen. The driver told us to help ourselves to drinks, before raising the glass privacy partition.

We just had to look. The first envelope contained one thousand pounds Sterling, and so did the second. We were totally gob-smacked. Disbelief turned to astonishment, and we felt on top of the world. We hugged each other with great enthusiasm, and plundered the bar within a giddiness of girlie gazumption. What a result!

The car stopped in a posh neighbourhood. A young woman got out of a nearby car, and opened the door for us. She was looked early-twenties, was early-thirties, and extremely well dressed. She was chatty, plus she already knew our names. Her name was Miss Constance, and she led us into a clothier that was very swish and select. We were measured everywhere, and told to return on Saturday for final fitting.

The chauffer was waiting by the rear limousine door when we came out. He extinguished his cigarette as soon as he saw us, and held the door open. Once we were settled, he asked us where we would like to be dropped off. I told him to take us somewhere close to Ben's shop. He chuckled and closed the partition once more.

When we got there, we discovered that Ben had not long opened shop that morning, and it was deserted. I told him our gig went like a dream, and we were open for select clientele on a regular basis. He tried to cut a deal for one-tenth of what we made. I fired back, "You're already getting your take, so don't be greedy." He accepted my words and apologised. That was a good call, and pure gambit on my part.

We were not only there to sound out the potential market, but confirm new business. I drifted through the shop looking for something I had glimpsed the last time we were there. Amongst the mockery of pseudo-female promiscuity, I found it, an Arab Strap: Leather straps and metal rings, called an erection enhancer. I asked Ben what it was, and we ended up having him demonstrate it. Two rings tightened around his manhood, whilst the other confined his paired appendage. The effect was obvious, everything swelled disproportionately.

We left some time later with free samples, and Ben with a contented grin on his face. Our plans formulating as we talked of consequences, and walked back to gaol. On the way we opened a new locker deposit bank in a different station. After window-shopping, we had a burger and checked in with Billie. She told us everything was fine, and we arranged to meet later.

The truth of the matter was, we had not been missed at all, and everything ran perfectly. Zoë and I worked the Sunday afternoon and evening, on the other side of London. It was gross. We did twenty men each, but it was better than doing it every night.

Ben arranged for us to meet an executive the following Friday, and yet another on Saturday. What can I say, it was easy loving and a lot of fun. It was also extremely well paid. The first punter was slightly weird, so we did not mind him not asking us for our phone numbers and a repeat. It was obvious he was trying to simulate a sexual fantasy with perhaps his own daughter, or the girl next door. Some holy grail of sexual depravity locked deeply away within his splintered sexuality.

The second man did want to keep in touch. By morning we worked out his predilection was for younger girls. We had Frog, and he seemed to like the idea of doubling her and Ellie, whom were real-life sisters.

We had a new business venture, one that demanded total inclusion and secrecy of my core team. My only question was, were they going to do this for themselves, for all of us, or because they felt they had to? I insisted this had to be absolutely and utterly on a voluntary basis, otherwise, it was rape. Zoë agreed at once.

In between clients, Zoë and I were fitted out for our new evening gowns. We had somehow moved into a world where the woman says what she wants, and the man pays. This did not just run to a couple of posh dresses and accoutrements like matching handbags and shoes. Oh no, it included jewellery and everything to make us look like proper young Ladies. Miss Constance gave us deportment lessons, and tried elocution with mixed results. All we had to do was act the part in public, and become whores in the bedroom. Yes!

Unlike Zoë, I knew this was important regards the new clientele we were becoming exposed too. I began aping the poshest girls in school, and after a while, registered for Finishing Classes. These were aimed to change girls with rich parents, from being normal kids, into well-mannered debutantes of elite society circles. Good deportment and elocution were pillars of these lectures. Followed by practical assessments, which were incredibly formal, for an informal class.

I did OK, but knew I would never pass as one of them. However, I learned the rules, and how to conduct myself within the ether the excessively rich inhabit.

I also learned which knife, fork, or spoon to use at table, and know there are dozens of them with specific usage. Zoë got confused, but of course, it was that maths thing again, counting. She copied what others and I did, and in the real world, that worked out just fine.

The next weekend was a total blast. Mr. Goldblum brought along his closest friend, and we were again in an astronomically starred, central London hotel. This time we had our own room between theirs. All had adjoining doors and we seemed to skip from one to the other, spending little time in our own room.

We ate at the finest tables in town, and were coached by Miss Constance, who must have come up through our side of the system, because she never so much as blanched. We became known as 'The Nieces', although whose was never defined. We stopped the men taking Viagra; the Arab Strap worked for Mr. Goldblum, but only partially for his associate. He was slightly older, a heavier drinker, and he did some light drugs with us as well. That was nice.

This became a regular thing twice every month, and we loved the escape. Mr. Goldblum's friend would be a different man sometimes, but overall, we had a done deal. We got eight thousand pounds for that first weekend, all in cash, no questions asked. We were given jewellery as a perquisite, and it was dreadfully expensive.

There were other rich perverts filling in the spaces, and we were making—I don't know, £15, 000 per month, each. It was always safe and consensual loving, given that we were being paid as whores, but what the hell. At least we weren't being raped by Paki grandfathers, and we had money in the locker bank to prove it. It was a big step up for us, and suited our independent streak.

On the Monday evening following, I drew my trusted to me and I made us swear an Oath of Sisterhood. I told them there was good work for us all, but one client wanted Ellie and Frog. I did not press them for an answer, but let them work through it themselves. After a few days, they agreed, and I had a new business.

One morning, I had something new to consider, the beginning of my film career. The summons to Psycho's workshop could not have been more inappropriate. She had become the owner of a back street film studio, the main output unsurprisingly, being pornography.

Psycho had called me early and asked me to run through the plot for her latest video ad. As I prepared to meet my new future, I had expected Zoë to accompany me, but she said the Paki's needed her. I left alone, taking with me my school uniform, the sexy one orchestrated by Ben and hand-made by the seamstress.

I walked out onto the street thinking nobody cared about me. I did not know at the time, every single girl was watching me, and wishing me success. I was going to a place they could not imagine: Psycho's lair.

It was nice to meet Deborah on equal terms. She was OK. We ran through the script, did drink, and drugs. There's not all that much to the script of a porno movie. I was to be royally fucked, but first I had to act all bolshie, like the prospective Pakistani audiences' imaginings of a typical, white and no-good, British pubescent girl. I dropped into character with ease, both on and off set.

Like some gross parody of a Bollywood movie, I was to be charmed on screen, before I willingly submitted my supposed maidenhead to a superior man. This turned out to be a masculine Adonis' of Pakistani decent, who would prove to be my heart's desire, after he fucked me real-good. Men!

Psycho had me ream a small squirt of tomato ketchup inside me, so the camera could focus upon my supposed deflowering. I couldn't stop laughing, so we had to shoot the scenes of my facial adulation of deflowering, the willing surrender of my maidenhead to this Paki 'god', and my newly awakened sexual desire, later.

After losing my maidenhead [sic], I was supposed to act all coy, admitting I was inferior to this 'MAN' that had 'TAKEN' me, my most precious female core. There was some religious shit to it, because I had to thank Allah for sending this man to save me, and convert to Islam.

Later I was shot wearing a devotees Niqāb, following my all-conquering man several steps behind, as he strutted the pavement outside Psycho's gaff. He swaggered ahead as if a Prince, neigh, a King of all women's pleasure, as defined by his most eminent manhood.

It creased me up, because the guy was anything but. He had a small cock and hadn't a clue how to use it. I think this is why they liked preteen girls, and sewed their wives pussy lips up so tight, that they could get off quickly. The needs of the female were their last consideration.

I already knew the guy was an illegal immigrant, and a part-time dishwasher at one of Mohammed's Uncle's lesser renowned Balti Houses. He was scared of women, and by the time I finished with him off camera, he was terrified of me. He was only doing the film, because he had been told to do it. He worked out and had a muscular body, which would help the viewing figures. I think he enjoyed the shoot. I found the bizarre episode something of a non-event.

Regardless, I got fucked. The Paki twist was, whatever happened to me, I had to be grateful and worship the man. A load of bollocks if you ask me, but I played for the camera, and we screened good.

I became a film star, but not a role model any female would wish to emulate. I was soon infamous in Pakistan, and in time, clients came to England just to have sex with me. It was still rape, but that was what I appeared to do for a living. It was all part of the job, but who gives a frigging toss?

Well, apparently there were many men in Pakistan, and the Arabian speaking world, that gave my film a really big toss. And so much so, Psycho became inundated with bookings, as the video I made went viral. With Mohammed's help, they offered sex tour holidays, for a large fee. Most of these perverts paid a large premium to shag the youngest girls. I heard Mohammed got one Grand for eleven-year-olds.

The Indians may have invented Bollywood, but what we created was better defined as 'Paki-Wood'. A-hem!

Chapter 25

We were cool, Psycho and I, equals. I would push her, and she would push me. It was a game. I was happy as I wandered outside, only to find a long car waiting for me. The chauffer doffed his cap to me and said, "Excuse me Ma'am, but Sir Richard has requested your presence."

I looked at him; "What? How the hell did you know where I was?"

"Zoë gave me the address. Your phone was switched off."

I switched it back on again and said, "I take it the bar is open?"

He bowed his head and said, "Ma'am," gesturing towards the rear with his arm, as he opened the limousine door.

I got in the back and tried to get David, the driver to have a drink. It was not easy until I stopped the limo, and sitting in the front, found out where the drugs were hidden, and that seemed to be his thing. I rolled, and I ensured we shared. It was good stuff.

The buzz almost took away the fact that he knew where I was. I mean Mr. Sir Richard Goldblum, if any of those names were real? Turns out they all were, apart from the Mr. bit. He was a Knight of The Realm.

Luncheon was fantastic, and between courses, I discovered Sir Richard wanted me to make friends with a thirteen-year-old girl. It became apparent she was a business competitor's daughter, and Sir Richard wanted to have her. It was his revenge for losing a contract. I will admit her photograph appeared cute, and she was definitely a virgin—by then I could smell one a mile away, even with only a photograph as reference.

I almost became embroiled in his plot to bed her, but I could not do it, become that hypocritical. I told Sir Richard plainly, "No way. You want her, then leave me out of it, OK?"

He turned his eyes to bore into mine. I stared straight back into his, closing the distance between us as he met total resistance. He knew it instantly. I flipped, and playing his male ego lightly, but making my point quite clear. "I will do anything as long as it is consensual, by all parties concerned. Anything else is rape.

"Fancy words, living the high-life for a moment of time, and petite pronouncements, don't mean much to a girl, especially when her virginity is the price paid."

He recoiled from me, but I had made my point, and potentially screwed our future. He gulped as my words hit home, and apologised. It was unnecessary, we were by then good friends. He asked me out for dinner, as an appeasement, and never mentioned the girl again.

David was waiting when I left after lunch that day. I refused to get in his car, limo or not. He bowed his head and said, "Isabella, you have an indefatigable spirit, one I find completely alluring. Please, let me serve you. You are worthy of so much more than this."

He was driving me home, but I made him pull over in a quiet place. We both got in the back. I probably made his small male dream come true that afternoon. That was my first experience of consensual sex without payment, and he was good at it. Mind you, I also garnered my own personal chauffer as a result—us girls can be real clever that way.

As a personal driver service, the only real difference between David and Asif, apart from the regular beatings, was that I alone chose when I allowed David to have sex with me. We were destined to become staunch friends.

Bilty

"You had me in stitches a couple of times, Isabella. This is such a light relief, after what went before. I guess it gets bad again?"

"Yes, but in different ways. The worst is probably over, except for the telling of other girls. I won't add too many, although there are thousands to choose from."

"Thank you Isabella, girls. I, like many others, will find it hard to differentiate between paedophiles as you describe them. Being say, Sir Richard and Asif. Could you explain a little more?"

"The big difference is consent."

Zoë added, "Yes, consent. That really matters you know. This was about easy loving sex, not that as practiced by the Paki's. That had grave overtones of abuse and physical beatings. They are worlds apart, to me."

Isabella added, "Bilty, I know in any British court, the far greater crimes committed by the never-ending cesspool of Paki's, would receive much lighter sentences than Sir Richard. And that is utterly unfair.

"Later you will learn why Sir Richard was the way he was, and I can say now, that all older women ripped him off. He wanted, needed, love from any female he could trust. Hence his predilection for younger girls. It's obvious once you look at the reasons why in context.

"Doing likewise with the 'Asians', their sexual slavery is debased, and all about women being lower than animals, and extreme misogynism. We are lower than their own women. Sexual trafficking, without pay. C'mon! Yet they are never prosecuted to the extreme, and are given soft sentences. The penalty as far as I am concerned, for what they took from me—basically my childhood, should be death!"

Bilty tried to respond, but all the girls spoke up in support of Isabella's statement. Candice said to her husband, "Listen, for herein lies the truth. These emotions are not an act. They are reacting to what their lives had become: sex slaves."

Isabella retorted at once, "This is why I believe there are degrees of rape, just as with Murder. Sir Richard did not rape us, but thousands of Paki's did. Why was that?"

Melanie answered, "Because they could, and because they knew they would get away with it—Play the race card, dance the religious fandango upon the cornerstones of British law and justice. I hate them. I repeat, they deserve to be executed!"

Bilty:
Personal Journal:

Notes:
1. The one thing that stands out a mile, is the distinction that Isabella and Zoë both apply to their sexual partners. The deep divide they both share regards relationships with Sir Richard, and those concerning the Pakistani grooming gang. They have a point. One Melanie supported.

2. One difference Candice just pointed out, is that Sir Richard never groomed the girls in any way. He paid for their services.

3. And what of the driver, David? That was consensual sex without payment. I wonder whom the courts would come down hardest upon, and doubted it would be the 'Asians', who were by far and away the worst of them.

4. One other aspect stands out. Isabella had come into the power of her own sexuality. The way she harassed the male lead off camera. I daresay the same holds true for Zoë.

5. That this was used as a promotional video in Pakistan, is almost unbelievable. The Middle East and Arabic speaking nations, no doubt. And the men came because of this. I now begin to see the scam revealed. It is all about money. Isabella is correct.

Comment
Isabella had been chatting aside, while I wrote up my notes. She seemed in excellent spirits, and we were all a lot happier. She shattered the illusion by coming over to me. "Bilty, time to go on. This time I will reveal the fullest depths of depravity these sub-humans inhabit.

"Prepare to have your eyes opened real wide. I will resume, now.

"What I will share is not common knowledge, but goes to show how sick these perverts really are. Strap yourself in. This will be a roller-coaster ride.

"Zoë, please see our guests have a very strong drink. They're going to need it."

Chapter 26 – Web of Lies

Isabella

Our days thereafter slowly changed. Like our own undercover operation, so the Muslims' expanded their own realm. Every month new destinations and associated clientele, from across Greater London and beyond, were added to the list of venues our girls serviced.

The SS continued to kidnap new, and younger girls into the system, so there was always fresh meat for our abusers to relish. I noticed the increase in inmates generally aligned with the increase in girls required, almost as if it were choreographed.

The demand was such, a new wing of rooms was added, and with subtle pressure, I and my closest managed to get rooms there on the same floor, and mostly adjoining.

During the summer holidays of my fifteenth year, both Zoë and I were required less, except for new destinations far from home. We continued to do a similar number of men each week, fewer venues, but more clients and time spent at each one. This suited us well, but in the process, I lost the school taxi service, and had to use the bus.

I was disgruntled at first, but later realised it put a barrier between the Muslims and I. They lost regular contact with me, and as a result, 'Out of sight, out of mind'. Zoë also returned to full-time schooling, and while in the lowest grade, she was holding her own. Slowly we were both breaking away from the daily horrors we had endured.

Billie continued to collect information about the Muslim operation, and Melanie upgraded the computer database. This concurred with the panties we collected, and other information Melanie included. We knew we were building an extremely strong case. But we still did not know how to use all the information effectively, given the police and CPS had already proven themselves incompetent, and complete waste of space.

The only pressure our cohort sustained came from Big Daddy Asif. He continued to force the bullies to expand Psycho's network of school recruitment. Under Psycho, the target age had been twelve year-olds, dipping latterly towards eleven. Preteens were proving easier to subvert than tweenies, and corresponded closer with the life of the Prophet Muhammad. Therefore, the recruitment of new girls included nine year-olds. I thought it was sickening, depraved, but what could I do?

The majority of the inmates managed to get to school most days, and they were up for a big reward should they enlist a new girl. However, the girls in most demand, or those who had fallen pregnant, were usually put into our 'Special Needs home Schooling Program', a fancy title for being allowed to recover during the day, and get ready for the next Paki gang-rape. They received zero academic education.

Pressure on us increased to recruit fresh girls from the inmate's schools, and many came from low-class schools. The recruiter got £200 for each new girl, which was ample encouragement. They were also paid for identifying future targets, either girls old enough to recruit, but directly by Asif and his team, or younger victims who were very pretty, and could be forced into the system by the SS for later abuse.

Sometimes Asif pressured me to recruit Academy girls. I said I would try, but told him they were all clever, and lesbians. With little contact between us, I got away with it, and the subject was dropped.

I looked at the girls from my academy regardless, and there were several candidates. However, I wanted to keep my own school out of Paki clutches, if only to shield them from what I had endured. And I also wanted to protect my own educational prospects. I am not proud to admit that, but it was a factor.

Our Kitty Logo worked glowing and golden. Zoë had actioned my request to secrete small cameras into the bags of all the girls. I called it our 'Assurance Policy', and so it was. We got them all, the bastards. Faces and continuity, having sex with girls they knew to be seriously underage. We reasoned they did it because they had the money to do it, and they thought they could get away with it *ad infinitum.*

By that time, most of the girls that had been abused for several years, understood quite a lot of Urdu and Pashto, Arabic as well. We would use it sometimes to talk secretly in front of English-only speakers. It also meant we understood most of what our rapists were talking about, although some would switch to another language, such as Sindhi, if they wanted to try and hide intent from us. Even without the language, we knew instinctively what they were up to.

The Muslims no longer wanted anyone above the age fourteen, unless they were still a proven virgin; meaning an official hymen inspection. There were not many left in Hammersmith. I doubt there was a single one in Shepherds Bush, of pubescent age or above. There they were in competition with the Albanians, Turks, and other paedophile rings, such as the Romanians [R 26.1]. Nevertheless, only the Paki's specialised in exceedingly young girls. That is Muhammad's legacy.

According to some of the minor local headlines, this was all about control and supply of drugs. I know it was also about vice, and especially underage sex girls forced to fuck for free. The man-fights sometimes made the local headlines, disputes about 'Turf' and all that macho stuff. To me they were boys pretending to be hard. That's boys for you. I knew I possessed what they wanted, right between my legs.

I believed the Muslims had reached their lowest debasement, but I was inwardly shocked one day, when Mohammed called, and collected me from school. He wanted me to implement his latest recruitment drive.

He explained, "Issy, you are clever. You will understand what I need. This is why I came to you with my new plan. There is a large pool of children waiting for foster care and adoption. Social services simply cannot keep up with demand, so they have asked me to assist them."

My heart quailed as he pulled the Mercedes over to the side of the road. It was a different model from the one he wooed me inside, thank God! Once parked, he pulled out a tabloid newspaper, one read by the masses. He pointed to an advertisement and said, "I am personally very interested in this girl. She is so sexy don't you think?"

The ad had her picture, and I was stricken, appalled at his open and utter contempt. It read, "Hi, my name is Holly and I am 9-years old. I don't have any parents and need someone to love me. Please call my mobile on 07963718454, or look at my Facebook, Holly Rock."

Mohammed said, "Holly Rock's, doesn't she. I simply have to have her. Isn't she so delightful?"

I internally switched off Mohammed's vile monologue from my conscious thoughts, because his continued existence — His still being alive, insulted the innermost core of my maturing femininity.

Instead, I stared at the page, stunned. There was a picture of a cute young girl. My mind somersaulted. I could not believe such a young thing could possibly know how to, let alone afford to advertise for new parents in an extremely popular national newspaper. In time, I noticed the small print, "Direct First Care UK."

Mohammed interrupted my seething outrage, only to compound it. "I have been personally grooming her for several weeks now, and we plan to meet soon. The stupid bitch thinks I am eighteen"

He laughed outrageously and continued, "Issy, there are hundreds of these girls. My initiative is to turn this advertising into a website, don't you think that is brilliant. I need you to select the prettiest and youngest, well, aged seven and above. Blessed be Allah, 'Assalaamu Álaykum' for sending Aisha to Muhammad's as his bride. You will groom these girls for me, and admit the most deserving to my operation. I know you can do it sweetheart — you will for me. I know you will. Thank you, my love."

"But why me, Mohammed?"

"Because you are the only educated girl, you are computer literate, and I do not wish the web developers to know the website content, they would have a fit."

Mohammed took my floundering paw and kissed the back of my hand before I could remove it from his grasp. Repulsion swept through me at the mere thought. Nausea filled my being. My mind went blank. This monster had discovered a new means to sequester young girls to satiate his disgusting appetite. Utter loathing coursed through my heart. I hid it well and replied, "Your wish is my command, my love."

He was so pleased with himself, he did not realise I was taking the piss, nor see the horror within my eyes. He began driving again, and I needed to be sick, but gulped to hide the fact from him. I focused on the name Aisha, and I did not know of her. To cover my dismay, I demurely play-acted, enquiring, "Tell me of her, Aisha. Who is she?"

Mohammed seemed pleased by my response, and spouted, "She was the foremost of the wives of our most Gracious Lord, The Prophet Muhammad. She was seven years old when she married him, but nine when the marriage was finally consummated. All Muslim men need to emulate the life of Muhammad, so as to gain enlightenment and succour at Allah's side. Seventy-two virgins await any man who enters Allah's domain. This girl will provide me with a path to heaven, Grace within the Court of our Lord, and everlasting life."

My wits battered senseless beyond any system of belief, I listened as the miles passed so slowly. Unfortunately, this disgusting male did not pass me by so quickly. I could not wait to escape this monster's clutches, but said "Yes" like a good little girl, and smiled the way he expected me to. My tattered psyche lay three-sheets to the wind by the time he finally dropped me back to gaol.

The creep wanted to wine and dine me, but I made the excuse that I needed to work on his brilliant plan immediately. My pretend enthusiasm gave way to obtuse outrage as soon as the car door slammed shut, and I hurtled back to the comfort of my boudoir.

I did not make the WC, throwing up in the bath. I knocked the wall urgently, and Zoë came through to comfort me. I was a mess, and in short time we both were. I still clutched the newspaper he had given me, as if it were the neck of a venomous snake intent upon killing me. My friend slowly teased the newspaper away from my grasp, and read. She soon joined me puking into the bath, and later, we got trashed.

We actioned Mohammed's plan, because we had no choice in the matter. It took a few weeks for his web designers to publish the site, and we met again soon after it was up and running.

Mohammed tasked me to enter the details of over one hundred children, mostly girls, and there was too much work involved. I persuaded him to include Melanie as moderator, which he was loath to do. After explaining the time involved, he acquiesced, allowing both Melanie and I limited administrative rights. We could add children, but not delete, and that gave us all the edge we needed to pull data.

I met Mohammed again before the month was round. I had a bad feeling about the get-together, and steeled my heart to endure. He told me the second phase of the website was complete.

[Bona fide example [R 26.2] used as illustration only. Imagine 'what if' a similar website was run by a paedophile – Mohammed perhaps?]

It would act as a meeting place for both children and prospective foster caregivers, and adoptive parents. The legitimate face of 'Direct First Care Placement Agency' fronted it. Superficially, most people would welcome such a website, if it were not under the complete control of a serial paedophile.

Melanie became our ace in the hole. She continued as moderator, now with access to prospective caregivers as well. She was able to track one of his main channels of selection and recruitment. For some reason, the pratt trusted us implicitly. I can only presume he had watched one too many Paki-Wood movies.

We protected the most innocent girls as best we could. But the reality was that most of them that were channelled into Mohammed's operation. With Melanie on board, everything was copied, correlated, and backed-up as evidence. We were even able to trace what became of them. This was supportive fact implicating the SS and care homes, as sex traffickers and providers of extremely underage prostitutes.

Melanie also monitored prospective caregivers, a few of whom she flagged to me as being bogus. We concluded a few were part of Mohammed's group, but one or two other's stood out as being wrong.

In truth, our amassed data, vitally important in itself, was not altering our daily physical predicament. The girls continued to get raped, each, and every, single day, as the number of clients and new girls continued to increase. We agreed that what we were doing was of the utmost importance, but there was no resolution. There was no end to our abuse, or preventing the abuse of newcomers to the care home.

I was floundering, and spoke to Zoë one evening when it all began to overpower me. I understood exactly what Psycho had gone through, and there appeared to be zero way out. I was castigating myself for being so consummately ineffectual. All my fine words and best of intentions, had made no discernible difference to the lives the girls in our prison. We were all just fucked.

Of all people, it was Mohammed who gave me the clue to unlock the next secret of the conspiracy. I was by then fifteen years old, and we normally had little direct contact anymore. Then one evening he insisted on taking me for dinner after school, to discuss his latest plans with me.

During dinner, I discovered Mohammed had designs to create a parallel social networking platform for young people. I was to ensure all our girls enlisted, and placed advertisements, or 'profiles', as he preferred to call them, of a sexualised nature.

211

He explained, "The website is hosted in Russia, and its primary purposes are to attract new male clients for the existing business, and act as a recruitment and grooming channel for new and extremely underage girls. I propose a one-on-one counselling service for full members, where we can offer them sound advice. Don't you love the idea?"

I already knew the outcome of that ruse: underage, unpaid prostitution. But he delighted in embellishing the finer details. Gross!

"Issy, I need you to persuade our girls at normal school, to share the website with their peers, encouraging them to join. They would be rewarded with a free phone top-up, burger meal, cash, or whatever. Brilliant, don't you think!"

In essence, they were to be insidiously victimised.

Inwardly I was nauseated, but outwardly, as before, I enthused. I reasoned this gave us immediate access to a larger whole, and probably all of the care homes and children caught up within the scam. With this thought, my eyes came alive, and I pressed for our wholehearted inclusion, my ruse to get at least Melanie within at a senior position.

Mohammed misread my gusto as being fervour for his latest abject schism. There is no gauge within heaven, nor upon earth, big enough to measure how much I loathed his continued existence. As my internal turmoil broiled to scorch my retribution upon him, so my outwardly doting doe-eyes entrapped him so easily, within my feminine snare.

I became two people, two minds as one. I was probably borderline schizophrenic by the end of the meal, given what I, what we had all endured for the bulk of our adolescent years. I separated my beliefs from my reality, and compartmentalised my madding mind, again.

Showing my outwards enthusiasm, I asked him what he needed us to do, adding for his distraction, that I hoped I would be well paid for promoting his brilliant scheme. He chuckled and handed me an envelope. It contained £500. He said, "That's upfront payment for fifty girls. All you have to do is get them to join the website and you get £10 for each one. Your target ages are nine to twelve, plus virgins up to fourteen. The more girls that join, the more money you will make."

I stared at the contents of the package for seconds, before the full impact hit me — he planned to take this nationwide and I was in prime position to make thousands of pounds for our team. I have no idea why I did it, but I flung my arms around him and kissed him full on the lips. We were both surprised at my reaction, and I mumbled unthinkingly, "This online Fuckbook is gonna cost you a lot of money, my dear. I hope you can afford it?"

It was a throw-away line, but he smoothly replied, "Kitty, Issy. This money is not mine as such, it is Company money, business money. I write these expenses off against tax, or am paid it as a company bonus. Our meal tonight for instance, will be chalked up as expenses, client entertainment. Regards this latest business venture, most of the money comes from Direct First Care UK as projected overheads, concerning setting up the new websites, which is also tax deductible.

"Social services, the local authority, and others have also contributed to this great initiative of mine. We helped them meet their targets, and made it easy for them to be fulfilled with the previous website.

"Local authorities in particular, pay us extremely well for advertising on that website, although to surfers it appears to be a free service offered. Nowadays, prospective foster and adoption clients have to pay a small fee. This gives us access to their financial details, if indirectly. It is easy when you know how, or have good friends — like clever web designers, and creative accountants and auditors.

"With this new website, all chat is monitored. It seems like a great and underage meeting place, a new and innovative social media. It is in fact a mechanism to recruit fresh underage prostitutes. Brilliant don't you think, and far less risky than doing it out on the street."

Later that night I sat alone in my room, remembering his words, and I even wrote them down so I would not muddle them later. I reasoned that if Mohammed was doing this, matron, and the care homes were in on the swindle. This confirmed the whole set-up was not about underage sex, which was just a bonus for Paki men. It was all about, mainly untaxed and untraceable money.

After that encounter, I began searching for a money trail, but it was extremely well hidden within the monster that was care provision, and professional accounting practices employed by Direct First Care UK. While our full team was included in the new website idea, I only confided in Zoë and Melanie concerning my tentative understandings about how matron's financial operation was set up.

§

Things were pretty settled as I grew into my sixteenth year. We had milked the local files and computers of all their information, and copied it far and wide. Melanie got a hack into an SS database using Matron's password, and that was a real revelation. Copied and traced, we were doing very well. Our gang had a line on the money-trail, and it wasn't pretty. However, it stopped dead regards matron and her covering company, as only official and audited files remained in her office. We could never define the monetary link between her and Mohammed, but there had to be one. I determined to find and expose it.

We did define what Direct First Care UK made out of us, and it was thousands of pounds per month. Matron and her deputy were directors of the company, as were a few names I did not know. Melanie dragged up a list of primary shareholders, and we were not surprised to discover Mohammed and his uncle's names listed.

What shocked me was that a Mrs. St. John-Smythe was also listed as an investor. I do not believe in coincidence, and she turned out to be the wife of the Judge that condemned me to my present existence––So that he could rape my virginity.

At my behest, Melanie did some online research, and by chance came upon a website that offered a massive amount of information, and references to the kidnapping by Social Services of girls just like us. It was a most startling discovery and buoyed us greatly.

She showed me a link, 'Forced adoption, family courts, social services, children in care' [R 26.3] and begged me, "Please Issy, spare a moment to take a look at this website I found, penned by Ian Josephs M.A. (Oxon). Regards care homes and the like, this is what he stated:

> 'The racket of child trafficking by employees of the state deserves to be exposed! More than 10,000 children are taken into care in England every year by social workers backed up by compliant family Court judges. Most come from loving homes as they reckon truly abused children do not make good adoption material and are troublesome in care so are best left alone.
>
> Care homes costing the taxpayer £200,000 per year per child, fostering and adoption agencies charging the taxpayer £1500--£2000/ week for recruiting foster families and placing children in them. It's a bonanza for those within the system with the "minions" getting generous commission backhanders for "recommending" these bodies!
>
> The National Fostering Agency [R 26.4] founded by social workers a few years ago was recently sold to "graphite" [R 26.5] for around £130 million! (See the net) Nice work if you can get it!
>
> Like birds of a feather, judges, social workers, guardians, hired experts, care homeowners, fostering agency directors, family solicitors and barristers all "flock together" making a living splitting up families for profit! No wonder the courts are secret and parents are frequently jailed for daring to reveal some of the horribly unjust practices that they have suffered at the hands of those who so profitably operate these parodies of justice.'
> sic erat scriptum

I stared at the screen, and said to Melanie, "There are well over one hundred girls in this care home now. Presumably, they are receiving that much for each of us, so that means matron is running a business worth at least Twenty-four Million pounds per annum!

"I'm going through her files again tonight. I need the costs of running this place. The profits are obviously shared between them."

Melanie concluded, "I'm with you. Oh, look at this—he lists <u>legal representatives</u> [R 26.6] that will take on these cases. We could never find one."

"Me neither. Send me the link, I need to seriously check out this website. It seems like a goldmine of otherwise deliberately obfuscated information."

Bilty

"So Isabella, let me get this straight. One: Mohammed is supplying a supposed legitimate website for all care homes owned by Direct First Care UK."

"Yes Bilty. And much of its operation is genuine. The problem is, Mohammed is running it, and siphoning off girls to meet his own, and his grooming gang's clients. Plus remember, this is nationwide in nature, so their influence grows significantly over time."

"Okay, I get that. But will he sell children to paedophiles?"

"Of course, stupid. Mohammed is all about money and underage sex girls. To the Matrons and SS, it helps fill vacancies and meets targets. But without administrator access, you'll get nowhere with it.

Melanie added, "I'll show you what we have when we break in a few minutes. I'm still a senior moderator, and trusted. But on condition I play by their rules, and don't do anything stupid. I add information to their database, and copy it to ours. That's all I do."

"Thank you. Two: What about the social media website?"

Mel continued, "At best, that's a can of worms, and there's little if any safeguarding. What there is, is to prevent paedophiles from outside getting a hook into the children on there."

"And Mohammed uses this as a recruitment tool?"

"It is quickly proving to be his main source of finding new underage girls, and occasional boys."

Isabella said, "Being online, and mainly hidden from adults and police, it is proving to be far safer than recruiting out on the streets. But the same pattern repeats once a child is hooked. A meeting is planned, and the children are inducted in the tried and tested manner. Taken to houses, plied with drink and drugs. Within a week, they are a part of his paedophile circus, and operate mainly from home to begin with. Later they are snatched by the SS into the 'care system'."

"Recruitment from schools continued I suppose?"

"Yes Bilty, it grew quickly, and has spread outwards. The catchment area is now larger than Greater London, and don't forget, Mohammed has people working in other cities, such as Manchester and Birmingham. His aim is to cover the country, and by and large, he is succeeding."

"So, any child, anywhere, is vulnerable."

"Yes."

Bilty became subdued, but his wife asked, "Isabella, The Forced Adoption website you mentioned. May I see it?"

With a nod, Melanie replied, "Sure. I'll bring it up now. I wish there were more people like Mister Ian Josephs trying to expose what is going on, and offering the type of support families in distress need."

Candice spent some time looking at the website, before asking Melanie to send the link to her email; her phone bleeped moments later.

Meanwhile, Bilty put his thoughts in order, and updated his log.

Bilty:
Personal Journal:

Notes:

1. The move to online sourcing of underage sex girls should have been obvious in this day and age. That I, and most others never considered it, is of major concern, regards our thinking and comprehension of the problem at large. In hindsight, it is such an obvious move, and much safer, unless hacked.

2. That there are people standing up for the rights of these unfortunates, be it family or child, does them great credit. I fear there are far too few of them.

3. Isabella has alluded to the money made, but I still await reliable figures.

Isabella

Bilty followed on from his last note. "Isabella, do you have any reliable figures? I need to know just how much money is being made, and by whom."

"Yes Bilty, I'll come to that now. I'll present our initial findings, because we did not discover full details until much later. Several years later in fact. Also remember, all these organisations were growing larger, spreading outwards like canker."

Chapter 27 – Breaking Free

With the assistance of my girls, I eventually came across the monthly and annual running costs for the current and last fiscal year, in the deputy's office. The figures were far higher than I imagined: rent, business rates, staff wages, insurances, certifications, food and welfare. Excluding planning permission for the extension and refurbishment, this amounted to outgoings of several million pounds per year.

I considered, "Some of this will be offset against tax, but without the full bookkeeping, I can only guess. It should be safe to assume the business in generating in excess of twenty million pound profit per annum. That is, just this care home."

You would presume we were taking great steps forward, but we were not. The money trail went cold with such instruments as shareholder dividends, bonus awards, and donations to and by charity's. That's not to mention indefinable claims for supposed and probably spurious expenses. Whilst these were alluded to in the files, there was nothing of any substance. I concluded matron was keeping the juicy information away from the premises, and retaining only the legal minimum.

When we returned to Melanie's room, she loaded up the information we had discovered, but the mood was of anticlimax. As an idle thought, I compared this to Mohammed's scam. We had well over one hundred girls in the operation, but I surmised that only two-thirds would be active on any one night.

We talked about the figure, and all agreed that three-quarters was nearer the mark. I reasoned that to be eighty-four girls. My team agreed with me, including Zoë, bless.

However, we also knew that many girls still out in the community also did tricks for Mohammed. Although we had met many of them in passing, we had no reliable figure to work with. We knew from snatches of conversational exchanges, few were as sexually active as we were on a daily basis, but if taken over an entire week, or better still, a month, their greater numbers pulled as many tricks as we did, if not more.

After a rather strange discussion, we finally agreed the operation included another ninety girls per day. We knew the standard charge was fifty pounds per girl. We had also discovered the hosts bought their drugs and alcohol from a central source—another of Mohammed's scams. That was something else we would look into. What better cover for running such an operation, than a under an Islamic front—after all, everybody knows that Muslims do not drink or smoke. Right?

I could never dismiss that idea, but there was zero proof, only our suspicions. My mind returned to the calculation, I simply discarded the premise, and rounded my figure down. I did the maths in my head, and came up with figures quicker than Zoë could write them down. Melanie tracked me with the calculator on her computer, and I was correct every time. That did not surprise me, but the others were in awe.

It went like this: 165 girls per day, x 5 clients each per day = 825, x £50 = £41,250, x 365 days = £15,056,250 pounds per year. Tax Free!

Melanie concurred with me, and the room was filled with silence. We stared at each other in utter amazement. Finally, we had begun to join the dots. Mohammed was making over fifteen million, tax free, in cash, each year. Just from us!

[Bilty: "Your figure is correct. Jesus Christ! He was making that much money. It's unbelievable.."

Bilty shook his head, but Isabella replied. "Those are conservative figures from this care home, only, at that time. It is larger now. They charged one hundred quid per client for age eleven and under. They had other care homes. I'll do the maths later, but think very large sums of tax-free, untraceable cash. I'll continue, while you catch up."]

Now we all knew this was not about sex, but money. The proof was in the figures. We, our young sex, were just a necessity of the job. I broke the spell by adding, "Don't forget of course, there are also Mohammed's special assignments, like when he relieved Alice and I of our virginities. Frog also [laughter]. Underage virginity sells for ten-Grand.

"What else is he into? Knowing him, he will mark-up two thousand percent on the drugs for an end user—I know about that stuff. Regards the alcohol, that is probably smuggled into the country, or stolen to order. Remember when a lorry-load of cigarettes went missing, and we ended up being given boxes of them. Mohammed is working scams within his scams, and making a fortune out of us."

Progress we had made, but despite Melanie's computer skills, we had to admit hitting a brick wall in our attempts to expose the whole rotten barrel of divisive, subversive intent and corruption.

I had become good friends with Vijay, and he was a decent and honourable man, even for a Muslim. I was indebted to his kindness. One day we chatted and he said, "I, and many other small shops buy much of what we sell through a wholesaler related to the larger family. Hussein Brothers, owned by Mohammed's Uncle, Usif."

We all played the circle game for half a year, and I was nigh-on sweet-sixteen. I was also cramming like mad for my final school exams, the biggest test of my young life. I was not taking the standard examinations the plebs did, but a higher certification called a Baccalaureate. This was most important for me, and for my future prospects. I also had other reasons to get out of gaol as soon as I could. I needed to drop out of the Muslims' orbit and re-create my life anew.

I worked on the deputy first, and got her full support. Next was matron, a more difficult obstacle. Zoë and I still had sex with Sir Richard often, and I planned to speak to him one day, when the time was ripe. Zoë was by then sixteen, and I was but a month away.

I had taken over supplying all of the girls Sir Richard enjoyed, a sort of specialist P.A. What I needed to do was extricate Zoë and myself from the care system at the first opportunity, and for that I needed Sir Richard. Theoretically, girls leave care at eighteen years old, but most usually approaching their seventeenth year. Why? Because they need our berths for new, younger girls.

I wanted out the day I was sixteen. I had a plan, but spoke to the team first. "I take it we are agreed that Mohammed's ploy of offering our girls a top-up or other treat has worked awfully well, regards the recruitment of new girls to his social website."

I waited for their response, and to a woman they agreed. Melanie spoke up, "In the first six months over twelve thousand kids have signed up, and it is becoming ever more popular as word spreads. I have identified about one hundred of them as paedophiles surfing for victims. However, Mohammed has his fingers on that pulse, and I tell the chief administrator of my suspicions. This keeps us well in with them, and they suspect nothing about our intent."

Satisfied, I pressed on, "So what do we need? We need information, especially regards the way Mohammed's operation works. We need to follow the money, and to our girls this is worthy of payment. I propose using the money Mohammed gives us to pay the girls. They must be utterly discreet. If Mohammed gets a whiff of this, he will kill us all!"

I did not for one moment think that he would, but I stated it as fact for the record, and dynamic impact, something else I was mastering in debating class. I said, "We need information about other care homes, and girls in the community. We pay on results, and any viable information is run through me first, before I decide on appropriate payment. Zoë, Mel, this is for you to organise and delegate. Billie, you are to choose the girls in first instance, and be wary of ones like Geraldine, because I have never completely trusted her, nor her clique."

My team agreed about how much money Mohammed was making out of us, but we needed to prove it with actual, referenced, and documented figures. We were lost within a rabbit warren, and the only way out was to follow the money-trail. The new plan worked well in parts, and intermittently in others. I expected nothing else.

I began staying late, and later at school, so I could keep up with the academic work I was being required to do. It wasn't until I began to focus solely upon past questions, that I found my equilibrium.

I spoke to the deputy head one day, and stated, "I need to become a resident for a week, so I can focus completely upon my revision."

She again probed me, but I wrote it off to distractions within the care home. Her eyes hovered over me for some seconds, before she sanctioned my application. I got my wish, and paid cash, something they were not accustomed to.

With the aid of tutors, I worked out the pattern of examination questions, and once I understood that, I knew which areas of coursework to revise most diligently. When they arrived, the examinations were monstrous, but I held my own, and knew I had done well. I stayed at the academy for two-weeks, barring a few night-errands. A precedent had been set. I needed to change my life, and I needed help to resolve my future. It was time to put my plan into action.

I requested a meeting with Sir Richard, and found myself in the boardroom of an eminent, international jewellery company. I was giving an ad hoc presentation to executives and departmental managers. Miss Constance was keeping minutes, because my presentation followed a scheduled strategic International Group meeting.

I had been asked to attend the same day, and within hours, so had little time to prepare properly. It was a tad off-putting, and scary at first, which was Sir Richard's design of course. He was testing me.

I began by laying out what I hoped for. While I addressed the assembly as a whole, everyone was aware my words were meant for Sir Richard alone. However, I rose to the occasion and said, "Ladies and Gentlemen, thank you for allowing me this opportunity to express my thoughts regarding the future of us all. Know that I plan to better myself, regardless of the current circumstances I find myself domiciled to endure. I hope that in the process I can assist you all as well.

"Sir Richard, you are aware of my predicament. I have just finished my initial schooling, taking a Baccalaureate, in which I consider I have done extremely well. I wish to continue my schooling into Sixth Form, again taking the International Baccalaureate.

"However, some of you may not be aware that my home life is 'difficult', to say the least. My aim is to kill two birds with one stone, and return to the Newbury Academy for Girls next semester as a residential student. Not only will this dislocate me from the intrigues of my current home life, but also allow me to dedicate myself to my studies in a convivial environment.

"My problem is, that in order to effect this change of personal circumstances in time for September, I need the support of a respected outside influence. Let me make one point clear, I am not asking for money. I am asking for credibility, something an appropriate letter from a company such as this would afford me."

Those gathered spoke into the round, considering points and querying their Company's level of commitment, should they decide to support me. They were talking about my future as if it were a business proposition. Their design to make me feel even more uncomfortable almost succeeded, until I remembered debating class, and in the process, adopted a new mindset. I stilled and listened intently to the discussion, noting points I would address, when it became my turn to speak again.

Debating is a class or club posh people devise. Its aim is to culture discussion, and promote the arts of persuasion and public speaking. It is mainly an extra-curricular activity, but one I had become fascinated by over the course of the preceding years.

The rigour was simple, we were given, or took potluck with a subject, and had to expound our views, whether we believed in them or not. It is a bit like political manoeuvring, or a barrister in court. I quickly learned that the views expressed were irrelevant. Becoming a good public speaker, and winning each point in dispute was all-important.

What mattered most was that I learned to argue my point in the most rational and engaging manner. I felt I was initially losing my proposal, until my mind-jerk turned it into a debating ploy.

After due consideration, Sir Richard responded by offering me a lowly position. "Sir Richard, with all due respect, I am not here to seek a menial job. Let us all be extremely clear upon this point.

"How much better would you all be served in the future, if I were to continue in full time education." I countered the points they had openly discussed, and from my notations, parried them one by one.

"What about your commitment to the Company?"

I replied, "New recruits to the Company need to be educated to a higher degree. You need the best people working for you."

I did not name myself as the benefactor, it was implied. Business people appreciate the finer points of dialogue.

After at first feeling turgid, my words took on a life of their own, as I endeavoured to envelope the ensemble, objections evaporating as my considered reposts hit their target. The tide subtly turned in my favour. Sir Richard was looking quizzically at me, a small but indefatigable smile toying within the corners of his eyes and lips. I could read him well. He was judging me, and was impressed.

I moved on quickly. It was like a game of swords, Epée if you prefer. We used words instead of blades, but the fighting, and feints were just as close and demanding as a rod of pure steel, our mental prowess to espouse or expunge at a will.

I dealt with the present first, "With no disrespect intended, the leading lights of this great Company are generally mature. While I know younger staff are regularly recruited, where is their commitment? Who will form the cadre of the next managerial level, after your day?"

Without overly embellishing what I promised on a personal level, I got the clearest message across, that by backing me, the Company's needs would be supported for years to come. This was my legacy.

I spoke over objections without regard, and suckered them with my punch line, "Suppose I were to dedicate my life to this Company's well-being? I am clever enough to excel any subject that will assist your long-term plans. I need your guidance upon which reading areas to specialise in.

"Most companies have a problem with high staff turnover, the brilliant leaving for pastures new at the first opportunity of advancement, usually more money or promotion. What if, by your show of loyalty in me, today, I repay with my loyalty to this company for decades to come?"

I departed the room with a deep look into every person's eyes, and a flick of my hair. I left the thought to hang. Miss Constance took me outside to await the verdict, and rounded on me as soon as we were out of earshot. She congratulated me on a brilliant performance. Apparently, she thought I was a natural. She bent in to kiss my cheek, and I swung my lips around to meet hers. The merest brush was fleeting, but palpable. She did not blush. Her cheeks turned the deepest shade of pale, before she voiced an excuse to turn her head away from mine.

I needed a drink, and a stiff one, neat. Instead, I was called back one minute later, and I got the support I needed. There was a proviso to volunteer, that is, without pay, for work experience over this and the next summer holidays.

I was grinning like a surrealistic feline, and feeling on top of the world, my world at least. I sauntered towards the seated, spread around the long table and said, "Thank you. Know I will not disappoint your faith in me. When do I begin?"

"Now." Their beaming smiles made my day. Miss Constance guided me outside. She gave me a wish list as I left, and squeezed my shoulder in feminine connivance. However, her eyes did not meet my own, but drifted with inner disgust, or perhaps longing, to dwell on my lips. I could have done so many things to her in that moment, but I liked her a lot. Instead, I blew her a provocative kiss, and left her to unravel her own inner demons.

With my future settled, Zoë and I searched for weaknesses in our prey, and looked at ways to use them. Regards matron and Mohammed, that meant following the money-trail, of which we still knew little of any worth. In some ways, understanding financial apparati is similar to driving a car. People don't just sit behind the wheel and off you go. First, you have to learn how the device operates, followed by how to use the controls, before driving it.

I took Sir Richard up on his offer of internship, and he delighted to indulged me, like he would his favourite niece. He did query why I wanted to work in accounts, and I told him, "I want to understand how money works."

Accounts are very boring. They are all about columns of figures that need adding or subtracting. This was not what I had imagined, but I endured. I learned quite a lot about balance, surplus and loss, plus spreadsheets in the process. However, the people were quite nice, and some would answer my more probing questions.

To Sir Richard, I guess I was providing cheap holiday cover, and I was of course, readily available for those times he needed release and companionship from the stresses of his office. It was inevitable that we were drawn closer together.

I also took a vocational summer course in therapeutic massage techniques, not ones of a sexual nature I might add. It added to my skills as a personal services provider. Nevertheless, by hard work and application, the team accepted me, and to the point, I was invited to attend their monthly get-together one Friday near the end of August.

We walked to a nearby pub, and that was when I discovered they liked to let their hair down on occasions. It proved to be a good night, even if I did have a client obligation later. I waited until they were merry, before I got talking to the two most senior, and they were qualified auditors. I asked them about financial swindles, and how to hide and trace the flow of money.

They laughed at my presumption, but indulged me, the apprentice of their art. Bit-by-bit, I began to get a handle on how money flows, and the ways it can be hidden, diverted, or manipulated. They were talking internationally of course, but some of the things they said had a lot of relevance for me. I stayed to finish my drink after their wives joined them. Once they had ascertained I posed no threat to their men, I spent time with other colleagues, before I made my excuses and departed.

By chance, my education continued, especially during the last week I spent in the department. The junior of the pair remembered my interest, and took to breaking the monotony of his day, by showing me several legal instruments that could be used to alter tax liability, or hide money. This was what I was after, and we became friendly as a result.

I was learning how the vehicle of finance worked, but still could not drive it myself. However, I knew what the controls did, and what to look for within the world of Direct First Care UK. I went over what we had already discovered with Melanie after the weekend. Pieces of the financial puzzle fell neatly into place, but although we progressed, we still needed direct access to full files to prove anything.

With summer fading and my new life about to begin during September, I took a week off with Zoë. We went to Cornwall and walked the beaches, swam in the sea, and did normal things. Our week was cut short by the demands of our burgeoning business, but we treasured those few days of normality, the first either of us had experienced for more than half of our young lives.

I became a border at school several months before I officially left care. All I had asked Sir Richard to do was offer me legitimate cover, so I could fund my own schooling. Don't you know, he paid for it all, and even got me a luxury suite to boot in the Sixth Form House 'A', or Alpha House as they called it. I in turn paid for Zoë' schooling.

I had broken free from the merciless Muslim oppression, and I managed to take Zoë with me. We celebrated our liberation that evening, and finally, our lives changed for the better.

Bilty

"I am gobsmacked, Isabella. I. Nobody ever looked at, never mind added up the money. But you did. Why did the press, the police not do the maths? This is horrendous, and puts a completely different complexion on the all of this."

"Doesn't it, Bilty. And Mohammed was working with four care homes, not just ours. They were all getting bigger. I doubt your maths can keep up. And this was happening all over the country.

"But we delved deeper, and the scams got bigger. Eventually we uncovered the all of it, before I went to Burma. Since then, nothing of any substance has been done about it.

"Candice, I need this book published. I need to expose the all of it.

"I'm sure we could all use a break, but I'm ready to go on. Genie, bring us suitable refreshments. Mine's a large, strong, Bacardi and cola."

Bilty:
Personal Journal:

Notes:
1. Isabella is special, and clever. She had decided to learn about finance, in order to understand how her enemies were using the system.

After a very short break, she resumes.

Chapter 28 – Private Investigations

Isabella

At the care home, we had procrastinated about many forms of reprisal, and gotten nowhere. Within my rooms at school, Zoë and I talked quietly about poisons and slow loss of bodily functions. What mattered was the suffering of our victim, his or her death remaining merely the inevitable consequence of our actions. It was the realisation and hoped for atonement for their sins, that drives the female, abused.

With only hatred and ourselves to give us away, our plotting matured. However, we determined to remain intangible, as if a part of the ether. We worked with all our hearts and sensibilities to perfect the art of murder. We knew we would never be discovered if we were clever. All we had to do was use the system against itself.

Unfortunately, the new system embroiled us. Given her lack of schooling, Zoë became accepted as my official Maid in Waiting. She attended some junior classes when she got bored — even Maths. She was not bothered much, no more than she could handle. By trick or treat, befriending, eluding, or punching, she made friends. She also recruited a couple of girls for our business. The first was Sybil, and a few weeks later Fiona. It was a small beginning, but a step in the right direction.

Whilst I was revising and taking additional prep classes, Zoë got to understand the alien world I lived in, a world of school that had for too long been denied her. Educated she would never be, but streetwise, the pick of any litter. I valued her worth higher than any other in the school. She joined the school Judo team, and quickly rose through the ranks.

At the beginning of our time there, she had signed up for archery and Clay Pigeon Shooting. These were not technically run by the academy itself, but by a couple of outside associations that used school grounds and amenities. The proviso being, facilities were available to sixth form students; the best had gone on to win Olympic medals. I ribbed her at first, until I tried it myself. I loved the revolver, while Zoë preferred a pistol. She said, "What's wrong with the pistol? Why don't you prefer it?"

I smirked, "It has no charisma, and after murdering someone, you would need to 'police-up' your brass casings. Mine are still in the chamber, so I'm away from the scene at once."

We were rather good with the guns, competitive, but the lethal arrows fired our maturing imaginations the most. At last, we had the weapon we needed within our grasp.

I loved the Long Bow, it was just so me somehow. I imagined being some modern day Robin Hood, a Cavalier or feminist righting wrongs and giving back to the poor. My imagery of daring acts of derring-do never did leave me.

To my side, Zoë was a Cromwellian character, stout, robust, and down to earth. Her crossbow was a far more needful weapon within the urban jungle we faced, it just didn't have the magnetism I preferred.

I became quite accurate over fantastic distances, well, two hundred yards at least. Zoë was one with the crossbow, and deadly within fifty feet. We took all the weapons classes, of which some involved taking a fuller event like cross country skiing. Fortunately it didn't snow often. I was accurate on the long-range obstacles, whilst Zoë was best at reactive short stuff. Like a mortise and tenon, we fit perfectly together.

Acting as my Maid gave Zoë a lot of freedom, and she still ran our operations in the City. Zoë met Billie several times each week, and also ensured Sir Richard was happy. There were a few other well to do clients we also maintained. We had the best and worst of both worlds.

Our plans coalesced over several weeks, but in the end, we had to admit we needed expert assistance to action our retribution. Melanie was the obvious choice, because we needed computer skills that all but the finest hacker or professional would never discover.

I got busy with schoolwork, leaving other concerns with Zoë. Melanie arrived at school one Sunday, and we were soon talking animatedly about our plans for revenge.

I had class to attend, and during the interim, they devised a plot to register Judge St. John Smythe with several child-sex websites, and flag it to the authorities. All they required was access to his home and computer when nobody was aware.

I liked it, but argued that to plant or manipulate evidence was wrong, and brought us down to our oppressor's own level. I mean, only the Bussies and SS stoop to such depths, and we had a higher moral code to follow.

I was convincing, but knew I did not have their full acceptance. I began with Right versus Wrong, but made my point stick by changing these to Good versus Evil. We knew the Evil existed, we had to expose it, not create a parody of self-sanctimonious deceit.

Melanie was first to agree with me, as experienced nerds would easily tell when the files were put onto the computer, and we would have exposed our intentions for no good reason. All we would do is alert our enemy to our existence. Zoë saw the reason also, and so we decided to discover what was already on the Judge's home computer.

How does one break into somebody's home? We didn't even know where he lived. Melanie said she would find out, and after dining in Kingston Town, she left in a regular Kingston cab I paid for. Two days later, I received an email from her giving us the Judge's address. She had tracked him down via his wife's charity work, having followed her interest in working to assist disadvantaged children. Her link to Direct First Care UK was highlighted, and appeared genuine.

Zoë and I talked our plan through, and we decided to break into the house and check her papers thoroughly, in addition to going through the Judge's computer and files. My best friend spent several days reconnoitring the house, a large, rambling building in the suburbs of Reigate. Her final report was most discouraging.

The house was heavily alarmed, although several people had regular access. One was a daily cleaner, and another a gardener. They also had several large dogs that were left in the house when the owners were out. The Judge was away most days, but his wife stayed mainly at home. We concluded it would not be easy to sneak in unnoticed, especially as neither of us had previous experience of housebreaking.

It looked as though we were thwarted before we had even started. Zoë was persistent, and went back the following week, as she was unknown to the occupants. Her plan was simple, to knock on the door and plead for some casual work. Knowing the old bat professed to be heavily into helping youngsters, we agreed it was worth a try, and we worked on her cover story the weekend prior.

To cover her identity, she chose a fictitious name, and bought a cheap and old mobile from a second-hand shop. On Monday, the cleaner denied her admittance, so she went back the following day and waited until the cleaner left for lunch. This is what she told me that evening, "I rang the bell and waited ages. I knew the old bat was in the house, but she took her time in answering the door. I was about to give up when I finally heard the catch unlock.

"I did as we discussed, feigning hunger and asking if there were any odd-jobs she needed doing. I could tell she was very religious and worked the Bible angle with some success. She questioned me at some length before accepting my cover story, but dashed my hopes by saying she needed no assistance that day.

"This gave me a small hope, and I left her with my new mobile number, telling her I was available whenever she had need of an extra pair of hands. She thanked me and told me she would keep the number just in case. She even wished me luck, and I quite liked her.

"I started to make my way back to the underground railway, but kept wondering how she could be mixed up in her husband's intrigues. I sat on a roadside tree stump and thought about it, because she certainly gave me the impression of a caring person, and not one remotely interested in procuring underage girls for sexual purposes. I looked around and realised the leafy, suburban community seemed a million miles removed from our world of care homes.

"By chance, I caught the glint of a car bonnet preparing to leaving her drive, and immediately started walking. I slumped my shoulders and waited until I heard her car draw near. I straightened myself, ignoring her approach, and went down the next drive, giving the impression I was trying every house in the neighbourhood. I know she saw me, and again on her way back from the shops, where I did the same thing at a different house.

"I had almost reached the same shops when my mobile rang, and it was her. She asked, 'Are you free next Thursday? I need a hand to clear out the box room'".

I replied, "Oh thank you. You are wonderful, what time do I need to be there..."

I high-fived Zoë and could not stop myself congratulating her. At last, we were almost inside the house. However, the waiting took its toll on our spirits as the days dragged slowly by. This was amplified on Wednesday evening, when the woman called to say something had come up, and asked if they could reschedule for the following week. Zoë fielded the call in good nature, but her disappointment was obvious.

Zoë's mobile rang again during breakfast on Friday morning, and we both knew who was calling, as I was the only other person to know her new number. By chance, the regular cleaner's mother had been taken seriously ill during the night and she would not be at work. Mrs. St. John-Smythe was in a quandary, as she had a party to prepare for, and asked Zoë how soon she could get there. Yes!

We were in, and I paid an extortionate amount of money for her to take a cab to the end of the road in question. Zoë was shattered when she arrived back late that night, but she had made a good impression. She had to go again on Saturday and help prepare for the party. I called David and asked if he was free to drive her, which fortunately he was. I also arranged for Fiona to cover her eminent weekend clients.

The party turned out to be some sort of club meeting called Inner Wheel. Apparently, this was the female version of the Rotary Club. I was at dinner the next day, when Zoë called from her regular number to say, "Issy, you won't believe this, but I was almost rumbled.

"Misses 'Sinjun', as she likes to be called, asked me to stay late and return early the next morning, and asked me where I was living. I had no answer and tried to think quickly. I was conscious she was staring at me intently, and thought I had blown my cover. She said, 'God forbid sweet child! You are not sleeping rough are you?'

"Unwittingly, she had given me my answer. I shrugged my shoulders, hung my head, and nodded. I made as if to cry from shame. Anyway, the upshot is, that I'm ringing you from what they call a gazebo, which is a luxury cottage at the bottom of their massive garden. It is quite nice actually. Hold-on, somebody's outside. Must go. Bye"

She called me back after I had returned to our room. "Issy, the Judge came to visit me. He was always disinterested in me, in the house, in front of his wife. This was reversed when we were alone together.

"That slime ball is a sexual predator, and had his wife had not called him, he would have taken me, willing or not. He disgusts me."

The man I hated most in all the world, the same man that took my virginity, raping my best friend. How could it get any worse? I tried to put my emotions aside and comfort her. I insisted we call the whole thing off, but Zoë would not renege on the chance we had to expose him, and finally get the hard evidence against them we needed. In the end, I agreed that she should fuck him, but only if there was no alternative. I hoped this impending rape would show results.

I met her at the local shops the next day, and she seemed fine. I gave her a camera to record whatever was to ensue. She made me laugh. I had missed her more than I wanted to admit, the truth be-known.

I did not see Zoë for the entire week that followed, although she rang me with regular updates. Apparently, the cleaner's mother was in hospital, and the woman had been excused from service until a week on Monday. This put Zoë in a great situation, and in time, she entrusted her way deeper into the household. She also got a cheap line on vodka from a local shop, and was happy, as far as it went.

The judge took her on Sunday afternoon, and she videoed it all. Unlike me, she was able to fight back. The recording looked like the grooming and rape of a minor, which is what it virtually was.

The next day, she managed to get sight of his computer when he logged on one morning before work. She also looked at his court files and managed to scribble some notes. He seldom used his computer, at least when Zoë was around, and all his personal data, as far as she could determine, was preserved in hard copy papers, and not digitalised.

I rang Melanie, and she sent Zoë a trojan that would allow her back-door access to the Judge's computer. It took several days before Zoë managed to load it into his PC. I was sure we would get great results, but although the man had several password protected folders, they were all concerned with Rotary Club business or court files. There was not a single hint of child-sex on his computer, even in erased files or browser cache. We were stymied once more. It appeared his only indiscretions were of the flesh, paid for with hard currency.

Zoë enjoyed her week, except for fucking the Judge every other day, or whenever he could get it up without his wife's knowledge. Misses St. John-Smythe had talked to her about her charity work, and Zoë gained the distinct impression she thought her support work was doing only goodly deeds for the unfortunate. Zoë was convinced she knew absolutely nothing about her husband's dalliances.

The woman called Zoë a few times more, but in the end, we decided to lose the sim card and keep the phone. We had all we could get, so it was of no use to continue the ploy.

I had put distance between our present lives, and our former ones in care. After all the horrors we had endured for so many years, I wanted it all gone. In my vanity, I had lost the connection between my own worth, and that of true friends. It was self-protection on my part.

Melanie proved me wrong. She came back to me the next evening with more information. She had copied every file of worth off the Judge's computer, and taken several hours to go through them thoroughly. She had checked his surfing history, and drew a blank with any sexually orientated website, there was nothing there.

On the other hand, Zoë had come up trumps regarding his business interests, which showed he had great influence over his wife's charitable works. Melanie had also garnered two-thirds of the Judge's online Bank login, but the last set of numbers had eluded her, until Zoë gave her their daughter's date of birth. Bingo!

Melanie printed off statements going back several years, and until the record began. It would take her some time, but she was already tracking the flow of money, which she would present to me later for deciphering. My fist pumped the air in release!

Although this was not the result we had been hoping for, it was something that in time would prove extremely useful. We needed to unravel the transactions and work through them. I was not especially thinking aloud as I breathed into the phone, "It's a shame we cannot do the same with matron's computer."

Melanie heard me and said, "Why not?"

I stared at the phone, and muttered, "Why not indeed. Melanie, could we get Mohammed as well?"

She replied instantly, "Of course we can, all we need is to set the latest Trojan in place, and I will have full access, at least for a day or so, or until the anti-virus software catches up."

It did not take a day or so to set up. In fact, it took us most of the Hilary Semester to access matron's computer, but again it appeared she kept all the really sensitive material backed up on hard-copy, offline. We could get nowhere near Mohammed's computer, unless we got lucky. I knew he was tech savvy and a nerd—another holy grail we sought.

[Isabella: "Bilty, unless you have any questions, I plan to continue. This is a preamble to what is of great interest, coming up next. However, I must put these pieces of the puzzle in place."

"That's fine Isabella. I have few notes on this section. Pray continue when you are ready."]

Chapter 29 – Revelations

The months passed into the next academic semester, and all too soon I was swatting for exams once more. Under the international baccalaureate, I was studying the mandatory six subjects on a par with A Level's. Although perhaps the content was not quite as deep, especially regarding the three minor subjects. Nevertheless, all six were much broader in scope. We were required to do a lot of independent research, and also had to prepare for an extended essay, as well as study world literature, and the theory of knowledge components. These all help prepare students for University.

I have an excellent memory, but was drowning under the sheer volume of work. This was brought sharply into focus when we had to write an essay for an old mock examination one day. I listed the main components required, and wrote it finishing well ahead of the clock.

As I read through, I realised I had overlooked one important argument that should have been included far earlier in the piece. I wrote it as an addendum, but presumed it would not be marked. Unlike computer documents, hand-written examination answers cannot be inserted into the original text. Subsequently, I remembered a couple of other things that would raise my mark, so added them at the bottom.

We had to hand our papers in as we left class, and I hung back to submit mine last of all. The deputy Headmistress came in before we had all left, and stood aside to watch, while she waited to speak to Iron Britches in private. I put my paper on the pile, and said, "I am sorry, but the subject is so broad I overlooked some related points and had to add them in at the end, instead of where they should have been. I am unhappy, because there is so much to get my head around."

The teacher looked up and smiled, which was always a bad omen. She said, "Then you better stop cluttering up my classroom and get to work, this time revising properly."

I shrugged and wandered away disconsolately. I was surprised when the deputy said, "Come to my room at break time, Isabella."

I went dutifully as instructed, and she bade me sit and tell her what was troubling me. I explained, "My memory is brilliant, but my problem is planning what to write before I began. The questions vary in subjective, and I need to identify what is, and what is not relevant before I began writing."

She smiled knowingly and said, "I thought as much. Other people's minds are strange places to visit, as you are no doubt discovering. You are studying English Literature, and sometimes you will be asked to compare books, authors, or even specified content, such as opinion. I will give you a tip, although please bear in mind, it is not for everyone, nor even the majority. I just have a feeling it may assist you.

"I use mind maps, spider diagrams if you prefer. Take the book's title as being the focus, and put that in the centre of a piece of paper, and draw an oval around it. From this radiate distinctly coloured main themes, lines, as being branches of a tree. These could be according to the main plot, subplots, and also include what the author is trying to say to the reader, what is the point of the book."

She showed me how to define these further into twigs, and leaves, marking each with a main word or clause my memory could remember. She even had some examples, and I realised what she was doing. She next drew lines from two subplots that interconnected, onto a separate diagram, marking another progression in a combined colour, as a branch, and worked that down to twigs and leaves. What she had done was make the diagram three-dimensional. It was a memory failsafe.

The deputy's method worked well for me, and although it took time to plan, once complete it reinforced my overall understanding in a much deeper sense. In future, I was able to picture, or draw the diagram on scrap paper, and select the relevant points needed to answer the examination question. It became very easy.

My examinations that early summer were important, but not finals. They consisted of lower qualifications and internal checks on progress. My exam technique was steadily improving, as I became more used to the stress they manufactured as a sideswipe.

I kept focused on the main objectives, and paid lesser attention to school orchestrated distractions. Many of the girls did not, and did worse than they should have done as a result. Being clever is not everything in life, how you use that knowledge is what matters most.

Without distractions, I got my best ever results at school, and made it into the top five across all subjects, for the first time ever. Later, the deputy Head congratulated me personally on a good year's work.

After the frenzy of exams, the summer recess came as a complete shock. We had nothing to do, and nowhere to go. I spoke to the deputy Headmistress, who allowed us to stay until the school closed. This gave me a chance to get on with my summer homework. I booked us both back in again for the following year, the one that really mattered. The deputy tried to probe me as to why we wanted to spend so much time at school, but given my background, she accepted I was more cast adrift than any other girl. She understood, if up to a point.

Once my holiday assignments were finished, we took a few days off, going down to Brighton. David collected us from Saint Pancras railway station when we returned, and we duly arrived outside Sir Richards's offices. I was due to begin my summer internship.

Miss Constance was waiting for us, and already prepared to take us on for work experience. I assisted in accounts and human resources for two weeks each, as holiday cover. Afterwards, I spent the rest of my time in Projects, even being given a small one of my own to manage. It was fun and I learned a lot.

Zoë was tried as an office junior for one week, but that didn't work out. After a talk with Sir Richard, she was moved to security, where like me she covered for staff holidays. She excelled in that environment, and they were sad when she departed.

While I was preoccupied with the business environment, Zoë was doing something equally useful, learning to drive. I knew she had been taking lessons for several months, but I was surprised when after intensive instruction, she passed both her car and motorcycle tests. I was destined to do the same, but with my overriding commitments, it took me a while longer. We celebrated her passes in fine style that evening.

Those weeks flew by so quickly. It seemed I was just settling into office routine, by the time we were due to return to school. Miss Constance gave me a glowing report concerning my work placement, which Sir Richard signed-off on, before inviting us both for dinner on the last Saturday evening.

It was like old times, and we stayed with him until breakfast. Later that day, Zoë rode proudly back to school on a trials bike she had purchased, while David took her bags with me in the limousine. I was using him, but in between times we shagged. We both experimented, and got very good at having sex: it's an art you know.

Once back at school, I threw myself into studies, while Zoë began targeting girls in the school. Being an all-girls school, interest in boys was disproportionate. The school was largely drink and drugs free, so the inmates' tolerances were low. We were recruiting girls for our own business, and by using our first-year converts, it became much easier. We introduced the "Hello Kitty" stuff again, and trained Fiona, to take over from us when we left.

That year passed by in a flash. My rage quieted, schoolwork mounted, and we were still servicing our elite clients at weekends. When the chills of winter approached, Zoë bought a car, and this allowed us a great deal more independence.

I took A Level's that fall. The additional qualifications would give me a stronger hand for University application. I completely switched off from everything after Easter, and did extremely well in my final exams.

That would turn out to be our last semester in school, and again we went to work for Sir Richard during the summer. This time I worked in finance, where at last I learnt how money flows, both nationally and internationally. I was good at it, and realised how we could track our prey. Zoë covered in security again, and kept in touch with our old friends and haunts.

I got my examination results at the end of July, and needed to share them with somebody. I called a number I had not dialled in some time, and was greeted enthusiastically at the door later that afternoon.

Sophie was looking a little older, but welcomed us both. I simply had to tell her my results—I got a Distinction for my IB, and already had four A's and one B+ at A Level. I had provisionally been accepted by Oxford University, but finally chose the London School of Economics (LSE). We had a great evening, and I repaid her all my school fees plus a bonus, adding as cover, "My boyfriend is very rich."

I would not let Sophie open the surprise envelope until after we left, so can only imagine how she felt. She was now quite wealthy, and my financial debt to her repaid in full. I could never repay the emotional one: For what is the cost of True Love?

That was a sort of Goodbye. My life was moving on. David was waiting with the limo, and Melanie scooted aside as we took over the rear. We enjoyed that summer more than any I can remember, before the dark clouds of personal reality streaked our skies once more.

Sir Richard was supportive, once he realised just how dedicated I was to making something of my life. He advised me on which courses to take, and his Company even sponsored me. He also ensured I got a couples room in Grosvenor House (Private) Halls of Residence. Everyone presumed Zoë was my partner, so we were left alone, which suited us just fine.

I thanked him the next time we were alone together, something he brushed aside. However, his eyes wandered to stare into the distance, as if trying to discern distant memories. In time he spoke quietly to me, his attention focused inwards as his true self was revealed.

"I can never have children. No doctor, no treatment can ever fix this. I am, and always have been sterile. Well, I have an extremely low sperm count, and most of those that are alive, don't swim right. That is why I never use condoms. What is the point?

"Regards my wife, it is a business arrangement, although we remain true to each other in public. It is basically a mutually beneficial sham. Her family are very well connected with mining raw gemstones in South Africa. Diamonds. We made our deal many years ago, and we remain contented with it.

"I have no idea how my predilection for young girls began. Perhaps a psychologist could unravel the cravings of my disparate sexuality, but I cannot. I have to live with it, and ensure I cause no undue harm. You and Zoë were my first, and I know it was of your own choice. That matters. I never did pursue that competitors daughter. It was wrong of me to even think, let alone suggest such a horrible thing."

I held him close, as he tried to explain the unspeakable. His drives, urges and desires. In the end he found words I could understand, "I was rejected in several proposals of marriage, when my fiancées discovered I could never father children. With one I loved deeply, we discussed adoption, but I always knew it was not for me. Others saw me as a way to make money, and one even tried to blackmail me. I grew to mostly despise the conniving bitches.

"Sexual rejection, or scams by marriageable women, became the norm. I needed children of my own, and by chance I found you."

His words held on the breath between us, before he admitted, "Isabella, you are like a daughter to me."

He cried profusely, and I held him close as his tears of what might have been, washed his conscience clean. Soothingly, I said, "I give my love to you freely, because I want to."

His eyes flooded again, this time in mutual respect and deeper understanding of what makes a man, a man. He held me so tightly, and for that instant, we became one.

I said, "Nowadays there have been great breakthroughs with IVF. Conceivably one of your good spermatozoa could be implanted into an egg. Perhaps one of mine?"

He stared at me incredulously, and gulped. The moment shattered when his mobile rang. He glanced, and put the call on hold. He looked me deep into my eyes, and said, "Thank you, but let's think on it first. It would be my dream come true ... but there is no need to rush into it. Let's wait until we are ready. I love you."

With that, he threw the bedcovers aside and answered the call. He looked back from the doorway, our secret to keep, and mouthed the last words he said to me, as if repeating them for absolution. All too soon he was gone, and soon was I, our sharing complete.

That word 'Love' had reappeared in my life. I knew what I must do. Before Uni began, I went back to Manchester to see my mum. She no longer lived at our old home, and nobody knew where she had gone.

I went to see dad in prison, and he was overjoyed to be with me again, if only for a few moments. He looked older, much older than the ten years since I had last lain eyes on him. It did not matter, I was thrilled to spend time with him again.

He told me spiteful neighbours and continued media attention had driven mother from our home. She was back living with her parents, who needed help around the house. I went to see them the next morning, and wished I hadn't. I still loved her with all my heart, but her tears flowed and she held me too tightly, much too often. She wanted to know everything that had happened to me, but what could I tell her?

I implied I lived with Sophie all the time, and had gone to a top school. When she learnt I was studying at the LSE, I became her idol. She wanted us to meet regularly, but I could not do it. Too much had happened to me in the meantime—Like Pooh-sticks cast unto unknown waters flowing beneath a bridge, times had changed for both of us. The murky flow of destiny had pried our lives irrevocably apart. By the time our vessels reached the other side, as if in a delta, her stream of life flowed one way, and mine another. I was no longer the innocent little girl she remembered. I was now my own woman in my own right.

I left with a heavy heart, knowing it would be a long time until I saw her again. That was the most brutal result of my domicile. The one woman who was central to my being, was no longer the same one I loved. The harshest cruelties of life had changed us irrevocably. We were both, by then, somebody else.

Social services were entirely, and utterly responsible. I would demand recompense, my pound of their flesh, like that Anthonio forfeits to Shylock, from each, and every single one of them.

Bilty

Isabella said, "Bilty, if you don't comprehend anything else, understand this. Sir Richard is not a sexual predator. He is a victim. He retains my greatest respect, because I went with him from choice. There was zero coercion. Zoë?"

"Yes. Same here. He's a lovely man, but too good for me. Anyway, I know who his favourite is..."

Zoë larked about, bringing laughter, as Isabella became the focal centre of her playful jibes.

I found the whole thing appalling, unfathomable. I made my notes.

I remain at a loss to explain why Isabella and Zoë do not consider Sir Richard to be a paedophile. He most certainly is. I shared my discomfiture with Candice.

"Bilty, I love you, but this time you are so very wrong. Trust me. With Sir Richard, it was not about sex, but about emotions. Same for Issy and Zoë. Have you so soon forgotten about consent? That matters to a woman you know. Level your rage at the grooming gangs, who denied these girls consent. They were forced to become unpaid prostitutes, for their master's financial benefit. And as we are learning, the girls were used and abused without humanity to make it so.

"Here, your job is not to judge, but to document for the record. You are the best investigative journalist in the UK, so investigate. Deal with the facts as presented, check them, but don't pass judgement on what you do not understand."

"I will do as you suggest. But I remain unconvinced in the matter. Regardless, I will do my job. Onwards!

"Isabella, you weren't serious about bearing his child?"

"Yes. I still am. It's just that I'm not yet ready to be a mother yet. I think? But maybe next year..." She left her words to hang.

Chapter 30 – Daniella

Isabella

After the regulation of a formal school, University life was so free, and being in the heart of the city was fantastic. I had expected our lives to be inundated by the intoxication of higher learning, but in fact it was our past lives that came back to haunt us later that academic year.

Both Fleet Street and The Old Bailey — The Central Criminal Court of England and Wales, are just along from the LSE. We took to hanging around the bars the journalists used, in the hopes that some media type would take an interest. We had to be most careful in what we said, but finally we met a journalist, whom I will call John, for no *bona fide* reason. He took us seriously, very seriously.

He was a columnist for a broadsheet newspaper, and a busy man. However, he guided and worked with us as directly as he could. In time, we finally managed to put something quintessentially coherent together with his adroit assistance, and Melanie's computer skills. We were all ecstatic at first, but over time, the onerous and overpowering amount of data we had amassed almost overwhelmed our valiant attempts to hit back at our oppressors where it could do maximum harm: Court. There was simply too much of it.

Remember how revenge works? Prosecuting our prey in a court of law, and exposing them internationally, fitted our criteria of retribution perfectly. This was not an area John was expert in, but he offered us a personal introduction to his friend Ian Josephs. We had already discovered the man's website, but now we had direct contact.

When we returned from our meeting, Melanie followed some links we had been given, and called me over. "Issy, you won't believe this. Have a look at this online report [R 30.1]. It's about a ruling by a senior judge, concerning a Staffordshire father who posted footage of the SS kidnapping his child, and he exposed the SS personal details online. Issy, the article is all SS bullshit, but read the comments below."

I was flabbergasted. Others were also trying to fight back against this iniquitous system. Melanie pulled up another browser tab and said, "I found this link site [R 30.2 - since removed: Strange?]. Also, check out Article 12 [R 30.3] of the UN Convention on the Rights of the Child. John was spot-on."

I read the short summary, and was horrified. The SS had broken every dam clause in their Nazi-esque quest to steal children from loving parents, and stick them in care. My mind was working, when Mel hit me again, "How does this [R 30.4] article fit into what you just read, Issy?"

I read the short tale, and nodded my head. "Social services do think they are god. When it comes to interfering in children's happy lives, their only concern is to make life as difficult and unbearable as possible, both for the child and parents, including the greater family concerned."

I read more links from online newspaper pages, astounded by the treatment of an American woman [R 30.5]. The follow-up [R 30.6] article made a more compelling judgement of the level of care the SS purport to bestow.

Although I reeled momentarily under the avalanche of information, I quickly recovered, because this represented life as I knew it. Life as every girl in any goddamned care home knew it also.

Our man from the press advised us to organise the testimony from girls who had been, or were currently in the system. He was convinced that once other victims came forward, they would speak out.

John was not wrong, and he, with Mr. Josephs legal insight, became our guides. The latter introduced us to a list of independent lawyers who would fight on the girls' behalf, for money we could afford. Nonetheless, the process seemed to take forever, and could flounder upon one girl's mood of the day, like precious China dropped shattering into pieces because of a soapy finger-slip.

Our targets were clear: Mohammed, Asif, three ex-Social Services managers, now matrons. They were all in league with each other. The umbrella organisation was called Direct First Care UK.

The rot extended to The Crown ~~Persecution~~ Prosecution Service, plus: barrister's, lawyers and solicitors. The Family Court judges were up to their balls deep within the mess of it. John insisted we look at the experts brought in to testify against the victims, our parents, and us.

John left us with a folder, and it made horrific reading. Many of the so-called experts did not even have proper qualifications. What they did have, was complete sanction by the Family Courts and the SS. The worst was that the best hustlers were making a ton of money, by providing the 'Expert Advice' the SS needed to work the system, and betray families.

The local authority and SS Duty of Care for us, which they were supposedly honoured to uphold, was in fact a rigged house of cards. To us abused young girls, they had zero honour, just our uttermost loathing and contempt. Their bank balances swelled upon our enforced and unpaid prostitution. We made our plans, and time moved on.

Perhaps because I had taken the International Baccalaureate, as opposed to standard qualifications, I had settled swiftly to life at University. I knew the reason why I was there, to get the best Degree I could. Others were still treating the place like a holiday camp, and hoped to find time between parties in which to excel in their chosen reading. There were not many of them, but they were a distraction I had no time for. I cut myself off from all of them, as well as from the outside world. I was doing what was expected of me, what I expected of me.

Life skipped several months and people's thoughts were turning to Christmas. I was drowning under the weight of projects, and revising like mad for my module examinations, when everything came to a head.

One of Billie's greatest skills was people. Even though I had seen little of her over the previous two years, Zoë had kept in close contact. Billie was the sort of person who was never in someone's life continuously. Instead, she brought pools of sunlight into people's days in dappled jets and bursts. She was never constant, but always within easy reach. She called me out of the blue one day, and told me her youngest sister had something important for us.

We met shortly after. There was a new girl, and she was 'hot'. OK, she was only nine years old, but she had everything a pervert required: Curly golden locks tumbled gaietously around her perfectly framed face, highlighting her bewitching blue eyes, and such an innocent look, even her snapshot affected me greatly. I was informed, that when she opened her mouth, it was only to bestow promises of candy forbidden. I knew I had to save her. She was completely naïve, recruited online.

Frog agreed with me and was determined to save her from our shared fate. The year before, one of the newer trusties in another care home had tried to save a girl. The trustie disappeared, and was found some days later, bloated and face down in a canal. The Coroner recorded Death By Accident or Misadventure. We knew it was murder.

It proved tricky to arrange, but I finally met the new girl two days later in secret. Ellie had helped her to escape from the care home, and told her where to go. Billie met her on the streets, and saw her safely to Camden Town, where Frog joined them.

I had to finish an important assignment that day, and was later than planned handing it in to the LSE submissions desk. However, that timed nicely, as it allowed time for Dani to get to Camden Town. We converged on an international fast food outlet and got seats upstairs.

Zoë's eyes kept darting to the stairs until finally the girl walked in, unsure of where to sit in the alien world. Melanie beckoned them over to sit with us. The girl stared at her, but Frog and Billie followed close behind, ushering her to our table.

Frog seated the girl and said to her, "Dani, you and these girls are going to become the best of friends. Do you understand?"

Daniella was gorgeous, and despite her initial timidity, she became outgoing and full of laughter. Her confidence grew as our meal progressed. Frog whispered to me, "Isn't she just your perfect?"

I choked on my food. My stomach was doing contortions, and a madding wind rose within my mind, howling: "Nooooo!"

I stared in disbelief as Zoë leant towards her and said, "I bet you are eleven years old."

The girl replied nonchalantly, her teeth full of burger, chips, and tomato sauce that dribbled down her chin, "I'm nine-and-three-quarters. My birth day was during the last full eclipse of the Sun, so that makes me extra special, so there."

The girl continued eating, oblivious of the quickening sands of peril she was already mired so deeply within. Frog said, "Daniella, Dani, I know you are so very special. When we get back, look around at all the girls you live with. Most of them are of little worth. Do you know you are the only virgin in that building?"

Dani looked around with eyes wide in wonder and said, "See, I told you so. I am really special."

She stopped eating and her brow furrowed with concentration. We all waited for her next words, which followed after she had thought them through, "I know what a virgin is you know. It is like if your name is Mary, and you give birth to baby Jesus. That's why she's called The Virgin Mary you know."

Her thought immediately evaporated as she tucked into her burger treat, and asked for another drink. My eyes flared in alarm and instantly locked with Zoë's. Dani had zero idea what virginity actually meant, Christ or no Christ.

I whispered to Zoë, "Mary was eleven years old when she fell pregnant, twelve when she gave birth to baby Jesus. Joseph was in his thirties."

"So the Christians were also paedophiles."

"Yes, but don't forget, life back in those days was harsh, survival of species the order of the day. Christianity has moved on, Islam has not."

Before the meal finished, I discovered there were five weeks until her Birthday. I had important exams to revise for, and module submission deadlines, all due within the next three weeks.

I already knew Mohammed liked to toy with his prey for several weeks, before selling their virginity to the highest bidder. Then raping them himself afterwards as a perk. I reasoned this would be the same, and we were determined to prevent it.

The first two weeks flew past, as I tried to revise through the drink and drug addled nighttime nightmares, and a never-ending stream of clients as the festive season approached. It was our busiest time of year. I was always wrung-out each morning, and chasing assignment deadlines each night. I also had to protect Daniella, but that could wait.

I did the only thing I could. I focused on my college work, and shut myself far away from the world outside. I reasoned that in my life, I had only one chance at this degree, and it mattered so much to me, and for my personal future prospects. When I was done, I would rescue Dani. Unfortunately, when I withdrew from my recluse, times had moved on.

I returned to civilisation knowing I had done well. I caught up with business, and was impressed everything was running smoothly. I asked about Dani, and there was silence. Eyes turned away from mine, and I knew the worst had happened. Her birthday was still a couple of weeks away. The bastards had taken her early.

I needed to see Dani at once, but Zoë and Billie stopped me, placing their hands on my protesting arms. Ellie came to their aid and said, "I saw her afterwards. She was a shell of her former self."

Melanie added, "She's now a part of the system. Even if you managed to see her, to talk to her, she would be so out of her skull she wouldn't know you were there. Remember how it was for us? Nothing she said would make any sense."

I wilted and cried. My shoulders drooped as the awful truth sank coldly into my core. I had failed. Not only the promise I made to myself. I had failed that most precious girl. I also knew my friends were correct. Daniella would by then be the hot new chick on the block, and in constant demand. I thought of her, and wept bitterly.

Daniella was nine-years old.

I berated myself in front of my friends, and chastised myself for putting my exams before her welfare. I was determined to get well drunk and stoned when Frog squatted before me, and held my hand. Her words were quiet and measured, "Kitty, it was a tragedy. We all tried to prevent, but Mohammed was too wily for us. We have all cried, and cry about the fates of all the other girls.

"Do you know that while we failed in one way, we succeeded in another? Come with me Isabella, and I will show you."

Others supported her and urged me to my feet. I felt like a leaf hurtling from end to un-end, enduring the turmoil of an autumn gale, the only thing to look forward to being the drab, desiccating cold of winter. I came to rest in Melanie's room staring at a dark screen. It matched the dank blackness of my mood.

The monitor came alive. Mohammed led an almost ten-year-old girl into a hotel room. I recognised the room at once. I had been there only once, for my own deflowering. My anger re-ignited spontaneously, and I began to rise from my seat. Billie said, "Think it through Kitty. Now we have real evidence, in addition to Frog. Like her, we have everything on record, including the grooming, Rohypnol, and rapes."

I was only mildly mollified as Melanie took up commentary, "Mohammed, Asif, they do not trust us fully any more. Sometimes they lie or change plans at the last moment. This is what happened with Dani. There was nothing we could have done about it, save dialling 999 and hoping for the best.

"Well, we all know far too well how the police deal with Muslim serial rapists, don't we girls—they give these paedophiles a warrant to continue raping us as they please, and chase easy targets instead, like the pensioner Grandpa riding his push-bike two yards into a pedestrian zone, before dismounting in safety from road traffic. Come-on!

"Dani was on her second date with Mohammed." Melanie started to pace the room as we all waited on her next words. Her fist crashed into a filing cabinet, and she winced. The pain was enough to elicit her words, as yet unspoken, "We all expected this to be one of several grooming dates. After dinner, he took her to get high. Later we followed them to a hotel. Zoë and I had been tracking her on the streets, determined to identify all of Mohammed's haunts. This one was a derelict factory. They left early, and we followed the route, as we had live feed from Dani's bag. That was an incredible idea of yours, Kitty.

"Zoë parked at the hotel he took her to, and we instinctively knew what he was up to. She went inside as soon as they left reception. I followed moments later and took the next lift to the floor they went to. I lost a bit of footage, but soon got it back when the lift doors opened. I didn't know which room they went into, so Zoë took a peek at the guest register. She managed to get the keys for the room beneath the one they were in, and we went inside. This is what we recorded. It was one of the most horrendous experiences of our lives. What could we do? Watch..."

Mohammed was true to form, and virtually repeated what he had done with Alice, Frog, and me. I had to give Melanie her due, because she had adapted the tape into a finished video. She managed to zoom in on the bottle contents Mohammed added to Dani's drink. The label read "Rohypnc..." Obvious this spelled Rohypnol as the label rounded and disappeared fully from view. It was as we had suspected all along.

I wanted to be sick as events proceeded, but remained with eyes glued to the screen. A sort of horrific fascination overwhelmed me, and I could not tear my eyes away. This was damning evidence, and it only got worse, or is that better? My brain was fried. Shock brought me fully sane. The one man I intended to execute knocked the door, and Mohammed showed him in. A colleague accompanied him.

Dani's mind was by then in a parallel universe, and whilst able to comply with what they told her to do, was clearly a dull-eyed zombie. The Judge dressed into his ceremonial robes of red with blonde horsehair wig. His associate dressed as Queen's Counsel (QC) in ceremonial attire [R 30.7]. They set video recorders to either side, and handed Mohammed a camera with which to record for posterity, close-ups of this most important of proceedings.

I sat forward in astonishment as the video continued, because Melanie was mixing in views from the new cameras also. She was seriously happy and said, "I searched for Wi-Fi feeds, and these dimwits had not the sense to password protect them, or turn them off. I got everything their cameras contained! This is where they keep some of their child porn."

I saw her smirk and probed her until she revealed, "Issy, there was a lot of it. Images, and videos of children being deflowered, most of whom we do not know about, yet. We have so got these bastards you know, up to their balls deep within virginal rape."

This compensation was small repayment to my heart, as my eyes were drawn with mounting dread to witness the events on screen. The Judge did not bother with foreplay, Mohammed had seen to that already. He lay on the bed in his ceremonial robes, and within seconds, their iniquitous coupling began.

The grossness of man revealed and reviled itself, as his face became a mask of ecstasy. She was forced to repeat the performance with the QC. Positions changed as they pounded, and compounded her innocence. She took far too much inside her and began to cry out in pain. Fortunately, the monster finished quickly, and before he ripped her formative cervix to shreds.

It was clear this was not the loving Mohammed sought. A fleeting image saw him head for the bar, and look back in disgust at the white men raping this almost ten-year-old virgin. I heard him say, "*alayhi s-salām*," and an indication of the depth of his inner turmoil.

I already knew this paraphrase was a corruption of the Hebrew expression of some millennia before: "*aleha ha-shalom.*"

Mohammed detested all Jews and Jesuits, and especially Christians. Yet he had no problem using the Prophet Muhammad's corruption of the Jewish phrase, and something all Muslims say many times each day. You have to wonder how wily the real Devil amongst us really is? "*Aleha ha-shalom.* Meaning: "Peace be upon him [her]"

Every time they say it, Muslims are using a Hebrew phrase. How quaint. That tells me a lot about their intelligence also.

This would be the same satanic, abominable entity that showed the entire Earth to Jesus Christ, and told him the World belonged to The Devil, but could be gifted to Jesus for a simple act of submission [The Temptation of Jesus: The Gospels of Mathew and Luke refer]. It sounded a bit like Bible verses Quran-Gate to me, but what do I know?

I will answer that question. I do know what is Right from what is Wrong. But, life is never black and white. It is made up of myriad, waterfall colours, sumptuous and indefinable hues, and shades of grey.

None of us are polarities. We are just doing the best we can that day. The scene before my eyes was a terrifying example of my inner moral and religious confusion. How could God exist, when he allowed monsters to rape me, Zoë, Dani, and all of us?

I looked away, but Melanie told me to watch. They were arguing about money. The legalese were adamant the price was £10, 000.

Mohammed countered with £10, 000 each, plus a bonus. They agreed at £20, 000, cash. I was stunned.

Melanie said, "We should post this on the net and let it go viral."

I retorted, still in shock, "We need to add a copy of the Judge's Court Order to the video."

Zoë said, "We got an angle on that yesterday. It is the same beak, Judge St. John-Smythe, who sentenced her in Family Court, to a life in care on especially shaky grounds. The QC in the video was at the Bar and his solicitor was acting for Dani. Talk about a set-up, a mockery of justice more like. These guys are choosing which underage girls they will fuck, and using Family Court proceedings to make it so."

I leaned to one side and whispered to Zoë, "I am going to ram a rocket launcher up his arsehole, and pull the trigger."

Zoë said, "Let me lube the grenade first so it goes in deep, very deep. One unexpected projectile deserves another, don't you think?"

My thoughts were crossing themselves in pieces, yet doubling interminably like a fertilised egg. I wondered if I was becoming schizophrenic, because I really, and I mean, I seriously liked the idea. Within the small evolvements and evolutions of my mind, I found a small pool of sanity, and with it came the will to go on. I was determined to purge this Judge, and his recalcitrant faeces from the history of creation. His entire being. But that story has yet to be told.

My friends managed to bring my mind back to the here-and-now. I watched the video conclude, with Mohammed fucking the girl twice, once with the lights on, and once after dawn. His brief display of genuine emotion was long gone. He got his rocks off and left, counting his money. We all made fingers of guns and shot him. Only I knew Zoë's intent—and as an adverse lift from tragedy, we laughed. We knew what we would do. He was a dead man, walking that day.

The video done, Zoë added, "We went in with a key card from housekeeping. Cost us a tenner, but we got Dani out of there, and took her back to our room to recover. Poor thing."

I had not noticed Melanie moving until she came back from a filing cabinet, holding a sheet in a plastic bag, "We took the bed linen too. I guarantee there is a lot of interesting and incriminating DNA on this."

I moved past my grief. We now we had real, hard evidence. My moods swung from despair, through horror, to exuberance. I knew we had the Bastard's fixed in our sights. We had a sort-of party after that.

In the days that followed, we should have let the video go viral. Instead, we worked to bring the case to prosecution. This is how it went: Acting upon anonymous information, police raided the Judge's home [R 30.8] and confiscated his computer. The press was alive with misinformation. The computer was completely clean, and yet we had contradictory evidence that digital recordings had been made during Dani's rape.

Melanie stated the obvious, "Only a fool could not see he has at least one other computer. What about the video's? None were recovered, yet we know he had to have at least one copy in his possession. He left the hotel room with it. Where is it now?"

We felt almost helpless once more, but we delivered a traceless copy of our video to the police, and even samples from the bed sheet. Although our semen samples were tested, the results stalled on a technicality, because there was no 'cohesive proof of the chain of evidence'. The results were not allowed as forensic substantiation in a court of law, as they could have been fabricated.

{Isabella: "Bilty, I have a serious problem here. Tell me how the said samples could be replicated on a hotel bed sheet?"

"Erm? The bed sheet from the same room of the hotel, plus the seminal fluid of the three participants. The blood of the girl and her secretions. That would prove extremely difficult to conjure. It is much easier to accept the fact as evidence."

"Yes. And those fluids would have been preserved in the mattress below. The vermin Bussies and CPS were zero interested in the crime, only in covering it up. That makes them guilty of subverting the course of justice. Correct? Dumbfucks!"]

The video was also discounted. We had sent them copies of our spliced film, and also full copies of each original. The edited copy we thought was most damming, was thrown out because it had been doctored. Sure, we combined it into one whole, so the truth was easy to see. The defence moved to disallow it, and all other video evidence because of this. The motion was accepted.

We had lost. Lost before we had even been heard.

We began to learn that once a legal precedent is set, it applies to all similar evidence of the said case in question, should the court wish it.

Would any normal person consider it wrong or right, for a Family Court Judge to rip a nine-year-old girl away from her family, just so he could in due course, take her virginity.

What he did was evil. We came to a strange conclusion. All British courts should have a primary duty to ascertain what is right from what is wrong, to discover the whole of the truth.

Within our personal experiences, we demanded the truth of any matter, when presented in a court of law, was the only interest of the court. Unfortunately, the truth of any matter is always neglected. Instead, prosecution or defence lawyers and barristers are allowed to tell lies in order to twist the outcome of the case. The court only listens to them, not often to the truth a witness is telling.

In Family Court, in utter contravention of Article 12 of the UN Convention on the Rights of the Child, the child victim, and parents are often expressly forbidden to speak. This is entirely at loggerheads with UN [30.9] and EU law. Those who make these decisions, need to be sent directly to jail. Instead, they domicile the child to a system that actually causes extreme mental, physical, and emotional abuse. Sexual abuse of extreme minors, the later virginal rape by some Family Court members would be a perk of the job, one should presume.

We were disgusted with the entire British care and judicial systems. They channelled us, abused us, and forgot about us. They deliberately covered their tracks under a mask of secrecy. We needed, demanded their support. Instead, its most prominent figures were allowed to rape us with impunity. Families were ripped apart so some old man in a red gown and horsehair wig, could rape our seriously underage virginity.

We were denied redress to the law of the land. Whatever happened to 'Putting Children's Welfare First' [R 30.10]?

Bilty:
Personal Journal:

Notes:
I am shocked to the core of my being, so is Candice. I have already heard how these Family Courts twist the truth, but know there is more to be revealed. What I cannot accept is:

1. That the rights of the child, and those of parents and greater family are brutally denied. This often ends in imprisonment, being the court's childlike retribution for challenging the system.

2. The heinous crime of the presiding judge committing the child to care so that he can rape her is unforgivable. Secrecy surrounding the court means he and other rapists get clean away with their crimes. Social Services are complicit in these rapes. They should all be sent to prison, and the key thrown away.

Isabella

Bilty turned to look at Candice, and after a whisper said, "Melanie, do you still have all this evidence. Could we be allowed to see it? The digital files that is, not the panties or bed sheet."

Isabella answered, "Yes Bilty. I was hoping you would find this interesting. Mel has already prepared a full copy for you. On the pen drive is everything, all our research going back years. It includes what other Muslim gangs have done. I'll take a break, but be back soon. Mel, if you would look after our guests.

"The memory stick if you please, Mel … thanks. There you go Bilty. More homework for you I'm afraid."

Isabella passed the device to Bilty, but Candice took it. "I better research this. It will add a depth of background to the book."

Mel added, "There are several folders on that. One includes all the online references I have found. Most are grouped and are up to date.

"I can open it on this computer if you wish, the background information should assist you assimilate all the facts and facets into a coherent whole."

Candice replied, "Thank you Melanie, but you get on while we take a look. I'll load it into my laptop, and give Bilty the pen drive."

Bilty

I became horrified by reports from other journalists, most notably Camilla Cavendish of the Times, who was followed by Andrew Norfolk, who continues the work she began. In the interim, others joined the fray, like Christopher Booker of the Telegraph. Unfortunately after several years of success, the courts have virtually gagged him. I also suspect the newspaper has been warned off from reporting similar in future.

The Jay Report was illuminating and equally damning. Only one MP took up the cudgel against child sex grooming gangs, John Hemming. Unfortunately he has since lost his seat.

I find the very existence of these gangs to be repulsive. There are so many of them, and the under-age sex ones are nearly always Pakistani Muslims. There are of course many more Caucasian, Christian paedophiles out there, but they tend to be loners, or small covert groups. They are not gangs intent on procuring hundreds of very young girls for sex, and never for prostitution.

Mel said, "Another hit the headlines [R 30.11], and the attitude of the leader is most disconcerting. But if you look at the pictures, you will see this was never fully investigated the first time [R 30.12].

"And where are the charges of threats to kill, threats to rape? The family were driven by fear to leave this country to escape. They feared for their lives, and the police did nothing until forced to years later. A gun was also used to threaten one victim, yet I see no charge relating to possession of a firearm. This is light justice, a slap on the wrist.

"In the first and last incidents, the police lost vital evidence, leading one to suspect they were in collusion with the Muslim gangs. They also ignored local reports [R 30.13] furnished by a whistleblower as early as 2005, as did all responsible aid groups in the region.

"I've compiled that large file on them. It began with Rochdale, twice, Rotherham [above] — twice, and again, then: Oxford, Derby, Preston, Telford and Stafford, Halifax and Northumberland, and Middlesbrough [R 30.14 – R 30.23]. When revelations at Teesside were released, the national press were so overwhelmed with cases of Muslim's grooming exceedingly underage girls, the details only made local newspapers. I find that disgraceful."

Isabella returned as Bilty stared at the webpages. He said, "This is horrendous. I cannot believe it, yet it is the reported truth of what happened in criminal court. We will both study this later at home. I've read as much as I can stomach for today. Candice?"

"Yes, same here, let's move on."

Isabella smiled conspiratorially. "Thank you Bilty, Candice. Now you begin to understand.

"Zoë, ask Vikki to attend, as we will need her opinion. I spoke to her just now, and she's ready when we are. Thanks.

"So Bilty, what do you know, personally understand about RAPE? We, have been raped tens of thousands of times, and I believe there are degrees of rape.

"What is of paramount importance, apart from the lack of consent, is the intention of the rapist, and in some cases, that of the girl. Listen-up. Sir Richard did not rape us, it was consensual sex, albeit for money. The Paki's raped and pimped us, and they remain unforgiven, even today. They raped us without consent. They used coercion and force, threats at least. Or like me, they drugged us and took us regardless.

"You now know they used us as chattels to makes millions of pounds of money. Cash. Mohammed treated our rapes with no concern. It was a means for him to make a lot of untraceable money."

At that moment Vikki entered, and Isabella said, "If your mind is now right, I'll resume."

Chapter 31 – Degrees of Rape

That same week I read a small thing online. It was in the States where an eighteen-year-old boy, already engaged to marry his long-term girlfriend, came under the spotlight. They made love for the first time. The girl was two weeks shy of her eighteenth birthday. Her father discovered them and called the police, a clear-cut case of sex with a minor. A minor cannot by law agree to sex, so the charge was Rape. The lad was imprisoned and put on the sex offender's register, that thing supposedly to track serial rapists who commit heinous crimes.

Just across the border, the next State had the age for sex set at sixteen. If they had done it in that State, nothing would have happened. Instead, the boy's future life was destroyed, and later the father of the girl admitted he had acted impulsively, and had made a grave error of judgement. You see, he realised the penalty far outweighed the crime.

I shared this with the others of my gang, and our debate about what constituted rape was re-ignited. Some argued the United States was a very different country to England. But the fact remained. The States treated an almost eighteen year old, as a rape victim, the same as they would a ten-year-old. The girl did not report it, her father did.

While we never reached a quantifiable consensus regards ages and all shades of rape, we did agree that there needed to be a sliding scale of sentencing, and many advocated degrees of rape, as with murder. We also agreed that if a junior minor [under thirteen] had sex, the case was extremely serious, should be fully investigated, and charged as rape — Regardless if the girl, or boy was in care or foster provision.

We all concurred, that if a child in Social Care reported a rape, the police had to investigate. That was vehemently supported for anyone under thirteen years of age. It should happen without referral to the SS.

A minor in British law is anyone under the age of eighteen, sixteen for age-related sex, with special provisions regards under ten. They are deemed to be incapable of making decisions of their own. Dani was nine. The Police, CPS, and SS ignored this. They should be prosecuted for wilfully failing in their duty, and perverting the course of justice.

Once we began talking about such illicit subjects openly, we found it was not so simple. Billie was the first to get us sidetracked, by focusing on the issue of consent. On this, we all agreed that the definition of consent lay entirely with the girl concerned.

Although Melanie agreed with us, she left us to mentally wrestle with a thistle. "This is all fine in theory, until you take into account, at what age a girl is able to decide for herself, if she wants to have sex or not? And what of the young boys that are raped?"

I replied, "The age of criminal responsibility [R 31.1] is ten-years old. Regards sex, a child under the age of thirteen cannot legally agree to sex, so the charge is automatically rape. Under thirteen is a watershed, as in law. They are considered to be children regards sexual offences.

"Notwithstanding case law, the SS turn a blind eye when girls like us are involved. Ask any sane person, how a girl of nine or ten years old, can make the 'life-choice' to become an unpaid, Paki prostitute. It beggars belief. Unless something else is going on? Yet, the SS state this as a fact of the girls choosing. It is not choice. It is coercion. It is rape!"

This drew intellectual divisions from us. While most of us agreed the current age of consent to marry was about right at eighteen years of age, sixteen with parental consent, we became embroiled with the age of consent to have sex. Many thought this was legally too high at sixteen - eighteen, except for homo's. But given our personal histories, that wasn't surprising. Some thought twelve years old OK, but the older ones tended to think fourteen, or fifteen--as [was] in Holland more appropriate.

The mood between us was genuine, but in a light-hearted and fun way. None of us were being completely serious, it was just a good laugh. Given my love of debating, I had to act as *agente provocatrice*, "Frog, you are adamant the age of consent for sex should be reduced to twelve years old. However, you also support marriage at eighteen. Didn't you tell me a few days ago that you wished you were still a virgin, so you could give yourself to your man on your wedding night?"

My observation certainly put the cat amongst the pigeons. Frog stood her ground and argued that both her highly conflicting views were correct. I thought she had dug a hole for herself, until she came out with, "Well, I see it like this. On the one hand is what you dream about, and in the other hand is what life has actually done to you."

I noted curious looks from Zoë and Mel. "So what you're saying in effect, is that the median is for marriage at eighteen, where you lose your virginity. However, because of what has happened in your life, you agree that the age to have sex should be many years younger. This is what I would term, life expectations versus personal experiences."

In the end, we agreed that our own personal experiences were not those of normal children. This brought us to admit a disturbing reality within all our lives. We were not normal.

Nobody in a position of authority would listen to our pleas for help. No one wanted to take action against our rapists. We were effectually cut off from normal society, and had been left to endure our daily abuse the best we could. I felt a mood of despondency about to settle, and knew I had to try to dispel it. "Why don't we ask the other girls what they think. We could put it to a vote, although it would have to be secret. Matron would have fifty-fits if she ever found out about it."

I had given us something new to do, and something that handled correctly, would be fun for all the girls. It took a month before Melanie was in a position to tally the votes. The consensus was a curious split.

Many chose ages eighteen and fourteen, for marriage and sex respectively. Almost as many went for sixteen and thirteen.

I had started something, and the girls talked about it often, but also for months, and even years after. It was interesting to note, that as the girls got older, so the ages of consent for sex they thought appropriate, invariably increased.

Zoë began a new theme. "There's also the problem with drink and drugs, say going out dressed provocatively, and get so smashed you can't remember anything. That is putting yourself in danger."

"But a girl has the right to do that, and not be molested."

"I agree," said Zoë. "It is still rape, but by a far lesser degree."

Vikki added, "True. But that's how I lost my virginity. I got so out of my skull, I didn't realise what was happening to me. That is my fault. It took me several years to admit that to myself. I put myself in danger. I was naïve to the ways of the world.

"My problem was, my rapist was a fit, hard-fisted pimp, who liked to beat me up. He kept me as a sex slave to do tricks, earn him money. I only escaped his clutches when he was killed in a turf war. By then I was in London and had nowhere to go. So what do you think I did to make ends meet? I needed to eat, find a room, and there were no paying jobs."

Zoë said, "The way the pimp treated you, is much like the care home bullies, and Paki's did with us. We had no freedom, no chance of escape. Many didn't go to school. We were sexual slaves. But the thing is, you were a lot older than us, more able to deal with it."

"I was just seventeen, and I was not able to deal with it. I felt utterly violated. I was forced to work as a whore, or suffer a beating until I fucked whoever. Having your life controlled by a pimp is rape. I had zero choice in the matter.

"Later, cast adrift on the streets of London, with nothing, except extreme hunger, I voluntarily sold my body to strangers. One reason I did so, was to repeat the enforced crimes against me, as a punishment to myself. I bet that sounds stupid, but it was how I felt: worthless. That was my choice. That was not rape, but the next best thing.

"I was forced to grow up quick, deal with my life, or die. Just like you girls. I'm glad I wasn't younger, but some of you were still at primary or middle school, and that's just plain wrong."

As our conversation of that day progressed, so Zoë stated, "Muslim, Pakistani rapists also seem to be above the law. The authorities allowed them to rape us daily with impunity."

We all agreed, and the conversation diverted, until Zoë brought us back on track. She insisted, "The supposed incestuous crime one of the other girls committed willingly with her father, was naïve by comparison to my own forced rape by my foster carers, and my daily abuse by the Paki's, both utterly against my will. Remember, initially it was anal and oral rape, as they were homosexuals. The police were forbidden by law to investigate, without the approval of Social Services. I have a big problem with that, and I was very young at the time.

Melanie put it into perspective. "I was first raped at seven-years-old, by my uncle. I knew it was wrong, but it felt nice. He was my mother's eldest brother, so it was family business. Some years later, this included my cousins, and the other uncle, also older than my mother.

"They were nice, but sometimes controlling. The younger ones began to bully me for sex, and it became rape. I don't class what my uncles did as rape. Does that sound strange? The cousins became evil for sex off me. They forced me many times. It wouldn't have stopped, but I got pregnant by one of my cousins, I don't know which one.

"That's when the SS intervened, and our family was ripped apart. My father, parents never touched me that way. They excommunicated the uncles and their families. But it was all too late by then.

"Regards degrees of rape? Yes there are several degrees. That rape of the American girl should never have been prosecuted as such. It was consensual sex by adults. That she was just shy of the official age is ridiculous. And as for putting the lad on the sexual offenders register, absolutely preposterous. It was fully consensual intimacy, by people more than old enough to fully understand what they were doing.

"In my own case, the rape by my uncle was consensual, in that I did not complain or tell anybody. I liked it. It was a new and forbidden game we played. But the continued rapes by my cousins were a degree harsher. They demanded and forced me. Neither uncle did, and apart from my naïvety, it was consensual.

"So, to protect me from that can of worms, the SS sent me to this nest of vipers, abandoning my protection. My life in care, as an unpaid Paki prostitute, a sex-slave let's be clear, is a thousand times more despicable, than what my greater family occasionally did to me. The result being, I was torn away from my parents, who never touched me once, sexually. Never. I don't get that part of the SS logic."

I had to agree with her. The crime of Rape makes no distinction between intent or consent. Only the actual fact of physical coupling, penetration, is admissible as evidence of rape, in a British Court of Law. Apparently, the law doesn't apply to Pakistani Muslims. We all knew we had been screwed up the arse by the SS.

Many people will state rape is rape. They are correct of course. Nevertheless, isn't that the minimalist view of those who have never been raped, or perhaps raped only once?

The first time we were raped, we all shared those same emotions, as does anyone who is raped. Female, or male, let's be clear. The self-loathing, the blame-game, the feeling dirty, violated, defiled. We were young children whose virginity had been taken. We were not adults. We were cut off from our parents, and left to deal with it ourselves. Usually our first experience was gang rape.

What about daily gang rape by ethnically and religiously alien males? Sexual slavery to the point it becomes all a child does in life. That is Human Trafficking, and demands a much harsher punishment, as does rape of those under the age of implied consent: Thirteen.

Billie stated the case of a Violinist who committed suicide, because a defence QC was allowed to interrogate her with lies she presented as 'possible truths' in court. I can only hope the woman's death comes back to haunt the haughty Bitch [R31.2].

Zoë said, "The lawyer made false accusations against a frail witness in criminal court, and the Judge condoned it, even though the witness begged him to intercede. The Bussies forbade her to seek counselling at any time since she made her complaint of rape, which she was forced to do at their behest. The female lawyer had no supporting evidence to back her character assassination of this fragile person. She laid into her deliberately and repeatedly. The woman denied the allegations, and pleaded for the judge to stop the tirade. He did not. Later, the witness took her own life.

"To my mind, the judge is a guilty accomplice to murder, and the female lawyer deserves to be publicly hanged for murder. They have no conception of what it feels like to be a victim in a legal proceeding, the Bussies also. Off with their heads!

"Why is it, so often within the realms of so-called British justice, the guilty are pardoned or handed soft sentences for sickening crimes, and the innocent, often the victims, are harassed by highly paid practitioners of law seeking to pervert the course of justice ... what of truth?"

I added sourly, "The reason is money. All they are interested in is making as much money as possible, for the least amount of effort. Few, if any lawyers have the slightest interest in their clients, or their professional codes of practice. They just want the money."

Zoë said, "Don't forget rape of children as a motivation, Issy."

We agreed, that if a legal person ever stated something in court, presenting it as a fact in cross-examination, by return, we demanded they be prosecuted for perverting the course of justice, if at any time, this was ever proven to be a lie. The legal profession needed to be above reproach, not active in letting the guilty go free, and imprisoning or murdering by suicide, the innocent: as is the current state of British law.

We already knew the answer regards Family Court. Guilty, despite being innocent. We had not been allowed to speak in our defence. It had already happened to virtually all of us. Sadly, this is indeed a fact.

I spoke into the pervading air of gloom, "I hope Criminal Courts are open to scrutiny, and not like the kangaroo courts that dealt with us."

Zoë answered me back quickly, "Well I for one hope that Mohammed and his gang of paedophiles are not allowed to speak in their defence. To me that would be justice."

A cheer erupted, but Melanie dampened our rising spirits, "You all know that won't happen. Criminal courts are open, and all defendants are allowed to challenge the allegations against them. You can bet Mohammed would have the best lawyers in the country fighting his corner. They would twist the truth to match their own needs. We all know this, even before the case gets to trial. Anyone disagree?"

Zoë answered the question instinctively, "These legal parasites are so far up the backside of the system, they believe they own it."

We burst out laughing, but after the joke was done, the truth of her words became the fact. Zoë for all her illiteracy was correct.

That night I sent a silent prayer, a wish to the essence, ethereal remnants of Frances Andrade. Our situations were markedly different, but the apparatus and central pillars of British justice [sic] remained uncommonly symbiotic, and essentially unequivocal.

UK is quite liberal in its views of underage sex without parental consent, as long as the children mutually experimenting with sex are of similar ages. The boy should not be more than two-years older than the girl. Ages sixteen and eighteen are also considered specific factors, particularly where the boy is concerned, but especially regards the girl.

This reads quite well, until you realise that judges, foster carers, and Muslims are above the law. So it appears, are Judiciary of the Realm. Not only was my own business booming, but that of paedophiles, it appears.

Bilty

"I will need to think long and hard about your assertion there are degrees of rape — Like with homicide you allude."

"Yes, First, Second, and Third Degree Rape. Instead of say manslaughter, we could use non-consensual sex."

Zoë butted in, "And of course, Rape by Misadventure."

We all howled with laughter. But her thinking was spot on, "Well, apply it to Vikki, or any females' drunken nights out on the town."

Vikki was straight in there, "Yes Zoë. I agree. That is what happened to me. My fault. I was too bladdered to get clear and safe; stay safe in the first place. Or even say, 'No'. It was rape, but I also brought it on myself. Yes, rape by misadventure is spot on, and the punishment should fit the crime. Nowadays they stick everybody on the Sexual Offenders Register, regardless if it was a misdemeanour or serious crime. That is wrong. That register should only include serious offences, or be graded.

"I my case, if it had been an ordinary guy, I doubt he would have remembered much about it either. Just my luck to get a mean pimp.

I added for clarity, "It reminds me of that case that's been going on, the footballer and the waitress. What crime was committed, and what should have come to court? Have you read the real details?

"The next day she complained to the police her plastic handbag was missing. That is all. The police coerced her into making a charge of rape. The CPS supported them. Now two out of three lives are ruined, and she is emigrating. This was rape by misadventure, and should have been treated lightly. All three were wrong. But was it nasty rape, or just drunken debauchery? Remember, she didn't voluntarily report the rape.

Vikki added, "Let's return to my rape. It wasn't all that different, but it was. My rapist did not stop because I belatedly said 'No', after the fact. Oh no. And that changes the degree of my rape. His intention was to rape me, enslave me, and sell my body against my wishes.

"To me, that is way more evil. Because of him, I was forced to endure rape by others. But, it is not as bad as what happened to you girls, and from such an extremely early age."

"Thank you Vikki. And that leads us very nicely into the topic of age. In the West, and as seen in tribal natives, the age of sexual awareness for a girl is generally taken to be puberty. Yes, same for boys, but it's the girls we are concerned with here. As a rule of thumb, this is twelve or thirteen years old; when they're old enough to bear children. In some societies, this relates directly to survival of species.

"In our own British society, under thirteen is the watershed as regards being able to make an informed choice about sexual relationships. If you are under thirteen, you cannot choose. Social Services are going against all asserted fact and case law. A ten-year old girl cannot make the lifestyle choice to become an unpaid prostitute."

Candice spoke up, "I cannot believe this. You have proof?"

"Yes, virtually every reported incident. Melanie?"

"Searching now: Rochdale, lifestyle choice, social services ... And immediately hits. Candice, I'll email you the links, and there are loads more, the Daily Mail [R 31.3], and the BBC [R 31.4],. There, sent."

Isabella stood to speak, "This is intimidation. And it is sexual trafficking. Let me be very clear on this point. These girls do not consent, regardless of what the SS say. If they are willing partners, then why do they try to report their rapes, as rapes to the police?

"These words are used by the SS as whitewash. This is only one reason why the girls are not allowed to speak out, or report their rapists to the police. It's an SS cover up for SS failings."

Isabella began a rant, but Bilty interceded, "Thank you Isabella. We will research and follow up the all of this. You have my word.

"The other question is, how did you became a Madame off the back of being a raped child. How does it sit with your personal history? What's your angle?"

"There is no angle Bitly. It was a wildcard chance threw at Zoë and I. It is not something I, we, ever planned for, or went looking for. But it offered us a way to keep the other girls, our friends let's be clear, relatively safe. Well fed and provided for also.

"But you do me an injustice. I am not a Madame by trade. I am a senior executive of an international jewellery company, one that supplies the trade. That's why I went to the Orient, remember.

"Zoë became my 'go-for', sometimes out East, sometimes here, or elsewhere in the world. Mel returned to Blighty, and supported my endeavours online. That is my work. Vikki runs this place on a daily basis, and she is damned good at it. I'll explain this place next.

Bilty:
Personal Journal:

Notes:
1. Isabella's point about degrees of rape is valid, and I will need to think about it deeply, and discuss it with my wife. IW may just be onto something in this regard. A campaigning newspaper may also take up the cudgel, so I will research and present an initial report to several broadsheets, and others.

2. The age of consent is a minefield, especially when put under an international spotlight. I personally doubt that most girls under fifteen years of age could make an educated decision about having sex. I know a ten-year-old cannot consent to being an unpaid prostitute. Isabella called that one out. This is denial of consequences by the SS.

3. I also partially accept her point that nowadays, virtually every sexual convict is put on the Sexual Offenders Register, even for minor indiscretions. This appears out of balance with initial intention. I am aware the offender's details can be easily discovered, but without reference to the crime committed. Unintentional indecent assault is classed the same as paedophilia, gang rape, and sexual trafficking.

4. They are different crimes, if crimes some are at all. So is the proposed rape by misadventure. A heady thought. I would not expect the man to be put on the Sexual Offenders Register for either crime, so long as it was a simple case of opportunism, or indiscretion.

Isabella
"I'll take a short break, then finish this for today. There's not much else to be said, except to introduce how I ended up here."

Chapter 32 – Super Escort Agency

I was probably raped by six thousand different Pakistani men before I was sixteen-years-old. I do not know the exact figure, but it is close, and perhaps on the downside. It is not the rape of my body I despise so much, but the rape of my childhood—salad days of growing up carefree and enjoying the discovery of life's simple pleasures and token treats with my family.

Daily gang rape was my life for the most important part of my childhood. It happened virtually every day. Do not ask me about rape, for I will tell you there are many degrees of intent. We continued to talk about degrees of rape. Melanie stated, "Prostitution is basically rape. I mean, girls do it with implied consent, but only to put food on the table, money in their pockets. Yet, it is they that are breaking the law. I believe prostitution should be legalised, and brothels, and be a taxable business. This offers the girls protection.

"Is prostitution just another category of rape? When a woman is forced into prostitution, if only to continue breathing, and not allowed any other choice, is that rape? My answer would be unequivocally, yes."

Zoë clarified, "I claim the right of profession as Prostitute—the oldest profession within any world dominated by men. Look anywhere, on any street, at any time of day or night, and even on Sunday's. You will always find a girl willing to sell her intimacy for cash."

Vikki chirped in, "We do not do it because we want to have sex. We do it to survive in this world, to fill our stomachs, if only until tomorrow. Is that so very wrong? To me, this is institutionalised rape.

"After a while, it becomes a habit, something we do--our job in life. It's a good job, and well paid, once you learn the ropes. These imbeciles in power are so stupid, yet the first to demand our services when they need them, willing or not. Like Mel said, why don't they legalise our profession, and admit that humanity is flawed. I have no problem paying them due tax, although I will administer Value Added Tax myself—That's personal, you know?"

I thought about Vikki, somebody who knew the difference between prostitution and rape. The difference is consent, for any reason, as long as it is not coercion. The simple premise that a girl invariably maintains the right to say either 'yes or no'. I reminded them of what Vikki had said after her later rape, when I lived with her and Sarah—she accepted the fact, protected her emotions, and got on with life.

Billie said, "I guess that's all I have to look forward to in life, being a prostitute. I could become a film star as well, just like you Kitty. Psycho's business has developed, and she now makes professional porno films. She lists her occupation as film director. She gave me an offer of good work, and it's well paid, if intermittent.

"You know, the adult film industry is the only one where women are the stars, and get paid much more than the men. Isn't that odd?"

I said, "No, it's misogynism. So, you gonna become a film star?"

"No. Well maybe. It'll put food on the table."

Melanie added, "Same here. We have no quantifiable education between us, so I have zero chance of a job in IT. What is there for us in life? We both have to leave care this year, and the deputy has already been pressuring me to begin my pathway plan. Apparently, she can get me a job on minimum wage as a shop assistant selling shoes. I'd rather be a prostitute and retain my self-dignity, and freedom."

Billie concurred, and we ended up talking about the futures of all the girls. They had both done tricks for me, and I told them we would look after them, and provide regular clients. I was already becoming aware that there were far more rich men looking for casual sex with late teens and early twenties, than those who sought only younger girls.

I told them both, "Press ahead with any pathway plan matron will sign-off on. Find somewhere to live, even if it's a shared room for now, and take any job offered. That gets you out of the system, and in the meantime, Zoë and I will build up our client base."

I confided with Zoë later that evening, and we knew we could offer regular work for both of them, but would it be enough to sustain them? It took me several weeks, but every time a client called to make an appointment, I ran through a pre-prepared script, first enquiring of any ways our service, or girls could be improved.

Most were satisfied, although one or two did reveal improvements we could make, which I actioned where appropriate. There was nothing seriously wrong with our service, but I discovered the girls from the Academy were better in the social situations some expected, while the care home girls were normally better in the bedroom.

I thanked them for their input, and spontaneously replied that we were currently instigating a training program. This appeased them; we prided ourselves on being proactive. A good whore needs to be most proactive, if she wants to increase her business.

Before each call finished, I added, "We have older girls, eighteen to twenties, with excellent credentials, and wondered if you, or others you know, may be interested?"

I did not dwell on the mention, even if it was the most important thing I said, I just left the idea to hang as I quickly finished the call.

I presumed I had failed. The phone did not ring, so Zoë and I looked at other ways of increasing our client pool. The following week I had a date with Sir Richard, and wandered up to his nearby office. I waited with Miss Constance, and she asked me why I was distracted.

I explained my dilemma to her, if briefly, and she pinpointed what I had been missing. She came right out and said, "Issy, you are one very special girl. Can you not see? This has grown beyond a couple of friends supplying a specific need. You now have your own business. Stop pretending this is still some part-time stunt for pocket money, plus shits and giggles. Admit to yourself, you are now running an escort agency.

Later, in the afterglow, I mentioned my idea of a super escort agency to Sir Richard, and he was supportive to the extent of saying, "Issy, these things take time. They do not happen overnight. I will put the word out, but first, you need a company name and a presence, a dedicated mobile and landline. Can you do that for me?"

I knew it was another of his tests, and agreed to do as he advised, and I did. Weeks passed and I was deep into one of my projects one evening, when the landline in my room rang. It had never rung before. I answered, "Kitty's Accompaniment services, how may I assist you?"

The male voice on the other end of the line introduced himself. "I'm Henry, and would like to partake of discreet female companionship this evening. A very good friend recommended me."

I left five minutes later. I needed to field this new risk personally, and before I committed one of my friends to servicing his requirements.

The meal was excellent, and the sex, engaging. He asked me for my business card, and I hadn't thought to make one. I pretended I was out, and promised to give him one next time. I left in the early hours with one thousand pounds in cash, and a repeat booking for a few days time.

I presumed everything was going perfectly, until after the next dinner, when we chilled with drinks in the hotel bar, before going up to his room. I had given him my newly printed business card. He drew it out, looked at it, and said, "Kitty, this card is boring. I know you are new to this game, and you, personally are excellent. Allow me to advise you about business, if I may be so presumptuous.

"You need to step-up where selling is concerned. What is this company name. Please, 'Kitty's Corral' is more appropriate. Men like straight talking. Instead of phone numbers, use a web address. Men may wish to dally with blue-eyed blondes who have a large bosom. Most marry brunettes by the way. If your girls are half as good as you are Isabella, know you have the makings of a great super-escort business. Make it professional, market it properly, or get out while you can."

I was shocked. I recoiled inside, whilst moving towards him physically. I placed my hand upon his and said, "Is it that obvious?"

He guffawed and said it was not, but added, "Kitty, if you want to make a success of this venture, you need to run it as a business. No half measures. I can recommend your services if you produce the website. Men of my standing require the utmost discretion.

"They also want to choose from a portfolio of girls. A short video introduction helps enormously, but nothing pouty or lascivious. Include an online booking form, and offer high-class escort services, never sex.

Keep it separate. All payments should be in cash, on the night. Your competitors provide this already, so let's say I am indulging you for a very dear friend, one who speaks extremely highly of you."

I knew he meant Sir Richard, but names were never spoken. I had much to think about, my future lay within those moments. What could I do, but call him out? I chinked his glass and said, "Bottoms-up."

He didn't miss my sexual innuendo, and ordered another round. As the waiter walked away, I put my pinkie in the corner of my mouth, and pretended to suck on it. In actuality, I was playing for time, time to think. The client's wishes are paramount, so I asked him straight, "Who would you like to accompany you to your room tonight? I do have several buxom blondes, but only one is natural."

As I said the words, I knew my bosom was smaller than his fantasy required, but this was business. I looked him in the eye and said, "I do have a natural blonde with green eyes..."

I left the thought to hang, weighing his intentions as he gauged mine. He asked me for her picture, and fortunately I had one, although it was not planned. I knew I had to get a lot better at business, and fast. I called Fiona, and despite her workload, she made it within the hour.

I left them in the foyer. As I watched the lift ascend that evening, I knew this was prostitution with full consent of the girl. Not rape. I smiled wistfully to myself, and made my way home.

By the end of the week, our part-time work had changed into an escort business. Melanie did the website for me, after she checked out all the competition she could find. All too soon, I was short of girls, not clients. We did not sell sex. We sold ourselves as the ultimate erotica-- demure, provocative, and unavailable—except to the select few.

Bilty

Isabella said, "Is there anything else? I feel we are about done for today, and it is almost dinnertime. You will join us?"

"Thank you. Yes please. Let me wrap up my notes first.

"So this is how it all began, off the back of daily and unpaid rape?"

"Yes Bilty. That about sums it up. It was a steep learning curve, but we created something that supports many girls. So no telling. OK?"

"You have my word."

"This was the first step, but there were several others, and a bit of luck. But that is for later. I'll be in the Raffles corner when you are done. Let's pick this up again next weekend. I've a busy week ahead."

"Same here. It suits me well. Candice?"

"Yes, admirable."

Chapter 33 – Forward Planning

Project Domicile
Interview: 09
Location: Fiddlers Court, The Oval, Holborn, Central London.
Time: 12:46 hours, Saturday, 28th October.
Subject: Isabella
Others Present:
Zoë, Melanie, Vikki, Genie, Candice.

Note:
1. We resume almost one week later, as both I and Isabella were busy. It seems she was in Amsterdam for much of her week. I ran checks regards her tale so far, and I also caught up with my backlog of work. Candice has picked up the online research, and is in regular contact with Melanie; that girl is a mine of information.

Ah. Time to begin again, and reveal the first tentative steps towards total revenge. All are relaxed, and Isabella takes centre stage once more. There is an aura about her, one that draws the attention.

Isabella
By the time we left care, we had each been raped more than once, for each, and every single day of our short lives. Imagine being forced by British Family Courts and people you do not know, into living that life. It was my life, and that of my few friends. Were we not justified in feeling deepest, bitter resentment?

It was gruesome, a violation of our right's to childhood, that had long since been replaced by everlasting and monotonous, Paki-rape. The sheer scale of our repeated rapes was horrendous.

My childhood should have amounted, accounted for far more, than to be used daily as a Paki fuck-toy. I hate the conniving brown-skinned liars, but I hate the British childcare [sic] and justice system that perpetrated this disgrace upon our young lives, even more.

To me, the system that supported our abuse was dastardlier, than those paedophiles that raped us, every day, for years without end.

I am not a racist, despite my rape by thousands of Pakistani Muslim men. That's not to say I would not be wary of any Pakistani male, but some were good to me, Vijay especially, and others. Their women lived a life of purgatory as far as I could tell, so I tried to maintain a sense of balance within my hatred. I still do.

It appears others did not. The media became a buzz with a series of killings. The sensationalism was way over the top, and credible reporting, limited. An outraged father had shot a Judge dead in cold blood. There

261

was a manhunt underway. The next killing was a solicitor, and the last was our linking clue, a psychiatric 'expert witness'.

Some days later, a bomb exploded in an office block, and several people died. It was a rare occurrence in the UK, so grabbed the headlines. What did not make the headline news was conspicuous only in its absence. Mel was the detective who eventually unearthed the real story. The powers that be tried to hide it, and we suspected press censorship, but the truth was out.

Mel pieced the true story together, "They were a family you know. The murdered judge was not any old judge. Oh no. He was a Family Court judge. The offices bombed were not ordinary offices either. They were the child protection department of Social Services no less.

"From what I can pull together, the father got so pissed-off with his family's treatment, that he took his revenge on them the only way he knew how. The solicitor and expert witness were involved in the case."

We all cheered. Finally, somebody was fighting back against this governmental secret society of child-snatchers and child-molesters.

Some days later, police were called to a terraced house. An unrelated report mentioned the 'parents' of a foster child, had been tied up, and the boy in their charge kidnapped. They were discovered several days later when concerned neighbours called the police.

The child was never found, his birth parents had disappeared, and the killer of the seemingly unrelated incidents we had already chronicled, was the boys biological father. The father's boat was discovered in La Rochelle some weeks later; the family long gone. Zoë quickly put together what had happened. She should have been a detective, because at least she had a lot of common sense.

Our frustration mounted, our inactivity, debilitating. The media and Bussies remained clueless as to what had really happened. That was, until we released something on the internet, and something else via a press contact.

Driven by mounting anger, Zoë and I plotted in private, wary of including others. We knew they all wanted to hit back at the system, but we wanted to protect them, if only from themselves. Our fear was they would do something stupid and end up in prison.

We became aware several girls were talking in groups, with the intention of killing judges, police, Muslim rapists, and other prominent figures. Over the days that followed, this included all of my cohort. I discussed implications with Zoë, before calling a meeting of us all. With inclusion came a flood of new ideas and useful deceptions.

Our main targets remained Mohammed and his Uncle, taxi drivers we knew had raped us repeatedly. Khan had physically branded Zoë: He would die. The matrons' in charge of all three care homes were more difficult prey, as were the offices that bred them in the first place, and any go-between we got a weapon's sight on.

The police were at best feeble, if not completely incompetent to handle such enquiries. After all, they only ever wanted to prosecute us victims; easy targets for bullyboy Bussies.

However, we did not know which people within the force were acting against us, because while the Bussies were always bullies, they had often appeared to be on our side — Before being over-ridden by a presumed, higher authority within the force. We decided to identify that source, and kill him, or her. We reasoned the ordinary police were so stupid, and afraid of Muslims, they'd never link anything back to us.

We continued plotting our bloodbath with the execution of all SS, CPS, and judiciary who were party to our abuse. I demanded the right to murder, Mister Ferdinand Aloysius St. John-Smythe, Family Court Judge, QC & Bar personally.

Our most important resource was revenge, and our second, information. We upload our own footage of Dani's rape and let it go viral. This time, Melanie and her computer would be central to our strikes. I had managed to get her a job in IT, working for an excellent webmaster, through one of Sir Richard's contacts. She was becoming impressively good at what she did.

Remember:

The Female studies her quarry, and acts subtly, before hitting her prey's bull's eye — like a female spider's conjugal visit, or that of a feral cat, she strikes without warning.

What if? Any male dominated 'Court of Law' would not, could not, give us young girls retribution — What of it? This time we would use the cunning of the Female, but using the 'Male means of war'.

One day we were out on the less travelled streets of London looking for specialised surveillance electronics. Melanie had researched what we needed, and we put the idea to our cohort. It was greeted with wild enthusiasm, and this was just the beginning of our true vengeance.

Melanie got the cameras and tracking devices she was after. The equipment cost us dear, but it was what we needed to give us the edge, and would preserve our anonymity during the war to come. Mel left to secrete our cache, and I sauntered back towards the LSE, to meet Zoë. We texted, and I met her on Drury Lane.

Zoë and I became so engrossed in our machinations of revenge. We did not realise we were close to Sir Richard's London offices, which we were ambling towards. It was late Friday afternoon and we had a dinner-date with him.

The big news was the woman now running Social Services was taking early retirement. She was the one that got me to dance Rihanna for her. She had already opened a care home with the assistance of Direct First Care UK, and begun to accept girls. Erin had been installed as the chief bully, which delayed her own pathway plan. I repeat, her pathway plan or life prospects, were delayed so as to suit Social Services shenanigans. I find that unacceptable.

Meanwhile, out on the streets of London, Zoë echoed my own thoughts by saying. "Issy, these girls are our friends, and without any structure to their lives, they will drift into prostitution and drugs. We have got to do something. Ellie is already out on the streets, and while we do our best for her, she is basically alone and vulnerable."

I pushed Zoë to see if she had come up with a solution. She said, "Well, apart from you, we have little education and are basically only good for DDF: Drink, Drugs, and Fucking."

"That's Paki misogynism for you."

"Agreed. If we accept that most of these girls will inevitably become prostitutes, can't we at least try to organise something safe for them? We already have more offers of business than we can cope with."

It turned out to be the same idea I had been toying with, the one Billie had mentioned. I said, "We'll need accommodation and a small office. I'll raise the subject with Sir Richard when the chance arises.

We weren't paying much attention to our surroundings when we reached the office block and went inside. David called out to us and we went to him. He warned us Sir Richard's wife was in the building, but she would be leaving shortly. We stayed with him until he left to take her to Heathrow. When the coast was clear, we were ushered up to Sir Richard's office by Miss Constance.

His dedicated PA buzzed us through, (Miss Constance ranked higher, and held a much wider brief). Sir Richard greeted us. "My dears, both as dazzlingly beautiful as ever. Do come in. Unfortunately, I have to attend a meeting, but I will be with you both shortly. Please make yourselves comfortable. Oh, and drinks are in the cabinet over there."

He was gone a long time, but we were fine and rifled his bar as we looked at some of his projects, between refining our formative business plans. We were not going through drawers or anything silly, just looking at what was left in plain view. Zoë had been leafing through some property brochures, and commented on the astronomical prices. Most were rentals, but a few were for purchase. They were mainly office premises, but one stuck out and I kept being drawn back to look at it.

There was permission for restricted use as an office on the ground floor. It was a double-fronted town house sitting in a typical, London residential square. There was a small communal green space in the centre of the ovoidly rectangular road that circumnavigated the petite park, with only one entrance to the secluded neighbourhood. It was in Holborn, right in the middle of the city.

I read further and noted it had large living, withdrawing, and dining areas on the first floor, with a library set to the rear. Below on the ground floor were modern reception rooms, and offices that espoused half-baked plans for an exclusive travel agency, one that never did any business, but did succeed in obtaining a business licence. Above these were four main floors that offered potentially twenty-four bedrooms. The price tag should have been many millions, but due to most of the property's semi-derelict state, it was on offer for a mere £2.3 million.

I turned to Zoë and asked, "How much money do we have?"

It was clear she didn't have the slightest clue. We had spent quite a bit of money: repaying Sophie, new clothes for our special assignments, and mobile phones, tablet computers, plus a car and motorbike. But I doubt it came to more than a few month's income. I said aloud, "We have been making around thirty thousand pounds per month since I was just turning fourteen. That's over five years ago. Let's call it sixty months since we began. Do you know how much money that is?"

I waited for her to do the maths, but it took her a long time. After due diligence, she replied with aplomb, "One hundred and eighty thousand pounds."

I had to hug her, her mathematics had always been hopeless. "No Zoë, you are one zero out. The true figure is "One point eight million."

Her jaw dropped and her mouth hung open as she stared at me. She shook her head in denial, and used a calculator on the desk to check my figures. She turned around with a look of wonder in her eyes. I stated, "Property is an excellent investment, and although it may take us time to renovate, I think this solves all our problems."

As if on cue, Sir Richard chose that moment to enter and asked, "And what, may I enquire, would solve all your problems Isabella?"

I held up the property details and replied, "Well, apart from your personal company, my love, this place Sir Richard."

He glanced through the brochure and said, "This is an exceedingly good investment opportunity, which is the only reason I was considering it. Refurbishment will cost at least half a million, if not more. Structurally the building is sound, save for some immediate attention to the roof, and damp in the wine cellar. The interior needs gutting. The place is riddled with woodworm, and all the windows need replacing. It will take a lot of work to put right."

He motioned towards the drinks cabinet and Zoë got him a whiskey. She handed it to him as he sat down behind his desk. He was thoughtful for a moment, before fixing me in the eye, "I would be tempted to take the ground floor, as prices for this place we are now in are becoming extortionate. We already pay upwards of ten thousand pounds per week, and they are talking of doubling it. To me that is a waste of good money.

He took a long drink, nodding his thanks to Zoë, and leaned forward, "How much money have you got?"

I never broke eye contact, but shrugged, "We have no idea, but it must be at least One point eight million."

He looked at the brochure and said, "Hmmm. Two point three million is quite close, given some bargaining."

Sir Richard stood up and paced the room, still holding the details of the house in one hand, and his whiskey in the other. He considered and spoke, "I am aware you have considered providing, shall we say, personal escort services to gentlemen. This property would afford a home for your girls, and offer discreet accommodation for an evening, similar to that of a superior class hotel, if you were to set it up correctly.

"Here's the deal, I make up the shortfall and pay for renovations. I get the Ground floor free, for five years, and take ten percent of whatever you make net. What do you say?"

I smiled and replied coyly, "We'll see. Five percent for five-years, and you fund the renovations, we have five-years to repay you.

We haggled, and in time agreed, "Eight percent, let's shake on it."

"Agreed. You're a sharp businesswoman. I admire that."

"Sir Richard, first, we need to get the cash somewhere safe. Do you know of a discrete banking service?"

I am sure his eyes almost popped out of his head. "You mean you have all this money in cash?"

I grinned back, "Sure, it's in our locker bank."

He dived to his intercom, "Constance, get me Sir Mortimer immediately."

While he waited for the call to connect, he asked how long it would take us to get the money. I said, "About one hour at this time of night, plus we need guards, suitcases, and a driver."

He smiled and said, "Consider it done, Mi'Lady."

The telephone rang and he spoke to Sir Mortimer, who at first appeared to be a little put out. As soon as he realised the size of the deposit, we were assigned security and David as driver. We did not collect all our personal money that evening, but did reclaim the vast bulk of it.

Bilty

"So that's how you came by this place. It seems a very good buy, and you two own it outright."

"Yes we do. We soon paid Sir Richard back. The irony that he was the largest single donor of our funds was not lost on him, but he humoured it well."

"Fresh drinks and some nibbles, girls, then I'll resume."

Chapter 34 – Building for the Future

Isabella

Melchett, Mortimer & Drewes was not a normal bank. It was a form of Merchant Bank. We handed over suitcases, rucksacks, and plastic carrier bags full of cash. The cashier, who had stayed on to service us privately after the Bank officially closed for business, spent ages counting our money; cash deposits were most rare. Zoë watched her like a hawk, and even with mechanical counting aids, it took a long time.

I joined the men in Sir Mortimer's office, and we discussed our banking arrangements in greater depth. He had our details and promised us he would arrange investment, personal, and business accounts suitable for our use. Some of those would be via a building society with banking facilities that they owned.

In due course, the teller came through with Zoë after processing our deposit, and handed her boss a piece of paper. It read, "£1,975,850."

The banker had been furtively glancing at me when he thought we were not looking, but now he turned his eyes fully upon us, and enquired, "And just how do you two young ladies happen to have so much money, and in cash?"

Sir Richard was about to intervene, but I leant forward provocatively, and cooed demurely, "Why Sir. They say it is the oldest profession in the world, is that not correct Zoë."

I licked my lips lasciviously and looked at his crotch. His face reddened, while the teller made an excuse to hastily leave the room. We had some paperwork to complete, and left the men to chat. I took some business cards from a stand in the foyer, handing one to Zoë, and asked the teller if they had safety deposit boxes. We took a large one and shared the keys one apiece.

The back of the business card was blank, so I wrote upon it in my best handwriting:

"Isabella waits to make your fantasies come true. Please call me soon: 0717967 583276."

The bank manager and Sir Richard came out and waited for the process to complete. They both seemed in an extremely good mood. We were shown to the door and Sir Mortimer shook our hands. I pressed the card into his palm, and we departed.

He called me later that night. I knew he would — men are so very predictable. We arranged for an all-nighter on Tuesday. Seeing he was rich, I doubled our usual fee to £2, 000 each, and he even left us another Grand as a tip. Five Grand for providing one night's entertainment is good money, although the fee included total discretion.

On Wednesday, Sir Richard called us from Italy, and asked us to check out the new premises. Miss Constance accompanied us to Fiddlers Court, where we met a surveyor. The house, although semi-derelict, was a dream. The surveyor made a damming report, offering an interim copy to the Agent. We were disillusioned before we met later for tea. It seemed he had made the worst possible assessment in order to give us leverage to bring the price down.

After several phone calls and trips to the estate agent, I got the price reduced to a whisker under £2.1 million. It was a snip. The process took almost ten weeks to complete, by which time Zoë and I had virtually closed the gap on the asking price. We were becoming seriously busy almost every evening. It appeared Sir Mortimer had many friends who were interested in our services, many booking direct, or via the website.

I did have misgivings about that, as my own past dwelt heavily in my heart. I could forgive Sir Richard and his few friends, but I knew it would be wrong of me to continue providing underage girls to new clients, as that made me a hypocrite. It was clear the main market was for late teens and early twenties, girl's old enough so there were no legal problems with age. They were adults and could make their own lifestyle choices, in full knowledge of all that this implied. Regards our earlier discussions about the age of consent, eighteen did it for me.

My main problem was, the girls I had easy access to, were mainly common. I mean no disrespect by stating that. But these high-flying men were looking for more cultured company. Fiona was still running things at my old school, so we dropped by to see her, late that Wednesday afternoon. David was our chauffer of course.

Fiona had eight girls between the ages of fifteen and eighteen pulling tricks on a semi-regular basis. The big difference between our operation and the care home scam being, these girls were volunteers. They had not been bullied into having sex, but did it because they wanted to. Most of them didn't even need the money, they were in it for the thrill. They called their liaisons 'dates'.

They were well paid, had regular health checks, and could leave any time they wanted to. Most of them were too young for what I needed. Zoë leafed through her file of older girls who had left, and we made a few phone calls. Three of them were up for it, but only two now lived near enough to be of any use.

I enlisted the services of a nineteen-year-old, and a twenty-year old before we left. I was still one girl short for the coming week. Business was prime on the run-up to Christmas. Zoë and I got back to Aldwych, and idled in the Grosvenor House common room while our dinner nuked in the nearby microwave. Carmel came in and flicked channels; she was an oddball just like us.

I was desperate, and she could turn out attractive, given some make-up and a proper dress. I also knew she was usually out with a different guy every night. I wandered over, and probed, "Hi. You seem down in the dumps. No date tonight? Care to share?"

She shook her head and said, "Get out of my face bitch."

I turned to leave it there, but looked back, and said on the spur of the moment, "I got money troubles as well Hon. But I just made a grand for fucking some old businessman. Not your thing I'm sure, but it pays the fucking bills around here."

I had not expected her to grab my sleeve, pulling the fabric of my blouse so hard I thought it might rend. Her words were as spluttered as my recalled dialogue, "One ... Thou—Oh my God! Whe... why—How? You mean, nice, not too old, and filthy rich?"

I nodded and added, "I call it 'silver service'." I dragged my sleeve out of her grasp, and motioned to Zoë as the microwave pinged. We collected our food and left at once.

Carmel knocked on our door before we had finished eating. She was edgy, jumpy, and so caught it was untrue. I told her to fix us all drinks. I needed the conquest so said, "Here's the deal: we get twenty-five percent. You get to fuck, suck, and maybe do anal with some old man for a whole night. What you do, and do not do, is up to you.

"You will go on Friday night, and not leave until after breakfast the next day. The client's needs are paramount. Never forget that.

"When you leave sometime on Saturday morning, his chauffer will drop you back here. You keep all of any tip, which if you are any good, will be about the same as your pay.

"Now, how much do you know about fucking..."

It turned out she knew very little. What can I say? We had to ask David to come round and help us train her. She was absolutely hopeless to begin with, and just lay there; although she knew her way around a woman's body—you gotta love all-girls schools. During the evening, we had to leave her practicing sex with David, as we had girls to place, and work to do. David didn't seem to mind, even when I confirmed he was not getting paid for training Carmel. Men!

The next afternoon, David was there to assist us work on the girl's techniques again, bless. She was learning, but we had to break her, and break her good. Fortunately, and despite Carmel's initial protestations, David proved to be an excellent teacher of sexual techniques. He got the angle of dangle just perfect, and it was not long before she exploded in a massive G-Spot orgasm, her first ever.

After a few more tricks, she became a regular member of our team. What impressed us most, was she was keen and willing to learn. When we got to our second summer at Uni, she was well into BDSM, and was taking vocational lessons to become a Dominatrix. By that point, our trade was flourishing, and demand for all persuasions of sex was a market driver for our escalating business. Delicately, as we moved out of the underage market, the over-age markets opened up to us, and this we had well covered. Given our girls proclivities from the Academy, we also moved into the female executive market, and that proved to be even more lucrative. But, standard of girl or, sometimes toy-boy, were higher and more defined.

Back in that present, I managed to squeeze in my exams and module submissions. I knew I had done particularly well, but I also knew this third semester amounted to little in the overall degree classification. On the other hand, we had been working seven days a week. New clients appeared out of the woodwork, and as quickly as we got girls into beds, so it seemed we needed more. There were by then, a few more LSE girls helping us, but everyone was going home for the festive break. This left us understaffed at the busiest time of year.

A few days before Christmas, things came to a head. We had too many commitments, and not enough girls. All work on renovating the building had stopped until sometime in the New Year. Disconsolate, I chose to walk home that morning, headed for Aldwych. There was a small café open just up a side street, and I went in.

I was sitting to one side, paying nobody any mind. My fingers ran with rivers of runny egg as I tried to demolish a bacon and sausage sandwich. I needed the tactile, hands-on feel of my food. Lost deep within my own world within worlds', I recognised her perfume before she spoke: "Bella?"

My hands a total mess of dripping protein, I whirled and grasped her in my mucky grip. I had not looked into her eyes properly before my fingers brought her head to mine, and my lips covered hers. Our tongues threshed together with an urgency I had not felt in many years.

We broke apart and stared at one another. She was much older than I remembered, like now she was mid-twenties. What impressed me most about Vikki was that her eyes were still alive. She had not fallen, but still soldiered on, still waiting on that dream come true.

Our time together was a blur, and by mid-afternoon, she was choosing her room in my new gaff. I knew I had to have her, just once you know — for old-time's sake. I guess that's why I jumped her bones. I wasn't expecting her response, as her unbridled passion for me appeared to be greater. God!

It was a cleansing of sorts. When our wracking rhythms within the wanton whirring whims of womanly wiles unwound, we held each other in the afterglow. We murmured quietly within secrets, and the softest longings of kisses.

The clock struck five *post meridiem* before we knew it, and Zoë came in to present our problems. We were three girls short on 23rd December, and there was no way to fix it. We needed fifteen girls all told. Zoë finished her delivery and looked at us. She said, "Vikki I presume. My pleasure to meet you. I now understand why you are so special."

The girls' army was called to battle the male libido once more, and we knew we would win, we always did. Vikki made a few calls, and within minutes, we had full coverage. Not just the three, but also the dozen other commitments. I worried Vikki's girls would be too common, or carrying [Aids], but it worked out. We were seriously busy all through Christmas Eve, and were all fucked-out by Christmas morning. Well, except for a special assignment Carmel and a true Dom took for Christmas Day. To me what they did was not sex, but they came away with ten thousand pounds, and a repeat booking.

I mused: 'The human psyche nary runs so deep, as the channels and causeways lust coverts most'.

I was still learning just how deep and miscreant those causeways ran. I had expected some of Vikki's girls to take the money and run. I was pleasantly surprised when every single girl came back to our new HQ, and laid their money on my table. They kept the tips, and Melanie deducted our take. Obviously they knew a good deal. Miss Constance rang, interrupting me, to enquire about our plans for Christmas luncheon. I told her straight, "We've not even thought that far ahead."

She asked of me, "How many are you?"

I replied without consideration, "A couple of dozen." I was going to say more, but the phone went dead, and I thought nothing of it.

We had finished cashing up in my room, and had thrown the bar open to the girls, in what was now, our makeshift reception room come saloon. A heavy hand knocked the front door. I locked the safe and went down to see who wanted us.

David doffed his cap to me, and stood aside as Miss Constance ushered in cooks and servants laden with turkeys, Christmas pudding, and all things for a great Christmas feast. I stood to the side in astonishment, as hampers and 'God knows what' were taken directly to our largely un-refurbished kitchens in the rear basement.

As if to answer my unasked question, Miss Constance purred, "We also have nowhere to go today. I trust we are welcome?"

I have no idea why I did it, even to this day. I grabbed her straight blonde locks and dragged her lips forcibly to my own. I delayed the final contact because I wanted to watch her eyes, which duly closed in subservience to me. Our kiss was brief, passionate, and public.

Her breathing was ragged as I pulled away. I looked into her eyes and lightly brushed her chest as I spoke, "Constance, you are definitely most well-come."

Her eyelashes fluttered to me, and she hurried inside. David adjusted his trousers, before he took my arm as we sashayed inside. One man versus twenty horny girls—I hoped he had the stamina to keep up!

That turned out to be one excellent Christmas party. David bestowed several presents that day, but I think the most important thing was, I had the cooks and staff sit and eat with us as equals. Not all of them could be with us, all of the time, but to me, that encapsulated true sharing of Christmas spirit, which in itself was over-flowing in rivers.

Time inevitably moved on, and by personal device, we were living in Fiddlers Court. Our first Christmas had just passed into history as a resounding success. We inherited a Chef from Sir Richard, the one who had cooked our first Christmas luncheon. He was extremely good, but a little too old for the cut and thrust of running a major, modern kitchen. Sir Richard's problem was the man did not want to retire, so we found him alternative employment.

The builders had first concentrated on major things, like rewiring and plumbing. The roof and cellar damp were fixed, new floorboards laid, before they began remodelling the major rooms. For months, the place looked like a tip. Many voices wanted everything taking back to the brick and starting afresh. I objected loudly, because the house had so much history and attention to detail, I made them renovate the existing, and it gave the place an overall charm of past glory; golden brown.

We created another world, right in the heart of central London. Once fixed with new drapes and carpets in keeping, and a grand piano at Sir Richard's behest, beset with candelabra and exotic plants to the side, the house felt alive and became a phoenix reborn in its own right. I engendered the mystique of understated charm from a bygone era, renewed and alive once more within impeccable discretion.

Reception was like a saloon from British Imperial past, where clients and girls could mix and match at their leisure. The restaurant had various sized tables, which could be combined when needs be. This was offered for small functions, private dining of 'couples', and for breakfast. The withdrawing room was set aside for couples and small groups, a quiet room for conversation. Nearby, the library was fitted out with several mini-offices, and also discrete terminals, so the wealthy could access secure telephones and computers with internet.

Below stairs, Chef Cuthbert was an oddball at the best of times, but was an excellent chef, and he pulled together a great team. I walked with him one day as he laid out plans for remodelling the kitchens. He insisted on keeping some of the old equipment, like a coal-fired Aga range, and a 1931 Leisure gas cooker that went up to gas mark 15. He whispered in confidence, "You need that intense heat for the lightest, fluffiest, Yorkshire Puddings you know."

In other ways, he was post-modern, laying out prep, cooking, presentation, and washing stations. He demanded all surfaces be made of copper or brass, as stainless steel promotes bacterial spread. He needed a wall demolishing, and it was a major support wall. I protested the expense, but have to agree his foresight was brilliant.

Old rooms with doors labelled: Scullery, Pantry, and Servants Quarters, remained in situ. The Dumbwaiter [food elevator] needed to be moved, and we required a passenger lift as well. Sir Richard insisted top-paying clients would refuse to climb stairs--we had a standard to achieve, and surpass.

The only suitable place was where the servant's stairs ran up the back of the house. We needed a rear fire escape also to comply with modern building regulations. I was talking to the building contractor a few days later, when Sir Richard dropped by. Our minimalistic designs were over-ridden, and he ordered state-of the art: Food, Staff, and Passenger lifts. A new fire escape was part of the deal, and Sir Richard was picking up the tab, more than one quarter of a million pounds.

One may wonder why I have spent some time describing this? The reason is the servants lift was built deep into the house structure. It also required two doors, one for each of the alternating floors. Every floor could be designed to allow access to the old servants' stairway. I worked with the lift engineer to make it so. At the turn of a key, and after punching in a code, I could reprogram the lift to open on the wrong side, allowing us access to the now defunct stairs, or secret hiding places if you prefer.

Once building works completed, I had one very special lift key, Zoë another, and the third was deposited with our Bank. Finally, Zoë and I were able to clear out our lockers, evidence remaining within easy reach, and completely hidden. We had covered our tracks and were home free.

You could presume Sir Richard ripped us off on our deal for the house. I do not think so, because while we had the cash, we lacked legitimacy. Total refurbishments came to over one million pounds Sterling, and we also acquired staff of the utmost discretion. His company would have paid a fortune in rent to stay where there were. With his offices, we had an unchallenged public face for working round the clock. But best of all, Zoë and I owned the Title Deeds outright.

I think Zoë could accept the way her life turned out, as did most of the other girls. I never could, and whilst the hypocrisy of becoming a Madame off the back of my heritage never sat comfortably with me, I carried a deeper wound that demanded many a blood sacrifice to heal.

Time moved on, as it invariably does. The next semester I took an additional module in Family Law. I needed to know, OK? I worked out what the law stated in actual fact, versus what had happened to me, and every other girl I knew. They were from completely different Universes.

"The needs of the child remain paramount" was, and continues to be, one of the key assertions in British Courts of Justice. In real life, we were gagged and never allowed to speak in Family Court.

Our needs became those of the SS, the Court, the Family Judge's whim. We had no voice, just like in olden days. This haemorrhage of a Kangaroo Court presided in triumph over our youth, and virginity.

In private times, I worked with Zoë to sharpen the imaginary arrow tips of our bows. The time of reckoning was overdue, and full repayment was demanded, and would be made.

For me, the killing was not enough. It was extra cream added after the trifle was served. I needed to undermine the entire system, and expose everything these sick bastards had done to us. All of us.

My course had been deflected by my new life, and my business was booming. We had extended into the attic to accommodate all the girls required to service our regular clientele. Most of our work remained off-site, but select patrons were given special privileges, and could meet us at HQ. It functioned as like a Gentleman's Club, and in that respect, Sir Richard's fatherly hand was a boon. To outsiders, we operated a female refuge, so as to deflect prying eyes and unwanted interest.

The seasons turned once more, but London always felt and smelled like London, 'The Great Wen' of William Cobbett's musings. It was special, select. A bit old school, a bit Nuevo and Modernist, ingratiating, always international, all wrapped up within some ever-evolving ether.

That summer, I scored several 1.1's, but just snuck down into a 1.2 overall. I was pissed-off about that. I worked with Sir Richard's Company during the summer holiday, although Zoë did not. That year my work mirrored that of my degree course, and I excelled in the business environment of a most successful International Company.

Before I knew it, the third year of University was upon me, and it's the only one that really matters — before, or afterwards. I was controlling one of the most lucrative businesses in London, but I decided to return to Halls for most of my final year. I needed the personal space.

Zoë and I were extremely close that last year at LSE, and we did strike back at those who raped us. But that is a story yet to be told…

§

"We'll take a break here Bitly. I need to get my mind right for the next part. If you will excuse me."

Isabella took all the girls with her, and left Candice and Bilty to their own devices.

Chapter 35 – Fighting Back

Bilty Steadman

"You seem reluctant to continue, Isabella. Is anything wrong?"

"No, not especially, but I need assurances from you first. You see, we did murder people, and I would get life imprisonment were these facts to be revealed. I need your vow that whatever I say, remains inside these four walls, and between all of us present."

"I give you my word of honour, nothing you mention today will ever be divulged. I will not make notes, so consider this a blank period."

Candice confirmed, "Same here. I will say nout; use pseudonyms."

Melanie had been filming every confession. "Mel, I want this recorded, but the only copy comes to me. Once in a memory stick, the all of it gets deleted, and I mean, wiped clean. You better hurry Zoë in here as well, she may remember something I forget. Nobody else is allowed."

"Of course. I'll get Zoë, and use a shredder once we're done."

Isabella

The criminal consciousness is critically, a conventional conformity of circumvention, containing clearly, a curious conundrum: deception.

We had all spent many years prevaricating, and in our own ways, fighting back against the system. We had achieved some success, and won a few good victories. Nevertheless, no one, not we, nor any other, had recompensed us for the loss of our families at such a tender age.

What of our childhood, our youthfully expectations of life? Were we to be cast adrift for naught, except institutionalised rape, condoned and emboldened by every agency and legal redress we were allowed, or more usually, not allowed to access? We were old enough to demand full redress of the crimes committed against us, yet the courts always sided with our abusers. Were they on the take?

This is the story of 'My Life'. That of Zoë's, and the lives of our friends, hundreds, thousands of other underage girls I either know, or know of. I will never be stymied, enslaved, nor cowed by those of great, though self-important worth, and even greater bank balances.

Social Services ran amok, as did the Family Courts they connived with. Mohammed, and Judge St. John-Smythe. They were never investigated properly, as neither were the QC that raped Dani, nor, so many others who raped us, repeatedly. They stole the most precious gift of all, that any girl can bestow: Virginity.

The first stanza of Robert Herrick's famous poem haunted me:

"Gather ye rosebuds while ye may,
Old Time is still a-flying;
And this same flower that smiles today,
Tomorrow will be dying."

Instead, our budding youthful femininity, was crushed between the judicial pages of reprehensible neglect, and the self-serving judgements of those with malign aforethought.

During my last year at LSE, we made a list of all those we would kill. It could never be called 'murder', because we were only calling-out those who were supposed to protect us, to justice. Our justice. They had failed, and acted knowingly against our best interests, and so many times before. Their lives had already become worthless in our eyes.

Each, and every one had a Duty of Care [R 35.1] for us, one they maliciously enthused to abuse against us.

We started watching boy movies, action movies — the ones where everything gets destroyed. People were killed and mutilated. Buildings blown up — it was not a pleasure, it was research.

That's when I discovered the real difference between the sexes. 'Men don't give a damn. Mothers do'.

The thing about female revenge, the one I have not mentioned so far, is that if our subtlety and laudable plots become unravelled, fraught, fritter away to nothing, then we as women, fight to the death. We are Deadlier Than the Male. [Hugh "Bulldog" Drummond refers]

Zoë and I still had access to Newbury High sports facilities. We were Alumni members, and could access the rifle range, and archery club. We both practiced on the crossbow, and learned about the different types, and their purposes. One was a professional compound bow that was able to kill a deer at distance. That was what we required.

To buy a crossbow, you need to be over eighteen, and checked by the police. We tried to buy legit, but it proved impossible. I mentioned it to Ben one day; we now paid him a handsome, one-off introduction fee. He knew of several gun merchants, but only one speciality salesman.

Our meeting with the guy was scary. He had the smell of someone who killed. I mean, we could not physically detect the odour, but, dogs were either beholden of him, or reared away in a gnashing of teeth. Animals sense a killer within their midst. Typically, humans do not.

Doing business with the guy was not pleasant, but we got what we wanted. A compound crossbow with excellent sights and discharge velocity of 400 fps [feet per second], or about that of a low velocity 9mm snub nose. However, penetration was a lot higher due to the overall weight of the arrow, and special arrow tips.

The bow had pulleys, draw assister, and came with telescopic and night sights, plus an inbuilt quiver. We spent money on piercing ammunition. His guns and blades were cheap, so we came away with a pistol for Zoë, and a revolver for me — I just preferred the style you know. Our deal was done, and he started to put his stuff back in the rear of his

SUV. We had already turned to leave, when he asked, "I don't suppose you are interested in a high-velocity rifle, are you?"

One of those weapons like on TV, and in films, where some macho guy assembles a rifle from bits and pieces, and blows a tick off a dormouse ten-miles away, right. Well, what we were offered was not quite that good, but it was accurate to within an inch over one thousand feet, wind allowing. It was all within the sights and ammo used.

We only met the creep twice. The next time we bought more arrows, ammunition, grenades, smoke bombs, and an RPG-7 that came with stacks of ammo. He did not have ready access to C-4, but sold us Czech Republic Semtex with detonators instead. The compound was brick red, looked like congealed blood, and we were one with the colour. We were on a mission.

Zoë and I set up to murder Mohammed first, he was our main target. We hid behind bushes in a quiet place we knew he used for abusing his young victims. The dark November evening was chilly with the scent of rain, which clung heavy with intent in the still night air.

We dressed in dark fatigues. Masks covered our faces so only our eyes were visible. Our boots were men's sizes, padded out to fit, and we wore heavy rucksacks to make our weight appear more than it was.

The taxi was early. I wanted to take revenge before the driver got into the rear. The child locks trapped some hapless girl on the back seat. She looked no more than twelve years old under the interior light. It was clear to see she was drunk, and not somebody we knew.

I momentarily thought to cancel when I realised it was not Mohammed, but Zoë was fixated, "That creep came inside me so many times, and laughed as he pissed on my face afterwards."

"Me too. He is so dead!"

He emerged from the rear some time later, and Zoë was running before I fired. The crossbow was silent. The arrow passed straight though his cranium. The girl saw nothing due to the interior light. Zoë wrenched the arrow out of a tree, and we scarpered. What a blast!

For the very first time, we had hit back against our oppressors, and do you know what—it felt so damned good!

We celebrated our first kill that evening in our room, exaggerating the worth and audacity of our first strike. The truth of it was, we both had blood on our hands, regardless of which of us pulled the trigger.

The police reports were slow to come through, and were confusing. They were looking for two men in their late twenties or early thirties, wearing size nine army boots. They believed they were members of some right wing neo-Nazi political group. We howled with laughter.

Later we adopted the media ruse, and offered the police what they were expecting, PBB, an organisation called Pure British Blood. I still cannot believe they fell for it, but they did, hook, line, and sinker.

There was no mention in the media regards rape of a minor — the girl in the back seat of the taxi. Zoë did trace the girl concerned, via Melanie. She was living at home with her mother, and was on the SS watch list. Her mother forced her to file charges, but guess what, they were dropped. The girl was not a credible witness, and as far as the police and CPS were concerned, no actual crime had been committed, semen stained seat and panties, or not, withstanding. Oh. And of course, the rapist was a Pakistani Muslim, and dead.

We tried again one week later. The spot was more public and dangerous. We waited until the rape was complete. We did not want to, but we needed the imbecilic Bussies to pick up and prosecute the rape.

The driver was Khan, another one we both hated intensely — not because he was Pakistani, or a Muslim, let me make that exceptionally clear. We hated him because, before and during our rapes, he loved to hit us, extremely hard. Just before he came, he loved to punch us viciously in the bladder, letting our internal convulsions bring him to his climax. He had also branded Zoë for life.

Zoë was ready to take him out as he opened the door to leave, but waited as he stood aside to take a leak. Zoë's aim was true. Within the pull of a hair trigger, we both became murderers, and sister's in arms.

She got him right between the eyes. This time I was running to retrieve the dart. So far, all ballistics were looking for was a pistol with silencer. Finding the arrow proved elusive. I had to line up with Zoë's position and our victim, and follow the line of fire. We could hear sirens in the distance by the time I retrieved it, half buried in the distant turf.

This time the girl was one of ours, but from a different care home. Enquiries stalled, and although semen was sent for analysis, all charges of rape were dropped before they were even initiated. She was considered to be making a life-choice. Impossible in Law: She was eleven years old! She was legally incapable of choosing to have sex. The crime was rape. The police did not even consider a charge of GBH [Grievous Bodily Harm], despite her hospitalisation for fractured ribs. But her rapist was dead. Obviously, this was not Operation Midland.

We were both mad. I reasoned that if we kept on hitting them, eventually somebody had to put two and two together. I knew that even Zoë could get that calculation correct, but could our forces of law and order? It felt like 'Zen and the Art of watching grass grow'.

Why do the police never bring rape charges against Muslim men whom habitually rape seriously underage white girls?

Melanie did some research, and discovered that every police constable in the United Kingdom, has to swear an oath before he or she is allowed to take office. This is what I read:

"I swear by Almighty God [Or other politically correct shit] to uphold the office of Police Constable. And in so doing:

To prevent the loss of life;

To detect the commission of offences;

To prosecute offenders to the fullest extent of the Law of the Land."

It was palpable that something was seriously amiss with the Bussies implementation of their sworn oath, and mission statement. We had garnered hard evidence at great personal risk. The police repeatedly failed to action. This extended to all three overriding principles of the Office of Police Constable. I accept there could be no court case to prosecute a dead man. But, there was zero follow through regards the rights of the raped child. Neither counselling, nor support of human nature. Let me be very clear: She, the victim, did not matter to them.

To us, their oath was complete and utter bollocks. They were the first to break their own directives, and protect these sinister Muslim paedophiles. As a result, our rage heightened.

Zoë spent some weeks tracking Mohammed, and also monitoring the gang's usual haunts. She discovered he was grooming a new girl, and we knew that meant he would be entertaining her on Saturday evening. We arrived after he had parked his car in the rear yard of a derelict factory. There was no clear shot without exposing our position.

We reasoned he would have to stop at the factory gate on his exit, as the entrance had high walls, the only pavement on the other side. The road was busy, so he would have to edge out into traffic when they left.

Opposite was a thick hedge, which partially hid a commercial vehicle repair shop. We waited, and were there for hours. I insisted on taking the shot, because I had vowed to kill the creep. In time, the car gingerly crept out onto the highway, and our plan was going perfectly. I was lying down peering through the sight. Mohammed had to wait for a six-wheeler to go past, and as soon as it cleared, I fired.

The car pulled away as I was about to rise in jubilation. Zoë put her hand on my back to hold me down. Mohammed stopped the car to examine the windscreen, before staring at the disappearing truck. We edged away and found a good place to hide under some tarpaulin. Moments later we heard a car reverse, and it stopped very near to us. The driver got out. Footsteps checked the hedge where we had been minutes before, and in time got closer. From the sound of shoes on gravel, he could have been no more than a few feet from us. We froze.

Now, we were being hunted, and I knew Mohammed always carried a gun. We were mere inches, and a chance away from certain death. My blood ran cold as adrenaline pumped through my veins. All my senses became acutely aware, as were Zoë's. I swear I could hear Mohammed breathing. It was so scary.

I felt great relief when his latest victim called to him from the car. He moved slowly away, and I presumed he was still checking around. When we heard the engine fire, we hugged under the tarpaulin. The car moved away and we began to crawl from within our hideout. I grabbed Zoë's hand and whispered, "Wait!"

We lay still as the Mercedes circled the yard, before it pulled out of the driveway. Cautiously we hurried to the hedge, and saw the car disappear from sight. At last, we could talk. I stated, "I hit him true, what happened?"

Zoë said, "The arrow hit the windscreen and careened off, the tip must have hit the glass at an angle, and I saw it go over the top of the car. We better find it, quickly."

The dart had hit the factory wall opposite, and dropped to the ground. The arrowhead was ruined, but the shaft was fine. We left at once, chastened by our experience. I was in a bad mood — Mohammed should have been dead, but instead he was very much alive, and probably alert to what we were doing. Next time we knew to fire perpendicular to the angle of the windscreen. Twice.

Our fourth hit was at another favourite haunt, the one where Mohammed had originally taken me. We both hoped he would show that night. We arrived early and waited. Nobody came and we left three hours later, hungry, cold, and disgruntled.

We returned the next evening and hid in the bushes. This time a taxi arrived, but it pulled up near the road and two men got out. They had torches, handguns, and were hunting us. We used stealth and lay in wait, separating to cover each other. Logically they should have headed in Zoë's direction, but the men were wary and circled around. I had my revolver in one hand, and my knife in the other. They were heading in my direction, and silence was our greatest ally.

I knew I had to lead them towards Zoë's crossbow, so chose my moment when one of them had to see me, and ran. I could hear them shouting to each other and glanced round to track them. I tripped over an exposed tree root and went flying. I rolled and brought my gun to bear at the bulk now coming to stand above me. He pulled out his gun and aimed at my face. The hole in his head stopped him, dead.

Zoë reloaded as I found a good place to hide nearby. The second man approached cautiously, drawn by the first man's now still torch and lack of verbal response. He was wary and knelt down to check for a pulse. His eyes searched the darkness, but he did not see the arrow that ended his life. He fell on top of his colleague. My gloved hand drew the letters PBB in the nearby earth with a stick.

We searched for the darts. No sooner had we found the second than another car arrived, and minutes later, we heard sirens approaching once again. We had already left. We raced through a copse and made our getaway, reaching a main road on Zoë trials bike. We were free, and onto busy city streets. We had at last administered justice, our justice on a few of our rapists.

Chapter 36 – Collateral Damage

Our kills made top headlines the next day, and everyone was talking about the PBB. It was time we changed our plan. Four low ranking men were now dead, all of them had repeatedly raped us, but we had failed to kill any of the larger fish, or expose publicly what was really going on.

I decided to lie low and let the heat dissipate. It was obvious the rapists would now avoid using the lay-bys and secluded places. All we had succeeded in doing was driving them into the safety of houses and businesses. Zoë was adamant we needed another plan to bring this atrocity to light. But, what were we supposed to do about it? The law was not doing its job, and neither were the courts.

We discussed in all seriousness, plans to destroy the taxi garage and headquarters, and also of hitting Mohammed's main offices. Both plans foundered, not so much for lack of military hardware or intent, but because innocent people would also become victims, and evidence would be destroyed. We relished the blood of the guilty on our hands, but to kill innocent people was murder, simple. I drew a line in the sand and stated, "No innocent person will die because of our actions."

Begrudgingly, Zoë accepted my wisdom. She would still urge me to change my mind at times, by attacking other public targets, but I said to her, "What if it was you in the collateral damage. You would be dead, and for no good reason. I need us to prevent this."

Turning her thoughts upon herself as target, quieted her, and so much so, she later lectured me on some of my more bizarre ideas of revenge. I guess we were too naïve, too immature to think it through.

Over the weeks that followed the hubbub died down. The worst place we knew was 119 Filbert Street. This was owned by a cleric who taught the Quran by day, and by night preached at, punched, and raped exceedingly young white girls. We had our target fixed, and discussed a means of attack. I wanted to use the high velocity rifle, but Zoë insisted the RPG was our best tool. We agreed to differ, and try one more time.

Our plans were made a few days before Bonfire Night, on which day in history, during the early hours of the 5th November 1605 A.D., a man named Guy Fawkes tried to blow up the Houses of Parliament, and almost succeeded.

We understood why he was driven to commit such an act. Centuries later, the common people of the United Kingdom still celebrate what he tried to do. Many still wish he had accomplished the feat, or that someone would do so in this modern day and age. The world was a madness of quasi-religious fervour, although few realised Fawkes was the fall-guy for a conspiracy to assassinate King James I, and return Great Britain to Catholicism.

We also knew the freaks at 119 Filbert Street would be beating up and heavy, while teaching Christian girls sutras. We had been using Zoë's black trials bike for our missions. It had false plates, and was kept in a lock-up near Battersea power station. We kept most of our weapons in the garage, but the walk back to the nearest underground station was a bit of a trek. The garage complex was isolated. There were also several ways in and out of the area, so we could come and go undetected.

We conducted a clandestine reckie of the house, and to my disappointment, we discovered the rifle was definitely out. That left us with Rocket Propelled Grenades. The front of the house was far too exposed, but the rear abutted the back of a pet clinic that had a small car park at the rear. To one corner was a stack of rubble that once scrambled, offered a great line of sight to the rear door of our target.

The range was less than thirty yards, meaning it would be an accurate shot. With imagination and empty hands, we practiced firing three grenades into the building, picking out individual targets carefully. We realised the alarm would quickly be raised, so planned only two missiles for best impact and speedy escape.

We intended to go in the next day, Tuesday, and had already ridden the area for means of escape. We knew from bitter experience the girls would not be released until after two a.m. Those men had beaten us too many times. We used to come away with fractured ribs, loose teeth, cuts, and so many bruises it was impossible to count them all.

We snuck out of Fiddlers Court after midnight, and twenty minutes later Zoë fired up the bike, as I grabbed the rocket launcher. The damn thing ran out of petrol and we had to push it for half a mile until we found a filling station that was open. The last quarter of a mile was uphill, which only added to our anger and fuelled our bloodlust.

Time ran away from us that night. It was just after 2 a.m. by the time we got to the house and made to drive by the front. As it came into view, we saw two badly injured and weeping girls being led out to a waiting taxi. They could not have been more than twelve years old, and were not a pretty sight.

Our emotions were blitzed and we needed revenge. Rage welled within us and we knew this evil had to be terminated. Zoë stopped the bike and said to me, "It is time these freaks were exterminated. Take the controls and pull up outside the front door."

I felt her moving behind me as I eased the bike up the street, and knew she was getting the weapon ready. I slowed quickly, and she fired before we came fully to rest. The front door exploded as I wound back the throttle and we got the hell out of there.

I ducked down a connecting alley and came up on the street behind. Once on the road proper, occupants of our target house were already running towards the veterinary centre car park seeking safety. Zoë fired a second missile into them, as running bodies were replaced by mangled corpses. We high-fived, before I rested my hands back on the handlebars, and wound the throttle back in earnest escape.

We made for a back-alley, and stopped in a secluded spot for Zoë to fold down and hide the weapon, losing vital seconds. I went to turn into our escape route, but there was already a police presence. I crossed a road and sped down another alleyway. Zoë said we had not been seen, but I was not convinced. We were also headed in the wrong direction.

We came to a dead end. We could either go back, or follow a dirt path that led down to the railway lines. I still had my bearings so went down and left, which meant we were headed west, and away from our true destination. The railway track veered south, and as we closed on a tunnel, I looked for a way out. The bike crested a rise as I dimmed the headlight, and we saw a large police presence. We were near the end of Filbert Street West, and police were cordoning off the area.

I eased the bike back down the pathway using the front brake, and looked into the black tunnel maw. It was our only means of escape. Zoë tapped my shoulder and said, "Go for it, Issy."

I felt her arms around me as I eased the bike into the tunnel. There were two tracks, but the third rail between each pair was electrified for Underground trains. If we fell off due to the uneven surface, we would be fried alive. I took it steady at first, but there was no end in sight. The tunnel veered left once more and there was a light in front of us.

It was getting closer.

I came to a stop and turned off the headlight. The train appeared to be on our track. We set the bike down and lay on our stomachs, holding the machine between us to prevent it being ripped away in the vortex of the train's passing. The look between our eyes said it all—Was this our time to die?

Luck was with us, as the train skewed to the side when it was dreadfully close, and passed by on the second track further away from our prone bodies. It was a close call. After it passed, we jumped up and hugged, whirling around in celebration.

All of a sudden, Zoë stilled and her eyes grew wide. She froze on the spot. I turned and saw the light of another train reflected in the concrete walls of the bend we had just rounded. The light was coming from the other direction, and getting brighter very quickly. We dived on top of the machine once more. Zoë had the rear wheel in her grasp, and I held the front forks and handlebars.

A shockwave preceded an inhuman electric howl. I felt the bike move and I'm sure I floated off the ground. The bike was trying to rip free of my grasp, but I held firm to the handlebars and rode out the storm of passing. Zoë kept us anchored, even though the draught moved us several feet, and tried to suck us under the train.

I have never been so scared in all my life. We rose in silence, chastened. Death had raked his scaly fingers across us that night, and it was a chilling experience. I smelled petrol. It took several kicks to start the bike. We did not speak. There were no words to express how we felt.

Frightened, Zoë said, "Get us the hell out of here, Issy."

That time I did not dawdle, but sped as fast as I could to escape the nightmare. Zoë's fingers dug deep, and deeper still into my stomach as we fled for our lives.

The track began to rise. I was dreading coming into an underground station, but fortunately we made it to fresh air. We had put several miles between Filbert Street and ourselves, but we had no idea where we were. I found a path leading up a small embankment, but we had to manhandle the bike through a rip in the chain-link fencing before we got out. In time, I found a main road and signposts. Soon we were heading out of Earlsfield towards Battersea. We had around seven miles to ride, and several more to get home.

Eventually we reached the lock-up garage and dumped the bike. We changed out of our army fatigues and began walking the last miles to our beds. It had been a long and eventful night. Our talk was stuttered. We were glad to be free and alive. I guess our minds were a little preoccupied, because in our disarray, we managed to attract the attention of one of the House Masters as we snuck back into Halls. In itself, that was not a problem, but we needed to cover our tracks.

Fortunately, he had not seen us directly, but he had heard a noise and was busy looking for anything out of place. Our luck held, when he chose the wrong direction and we scampered back to our room. We just had time to undress and get into bed before there was a knock on our door, which opened far too quickly with the master key. His torch shone on us and we appeared to be fast asleep.

The door closed, but there were no footsteps leading away. My night vision was coming up, and I shook my eyes at Zoë, intimating for her to remain as she was. The door reopened some thirty seconds later, before closing quickly, and this time he did walk away. We heard him check all the rooms on our floor, and in that time, exhaustion overtook us. The luminous hands of my alarm clock were approaching four o'clock when Hypnos took me for his own.

The fire alarm sounded at precisely six a.m. Of all nights, why did it have to happen on that particular one? Fate can be a fickle friend, but she is a good provider.

We dutifully drilled out to be accounted for in the cloying and chilly blackness of a mizzling late November morning. It was damned cold. The damp settled within us, and we were shattered. Our day started early with a mug of warming soup, the biannual regulatory fire check completed successfully.

I have no idea what the Gods were thinking that morning, a ramshackle day in-between what had come to pass, and was yet to be. We watched the news bulletins, and the house became a fireball.

There was more good news: Three of the occupants were dead, and the fourth was in critical care. He died a few days later. Our celebrations were abruptly censured when we discovered a girl was still the house. She had suffered from smoke inhalation, sustained broken ribs, fractures to her arms and legs, and was stretchered out into an ambulance.

Zoë and I clung tightly to each other. We traded guilt, shame, and remorse. We needed a new plan. The one we had was a dud. We were hurting the innocent as well as the bad guys. We decided to stop direct action, but maintained our stockpile of weapons and ammo, just in case.

Our mood was sour for several days, compounded by lack of news coverage. Hurting our own was not what we ever imagined, and we were to blame. Our contrition lay ice-cold. The heavy weight of the frozen dagger of revenge, lay like a shard buried deep within our hearts. We shared the burden of culpability between us.

Some days later, Melanie unravelled what had actually happened that night. I blanched when I discovered the whole truth, because it seemed impossible, but there it was in the report I read.

The girl in question had been bullwhipped and bullied into saying she wanted to become Muslim. They had kept her to teach her the words of Muhammad. She became their slave, and was made to wear the burqa at all times, and attend classes of religious instruction. She had to pray in an outhouse toilet, as those men decided she was not worthy of joining the men's prayer group.

In time she learned their rules, and argued with the cleric, stating her rape, her prostitution, were against the words of the Quran. She was given extra Sharia instruction, before protesting more and being called to account for her sins. She tried to escape, but they caught her, and dragged her back inside to face trial for her sins against Allah. It became patently evident the worlds of British Justice and Sharia Law inhabit divergent, bellicose universes, regards the reality of any truth.

The Muslim bastards tried her in an unofficial Islamic Court, passed sentence without her present to defend herself, and tied her limbs to all four quarters of her bed. After beating and raping the two girls we saw leave, these 'brave men' began to stone her to death for breaking Sharia Law. The mattress was soft, the girl was English, and brought up as a Christian. Our actions saved her life, ain't that a fact to live with? Police had put a blackout on news, fearing race and religious ramifications. We spread the truth via our own connections.

My tears fell heavily, and smudged with those on Zoë's cheeks, as we sought sanctuary together once more, from this most heinous act. The girl was supposedly 'in care', and was only just thirteen years old.

Our layers of liability were washed away in the acknowledgment that we saved her from being stoned to death. Had we not acted, the girl would now be a corpse. For the first time ever, Zoë and I went to a nearby church, and took Holy Communion. It was not a duty we had to perform. We went because we needed the succour. We prayed for forgiveness, and guidance. I guess it was an extravagant emotional release, but one that fortified us to continue the good fight.

When we came out, Zoë started to sing a Sunday School song.
"Muslims love the little children,
All the little children of the world.
Red and yellow, black and white,
All are targets in their sights.
Muslims *love* the little children of the world."
"Jihad, jihad, jihad..."

It was wrong. It was racist, and hit the nail on the head. It became our anthem. Afterwards, we made a vow that before the next year was out, we would vanquish our enemies. I had intended to only include Zoë, but Melanie insisted upon standing with us, and so did Vikki. She bore a deep-seated grudge against the Bussies, who had targeted her remorselessly out on the streets. She told us she was even arrested for soliciting, even though she was out shopping innocently. As usual, the police focused only on the easiest and known targets.

Prostitution in itself is not a crime in UK, but everything associated with it is, just like smoking. However, unlike smoking, the police only ever go after the working female struggling to get by. The male clients that used and abused her services were never suspected of committing an offence; any pimp noted, and above the law — 'Carry on the good work son'. Just like the misogynistic Muslims. Vikki's anger and deep-seated rage made her a force to be reckoned with.

Predictably, the police once again wrote off the investigation into 119 Filbert Street as a Muslim issue, and enquiries faltered. They were still fixated upon the fictional PBB.

The bottom line was always the same: These supposed Muslim bastards hid behind, and used religion to get away with stuff that would automatically imprison any other British subject. Our namby-pamby police were a disgrace to their uniform, the British Government, similarly exposed. The girl was sectioned, and put in a loony bin so she could not have recourse to the law of the land. They shut her up, and locked her away, such a caring society: Not!

Bilty Steadman
"My lips are sealed, even if that was some admission of guilt Isabella, Zoë. I believe you tried to do the right thing, in the only way you knew how. It was the wrong means. You both realise this."

"Yes, Bilty. But we hated them, detested what they had done to us. Even now I don't feel remorse.

"There are degrees of rape. Repeatedly gang-raping a nine-year-old girl deserves the death penalty. Instead, these Muslim freaks are found guilty of lesser crimes, and given four years. Out, back on the streets in sixteen months. They are gloating. The system is stacked in their favour. How do you think we feel?

"I remind you that I, we three girls in this room, have each been raped by over six thousand Pakistani Muslims each. Technically some were Afghani. This is not one pervert in a bedroom lusting after jailbait. There is an endemic cultural acceptance that raping women [R 36.1] — including other Muslims [R36.2], and especially, seriously underage white girls, is acceptable. Revenge rape; I'll add that to our Rape category.

"This is a religious problem, because to them, we are considered captives of war. That means, by extension, that they are at war with us [R 36.3]. Except our loony left fawn all over them. They use any excuse to appease these monsters. I remind you, they are serial child rapists!

"Bilty, why are there so many of them? These are relatively small communities. If you count the number of Pakistani men, and compare that to the number of enforced child prostitutes, you will discover that the majority of Muslim men of the area have been fucking us. Their ages range from teenagers to grandparents.

"Do the maths. You're supposed to be an investigative journalist, so work it out. We have been raped by over six thousand, different, Paki men each, most of them local. Like an infestation of rats, it's an epidemic, a prevalent problem of the local Muslim community. As a percentage, that's most men in the community.

"They need to be executed!"

"Isabella, isn't that a bit severe?"

"No! It is just. They replaced our childhood with sexual slavery."

Zoë shouted angrily in support, "I demand the death sentence for the ringleaders. Life imprisonment with consecutive sentences for the others. They should never be allowed out of prison.

Mel supported, "Deportation for all others, and sod their human rights, they denied us ours."

Abruptly, Bilty became aware of exactly how deeply all the girls felt about their systematic, and systemic abuse.

Bilty:
Personal Journal:

Notes:

1. I cannot report on what I have just heard, to protect the seemingly guilty. However, the vehemence of the reactions from the girls present, suggests their actions are not without foundation. As a female, I'm sure my wife will have a better angle on what we just heard.

Candice

"Isabella, may I have a word with you. I know that you know, that what you did was wrong. But given the circumstances and your ages, I find it hard to blame you. At least you did something, even if it were the wrong thing. It shows how deeply you resented the men that habitually raped you. It also, implacably states how you felt about your personal circumstances. None of you were being cared for by the authorities.

"Thinking ahead to the book about your life, I would like to include this episode. I can write it as fiction, change the names of everybody, and those of places. I can even set it in a different city."

Isabella looked enquiringly at Candice, before saying, "Why?"

"Because this episode shows how bitterly you resented what had happened to you All of you. Has any other girl in this 'abuse system', had the balls to do what you and Zoë did? No."

"I'll think about it, but I retain final veto. You do understand?"

"Yes, fully. Let me write it, and later we can discuss, and delete as are your wishes. I may even publish it under a pseudonym."

"OK. But nothing gets published without my express approval. Shake on it." And shake hands they did.

"You stopped direct action after that I presume?"

"Yes. It was pointless, and dangerous. The police couldn't charge the rapists, because they were dead. If one had survived, a court case may have resulted. Neither the SS or care homes were ever questioned as to why girls in their care had been raped by Muslim taxi drivers. It was at best a farce. Neither was it the public exposure I sought.

"I'll come to the art of female revenge a little later. Was there anything else, as a short break is on order."

"No. Thank you Isabella, this is fine for now. What's next?"

"I'm going to introduce one more young girl, and this ultimately led us to the correct path of revenge. You see, we finally found means to let the police witness the rape of a seriously underage girl."

At that moment Genie entered and said, "There's a light buffet available in the saloon. Our *dabbawalas* have been busy between stairs. Come everyone, it's time for Tiffin."

"Thank you, Genie. Perfect. So, were our rapes revenge for past perceived Colonial misdeeds? I'll leave that thought to hang. Come."

Chapter 37 – Charlotte

Isabella

The month passed into the next, and our business was greater than ever. Our girls worked flat-out during December, pardon me for the pun. I left it all for the others to cope with, although I did turn the odd trick when they needed me, or when I fancied a break from studies.

Again, I cut myself off, swotting hard at the LSE and Grosvenor House. When she was not helping me, Zoë liaised with the LSE girls working for us, and selectively recruited newcomers when she could.

My assignments were completed with days to spare. Unlike everyone else scrabbling frantically to complete their own, I reviewed them to gain the highest possible mark. Once submitted, I returned to Fiddlers Court, and was soon embroiled within the confines of our business. Christmas came and went, and was an even greater success than the year before. Miss Constance and David stayed as our guests for several days afterwards, and let's just say, they both fitted in real-swell.

An uncanny solitude enveloped me during the lull between Boxing Day and New Years Eve. The 28th of December was a throwaway day betwixt, being neither one thing, nor the other. Curiously, the winter chills waned to warm, the shrill and biting wind dropped, and snow fell like a fluttering myriad of magical blessings for the first time that year.

I was entrap't, enrapt. My mind's-eye besotted within the miraculously whitening wonderland. The constant throb of the city was muted, and the solitude of sharing-alone, settled with each snowflake.

I stared out of my window. I watched young kids larking around with gaietous abandon in the park opposite. My forehead pressed the icy pane, as my spirits rose to watch something so perversely normal. If there is a window to the soul, I knew I was looking out from it. The children's small play of fun and life raked my emotions unexpectedly. This simple pleasure of playing in the first snow had been denied me, and every other girl I knew.

Instead of family fun, we were raped. I cried. My tears did not fall for myself as such, but for how a child's life should be. Instead of despair for myself, I shared their unbridled joy. I became one with this simple pleasure of the innocence of youth. It was a cleansing of sorts.

Drawn inescapably into this unravelling of time, I made my way down to the park, and sat aside to watch them playing, until I felt the need to move-on. I envied these small-people their innocence of childhood. But I had to move before my own bitter memories replaced the vision of happiness that contented me that day.

I wanted to expunge the festering stone cold welt my heart had become, and replace it with those children's innocence, if only for one brief moment. I decided to walk, because doing 'normal' had no place in my life. I had no destination in mind, but my warping thoughts were already away with the faery', as with the fall of snow, this non-day had become mystically enchanted. I passed a small street, and smelled the welcoming waft of warm food. I turned to walk down to the café, not more than a few yards from Grosvenor House. I remembered meeting Vikki there, was that only around the same time last year?

My fondest reminiscences were rudely interrupted, when I was hit on the back of the head by a snowball. I cursed, whirled, and hastily balled the angelic crystals to throw back at my tormentors. Billie, Ellie, and Frog let fly with another barrage before I could respond.

I cursed them rotten, and did get them all back. I managed to bestow an icy mush down Frogs back, and secreted another inside Ellie's bra whilst her younger sister's screams distracted her.

Billie was wary, but I pretended to give up to her evasion, before dropping back to scoop afresh, and moulding an icy bomb, unseen. I toyed with the outer door lock of Grosvenor house, before stepping back to usher my dearest friends inside. I caught Billie completely unawares, driving my hand down, deeply, into the front of her jeans from behind. I got her so good, and laughed as her ammunition had already melted.

I know she turned to hit me, but a strange look came over her face, and she gripped her girlhood, right there in the main entrance. Her eyes seemed to twirl within their sockets, and in time she spoke, "Kitty, I would kill you now, except you have no idea how hot this ice feels. Damn you! We better tell Carmel about this."

Ever the instigator of dark, satanic vengeance, I replied impromptu, "Better still, let's get her later. Here's the plan…"

When our laughter and curses diminished, I ushered them to my room. They were already working for Fiddlers Court, and I waited for them to make their presentation. What they told me was one of my most macabre nightmares, and also, the stuff of a dream come true.

Frog was more ebullient and said, "Issy, we just found out, Mohammed has a new girl he wants, and she's only just nine-years old."

I looked up and meant to glance at her eyes, but was distracted by a photograph of a lovely young kid she thrust into my hand. She was an angel. I looked up at her to respond, but Billie interrupted, "Mohammed is planning to rape her today, and we know where."

I was all action within an instant, but stalled. I asked pertinent questions, and it transpired they had some half-baked plan to kill Mohammed and rescue the girl. I stated for all with me to hear, "Mohammed does not work like this. He will drug her in a hotel, and sell her virginity. Remember me. Remember Alice, and Daniella? He won't do this now, but tonight. Monitor the usual hotel room. Check if he's booked. If so, I want our own camera in the smoke detector.

When we reached our operations room, we checked and confirmed he'd booked room 101. Genie took a nearby room in the hotel on the floor below. Mel installed and connected to our smoke alarm camera in the room, and got good reception as events unfolded. That night, Mohammed got girl drunk and high, before using the Rohypnol.

Vikki was watching the main door from the foyer, and saw two men enter the hotel. One of them was the Queens Council from a previous rape, but the other man was unknown to her. I cursed Judge St. John-Smythe was not there, but I planned to get him later, regardless.

As soon as they entered the lift, Vikki called the police, switched off the mobile phone, and left. The phone only ever made that one call, and was cleansed thoroughly before being dumped in a rubbish bin some time later, and many miles away from both the hotel, and the sim card.

Our plans did not work out perfectly. Family Court Judge Selwyn Lewis had already raped Lottie, and the QC was taking his turn, when police broke into the room. The officers witnessed what was taking place, and all three men were arrested on charges of raping a minor.

Charlotte was taken to hospital, and DNA swabs confirmed her rape. The use of Rohypnol was identified, as was ecstasy, cannabis, and alcohol in her system, plus a hint of heroin.

Despite the legal profession closing ranks, they didn't succeed. The evidence was much too clear-cut for even the police to ignore. The room was crawling with forensics for many days after the event. We sent the video viral from an internet café way across town. It attracted a lot of interest, especially once the mainstream Press got hold of the story.

We re-released the footage of the rape by Judge St. John Smythe. It carried less weight, but added to the breadth of the police investigation, if only by sheer public outcry on social media. Nevertheless, Judge Lewis and the QC were duly processed and remanded in custody, eventually receiving very long prison sentences.

Mohammed was charged with various minor crimes, but was allowed bail at the second arraignment. His Barrister was incredibly good, and after our video evidence was disallowed, all charges against him were dropped. No surprises there then.

Using our female wiles and intelligence, we had struck back decisively against our enemies. This is where the female differs from the male. The rapist's crimes and subsequent humiliation were exceedingly public, and the stigma would never, ever, leave those men.

Unlike a man on the high of one success, we did not push further, but lay low until the attention shifted. None of us went to Court. We followed developments on TV and various online media offerings. That is not to say we did not celebrate, because we did, greatly.

However, I still felt remorse for what happened to this pure, young innocent. She was raped, something I desperately wanted to prevent.

Vikki eventually prevented my malaise from overwhelming my sanity, and we got quite drunk that night, but that's another story.

From the next morning, I began to pull my life around. I stayed with my friends at Fiddlers Court for several days, and held a grand party on New Year's Eve. It took us several days to recover, and before the urgency of study focused my mind once more.

During January, Zoë and I rode the motorbike up to Waterloo station and parked it with the keys in the ignition. It passed us with a new owner before we even reached the main terminus. I knew by the next day it would have new number plates, and have been re-sprayed.

We burned our fatigues, and gifted out boots to charity shops, leaving them outside for collection. They never made it inside. We kept the crossbow, high velocity rifle, and everything else of our arsenal, except the Semtex; which had gone a bit greasy. We disposed of that safely. The rest was secreted within the old servant's staircase.

I dropped off the radar for half a year, leaving Zoë in charge at Fiddlers Court. I returned to find Vikki running my domain. Melanie was riding shotgun, and said, "Vikki hasn't put a foot wrong."

Zoë kept an eye on them, but she was not a businesswoman.

I finished my Degree at the LSE, and achieved a 1.1. My father still carries the picture of my Graduation closest to his heart, although I do not. I considered taking a Masters but remained undecided. I still wanted to fight the system, but we were becoming seriously busy most evenings. Our business was thriving, and we were making more money per month than the majority of wealthy people earn in a year. It was all cash, and tax-free. I returned to Fiddler's Court, and we chilled.

I spoke with Sir Richard the following day, and was offered a job with his organisation. I'd work a normal office week. He had created the position for me—we both knew it, we just never spoke about it.

Later that day he spoke candidly, "Isabella, I took offices at Fiddlers Court, for five years, for a reason."

After due consideration I volunteered, "You plan to retire?"

He responded with a delightful smile, "How perceptive of you my dear. Retirement is a very big word, so let us just say, I am considering taking a back seat, and letting younger blood attend to the daily grind.

"Jetting around the world may appear to be exciting, but it becomes most tiresome. I'm thinking an executive position, but will remain Chairman of the Company. What are your personal plans for your future, Isabella?"

I was about to reply impulsively, as is my way, but stalled deliberately to analyse his words. It is a British way. Sir Richard was his amiable self, but asking me a different question. I was reminded of how educated people would talk around the focus of their attention, until one spoke of what they wanted to discuss. My question was, what did Sir Richard want me to say?

I took his glass for a refill, allowing a ruse whereby to think clearly. I returned a large measure to his hand and purred, "The question should rightly be, how can I best serve you?"

He smiled and said, "I hoped you would say that..."

The outcome was we enjoyed leisurely sex that summer's afternoon. It was not the urgent grinding of needful lust, but making love and sharing companionship. Neither did he need a pill or a strap.

I enjoyed it immensely, and in the process realised, I was growing older, I was becoming grown-up.

Later we took dinner at an exclusive restaurant, and during it, my mentor guided me to enrol for my Masters Degree in International Business Finance, which turned out to be a ten-month, internationally accredited course. What he actually wanted, was somebody he trusted on the inside when he stepped back.

The initial position in his company would be lowly, so as not to arouse undue rivalry or concern with ensconced staff. However, he made it perfectly clear, that if I performed as he expected, I would be fast-tracked. I took great comfort from the admission he wanted me there for the long haul, as his ears and eyes on the inside. It was mine for the taking, and I knew I would not let him down.

I reasoned, my own business would run in parallel, as we were based in the same building. I doubt I ever felt true adult love for any man before that moment. I left feeling as if I was floating on air, and enrolled for my Masters, again at the LSE with Sir Richard's Company sponsoring my studies.

I settled in quickly, but one must never lose sight of what is of the utmost importance, at least to a woman whom has been repeatedly, and systematically wronged and raped since childhood: Revenge.

The dispensation of appropriate justice was mine alone to bring to account, full retribution my only desire. British Courts of Law had zero interest, so I would see to it myself.

The only person I could depend upon to see it through, was me.

Bilty

"I must say, that was a brilliant move. You nailed two of the three, and seriously difficult targets. You must be well pleased, all of you."

"Yes, Bilty, it was a result, and the one we needed. It changed our thinking. We wanted to repeat, but Mohammed is a wily adversary. Now ask yourself why the SS and care homes were never questioned about Lottie. She had been in care for two weeks. So, still a cover-up.

"I should point out, that Judge Selwyn Lewis was the same Family Court Judge that supported Child Services up in Manchester. He sent Lottie to Hammersmith. And to his friend, Judge St. John-Smythe. They did the same to me years before. Together, they presided over the fate of very young girls they intended to relieve of their virginity. That is sick."

"Earlier, you told me to join the dots, and now I have: God forbid."

"Bilty, this is every child's nightmare. Why did the judge know Mohammed? Take this further, much farther when you investigate."

"I'll see to that, although it's hard to know where to begin. These are very big fish we're after."

"You will know by the time this tale is told. But in the meantime, where would these men meet? Perhaps at a certain Gentlemen's Club? I do not know, but it is a good place to start. Candice, are you OK?"

"No. This is all too sickening. I would not have believed it possible, but you have shown me the proof. I am coming to admit, that harsher penalties than Life Imprisonment should be handed down. And that sentences should be consecutive, as in the States.

"Excuse me, I need a moment."

She departed with Bilty, Genie guiding them downstairs, and for a breather. Zoë said, "How far you going with this tonight?"

"I'd like to be done with the all of it, but that won't happen, they are too wrung out."

"Yes, but at least they are listening and taking note. That's a first."

"I guess so. Let's break for a few minutes as well."

Bilty:
Personal Journal:

Notes:
1. Isabella has provided indelible proof of one Family Court Judge, and a QC, whose solicitor was acting for the defence, who raped a nine-year-old girl. A virgin. Mohammed got off scot free, and that is a miscarriage of justice.

2. I will need to research the case, and pull court records to discover the all of this. Candice will expect as much.

Ah, Isabella returns, looking fresh and composed.

"I perceive a change is coming. What gives?"

"It all gives. I found the money trail. I'll take us up to the finale this evening. OK with you both? Let's resume."

Chapter 38 – Sisters' In Arms

Project Domicile
Interview: 09 – C

Note:
1. Evening is approaching, and we are becoming wrung out. The monstrous scale of child abuse is undeniable, grotesque, and persistent.
2. Isabella remains calm, perhaps overly relaxed, as we begin to wrap up this sordid tale. She said we will be done by tomorrow, and that means Sunday will be a busy day.

Isabella
Sir Richard really put the pressure on me the following semester. I was expected to run a small department of his Company, and side-by-side, run my own business, plus study for my Masters in my spare time. I knew he was testing me, and I prevailed. Nevertheless, there was something else on my mind also, completing our retribution.

These twism's of fate walked hand in hand one evening, when I had the option to either: pursue my rapist, Judge St. John-Smythe, complete an assignment on time, or attend an extremely important business meeting in Milan. That night I had to separate personal goals from practicable ones. My past, present, and future, all hung within the choices I had to make before daybreak. I was halfway down a glass of Bacardi by the time I found a resolution. I also knew I was being judged on the outcome of all three options.

I made a call to Melanie, telling her to action the Judge, and this time, put him away for the rest of his life. I flew business class to Milan, and completed my assignment on the aeroplane. I slept little, but emailed it to Melanie as soon as I landed. She would compile the submission folder, and Zoë would hand it in on my behalf. I was fucked by the time I arrived in the intensity of an unknown, and exceedingly foreign country. The Italian language overawed me, until my Latin base linguistics kicked in. I also remembered some words the Arts Master had used at school. Despite my need for sleep, the Country was hot, the wine chilled, and the male attention, quite invigorating.

I controlled the meeting and closed the deal, declining their magnanimous hospitality as much as I dared. That was, until another bottle of Chianti at dinner brought forth my second wind. I danced all night, and in the early morning, slept on the plane. I did it all, and that was the truth. I knew I had passed the test, although there would be a few more to follow. I was ready, and having succeeded once, knew it would be a lot easier the next time.

Sir Richard greeted me profusely, but was too busy to congratulate me properly on the deal I had made until the weekend. But it showed he trusted me to get the job done, and that was more important. If the boss is breathing down your neck all the time, you know you are in trouble. Or he is a workplace bully, which Sir Richard most definitely was not. If the boss leaves you alone to get on with it, you are doing it right.

Zoë handed in my assignment, but had to take several goes at it before she got the hang of submission guidelines. Nevertheless, she managed to do it correctly in the end.

Back in the world of child-rape, things did not go down so well. The Judge did not show, and Melanie was left feeling frustrated as her immaculate plans came to naught. I was left wondering if this was another false lead.

On Sunday, I held a meeting with the girls, and discovered what went wrong. They were expected. The lust took place elsewhere, and we needed to cover our backs. Retreat, regroup, and strike from an unexpected direction. I had been studying the I Ching in my seldom-idle moments, and the Art of War by the great Chinese strategist Sun Tzu. His book offered similar thoughts on warfare — battles sacrificed to secure a greater victory, much like a pawn in a game of chess.

I heard the girls out and stated, "The enemy is evolving to parry us. Know your enemy, intimately."

That caused howls of laughter from my friends, because we had all been intimate with these barbarians frequently, and many times too often. What I did was drop a seed, and let them think about how to use the information against our foe. I left that kernel to fester, wilt, or grow. Sir Richard was doing exactly the same with me, but in a different and business orientated context. So far, I was ahead of his game. I needed my girls to catch-up, and fast. As the laughter subsided, I continued.

"Focus upon what is most important, and action it. Study every aspect of your enemy, until you each know all their ways and their habits. Keep yourselves anonymous, otherwise we are all undone.

"Be prepared for other false leads, and check each one carefully. After that, double-check from a different angle. We will stop all direct action until I sanction it, which will be after they have dropped their guard. Remember, if the information comes from them, it is likely to be false, or a half-truth. Time is on our side."

My brief talk worked well, as we were all becoming a little wiser. I spoke with Zoë, Melanie, and Vikki in private afterwards, elucidating what we were about in ways they could comprehend. I left them to celebrate their new understanding, and returned to my studies. I now had three Generals at my command, and each was ideal for the roles I had tasked them: monitoring, technology, and business.

Later, I reflected, that this was exactly what Sir Richard expected of me also. I was amused by the fancy, and opened a new bottle of Bacardi to celebrate my deeper perception.

Truth be told, I drank little that night, as I needed my brain to function properly early the next morning. By putting our revenge on hold, I had also freed myself from the extra stress associated with plotting the murder or exposure of high-ranking, and very public figures. Time was the one thing I did not have enough of.

The girls came to me with plans that were more serious on occasions, but each was flawed in one way or another. Most involved murder, and while we all agreed this was justified, it was less than the complete retribution and public exposure I demanded. I wanted to humiliate them and eviscerate this cancer from the heart of British childcare, forever. We had done that with the Judge and QC, but the system they used and abused remained.

That in turn meant, showing the world what they had done to us, and sending them to prison for their crimes against our fledgling humanity. I determined we had to find a means to reveal all.

The months flew past and my studies were going extremely well. I was rushing to meet submission deadlines for my main Masters projects, and associated dissertation. The time was just before the summer break, when Sir Richard called me to a meeting. This was normal, and I prepared the usual progress report. My project for him was virtually completed, ahead of schedule, and under budget.

However, the emphasis of this assembly was entirely different. The group was composed of senior management from all over the world, and I was given a new and major project to work on. I was required to develop sourcing of gemstones, grading, and sales in the Far East. It was a promotion to manageress, and serious raise in pay. It also meant I would be spending much time out of the country.

Aside, Sir Richard said, "This is your big chance Isabella. Make a success of this, and you will have earned a place at this very table."

I was just about able to balance my schoolwork, complete the existing project, and begin my new job. They were all extremely demanding. I am sure The Fates must have had it in for me, because one afternoon while I was chasing my final submission deadline for the LSE, my stalwart source of information came to visit me.

Zoë related, "It was earlier today, around lunchtime, when matron made a big fuss before leaving early. We all know she does this sometimes on a Friday afternoon. Frog, who gets out this year, got wind of it, and thought she might be meeting someone. You know Frog still has the keys for matron's office and secret drawer, the ones we borrowed and copied all those years ago. Well, she slunk into her office when staff either left for the day, or went to the dining hall.

"She sneaked a peak at matron's diary, and discovered an entry listing for the coming two weeks: 'Holiday'. She found brochures with circles indicating a trip to the Maldives, and put two and two together."

I knew Zoë far too well, and she was holding something back. I pressed her to tell me all. With a smile of delight she posed enquiringly before adding, "Well, Frog knew matron had a new front door fitted last month, and she found the old set of keys in the secret drawer of her desk. There are five keys on the key ring. Three of them are door keys."

I was still not getting it, until she elicited, "The old front door needed only two keys, so what does the other open?"

I looked at her incredulously, and uttered, "The side door?"

Zoë said casually, "Care to check it out with me later tonight?"

She dangled a set of keys in her hand, before spinning them around her index finger. We were on a mission, one that had eluded us for many years. I sent her to watch the residence, and some hours later she reported matron had left in a taxi, taking with her two large suitcases.

We both returned to the house at three a.m., entering via the back garden. Our pulses raced as we crossed open ground, our breathing ragged. Not from exertion, but from fear of being caught.

Zoë offered the keys to the secluded side door, and it unlocked. We were ready to bolt if an alarm sounded, but as her gloved hand depressed the handle and pushed the door open, all remained silent. At last, we were inside Matron's lair.

We waited for sunrise, which was half an hour away, it being nigh-on midsummer. The house was large, modern, had four bedrooms, was detached, and somewhat secluded. We had presumed matron lived alone, and were surprised to discover she was married. We took our time and methodically worked through the main rooms, before discovering her study upstairs.

The place was a mine of highly sensitive information. We found files relating to Direct First Care UK, Mohammed and his organisation, details about our care home, and all the others. We even had contact numbers for highly influential people, including Judge St. John-Smythe. We worked quickly. I was pulling information as Zoë photographed it. The evidence was highly incriminating, once you understood what was happening. Due to my work and education, I did.

We left at 6.30 with a stack of data, although there was one locked door downstairs we did not have time to investigate. I went to work after a short debrief at Fiddlers Court, and felt shattered all day. I left instructions for Zoë and Melanie to go through the entire house with a fine toothcomb the next night. They spent most of the week there, Melanie photocopying everything, and probing the depths of matron's home computer at other times.

My thoughts distracted by my new job, and our discoveries at matron's home, I was becoming engulfed. I got back to my room, got out my LSE project, and fell asleep in an instant. I woke early, and examined my priorities. I needed to delegate in order to do it all.

On Monday morning, my mind was made-up. I told everybody I would not be available until Friday afternoon, when I would have completed my submission for the LSE. I gave my new team at work a series of tasks to do, and waited for objections. There were none.

I bumped into Sir Richard as I was headed for my studies, and told him straight what I was doing. He smiled at me and said, "I judge people only by results, not timekeeping. Your team are experienced workhorses, not high-flyers. Use them wisely. Congratulations my dear, you are learning the art of delegation. I knew you would, eventually."

I checked in with my team every morning, before speaking briefly with my girls, but waited until the weekend before calling for a review. I was always a mere phone call away, but both teams soon learned not to distract me with trivia.

During the interval, I finished my final Masters submissions, including the dissertation, and felt good about it. After submitting it, I spent the remainder of Friday on my work project, before clearing out my room at Grosvenor House. I had been there for four years, and knew I would miss it.

I moved fully into Fiddlers Court, and had a meeting with my girls the following morning. Melanie had been working on her presentation, and it showed. We had more than enough information to expose the entire swindle, but it was out of our league.

Over the days, they had discovered the key for the locked door; a study that belonged to Matron's husband, Dean Holdsworth. It became apparent he was an accountant, and the Company Secretary of Direct First Care UK. We had finally uncovered the money trail.

I spent the entire evening going over all they had discovered, and did not even have a drink. There was an avalanche of related and intertwined information. It took me into the small hours to unravel the jist of what was going down.

On Sunday, I began pulling the disparate financial strands together. It was a scam, as I had suspected all along.

The following Monday I went into work and dedicated the morning to my team. They had done really well. After due review of progress, I instigated phase two of our initial program, and added another which I had planned for much later, but it would keep everyone busy, as again, I was short on personal time.

I have no idea why this happened so often, but yet again, I bumped into Sir Richard as I was leaving. It was as if he had his finger on the pulse, or a camera in my office. He asked me how it was going, and I replied, "I'm trying to get ahead of the clock, so have set the team several tasks. Last time they…"

The man cut me off mid-sentence, and asked, "What are you really up to? I know you much too well, Isabella."

I laughed and rejoindered in kind, "If you know me that well Sir Richard, you will not worry. Let's just say, something came-up, and I need the personal time to deal with it. There is some legacy from my past I need to finish, once and for all"

His voice was businesslike, but his fatherly eyes told of a deeper understanding of his wayward protégé, "This is why I generally prefer the company of, shall we say, younger women, for they do not have the febrile machinations of grown-ups. So be it, or be damned. Get this— whatever it is, dealt with, for-ever."

He sauntered away, like The King holding all the cards. I, as yet, unproven. I knew he turned at the end of the corridor to watch me leave, but I did not look back. I had a curse to end. I took two days off to understand all the evidence gathered by Zoë and Melanie. They became central to my formative plans, as in short measure did Vikki.

I worked late on Friday evening, and did a full day on Saturday. Sir Richard came in, and was impressed with our progress. He said, "Time you finished for the day. I would love your company for dinner."

"I'll need half an hour to complete. But yes, that would be admirable. It's been too long since we shared personal time together." He did not miss my innuendo, and smiled profusely.

On Monday afternoon of the following week, I returned from lunch and went to see Sir Richard. I briefed him on my progress and concerns, before saying, "Myanmar is the biggest regional producer of gemstones, virtually everything except diamonds. Foreigners are hardly known there, so I think I should go to Burma in the near future and see how the land lies, get a personal feel for what we are about. I'll make a supporting presentation on Thursday, if that suits you?"

That evening I spoke to John from the Press, and later Mr. Josephs joined us. Both offered us their assistance, but what we had unravelled was all way too big, even for them to get their experienced heads around. They did give me contact numbers, some of which I pursued. One was a freelance investigative journalist who became especially useful to our plans. His name was Bilty Steadman, a pseudonym I concluded. I also gave Zoë a special mission that week, which was to become exceedingly important, but I will come to that in due course.

[Bilty: "So this is where I first enter the story. But I was a long way behind where you were. I spoke to both of them later, and they persuaded me to support you; then Candice came on board. My misgivings now make total sense, and were unsupported. Pray continue."]

We would have acted as soon as matron returned from holiday, but two things were against us. The first was an entry in her private diary, detailing a meeting with other care chiefs and executives, scheduled for the coming weekend at Mohammed's office. The second was that we needed to purchase some particular chemicals and specialised equipment. In the meantime, we refined our plans, and work kept me nicely preoccupied, although the waiting was excruciating.

Meanwhile, Melanie prepared files for viral exposure on the internet, but we knew that was a support plan. She, with Zoë and Vikki worked on the more practical aspects of our proposed siege, and by Friday evening, we were as good as ready. If everything went to plan, we had the evidence no jury, nor journalist could baulk. Ensuring the plan worked perfectly kept me awake until after midnight.

I slept until 6 a.m., because Zoë and I had something vitally important to do that morning. When we returned, I rehearsed my lines, because our main play was about to centre in the round of public exposure. There was no room for error.

It would have been very simple for us to act like men, and send a few Rocket Propelled Grenades into Mohammed's meeting room. It was much too easy to kill every last son of a bitch, plus the bitches as well.

I guess my belief in any religion had been fucked out of me. I still bear the scars of institutionalised rape from an extremely early age. So, do my comrades, Aisha's latter-day warriors against the misogynism of Muslim men and their compliant women: My Sisters' in Arms.

Bilty
"That was certainly a lucky break, Isabella. Access to Matron's home, and all the information that had eluded you. You must have been delighted."

"Yes we were. That was the turning point, the holy grail we had been seeking for years. With full access to Matron's home, I was able to follow the money trail. We had at last obtained substantiated facts. That her husband was the accountant responsible for the care homes and Direct First Care was a stunning bonus."

"Could you have done anything otherwise?"

"No Bilty. Even with my understanding of the vehicle of finance, it took me some time to piece the all of it together. Without the data from Matron's home, we would have remained as lost as forever.

"What it did was, allow us to take action."

"Can you break down what you discovered, in simple terms?"

"Yes I will. But I'm calling this off here, and will finish this tomorrow. Melanie and I will prepare a document summary for collection tomorrow.

"Bitly, Candice, you will stay?"

"No, this time we will go. This should have been our monthly date night, so Bitly will be taking me for dinner, won't you."

"Yes dear. I fancy Curry."

"Italian it is then."

"Isabella, when should we return, it will be a long session I presume."

"What? No Bilty, it will take the afternoon, and then we will be done. Candice, afterwards keep me informed of progress. I need to leave shortly to prepare, I have a busy evening ahead. Until tomorrow then, *au revoir*. Genie, please see them out and call a driver to attend."

The girls departed, and Bilty filled in his journal, whilst conversing with his wife.

Bilty:
Personal Journal:

Notes:

1. I will be most interested to learn about the money trail they uncovered. I have some experience regards investigating creative accounting, so this will be fascinating.

2. What cannot be denied, is that these girls were putting a very serious and far-reaching operation together, one that today, years later, still sends shudders through the foundations the legalese and authorities concerned, built their empires upon. Respect Girls.

3. The early night was a surprise, but most suitable to my wife. I would have preferred to be done with the all of it, but life doesn't suit everyone all of the time.

Chapter 39 – The Art of Female Revenge

Project Domicile
Interview: 10
Location: Fiddlers Court, The Oval, Holborn, Central London.
Time: 13:02 hours, Sunday, 29th October.
Subject: Isabella
Others Present:
    Zoë, Melanie, Vikki, Genie, Candice.

Note:
1. We settled down for the afternoon, all feeling refreshed. Isabella has said the session will be the last, and will be enlightening.
2. Before beginning, Isabella handed me a dossier, and Melanie added a digital copy. "As promised, Bilty. A referenced summary of their financial scam, at least, as far as I understand it."

Genie handed her a large glass of brackish liquid. Isabella stared at it, before saying, "Vengeance is such a sweet chalice to sip upon, on this, such a bright and sunny afternoon.

"If there's nothing else, I'll begin: The art of female revenge."

Isabella

Female vengeance is not the stuff of male-dominated action films, a hellfire of bullets, nor explosions of blood and gore. Sometimes it carries with it explosive impact. At other times it is slow, public, and designed to cause maximum distress. Female revenge is a consuming fuse, leading to revelations that envelope the unwary, entreating them to endure damnation for all eternity. It embodies fullest exposure, public humiliation, and personal suffering.

Until my release from the clutches of Paki-rape and daily abuse, I had not been able to focus properly upon my retribution. It was always a beholden objective, but never a fact. During Sixth Form, I cut the ties that bound me indelibly to my sexual abuse.

It matters to a girl that she maintains the right to determine which male will, or will not be, her lover. The art of female revenge is not about what you do, but the way in which you do it. For any woman, it is not enough to defeat her enemy. What matters most is that the enemy is aware of why he or she is suffering, publicly pilloried, before summary execution. This remains almost inclusive of females, exclusive of males.

One big difference is that men usually strike back immediately, while a women is inclined to bide her time, to expose disproportionably, the slightest weakness. In the world of school bullies and care homes, I learned to attack first. Now, I faced a bigger challenge, and one that required precise aforethought and meticulous attention to detail.

Matron's meeting was scheduled for 7 p.m. Saturday evening, after regular staff had departed. Zoë and I went in via a rear fire door at 18.50 and waited. We avoided the guards. Their patrol schedule and security cameras had been hacked by Melanie to ensure our safety.

The delegates arrived, and security completed their rounds. We introduced industrial grade chloroform into the air conditioning system. Zoë let in our backup crew, and soon everyone in the building was accounted for, asleep, and tied up.

We were wearing full body protection that was untraceable, except for the soles of our shoes, which we put on just before entry, and removed on exit. The shoes had platform soles to make us appear much taller. The padded suits were male sizes, and the helmet included a gas mask. The overall design was menacing.

Before the tranquiliser wore off, we rearranged the delegates at the meeting table, tied them to their chairs, and covered their mouths with duct tape. The girls hoisted me, and I replaced the fire alarm with one that appeared identical, but had cameras and audio. I hid a powerful transmitter in the tiled false ceiling, and Melanie confirmed reception.

I took control, and waited for them to come round. Vikki was nearby, ready to record every confession on a hand-held camera. Zoë would remove and replace their gags. My focus was for them to tell us their individual parts of the plot. They didn't tell us without persuasion I might add, but the fear of pain proved to be our greatest ally.

I began with Matron, as we had more than enough data from her home. It was impossible for her to deny the evidence. Once she spilt the beans, the others admitted supplying girls into care as a requirement of their jobs, and targeting the easiest prey to meet their targets.

How can anyone put targets on getting children into care? There is either a need, or there is not!

Most often, those at serious risk are ignored for easier prey.

I began my interrogation with Matron. "We went after the young girls Mohammed specified as being at risk."

"Let us be clear. Mohammed told you they were at risk."

"Yes. He knew how the local streets worked, and which children were vulnerable. We followed up his leads, and it helped us meet our targets. So, everyone was a winner."

"Except for the targeted girls. He had a market for their services?"

"I don't know."

"Yes you do. You knew they would become unpaid prostitutes."

Matron refused to answer, that was until I got the pliers out. "No, it wasn't like that. Often, the chosen girls lived at home, and were mostly unknown to us, let alone on the 'At Risk Register'.

"We would initiate a complaint, monitor the targeted girl, and suggest they should be taken into care outside of the area. In return, Mohammed rewarded me."

"So you admit to targeting specific children. How?"

"I can't say."

"Oh yes you will. How much money did he pay you?"

"You know? Oh my God. He paid me two thousand pounds in cash, for each girl we brought into the system."

"You admit taking bribes for putting kids into care. Let's move on."

I discovered which SS offices and local councils they had liaised with. They gave up the names, but refused to take any direct blame for what became of the girls in their care. "It was the girl's lifestyle choice."

Melanie had previously discovered a list of girls' names at matron's house, and I demanded, "Specify which girls on this list you targeted."

My name was one of the many she identified. I intended to return to the same point later, but from a different angle. I knew most of the girls mentioned, and chose one that I knew had been identified by a taxi service. I pressed her for details, and in due course, she said, "The girl was taken because of information Mohammed supplied. We would do school checks, search hospital records, looking for means to intervene."

At last the truth was out—why my own family had been ripped apart. It was due to the taxi driver who took me to hospital. Relief, justification for my beliefs, and euphoria flooded my psyche. The barbaric bitterness of unrequited retribution was strongest of all. I kept my boiling emotions in check. The communicator masking my wrath, turning my warranted outrage into an intimidating male voice.

I pursued the connection to Judge St. John-Smythe, and his peers. Nobody wanted to speak against the judiciary. I began to pull out her fingernails with the pliers. I did not use much force at all, but she cracked just after her nail varnish.

She said, "I was taken into care when I was thirteen years old. Judge St. John-Smythe took a liking to me, and reserved my case to himself. We kept in touch, became good friends, and he had sex with me for the first time just before my fifteenth birthday. He did so on regular occasions thereafter."

I believe her tears for herself were genuine. What I could not forgive, was how she sought a position in life where she could force similar abuse upon others. She also made a lot of money from it.

I pushed her on the point. "The Judge persuaded me to work in Social Services. He used Rotary Club contacts, and gave me a personal letter of recommendation. The requisite was, I look the other way when a young girl he fancied passed through his court."

"Name the other judges."

"No. It was only him."

"Liar! We know Selwyn Lewis is one. And a QC. Let me show you the video of Charlotte losing her virginity. She was nine years old, and she was in your care."

Matron quailed, and names of complicit Family Court judges were added to the list, QC's, police officers, local councillors, Social Services, lawyers, and the CPS. Each matron told a surprisingly similar story. They all added more names to their declaration of guilt.

After they confessed, I said, "Time to move on. Let's define the role of Direct First Care UK. It is a legitimate enterprise on the surface. The main shareholders are you four ex-SS managers, Mohammed, his Uncle Usif, and Dean Holdsworth, plus one other. How did you finance it?"

Matron replied, "They used stakeholder investments to finance their operations. Pension funds, city fund managers, and charitable donations. Once favourable dividends returned from the first care home, other homes were quickly financed to increase fiscal yield."

I delved deeper. "Direct First Care UK is a holding company for many other associated frauds. Your website allows you access to prospective foster and adoptive parents, in addition to the children themselves. The associated database must be chock-full of highly sensitive and personal information. Explain."

"It enables team and Social Services staff to check and prepare matches, before making direct contact. The key to success is that only children can advertise. Foster and adoptive parents can only register, and submit an online, and exceedingly detailed form. It was a Godsend. We were able to quickly match children to prospective foster and adoption clients. Everything was legitimate as regards general operation."

I retorted, "The problem is, the administrators were in it for the money, some running a child prostitution racket." With a little persuasion, the care home matrons all admitted they did it for the money, but claimed to know nothing about the sexual slavery scam.

Mohammed was doing the same, selecting girls for his operation, and using the care home facility as domicile to be easily available. Sometimes Mohammed needed to know if the girl was a virgin. Matron admitted, "We would make an allegation of sexual abuse, and send the girl for physical examination, which of course featured a hymen check."

As in my own case, twice. I was astonished how matter of fact it was stated. I set about the point with gusto, until each matron admitted, they knew the girl's virginity was important to Mohammed.

I stated, "Each of you knew these girls would be raped."

"No, it was their lifestyle choice. We could not stop them."

I shouted, "The law clearly states, sex with a child under the age of thirteen, is automatically rape. How can a naïve, nine-year-old virgin, make the choice to become an unpaid child prostitute? Your double standards are a disgrace. So is your dereliction of duty, of Guardianship.

"Further, Mohammed's Russian based website is an abduction tool. When Mohammed found a girl he wanted, no matter where she lived, he told you, and you actioned the girl being taken into care locally.

"'Direct First Care Placement Agency,' as the name implies, is a separate arm of your company. They supply prospective foster carers and adoptive parents with children. The Local Council rate for each foster caregiver was £1,200 per week. Regards private adoption service, this figure leaps to £22,000 per placement, and is increasing annually.

"Each of your care homes is taking upwards of £8,000 per week, per child. This rises to £20,000, per child, per week, for troubled children. The latest care home caters for this class of inmate, and operates like a prison. The kids are more troublesome, but are still used as regular prostitutes. You are all directors. Your sins are many.

"I notice you are paying yourselves an annual wage in excess of £300,000 per year, ten times your pay grade if you had remained in the SS. This does not include backhanders, bonus awards, expenses, pension and share rights, nor the profits from any future sale. You are all, only interested in money. None of you give a shit about the lives of the kids you are paid to protect. What of your Duty of Care? You sicken me!"

I strolled around the table, needing to quiet my surging venom. "Henrietta Allardice!" I whirled back to a matron I had just passed.

"Does the name Tom Cousins mean anything to you personally?"

She shook her head vigorously in denial. "Liar! Let me explain. Tom was Henrietta's unofficial guardian, in the days before foster care became a modern moneymaking racket. I notice you still live with him. Do not deny it Henrietta. This is a fact of your life. It is also a scam you cooked up together. So, let's get down to the real issues.

"Tom is an Expert Witness by trade, and provides reports for Social Services, especially on the mental state of unwitting mothers who are fighting to retain their sons and daughters within a family environment. He scraped through his GCSE in psychology, at the second attempt, and has no other medical qualifications. Is this not so, Henrietta?

"Well, he does have an Associate Degree, one bought online from a well-known, and spurious Academy in the USA. It is a phoney qualification. You pay your money, and get an Associate Degree by return of post. In British English, that is a Diploma, not a full degree.

"But, what makes Tom special, is that he is the preferred 'Expert Witness' for mental health examinations [R 39.1], and usually does these without bothering to see the victim in person. Fact.

"His minimum fee for a short report, and Court appearance is £37,500. In the last year accounts are available for, he was paid just over half a million pounds by the British taxpayer, via Social Services, from the same office you used to run. He also works for other SS offices.

"How do I know this you may wonder?"

307

I nodded my head, at which, Zoë dropped a piece of paper in front of each person. "Dean Holdsworth just so happens to be his personal accountant. This is turning out to be a most nepotistic, and lucrative world you all inhabit. Isn't it?"

Matron was visibly shocked when I stated, "Patricia, I notice your husband, Dean Holdsworth, is Company Secretary of Direct First Care UK. Graham Holdsworth, of Holdsworth & Holdsworth Associates, just happens to be the auditor for the last set of published accounts. That would be your husband's brother, would it not?"

"How do you know this?"

"The information is in the public domain. Answer the question."

"Yes. They are brothers, and Dean is my husband. They are also excellent accountants, which is why we use them."

I pressed onwards mercilessly. I stood behind Mohammed, and put my hands heavily upon his shoulders. "So which of you is going to tell me how this paedophile became central to all your scams?

"Not only does he fuck nine-year-old girls, but he makes millions of pounds per year from underage prostitution rackets. Look!"

Zoë laid another piece of paper before each person. The maths were so simple, even Zoë had got them right first time. "This is what Mohammed is making out of girls in your supposed care. Millions of pounds per year. It is all in cash, untaxed, and untraceable.

"Then, there are many more girls out in the community, if turning fewer tricks. But, they will be earning more for him overall. Those of you that missed the money-trail, should bow your heads in shame. Inzamam Mohammed has been making even more out of this scam than you were, isn't that the truth. Just look at the figures.

"Of course, the price goes up, as the age of the girl gets younger. Older girls, like those above thirteen years, well, the punters only paid fifty quid a fuck. The market demand was for nine-year-olds at one-hundred or more pounds per go. Sick, isn't it. You all, knowingly, supplied these girls for him. That is even sicker!"

Eyes bugged as I watched the matrons squirm. Zoë un-gagged them. They protested their innocence, before venting their wrath at Mohammed. Sharon Hayes, matron of the first care home let rip. "You bastard! You gave me only a couple of hundred pounds for each girl I got into care. You and your Uncle have been ripping us all off from the beginning."

I judged the moment before re-entering the fray. "So, the scammers have been scammed, and it serves you right. What of your Duty of Care to the girls left in your charge? You have all but confirmed you sold them into prostitution, some as young as nine-years-old. You deserve to be in prison. Hanging your worthless hides is too good for you.

"So Sharon, tell me how this all began?"

"We didn't..."

"Oh yes you did. Knowingly. You've already admitted it. Tell me."

"Usif Mohammed was the man with the money. Inzamam controlled the day to day running of the business. When I was introduced to Usif, he was a charming and a most concerned businessman. He was one of the leading lights of the regional Muslim Conference, and he needed advice regards founding a charity.

"He told me about vulnerable youth cast adrift on the streets, and asked for my support. It all started innocently enough. I became engaged with his idea of saving young girls from drink, drugs, and prostitution. I believed what he was saying." She had the nerve to weep. "He was so very sincere."

"Except that in your care of guardianship, they did drink, drugs and became sex slaves."

"No, it wasn't like that."

"Yes, it was exactly like that. You disgust me. Go on."

"Over time I became his advisor, and we met often. I introduced him to other leading charity workers. I remember he got on really well with Misses St. John-Smythe, and her husband took an active interest.

"We met for a dinner-dance at the Rotary Club, and that is when Usif asked me about opening a care home. The judge supported him, and I was so taken with their idea, I offered to quit my job to open and run the first care home, as my focus was upon helping the children."

"But you became their pawn and face of legitimacy. Continue."

"Patricia's husband was an accountant, so I asked her advice, as she was my underling at the time. I was wary about being ripped off, and losing my pension. Dean checked it all out, and came up with a redundancy solution. The result was, we formed Direct First Care UK."

"To be clear, Sharon. Dean is very good with accounts, and manipulating the law, as regards legal process. I do not mean illegally. But he knows a lot about the vehicle of finance. He also knew local authority employment law, thus allowing you to extricate yourself from your employment. With a pension and lump sum?"

"Yes, Dean is a very good accountant, and auditor like his brother. They have done nothing wrong. They had both done work for the council before this. I invested the lump sum into my pension, which I get at the official retirement age. So far, I have not seen one penny of it."

"I understand. Go on, Sharon. Tell me about how Direct First Care UK came into being."

"Well, they sorted out the legal minutia, financial details, and arranged funding. I have no idea how the fiscal side worked. You have to believe me. But I did know about how care homes were run.

"So, I quit my job and began the first care home. We had twenty-four children the first year, and that rose to almost sixty kids the second year.

"Pat took over my job, and helped find new children in need of care. She had targets to meet. To avoid trouble, Usif suggested we take only girls. That saved us many problems. I believed I was doing God's work. Mohammed, I hate you, and your God-forsaken Uncle!"

"So, judge St. John-Smythe and Usif were the ringleaders?"

"Yes, they set it all up, if that's what you mean."

"Sharon, who drew up the rules and Mission Statement?"

"All of us agreed the Mission Statement, although I wrote the draft rules for the care home. Why do you ask?"

"What about the daily running of the Company, and the care home?" I waited for Zoë to drop the share issue statement before them.

"I see from this document, judge St. John-Smythe owns ten percent of the shares, Usif and Inzamam, own seventy percent of the shares. That represents the power they hold in the Board Room, and over you. In other words, Inzamam told you what to do. So does the judge."

The matrons tried to deny it, but after we produced more evidence, they admitted they did as they were told. This was turning out to be an incredibly nasty nest of vipers. Zoë gagged them.

It is a human frailty to do wrong for all the right reasons. It is culpable iniquity to do wrong, for all the wrong reasons. Buoyed by Sharon's confession, I moved on to the next part of my interrogation.

Bilty

"Isabella, this is amazing. The SS and Matrons accepted bribes, and were aware these seriously underage girls would become prostitutes. That is complete dereliction of their duty."

"Yes it is. I call it child trafficking, which Social Services are guilty of. They need to be charged as such in court, and sent to prison.

"And no, Bilty. The Matrons have not as yet, categorically stated they knew the girls would become child prostitutes. So far they have only admitted to the use of the cover-all phrase , 'it was the girl's lifestyle choice'. That is not the same. Whitewash if you prefer.

"In debating class, I learned how to leave triggers in dialogue for later exploitation and exposition. It's a ruse lawyers and politicians use to deceive the subject, lure them into a false sense of security.

"They do admit it, but that is yet to be revealed."

Isabella took a moment to finish her drink, and look around, before saying, "So how come, in the intervening years, not one has been prosecuted? I intend to change that."

"You have our undivided support. Anything else?"

"Yes. Tom Cousins is still a preferred 'expert witness'. He should be in prison, and also those who use his services. No one, not the Press or Bussies, have even bothered to look for links between these people--say co-habiting, or plotting scams together. I have returned to put the record straight, and do what the police have conspicuously failed to do. Prosecute the perpetrators of heinous injustice.

"Inzamam and Usif Hussein are still running their company and their scams. The police and local authority have barely acted against any of them. It seems more like a cover up, and denial of information to the press. Mel you got that new link we found last night? The article that reads like a case resume."

"Coming up now: <u>Rotherham</u> [R 39.2]."

"Please show it to them, and email Candice the link. For once, it was a most credible piece of journalism.

Bilty:
Personal Journal:

Points of Note:

1. What stands out, is that the SS went after unknown children at Mohammed's request, and found means to bring them into the system. That is atrocious behaviour, a misuse of their overly powerful authority, and should be a criminal offence. It is kidnapping. That means misuse of childcare provisions is considered irrelevant by the authorities.

2. The SS and Matrons knew the girls taken into care would become seriously underage, child prostitutes, without payment. I must wait for the final revelations, but if this is so, it proves a most grievous misuse of the fundamental objectives of their profession. By setting out to take the children into care, on any pretext, in order to facilitate them becoming child prostitutes, is child trafficking. They were breaking the law.

3. The proof that an 'expert witness' has no qualifications, but makes a ton of money, as spouse of one of the directors is troubling. That he is still practicing is unsupportable.

4. Mohamed paying cash, backhanders as a bribe for his chosen girls being taken into care, needs to be followed up. This should be the job of the police, but then, I am already aware that after Isabella's revelations, they tried to cover matters up, and at senior level.

5. Regards Holdsworth and Holdsworth Associates, their use of creative accounting is not against the law, if done within legal framework. I take no immediate issue with their accountancy practices.

What I do understand, is that auditors are supposed to be entirely independent of the company books they are auditing. They often work for the same accountancy company as holds the account. But in this case, it is a small company, consisting of two brothers, and I find this too nepotistic to be clearly an independent audit. Something else I will need to examine in greater detail.

6. Perhaps the most telling point is regards the judiciary. It is clear that judge St. John-Smythe and Usif made a deal. They were both interested in gaining access to extremely underage girls for sexual purposes. That the judge has a ten percent stake in Direct First Care UK is a gross conflict of interest, seeing how he is a part of the system that sentences these innocent children to a life in care. And he often appears to do so for his future sexual gratification. Untenable.

Candice said, "Are you about done, love. It looks like Isabella is about to resume."

"Yes dear."

I will continue to add notes, and watch the video, later. Isabella is about to resume, so a clean page of my notepad.

Chapter 40 – Smoking Gun

Isabella

I picked upon Mohammed for the first time, leaving the others to think about their crimes against the minors they were paid to protect. Children they had a duty of guardianship over, let us be very clear on that point. It's an inherent part of the domiciled child's conditions of life.

I had deliberately saved him for the last. I pursued my questions, and asked him to tell the group about his bail, and the reason behind it.

Charlotte's case details were *sub judice*, but because of us, the whole world knew about it. When the tape covering his mouth was removed, he refused to say a single word, which I had expected and prepared for. At my nod, Zoë came forward with a streaky rasher of smoked bacon, and dangled it menacingly before Mohammed's eyes.

His eyes fixated on the meat, as if it was a Cobra inflating its neck, preparing to strike a deathly blow. Zoë moved the rasher to his lips, and he tried to move away. I stood behind him and held his nose. He began to shake. Mohammed made rapid acknowledgement through all but sealed lips, "Do what you will, but I will never tell you."

I said, "Mohammed, Allah may welcome you into his domain with gratitude, for raping Charlotte, who was only just nine-years old at the time, and so many other underage white girls. However, you would be cast out and damned to hell for all eternity, were Allah to discover you had eaten pork, a far more heinous crime, don't you agree."

"Yes it is." His words exposed the brutal divide between the moralities of our disparate cultures. Once stated, he remained silent.

I looked at the women and said, "There you have it. The rape and sexual slavery of a nine-year-old girl, is a lesser crime in Inzamam's belief, than eating pork. Yet you all put personal profit before the childcare it was your duty to provide. What about the children in your supposed care? What if they were your own children!

"They were domiciled to a life where you were their guardian. Yet you ripped them away from their loving family environment, and you were active in sexually trafficking them. You are each beneath contempt. I could so kill you now. Each and every one of you monsters."

Zoë left the bacon in front of him, taped up his mouth. Out of camera shot, I sprayed a small amount of chemical up his nostrils, before moving quickly away. I watched his chest heave several times, before the tape over his mouth was carefully removed and discarded.

I had used a refined preparation of an evil drug named Scopolamine [R 40.1] [R 40.2], also known as The Devil's Breath. It would render him incapable of exercising free-will. It was highly illegal and quite expensive. However, he would have no memory of what he said or did. That was revenge for my loss of virginity.

Chapter 40

I still retained only stroboscopic flashbacks of the biggest moment of my life. We had tested it beforehand, Zoë volunteering, and she could not believe the video we shot of her during the few hours she was under the influence. She became our puppet. It was administered exactly like Mohammed's dose, and he would tell us everything.

I was also aware the CIA had used Scopolamine for several years as a truth serum, but it had proven open to suggestibility. Therefore my questions were simple and precise. So were his answers. I had planned them as a mind map, and kept to the script.

Once in thrall of the drug, Mohammed answered each question immediately, and truthfully from memory. He told us about Lottie. He explained about several other girls taken from home, and ones from each care home, who had suffered a similar fate. One of them was me.

He told us how much he was paid for each virgin, and whom by. It was also a ruse to distance ourselves from one particular care home, and included girls who were still at large within the community.

He with detailed payments made to the matrons privately in each instance, confirming the cash bribes. The amounts were not the same.

"What happened to the girls, Mohammed?"

"Proven virgins with hymen were sold to elite clients."

"How did you do this?"

"The taxi driver would take a picture, and I'd sell the slut."

"How much money?"

"Ten thousand pounds for under thirteen-year olds."

"Who were their virginity's sold to."

Mohammed stated from memory, naming judges and elite from British society. Judges St. John Smythe and Lewis were his most regular clients, and he told us where his records were kept, which we copied.

"They lost their virginities in hotels. Why did you drug them, and what with?"

"So they would remember nothing, but remain pliable to suggestion. You see, I needed them to act as if they were a bit drunk, but doing it of their own free will. I'm good at this."

Mohammed explained it all in great detail. He named drugs, and concoctions made from them, refining all the time. He included more than we knew of, and seemed content. There was no remorse. I had what I wanted, and Mohammed was gagged with fresh tape, until his next confession was due.

Henrietta surprised me by wanting to speak. She stated, "I never knew those girls would be drugged and raped. But what could I do?"

"You could have said something. Exposed the scam."

"No couldn't. They would have killed my husband, enslaved my children. There was nothing I could do. Once you are in their clutches, there's no turning back."

The self-serving bitch cried false tears for her own failings. I wondered if she were playing games with me. "Henrietta, we both know that is a load of bollocks. You are only trying to blame another for your own misdeeds and failings. Focus, or I will kill you. Right here, right now. You will only live, if you tell me the whole of the truth.

"Admit, that to prevent your own children becoming trafficked as sex slaves, you did that to the girls in your care. At least, allowed it to happen, unmonitored, and accepted."

"No, I never…"

"Oh yes you did. Be honest for once."

"No. It wasn't like that. I had to do it."

"For Inzamam Mohammed."

"Yes. He would have had us all killed, to look like suicide. Or made into sex slaves, don't you understand?"

"No I do not. You should have reported it to the authorities, instigated charges. But no. You took the money instead. Meanwhile, those in your Guardianship suffered as sex slaves instead. Admit it!"

Henrietta drew in a long breath and shouted, "Yes. Damn you."

"Unpaid sexual servitude, as held in dominion by the child's Domicile. Tell it all."

"I cannot. It wasn't like that."

"Yes. It was exactly like that, except they were somebody else's children. Not your own. Tell me now."

Defeating and blubbering, Henrietta admitted, "Yes. I knew they would become unpaid prostitutes. I did it to protect my family from them. We agreed to call it, 'making a lifestyle choice', so as to deflect interest from unwanted parties."

"Yes, like parents, and proper courts of law. The family court judges were also running a similar scam. Their angle was to fuck the young virgins, wasn't it."

She nodded her head, a broken woman. I felt no sympathy for the cretin. Her plight only aroused my uttermost loathing of her kind.

"So, to save your own family, you kidnapped innocent children from loving families. Families whose children I note, were not on the At Risk Register, and knowingly abducted them into care.

"No."

"Yes you did. Many times."

I looked at the others by turn. "So did you all. I will not leave until we hear the truth. Henrietta, it is now, or never. Admit it."

She nodded her head, before sighing, "Yes," on an expiring breath.

"Again, louder."

"Yes."

"Yes what?"

"Yes. At Social Services, we worked on any angle to get the chosen children into care, and the courts transferred them here."

"Finally we are getting to the truth. And you knew what would happen to the girls."

"Yes. I knew Mohammed would use them as sex slaves. We had to turn a blind eye. The judges also. They were also under threat you know. We all were, everyone was. He has stuff on all of us."

"I need your full confession now."

Henrietta finally told all, becoming open and forthcoming, as if in remission of guilt. She implicated all at the table, and others in Social Services, and outsiders we knew nothing about. Her confession was so all-pervasive and damning, the other Matrons had no option, other than to admit their own parts in the process. I'd prepared to administer further physical encouragement, but not one of the Suidæ kind. As it was, I didn't need to. With one broken into admission of acknowledging the true fate of these very young girls, the others followed suit.

The stories were repetitively similar, although other names of abusers were added to the mix. I had the writing hand of each matron released, and they all made a list of girls not at risk, that they targeted on Mohammed's behalf. I had done similar before, but this time there were new names we did not know of. That is the difference between checking a list, and writing one afresh.

The names of Zoë, Melanie, and I, were noted, as were contacts in other SS offices who did the legwork. I wanted everybody involved in these scams prosecuted for child kidnapping and human trafficking.

Once done, Zoë taped their wrists to the chair, and I recapped. "You still don't get this, do you. You, as Guardian, had a legal responsibility to see all the young girls in your charge, were treated the same as you would your own children. You disgust me!

"What I find intolerable, is that you were party to sex-trafficking them for financial reward. May you rot in hell for all eternity."

I returned to Mohammed. He remained fully compliant, confirming all the Matrons said, even adding details from his own point of view. They say ink is mightier than the blade? Not for me versus my Muslim enemies, give me a bacon buttie every time.

I returned to hammer the final nails into Mohammed's coffin. I knew what he said would never be admissible in a court of law, but having once admitted the truth publicly, would render him likely to confirm what he stated for the police, especially with our backup files. The police would also know where to search, and what to look for.

With great enthusiasm, Mohammed told us of his part in sourcing young girls, and his part in raping them. He specified how his operation worked, and had already confessed to selling very young girls' virginity to the highest bidder, and given us a list of names.

I worked my questions to a rehearsed script, and kept him on point.
"What about the other girls?"

"Who? Oh yes, the slaves. They went out to make money."

"No. To make you money."

"It's the same thing."

"But different men every time. How did you do that?"

"It was easy. I adapted an application, and it ran like a non-repeating roster. I coded it myself, places, times, girls. I am a genius."

"I need a copy."

"It's on the computer in my office."

"Password. Folder? The containing folders with everything inside."

Mohammed gave out, and Ellie went to make copies. Her gloved fingers handed me duplicates of his assignment log, a fancy title for a roster. It detailed the girls, the venues, and the clients, if many were numbers of men only. It went back to the very beginning, and contained years of incriminating information. Ellie copied, printed, and left copies for the fuckwitted Bussies to follow up. She also left the computer on.

The folder was a shock to me. He was a 'Landlord'. He controlled seven other operations in London. Each had a dedicated lieutenant.

Non-virgins entered the underground paedophile circus, and in time, regularly did tricks for other lieutenants of his operation. That's why we were active across Greater London. We became regulars in Islamic hotbeds, such as Tower Hamlets, Newham, and Waltham Forest. The lieutenants were different, but acted like Asif. They were all controlled by Usif through Mohammed. One must embrace the fact, these were not isolated groups of paedophiles. This was a large scale business, and run as such. I would guess, but I have no proof, that some money was used to fund Islamic terrorism. This was just the tip of the iceberg.

Moving on. After a few years, some were sold to the ringleaders of other 'Asian' gangs, once their faces, their vaginas actually, were no longer the latest thing in town. Later, older girls were traded with other groups, especially the Romanians who specialised in older teens.

With ferocity I shouted, "These are not chattels of war. These are ordinary children. Just like your own. You disgust me!"

He admitted giving Asif his orders, and that the paedophile ring remained highly active. He said, "We are feudal landlords in Pakistan, and can do as we wish. No one can challenge us. We brought this system to England, to enhance your peasant lives. Therefore, the care homes are breeding grounds for enforced prostitution. We trade with other feudal landlords in UK, of which there are dozens."

"Write down their names. Name them all, Mohammed, and brief details of the deals done." Zoë freed his right hand, and he did as told.

He had supported what the matrons had already told us. But his understanding of humanity was that of a despot. He acknowledged, "We use other people to work for us. They are only important to produce food, or to make money, otherwise they have no value."

"So these downtrodden masses of serfs in Pakistan, turn to the Taliban, who offer them succour."

"The Taliban are evil, usurpers of the true Pakistani birthright. But now they are so strong, we have to deal with them. This is one reason why England is the land of fortune and promise."

We were disgusted. Later, Melanie checked the web, her search for Pakistani feudal landlords [R 40.3]. The results were surprising. At last we understood our enemy within. They were tribal tyrants. They owned 'farms' covering hundreds of square miles, and all the people within.

With subtle prompting, he confirmed the money link, and Direct First Care UK as being a front for illegal activity. He detailed how his own, and other gangs of Muslims across the country, worked as a loose federation, swapping information, and trading unpaid, and underage girl prostitutes. This was their largest growing market, which did not surprise me. Social services would rubber stamp the girls' transfer. His father ran the scam in Birmingham, and Mohammed provided vital information.

One key proviso was to target pretty, young girls of potential sexual value, and rip them away from their loving families via Social Services, on any pretext. They were left at the mercy of his gang, all-alone in a strange and hostile environment, one where they knew nobody. The care home bullies, who were paid a little, did the rest. He was no Julius Caesar, but he knew how to Divide and Rule.

Mohammed explained how his drivers targeted girls playing truant from school, and even going to, or returning from school. The recruiters received a relatively large payment for each girl who became a regular, and a bonus for those that became popular with clients.

He started to give up a list of clients, but it ran into thousands of names. Time was pressing, as we needed to be out of there—security had to call in with a monitoring station. Mohammed told us where the list was kept, which Zoë retrieved from his office, and he identified the main contact person for each cell. He also confirmed how they used the website to find and subvert new girls, and he admitted age nine years old was their preference, in honour of The Prophet, Muhammad.

I wheeled on him and spat, "In honour of Aisha, don't you mean?"

Several Matrons tried to speak, but after each confession, the duct tape had been diligently reapplied to their mouths. I presumed they did not know the depths of Mohammed's true intentions and abuse. One of our girls came in at that moment and signalled. Our time was up.

Vikki said, "Mike, it's time to go." We had all chosen male names, a ruse to deflect the Bussies' inquiry.

"I told you not to use our names. Damn, you." A rehearsed ruse to throw off the Bussies. I dallied to press Inzamam about his uncle.

He confessed, "Usif is our leader. I am second in command of his empire. Iqbal, my father is another. We deal with other Pakistani leaders in England, and are constructing a nationwide exchange scheme, so new girls are never a problem. Using Social Services, we send them to other areas. I am now coming into my own power, as Usif grows older, and takes on a more fatherly role. It is I who will succeed him."

"What about the websites?"

"Ah. Those are my invention. Numbers are growing quickly since I met with other Landlords, and they agreed to use the website services I provide. I keep the best girls for ourselves, but the others go to different areas. Regardless, many are swapped later for a small commission."

"And regards the company, what was Usif's role? He set up the company. Was he the first to rape white girls?"

"Of course he was. He was the first to woo dishonourable white sluts and save them from being educated. He created our first care home. The man is a genius. None of this could have happened without his intellect, foresight, and connections."

"And what about the girls, the women. Do you idolize any?"

"What? Allah created females to serve man. If the wife is no good, or she only produces girl children, she is beaten. If she does not improve, she is killed and replaced with another. They have no worth."

"Except for fucking, you egotistical, self-centred bastard!

"Why do you venerate Aisha?"

"Because she was Muhammad's favoured wife, and she also fought for Sunni."

"Yes, I understand––The Battle of The Camel. Is it true that if a man is killed in battle by a woman [R 40.4], he will not go to heaven?"

"Yes. It is a grave crime, and denies the man a seat at Allah's side."

I got a few names out of Mohammed, regards his uncle's activities: the supply of liquor and cigarettes, drug smuggling, and terrorism. He said, "I'm not directly involved with that side of the business." Under threat from a bacon rasher, he told us who was, but that he controlled them in London. The drug was wearing off, but there was a trail to chase, and I would ensure the police followed it in full. We had it all!

I had been awaiting that moment for an extraordinarily long time, virtually two-thirds of my life. We had them in the entirety, and there would be all hell to pay if those present at the table, were not indicted and locked away for the rest of their miserable lives.

The girls acted swiftly as I revelled in my moment of total revenge. I heard the rattling of a can of spray paint, and watched Zoë graffiti the letters PBB prominently on the boardroom wall. I reflected that Mohammed's testimony was damming. It mattered to me that he knew who I was, but I could never reveal my true identity, without exposing all of us. Herein lies the crux of female retaliation: Do unto others, as thou would have done unto thyself. Not!

Regardless, I would soon have the public exposure I demanded.

We opened all the incriminating evidence and laid it out before each one, adding selected titbits and untraceable copies Melanie had prepared specifically for that moment. Our victims remained tied to their chairs, so they could only look at the documents. I hoped they would reflect upon their avarice, dereliction of duty, and woeful lack of humanity.

Zoë left to complete our plan, the second dose of chemical. This gave Vikki time to copy the recording she had made, and leave a pristine duplicate for the police, in the centre of the table, somewhere these sub-humanoids would never reach in time. We left immediately they wilted from a second dose of industrial chloroform, and soon, we blended into the madding mayhem of Marylebone.

I called Mel as soon as we were out and clear. She decamped, after she actioned Genie. The latter had already entered matron's home and laid out a few of the main evidential leads, as if Matron and her husband, had left them out on their desks. She was waiting along the road, and dialled the police at the same time I did.

I sounded like a man, and screamed in supposed shock. "There's been a gun battle at Hussein Brothers offices. I saw people being killed. I think it's the PBB." I shrieked, and cut the call dead.

Across town, Genie played a young housewife, and complained she had been raped. Melanie had manufactured both recordings during the previous days. Both were compelling and untraceable.

I called the Press at once, repeating the recording. Nearby matron's home, Genie did the same. We would see who responded faster to these emergency calls, the Bussies, or the Press. In both cases, the Press arrived first by several minutes, but they did not have legal power of entry, nor enough time to find a way inside. Perfect.

I also made one last phone call from the mobile before I threw it away. My contact was the investigative journalist, Bilty Steadman. He had agreed to monitor the police response, because, like us, he was after the bigger picture. We arranged to meet a short time later.

The girls were long gone when I heard the sirens approaching. I had waited out of sight, mulling over a clothes purchase inside, and near a shop window. I looked up at my reflection, and brought my hand up to form the pretence of a cocked gun. I turned and pointed in the direction of Mohammed's office, and fired my imagination. "Got you!"

I was looking at my hand, knowing I was holding a smoking gun.

In due course I watched armed police enter Mohammed's HQ, and I too melded into the congested ether of modern London.

I met Bilty, if briefly, in the Jamaica Inn 'Wine House' a short time later. I wasn't there more than a moment, but the physical meeting boded much more for the future. We remained in regular contact, and I, well Mel, gave him access to camera feed, plus the frequency and decryption key for the transmitter I had fixed in Mohammed's offices.

The story was all over the news for weeks to come. Melanie released selected footage before we arrived back home, and again it went viral. The Press couldn't get enough, especially when they worked out what it was all about. We sent full copies to John, Mr. Josephs, and Bilty Steadman. As a matter of public courtesy, every time the hubbub died down, a new revelation was timely and forthcoming.

It took Scotland Yard a lot longer to piece the incidents together, but that's the Bussies for you, just like the SS, only interested in the weakest targets, and protecting their own. I remain sure they were all double-dealing to try to keep the issue in-house. Like in Rotherham.

This time there would be no escaping the facts of organised, pre-planned child rape and trafficking by people in offices of total faith. Those entrusted with a Duty of Care towards the most vulnerable of our society.

Bilty Steadman

"So this is where I entered the story. I did not know what you were all about in those days, but your initial contact was intriguing, Isabella."

"Yes Bilty. We knew we needed a reliable contact with the press, someone who would not balk at exposing the truth. You came highly recommended, and let's just say, I had a feeling you were the one."

"Thank you. So that's how it went down. I must admit, the video you sent me was damning. I remember we all video-conferenced some days later, and discussed how to keep the pressure on.

"I did monitor the cameras you fixed, intensively that day, and the recordings on daily check. And you know what? I got footage of senior investigative officers trying to limit the damage, trying hide or destroy evidence. I have since ascertained, one of them was being paid off, and likely the other one also. I am still after the pair of them. They still don't know about the cameras and transmitters you put in place. They will as soon as we release the footage of their corrupt police practices.

Bilty:
Personal Journal:

Notes:
1. I remain astounded by Mohammed's attitude. That he considers eating pork to be a far graver crime than raping and sexually trafficking nine-year-old virgins is beyond my comprehension."

2. I note that Mohammed considers himself to be a clan leader, and tribal landlord in waiting. In Pakistan, he is of the upper caste, and acts like a despot. He would be above the parliament and law of the land. That he has brought this culture to our green and pleasant land is an anathema to all, and everything that is British.

3. Following this observation, leads one to a deeper understanding of their alien thinking. I must conclude, Mohammed is not of our culture, or religion. He has zero intention of integrating, but will use all the civilised British tools at his disposal to subjugate the next generation of British people to his will. His aim, to corrupt the British bloodline by impregnate white, Christian girls.

This is an issue concerning ethnicity.

This is an issue concerning religion.

And this is an issue concerning the racial belief, that white people are subservient to Pakistanis.

4. The problem, clearly, is to find police untainted enough to do their job, and bring justice to these young women. Following through with substantive, if supportive evidence, will largely be my job.

There is much here to follow up, and with Isabella back, I feel empowered to follow through. She has the moral fortitude to seek right over wrong. It seems, few others in positions of great power have similar thinking. They will fall.

"Candice, you have any observations?"

"No love, not coherent ones yet. This is way more than I imagined. The depths of depravity Isabella and others were exposed to is evil. That with her gone, nobody followed through, is unworthy of civilised society. I intend to set the record straight, and I will write her story. I'll need you to dig deeply into the all of what she has said."

"Yes, consider it done. There are many that should have been brought to book, that have been overlooked. Time to wring a snowball, and roll it from the top of this mountain of deflection and deception. I have some ideas."

"Does that mean we are about done here. It seems a bit early."

"I know there is one more scene, one that will blow your mind. I think it's time to finish this, if but for the moment.

"Isabella, I believe there is still one last tale to tell; if you please."

"You will be taking action, following up?"

"Most definitely. But it needed you here as the leader, no disrespect to any others intended. You are the one. You know that."

"Yes I do. Thanks. But before I get to the last act, as it were, I wish to take an aside, so you fully understand the breadth, depth, and the all of the problem. Time to crunch some numbers."

Chapter 41 – Number Crunching

Isabella

"The cases that have hit the press, Rochdale, Rotherham, and many others, were hampered by lack of information. They needed girls to come forward, and from them, were able to identify the main rapists. We had access to the Landlord's files, which gave us names of girls, venues, and client contacts. That means that our information can be easily verified. The police should be building a similar file regards these other atrocities.

"Bilty, how many Muslim men were knowingly paying to rape children in Rotherham. Come on, do the numbers of men."

"Hundreds?" Gulp. "I have no idea."

"Typical. I've led you to the iceberg, but you take only chips off the top to add to your Whisky. Let's get real and extrapolate figures in the public domain. I'll return to this later, but for a different reason.

"The real figure in Rotherham [R 39.3], now suppressed by the Press and everyone, was at least two if not three times the used figure of 1,400. That figure is also rounded down to an even number. Why?

"So, each night, these girls serviced at least four different men. Say 4,200 girls, so that means there were at the minimum, 16,800 Pakistani Muslim men fucking them. Every night. I thought it beyond time somebody took the highest figure, and rounded it up."

"Oh My God! That's more men than in the entire community. Wait. Some would be the same men. Weren't they? Same men, different days."

"Good try Bilty, and a question I need you to answer. In my own, our personal experience, few were the same men. Occasionally, yes. But with so many girls to choose from, they'd ask for different ones each time. I can prove it. I've already revealed Mohammed kept an assignment log like an operations manager, so each client regularly had new faces. Mel?"

"That's true, Bilty. But he was clever and used the computer. I have a copy of the application used, and folder; I'll forward it to you. Mohammed assigned codes to clients, locations, and girls. Each week, he would run the program, a bit like pressing a button on a one-arm bandit, and he would have all new faces at each client venue. Neat eh. It was clever, but the computer did the work, not him. Then he'd give the list to his lieutenants to action."

Isabella took over, "Reliable figures. I don't know. We all shared information about our rapists. We older girls did many shifts out of town, out of the closed community. I'd say we fucked at least treble the number of different men, for each girl listed, but four times feels about right.

"You stated earlier the Pakistani community was in denial. What if it wasn't? What if this went on with all knowing. This is becoming insidious victimisation of young Christian girls."

"I'm on it."

"No you are not. You haven't a clue. Just like everybody else. Why didn't you, or anyone else, extrapolate the figures? Let us relate the figure in the public domain, to the facts of life in Rotherham. The numbers of girls, and abusers. Let's do it now, then you'll know what to look for. What is the population of Rotherham?"

"Er … I don't know."

"Mel?"

"Searching the internet now … Got it, 257,280 in the 2011 census. Current estimated population in 2014, is 262,446."

"Ethnicity?"

"236,438 white British. The largest 'Black Minority Ethnic' or BME, are Pakistani and Kashmiri, who numbered 7,912 in 2011. That would represent a total of roughly 3,600 males of sexual age."

"Hmmm. So these figures do not add up, or even come close. Thanks Mel. Bilty, this is what I mean by looking at the figures.

"Now let's do some simple maths. How many of the white British population would be girls between the ages of say nine and nineteen? That's to account for those that were abused younger in life.

"Let's halve the number for females, equals 118,219. Presuming an even population spread of ages, which it won't be, females are slightly more, and up to age eighty, and for easy maths, the female population is about 120,000. For girls in Paki thrall divide by one-eighth, and I make 15,000 young girls. Using the lowest figure from Rotherham, that means that one in every ten girls of school age was in thrall to the Pakistani grooming gangs. But the figure is likely to be three times higher at around one in three of all female children, so what's wrong?"

"The catchment area, Isabella."

"Correct, Bilty. Those figures are only for Rotherham Metropolitan area. Good. Rotherham is five miles from Sheffield city centre, and parts of Rotherham borough are a best one mile northeast. Let's define Sheffield. Mel, same again, larger catchment area."

"Working … got it. Sheffield City has a population of over half a million at 569,700. But Sheffield Metropolitan City is the third largest in UK, with a total population of 1,569,000 approximately, estimated for 2015. Sheffield in these figures includes Sheffield City, plus Rotherham, Barnsley, Doncaster, and Chesterfield."

"Go on."

"I'll break down the stats … Sheffield: population 462,554. White British, girls of age interest, say roughly 30,000. Pakistanis = 22,000, so men of sexual age is about 9,000."

"Good work, but we are still short of numbers. There are not enough girls or men. Do it for all the areas mentioned."

"OK … for other areas of Sheffield: total for Doncaster of about 16,000 for white girls, and 3,000 for Muslim males of sexual age.

"Barnsley … about 5,000 girls, and 270 sexually active Muslim men.

"Chesterfield … say, about the same as Barnsley."

"Thanks Mel, I could see that took some research and interpolation. Candice, Bilty, do you want Mel's links."

Candice replied, "No, it's all on the web, so I'll check your figures myself. You searched for 'demographics' Melanie, so I'll do the same."

Isabella said, I've added up the figures for greater Sheffield, and I get approximately 71,000 white British girls between ages nine and nineteen. If four thousand two hundred were targeted by the Pakis, that means that one in every seventeen girls was in thrall of the Paki grooming gangs.

Regards the Pakistani men, I get a total of sexually active age paying for these children's sexual services is 16,140. Taking the lowest figure of 1,400 girls, x 4 men each night, gives us 5,600 Muslim men, or one in three men. If however, I take the figure of 4,200 and times that by four punters on any given night, that makes 16,800 Muslim men, or more than the entire total.

"Are our figures incorrect? I doubt it. Perhaps we should add in farther afield places, like Dewsbury, a hotbed of Islamification. Or were some girls sent to the nearby city of Leeds, and its satellite boroughs?

"Because what I am seeing here, once the figures are revealed, is that virtually tantamount to a sexual war against white, Christian girls. The entire male Pakistani Muslim society were fucking these seriously underage girls. This cannot have gone unnoticed by other Muslims in the area, it is too widespread. The whole community is in denial.

"There can be zero mistake on this point.

"I expect you to do the research Bilty, and report the outcome. Candice, this is insidious victimisation of the flower of white British youth. Christian youth. I won't let this drop until the all of it is revealed. Check my rough figures here, and make them into real statistics.

"Here's something to think about. What if, the true scale of this atrocity was also happening in Rochdale, Birmingham, and elsewhere. You better have a look at places like Telford, Bristol, and Oxford also. I need this to be a thorough and damning exposé. Bilty, I need your undivided attention in this matter. Go digging."

Bilty

Isabella should have been a detective. She alone had the wherewithal to pose questions nobody else even thought to ask, or if they did, preferred not to answer.

She caught me cold with this revelation, and I am good at what I do. Not good enough it seems, so time I stepped up.

Bilty:

Personal Journal:

Notes:

1. Isabella used the figures in the public domain from Rotherham. To myself, most others, they were simply figures. She took the whole thing several stages farther, and brought the reckoning down to core numbers. She then extrapolated figures of girls and Pakistani men, using census and demographics from freely available, and governmental sources.

The information was available to all, but only she had the wit to crunch the numbers. Her guile to focus on the numbers of girls in the community, and Pakistani men, and use those figures as percentages of victims and perpetrators brings with it a harsh reality:

2. The horrendous scale of sexual trafficking.

3. The great number and colossal percentage of Pakistani men involved. Only with these figures and application to real life demographics, do we begin to understand the iniquity of what occurred in Rotherham. And elsewhere.

The demographics are based on the UK census, a collation of data of registered individuals and families. It does not include illegal immigrants, refugees, asylum seekers, and those of no fixed abode. If this percentage is high for Pakistani Muslims, then that may go some way to explaining the discrepancy in the figures. But, this still represents the majority of all Muslim men in a metropolis of one and a half million people.

I now understand what to expose. It amounts to a jihad--a religious war against white and seriously underage, Christian girls.

I spoke to Candice about the implications, we were both horrified by the revelations. Isabella interrupted, "One last thing, Bilty. In Rotherham, Sikhs and Hindus protested the use of the word Asian, stating it should be Muslim Pakistanis. There's not much love lost between those religious tribes, but I find they were correct on this point.

"They were ignored. So were the Christians, the Chinese, and others. This means that the Muslim minority were being favoured over all other races, ethnicities, and religions. This was called political correctness, but how can it be, when only Muslims from Pakistan benefited from the deceit--which is what it was.

Isabella added, "Time to finish the bulk of this. Onwards!

"You know I adore Latin, so I'll call the finale *In Camera*. I love the pun. Fresh drinks—more ice Genie, camera, action!"

Chapter 42 – Caught *In Camera*

Isabella

I still sought my personal retribution on one Judge. To tell of how that played out, I need to go back to the week before the meeting at Mohammed's offices. On Monday I'd discussed Burma with Sir Richard.

David was hovering nearby on Tuesday morning, which was unlike him. I was quite busy with my team, and with a word, he melded into the background, that was until lunchtime. He insisted we go for lunch together, and I was intrigued to know his angle. He had been with Sir Richard far longer than most staff, and like Miss Constance, had access to the man's random idling of thought.

David drove us to an exceedingly good restaurant, and his mischievous grin was compelling. I was still waiting for him to say something of interest as we finished the main course. I chose sweet delights from the dessert trolley, he preferring a menu dish. After we were served, I asked outright, "David, what's this all about?"

He looked away before he spoke, "I know what you are doing, and I agree with you. Do not get me wrong. However, it would be much more within your best interests, for you to leave London for a while, and I don't just mean the city, I mean UK."

I was startled, but there was no way either he or Sir Richard could know what we were planning. He had to be discussing work. Satisfied, my momentary doubt stilled. He calmed my fears by saying, "I know Sir Richard has been looking at buying rough gemstones from Burma, or Myanmar as you may know the country, for years now. He suffered a bad experience in the Orient, and has been loath to follow through."

"A woman?"

"Yes, a female who scammed him both in love, and in business.

"Nevertheless, the emerging market is there, but he always stalls. He is also getting too old for long-haul flights, so needs a lieutenant to do this for him. I suggest you complete your planning, and go there at once. I can take you to Heathrow as soon as you are ready to leave."

This was all very sudden, and reeked of a set-up. I looked him in the eye, and saw the deception so plain upon his face. He was offering me a leg-up, and insight into what my boss required of me. David knew that I knew, and shrugged his shoulders. I realised in that instant, both he and Sir Richard were looking out for me.

I had already made the decision to go to the Far East sooner rather than later. I had been thinking indefinite time, but David brought this into reality and focus, like a number of days.

We were interrupted as coffee was brought to the table. Once the waiter left us, I winked at him and said, "I have one more thing to do first, and before I can leave. Will this be a problem?"

"No." David surreptitiously produced a manila folder, and moved it towards me. "Miss Constance asked me to give you this. Inside are copies of Sir Richard's provisional plans for Burma. Improve on them and make the presentation on Thursday. You should leave on Friday midday. I will have Miss Constance book your flight and attend your visas when I return to the office."

I smirked and said, "Please make it next week, business class. I hate cattle class. Wait, I'll speak to her, I have a cunning plan."

"Not one devised by Professor Cunning of Cunning University?"

"No, my own, and just as good. Leave it with me. David, thanks."

Within his smile, our deal was done. All I had to do was expose the entirety of the care system, a horde of Pakistani child-rapists, and a paedophile judge, all within six days. Easy!

That evening I set Melanie to a new task, tracking the Burmese gemstone market. I already knew peasants took most precious and semi-precious, rough gemstones, across the mountainous, unguarded borders to either Thailand or China. My team at work had dug deep to find the clues, what I needed were the personal contacts of the mining enterprises. I knew they existed, behaved like tribal clan leaders, and were wary of newcomers. I needed local introductions to the highest quality suppliers. I also asked her to look at options others had not tried as yet: Laos, Cambodia, and Vietnam. She began with those who bought the stones, and traced it backwards.

The Far East international gemstone market revolves around Hong Kong, and to some extent, Singapore. Most jewellery manufacturing is done in Shenzhen, a new Chinese city just across the border within Mainland China. Bangkok is a major regional player, most Asian gemstones being cut there, but they are adepts, not master class exponents of the art.

Sir Richard's traditional plan was that the stones we prized would be cut in Europe. Quality matters, often more than size—I should know.

Regardless, my innovation was to have European expertise on hand in the Far East. From these initial thoughts, a new stratagem was born. I would tell about those intrigues and double, double crossings' now, but the mysteries of the Orient are best left for another tale of my stranger than fictional life.

What I will recount, are the ways of female reprisal, as I ravaged my personal wrath upon the latterly pitiful, Judge St. John-Smythe.

That week we worked on two plans of revenge. Melanie was in charge of information gathering, and all things computational. She researched, as we prepared for the day in question. Zoë had gone into action on Tuesday evening, to fulfil the special mission I had given her. I left her to pick her team. The St. John-Smythe's were out at a Rotary Club function, and their house was left unattended.

Zoë stationed lookouts in appropriate places, and did all the work herself. She was overly familiar with the house, and had one goal. Steal, copy, and replace exactly, the Judge's work keys. She already knew where he kept them, it was all a matter of access. Zoë, you tell it, go on.

Zoë

I discovered the old patio doors had been replaced with modern ones, and alarmed. That left only one way in, above the garage at the back. A window leading onto the staircase. The double garage itself had a pitched roof, but the addition of a downstairs utility room had a flat roof, just where this window happened to be.

It took me a while to jimmy the catch, because I wanted to leave no trace. Once inside I found the keys, and passed them out to Billie, who went to copy them. I also soothed the dogs' emotions, locked in the kitchen. They remembered my voice and weren't a problem. I didn't go in to fuss them, but looked around to pass the time.

My imagination ran wild. I was sat in the Judge's chair, and gazed at his domain. In one sense, I was killing time. In another, I was imagining, seeing his world, through his own eyes.

My eyes looked at the antique wooden desk, and I studied the inlaid crosspiece above the central drawer, but below the top. It was over two inches deep, and had curious designs embossed all over the surface. My interest roused, I tried to define what the carvings were, only to notice the telltale signs of scrapes, the wear of ages, to the sides of the frame. I examined the marks closely, and they appeared to be drag marks.

Carry on Issy, I get confused.

Isabella

Zoë will admit that she is not brightest at maths, but she is a keen student of human deception. Opening the central drawer beneath, her gloved fingers searched upwardly for a catch, and found one. She operated the lever, and a secret drawer above slid open. Revealed, lay a pile of CD's and DVD's, plus memory sticks. She could never copy all of them in the limited time available. Neither was she that skilled.

There was also a photograph album. She opened it, and found images of young girls going back decades, all with names, and brief annotations in code. She photographed every page with her mobile, and reset the visual record back in place when she was done.

There was one picture of matron near the beginning, and later one of me, just before I was seized. The latest entries showed other girls we knew, including Alice, Daniella, and most latterly, Lottie. Zoë knew instinctively what it was: a virgin rape-list.

I am sure she would have done something most stupid, if her accomplice on the outside had not returned at that precise moment with the original keys. Fortunately, I was that person. Through the small top window, she told me what she had discovered. To her frustration, I told her to leave it be exactly, and get the hell out of there.

Later that week, she returned with Melanie and I, and we copied the lot. We had a mother lode, but I knew there was more, much more, but where? There could only be one place nobody would ever be allowed to look, to search: The judge's private rooms at court.

[Bilty: "You did it Isabella. That's fantastic! You nailed him at long last."

"Yes, but no. We had hit the Bull's Eye, but later I was to nail his balls to it. Publically. That is female revenge. There is more."]

Between times, I stared at the photograph of myself, because I could not place it. The location was a stairwell, and eventually something about it triggered a distant memory. I scrutinised the pictures, and noticed the gash to my knee, and puffy eye. I realised, the taxi driver who took me from school to hospital had taken the photo. That was when all my troubles began.

Social services had slightly more recent pictures of me, and a video. I asked myself, "Why did the Judge have this particular picture?"

There could only be one explanation — he received my photograph before Social Services became involved and kidnapped me, but from whom? My instinct told me it was Mohammed, something I was later to confirm as correct. By deduction, I could only assume Mohammed had already sold my virginity to the Judge, before the SS became involved. I had proof of how the system worked, and would use the it against them. Our targets identified and accessible, all things came together.

Due to an upsurge of <u>angry parents</u> [R 41.1] venting their wrath, Family Court Judges' worked within a protective shield of heightened security. That would be on weekdays, when the Court was open and expecting trouble. One could ask why. The answer is patently obvious to any virginal nine-year girl kidnapped into care. The comprehension of most adults appears to be extremely limited by comparison.

I admit, there are times when one person cannot do it all. There were skills others possessed far in excess of my own limitations. Melanie's research found our elusive way into Court Chambers. It cost me a large sum of money, but it was worth it.

She discovered one of the cleaners was an ex meth-crazed prostitute, who was still trying to survive child-rape, and worked in the Family Court. Mitzi Logan had been given a work placement as part of her rehabilitation plan. Otherwise, she was ruled by addiction and deep-seated bitterness. I was to discover her plan was to stab the Judge in the heart, but she didn't have the balls, the 'vag', unsurprisingly. She reminded me of the worst cases of human desperation I saw on the streets of Waterloo, all those years ago with Loady.

Sure, the system had given her a job, to be shot of her, but nobody was looking out for her. She was not my problem.

She demented over half-baked plans to get back at Judge St. John-Smythe for raping her, at the grand old age of fifteen. Mitzi Logan was not someone I would normally trust with my life, but she was a cleaner where we needed to be, and my disguise at the time we met, was most professional. She was supposed to work on Saturday morning, the same one of the evening meeting at Mohammed's offices.

I made myself up to look like Mitzi, copying her accent and body language. She was two thousand pounds richer, simply for lying in bed blitzed. She lent me her security badge and some clothes, which I washed, twice, before donning. I returned her badge later that day via the letterbox, wiped clean, but burned her clothes.

The weekend guards at court were lackadaisical at best, without some of Vikki's girls dropping by distraught, to distract them further. I got in late and worked, trying to become a typically bad cleaner. I was left alone and nobody bothered me. As I presumed, Mitzi was not a popular co-worker. I kept my eyes down but peeled, and noticed there was no surveillance in the restricted area I was working in. Having got to the Judge's rooms quickly, I let both Zoë and Melanie in unobserved.

At last, we were *in camera*, the common legalese jargon, and Latin name for a Judge's private chambers. Our only purpose was to turn ancient Latin into the modern-day evidence. Our focus set, our gloved hands began a full search of the room.

Meanwhile, Melanie used the computer and discovered protected files, which had the same birthday password as his home computer. She opened sample files at random, and left them open. She copied relevant folders to a pen drive, and found a stash of secret documents.

I fitted a fire alarm and powerful transmitter, as I did later in Mohammed's offices, before joining Zoë as we searched for physical evidence, which Zoë photographed. During the hunt I came across details of a second bank account, one used for funding his illicit activities. I gave the account number to Melanie, who managed to login. She printed off details of his account going back for years. We took one copy ourselves, and left a second in the printer tray, so as to assist the fuckwitted Bussies with their latter-day investigation.

Zoë was not idle either. We would never have thought to check underneath the bottom drawers of his metal filing cabinets, but she did. There in full colour, were recordings of his rapes and rape victims, plus many other child-porn movies of black market origin. We viewed a few seconds of several, and they were vile.

Chapter 42

The evidence went back years, decades, and longer. Some of them were made using ancient recording equipment from a prehistoric age. At the other end of the spectrum, the latest files were on mini-discs and pen drives. Zoë even uncovered a secreted laptop he used for viewing his stash of pornography. The Judge was one extremely sick individual.

We had just discovered a diary and associated list of 'Friends', when security checked the door. Fortunately, I had locked it. We remained quiet until the guard's footsteps faded away. He suspected nothing.

We took pictures of the most interesting personal journal pages, and later released tantalising snippets when the furore surrounding the investigation waned. The information was stunning. The cretin was a parasite. He targeted virgins, and we confirmed the money trail.

However, our time was quickly running out. We copied as much as we could, and left copies *ad hoc* for the Bussies or Press to find. We laid telltale snippets on his desk. The judge's prints would be all over his stuff, his image on many of the videos. We put most stuff back where we had found it, so the Bussies could discover it, and prove the continuity of evidence. We did leave the filing cabinets unlocked though. Once the bottom drawers were back in place, we scarpered.

Although we were wearing gloves and body suits, we wiped down all surfaces touched, and I finished a very thorough cleansing — the only one of that morning. Satisfied with our work, I locked the door from the outside, and escorted us to the fire exit. We disappeared into the Saturday shopping throng, leaving the evidence to be discovered. That was not as easy as it sounds.

Come on! It was dead easy, if you are a practitioner of the arcane, obscure arts and intricacies of female revenge.

On Monday morning the Judge headed for work, unaware he was being tailed. As was his observed pattern, he drove his Bentley to Reigate railway station, and travelled first class on the 8.09 to West Brompton, arriving at just after 9.10. Zoë watched him enter the back of a private car, and called me as soon as he departed.

We had already timed this trip on previous weekdays, and knew it usually took around fifteen minutes for the journey to Family Court West London. Melanie was loitering nearby the destination, and at my call, made another to the emergency services. She posed as his secretary, and said, "The Judge had just been beaten by thugs, his office ransacked, and he has suffered a heart attack as a result."

The ambulance arrived first, followed by the Press, and last, the Bussies, unsurprisingly. That Monday morning, the Judge's secretary was surprised by the arrival of emergency services. The police insisted on inspecting the judge's rooms, and began to investigate. As soon as they realised what was before their eyes, the room was sealed for forensics.

The Judge was the last to enter his official chambers that morning, and was immediately cuffed and taken into custody. This time he would not escape the iron fist of justice.

Family Court Judge, Ferdinand Aloysius St. John- Smythe was arrested after the Bussies finally decided they had to begin investigating the pervert properly. That the free Press were there to hound the police investigation at all stages, perhaps compromised by the fact I rang the media first, regards the secret drawer in the Judge's home desk. One photograph I gave them, showed the secret drawer open. I considered, as the Bussies had never been there for me, it was time a little more of the highly guarded information fell into the public domain.

After that, we no longer bothered with the Bussies, they were a disgrace to their uniform. We sent original pictures of the judge's rooms to our press contacts, and let it go viral on the internet. We kept on releasing selective information, but still nothing was being done.

During a private discussion, our hidden camera at the judge's offices recorded a Chief Inspector of police talking in confidence about limiting the damage and hiding evidence [R 41.2]. The same happened at Mohammed's offices, but on that occasion, the police officer held the rank of Chief Superintendent.

I had not expected to actually catch the police in collusion, but this is what we had. I left the Press to run with it, and another force was called in to investigate the workings of Scotland Yard. The press release was delayed until a timely moment, and just after all initial investigative work in both locations had ceased.

We actually compromised the investigation and subsequent proceedings, by making some information public, but it added to the outcry and publicity against those trying to dismiss the incidents, and hide these crimes from scrutiny.

The Rule of Law seems to be that, everything is OK and will be hidden, unless the Press gets hold of it. Apparently, it is something to do with the chain of evidence, and privacy, although for whose benefit, I never could work out to my personal, nor complete satisfaction.

Scandals continued to be revealed, the newspapers opening any can of worms at our biddance, ones the police preferred to keep under lock and key. Our tactic of telling both sides the same information, worked spectacularly well. The police began with a small investigation of localised crime, and ended up with a nationwide special task force. They code-named it 'Candy Monster', out of undue, and misplaced respect for one of our most resilient tormentors.

The Press queried and pried, contesting the at first limpid investigation, which brought forth a wave of public indignation. Once the national task force was established, waves of abused girls came forward to make their personal complaints. The operation was drowning under a mass of information regarding systematic abuse of under-age girls.

Many more victims were drawn to our own (supportive) website, seeking succour, and reassurance. We held true, whilst all around us, people in authority prevaricated and blamed others.

We publicly, but anonymously, served our entire stock of evidence at police headquarters, Scotland Yard, very early one morning. Only the press were there, except for security guarding what would prove to be the police's downfall. We gave the Press copies also.

Questions were raised in the House of Commons, and a Public Enquiry initiated. That got nowhere, because it was a countermeasure aimed at damage limitation. I found it hilarious, that several highly influential people on the list Mohammed gave us, including a judge, were on that very same committee. Strange? The press thought so too, and pursued the matter with great enthusiasm and alacrity.

Our move was to tell the Press the names, and what they had done. The Enquiry was eventually abandoned, as our own lives moved on. It will be years until the Independent Inquiry reports its findings. We were proved right, but during that time, most of the big players disappeared into the woodwork, nary to be seen or heard of again.

Such are the ways of seriously underage child-prostitution, when applied to Ministers of Her Majesty's Government, and Members of the Houses of Parliament, Knights of The Realm, and the British legal profession, childcare professionals — Oh. And followers of Islam.

If you are a girl, a woman, a mother, or Grandmother, you will understand my deepest, utter loathing of all these creeps.

Candice

"Congratulations, that was some story. You are aware the press have lost all interest, and the Independent Inquiry will take years yet to report. As you suggested, there is way too much of it, and those most responsible, have the money for the best legal representation. They use political correctness as a ruse to deceive by generalising. How do you want to play this?"

"Simple, I want justice to be seen to be done. What has happened in my absence has been a charade of posturing and petit politick. I am fighting for us, the girls ex of, or in the system. They are still recruiting new girls! I am seriously at a loss here."

"We both support you, and will help you to gain full retribution. But, for the book I need an ending. What have you got?"

"Something poignant, whimsical, and nice? Listen-up."

Chapter 43 – A Gael Blows

Isabella

I was booked on a flight for Monday evening, but had a presentation to deliver the Thursday prior. I had studied the contents of Sir Richard's folder, and had realised he was expecting me to step-up.

At first, I adapted his notes, before rethinking the whole approach. The Orient is a different world from the Occident, and Melanie's research gave me the defining edge I needed. Zoë was forever at my shoulder, offering me her considered advice, as were my team at work.

During my little time remaining, I worked Sir Richard's angles, and made a far-ranging proposition. It was in essence his original plan, to include control of supply, manufacturing, and sales. I took it several steps further, and by the time I was done, it was my baby.

The presentation was a great success, and was accepted in its entirety. Afterwards, Sir Richard complimented me on the idea of bringing Western experts skills, and technology to the Far East. In particular, he liked my addition of creating a free market of highest standard, one that he controlled. This would have our competitors coming to us for their highest quality work, until in time, they developed their own facilities.

I proposed to use the intervening period to establish our name as the market leader in the Orient. On the spur of the moment, I pressed him to include Tokyo, Taiwan, and Singapore in my brief, and he obliged with one of his largest smiles. I knew I would miss him dearly, and with no words necessary between us, pecked him on the lips.

A few days later, my bags were packed, and I was ready for a new adventure. David collected me for the drive to Heathrow. We were thwarted, as a major accident closed all roads West, into and out of London. I found myself pacing the futility of Euston railway station, trying to contact my dearest, and tell them about our change of plans.

I was dressed in my best business suit, and squawking with desperation into my mobile phone, when a youngster stood in front of me. She was an urchin child. She said something to me, but I paid her no mind, so concentrated was I upon my escape from Blighty. I got resolution, and Miss Constance ended by telling me, "You are just the same as Sir Richard—cast from the same mould, don't you know it yet?"

The line went dead, otherwise I would have said something. I was still mulling over what she had said, when the young girl's words came back to haunt me. I remembered saying them myself many years before: "Excuse me miss, but I want you to know that when I grow up, I want to be just like you. What do you do?"

Her words were a seed I could not dislodge; needy, in-submissive. The world I lived in was æons away from her own, and yet, I could not dismiss her want. It was already an integral part of my substance, my unique identity as an individual, a human being.

From being cast-adrift, a child on the run, I had become my own worst enemy. There was zero mistake. I looked for her, but she was gone. My mobile rang, and it was Melanie trying to complete an impossible connection. She needed Station info, and British Rail's online information system was down, frozen one day previous. I told her, "Use your initiative. Talk to Miss Constance," and abruptly ended the call.

I was overly worried, and looked for the girl. I found her in a quiet spot, blowing bubbles from a dip stick. There was a man beside her. I told him to go. He refused, and I hit him with a good boy punch to the jaw. He left, cursing me. The child said, "Thanks. I didn't like him. He was shifty. But the bubbles he gave me are great!"

See how easy it is to manipulate a child.

My eyes scanned the crowded foyer, and there was not one single person looking for a child — Years of abuse makes one streetwise. I knew I was looking at my former self, escaping. I had to become proactive within her cause.

I offered her fast food, and she took my hand. She was starving, and wolfed-down a large burger treat. I went to the toilet, not to relieve myself, but to call my team to action. A young girl's life needed saving from the future we had all endured, to our uttermost displeasure.

I discovered her name was Gael, and she wanted to go home. She was trying to escape foster care, just as I had once done. I did not think, without assistance, she would be so lucky as I.

In time, my friends joined me, but I waited for one special person to appear. Traffic was against everyone that day, but she made it, just as Zoë was beginning to panic about missing our last Heathrow Link. It was a very close call. I swapped innocent kisses with Sophie, and asked her to take care of Gael at my personal expense.

As I turned to depart, about to dash for the platform, I heard the youngster say, "She was nice to me. Are you my new mummy?"

I ran for my train, our last connection for the flight. I did not even question why Social Services were not prowling Euston Station foyer on the lookout for runaways. I already had my answer. They caused it.

I had saved one soul that day, but how many other lives could I rescue from abuse? Would I crush The System, or would it crush me?

I arrived at a very far-reaching decision within that moment. I vowed to protect the innocent, and garner the rich that abused them unto their own hell. My thoughts turned to opening a proper care home, for all the right reasons, at total exclusion of the wrong.

That was destined to be my last day in Blighty for many moons.

Sophie was trying to run a legitimate foster home, against the odds of corporate concerns, or shenanigans, as I prefer to see the swindle. I realised the powers that be, were only using her service for legitimacy; as an acorn to promote their own claims for authenticity.

Unlike the businesswoman who walked away from my younger self, totally ignorant of any others' worth, I had made a difference to one child's life. It was no big thing, within the population of the Earth, but it was something I could do, or choose not to do, should I choose to take the time to do so. I was proactive, not driven by avarice or misplaced self-worth. I wondered again, how many others I could help.

Two others accompanied me onto the aeroplane, Vikki remaining to run my business in my absence. I managed to upgrade both Zoë and Melanie to Business Class on check-in. I was lucky that time.

I sat between the two as we ventured tentatively into our latest acts of international derring-do. Perhaps in times of solace, I missed my third General equally deeply; for Vikki was the very first person I fell in love with—Oh, so many years ago.

Domicile

Hmmm. Domicile is a place where people in authority—and with only their self-interests [R 42.1] at heart, put you, just to be rid of you. Let us be extremely clear upon this point. They disregard your personal and best interests, gag you, and sell you out for the highest profit.

The needs of the child are irrelevant!

It is never, and can never be, any moral person's personal wish: Domicile … some made-up laws of men are simply, and significantly, something we preteen girls were bound to—Were subjected to comply with. We were not allowed to speak in court. Neither were our parents, and we were not allowed independent legal representation. This is child-snatching. Kidnapping of young girls, on legal pretexts of false evidence. Evidence, we were not allowed to contest in our defence.

I wasn't. Neither were my parents. They were locked up for trying to tell the truth of the matter. Irrelevant in Criminal Court, and seemingly a superfluous and an unwanted distraction in Family Court.

Their illegal apparati amounts to pre-planned child trafficking.

I kept my gun and my bow. I will use them, unless Family Court becomes accountable for the lives of the children they deliberately ruin, in order to make money, or favours in kind.

To misquote Bogart, "Here's looking at your kids."

As so was it in Aisha's time. But she dared to fight back against Ali, the Fourth Caliphate, Muhammad's adopted nephew, and instigator of the Shia, an abbreviation of the Shia-ne-Ali, *Shīʿatu ʿAlī* sect. Our oppressors were Sunni, but they seemed all the same to us.

I doubt but few have worked out the simplest of truths.

Aisha gave her name to Asia.

That is her enduring soliloquy — One spoken everyday in the round, with minimalistic comprehension. One third of our modern world bears her name. The Politically Correct labelled our rapists, 'Asian'. That means paying homage to Aisha. I saw no Chinese, Japanese, they were all from a small area of northern Pakistan.

Religion, like the law, the governmental machine, remains, ultimately — a weapon used to control the general, and vaguely principled populace ... wholly within the interests of those that create, adopt, manipulate, and are/or adept to run those scams.

I intend to rip the system apart. I will expose all within, who made money out of my sexual slavery.

Muslim Pakistanis and Afghanis, seem to think it is their right to rape exceedingly underage girls. This is not a nationwide problem, but an international one, that has singularly never been addressed as such.

Mohammed admitted that he considered himself to be a Landlord, and all within his sphere of influence were his slaves. Remember, he spoke with other UK Landlords, and was instigating a national network of child sexual trafficking. And he was using the SS for legitimate transfer. The police, the authorities, seriously need to get a grip of the larger situation. It is happening in every city and town in UK.

Candice

"That's perfect Isabella, and fully rounds the story. Excellent. Despite all that you have suffered, your humanity shines through like a bright beacon in the night. I will try to show that when I begin writing.

"Were you serious about starting your own care home?"

"Deadly. I've already spoken to Sophie, who will run it for me. She had been thinking of expanding her home, but I offered her somewhere much larger. She needs a qualification first, so it will be a few months.

"That fits nicely with completing the purchase and renovating the property. It will be able to take two hundred children of all ages."

Bilty said, "Isabella, I know you well. What's your angle? I know it's not money, and yes, you want to protect the children. What else?"

"You read me well, Bilty. I aim to run it like a boarding school, and warn them of the dangers. The difference is, we will employ a fulltime counsellor to offer succour and support. Interviews will be recorded. This time, if a child reports being raped, there will be prosecutions. That's the purpose of Sophie's course. So, next time, we will be fighting the system, but from their side of the fence. Neat eh?

"We're as good as done. Just one more thing. The money trail."

Chapter 44 – Following The Money Trail

Bilty Steadman

"That's one hell of a story, Isabella. An excellent result, and the ramifications of what you discovered and divulged, will go on for years.

"What I, and other journalists, the police, and everybody including Doctor Alexis Jay missed, was the money-trail. Yet you found it."

"It was obvious to us. We were being fucked twice each time, once by the Paki punter, and the second time by the Paki pimps, who kept all the money they made from us. We were held in the yoke of sexual slavery, and trafficked all over the place. We hardly saw one penny.

"I read the papers, the Jay Report [R 43.1] in full, and I knew at once, it was all about money. Why do only us, the victims, understand this? The figures are in the public domain, and yet were either wilfully covered up, or people were too stupid to do the maths.

"You have our own figures, Bilty. Why not be the first person to follow the Rotherham [R43.2] money trail. Go on."

"I'll use figures in the public domain, Isabella. There were at least 1,400 girls involved, an exceedingly conservative estimate. The true figure is likely to be at least two, and nearer three times higher. Okay. Just like you did, using the lowest figures mentioned.

1,400 girls x £40 a go, times 4 men per night x 4 nights per week. Multiply by fifty-two weeks, and I make that ... Oh My God!

"**£46,592,000!** All in used notes, untaxed."

Isabella hammered the final nail home; "Forty-six Million pounds! The true figure is likely to exceed one-hundred million pounds, per annum. This happened across the country.

That went on for sixteen years: The true figure is several **Billion** pounds. Now tell me this was only about extremely underage sex?

"Why is nobody following the money-trail?"

§

A famous Irish comedian once said:

"Thank you, goodnight, and may your god go with you."

I do not believe he was joking.

yours truly,
Isabella Waites

The End

Epilogus

Bilty sat in his office. The hour was late, and his whisky, like his mood, sour. He glanced at the banker's lamp, turning the cover slightly downwards, so as to reduce the glare.

He felt as if under a spotlight, and he needed to respond. Why was nobody following the money trail?

There could only be one answer. They were all in the scam together. Each and every one of them, taking a slice of the pie. Isabella had detailed as much, yet even he had become too busy with other matters, to follow through.

But it was Isabella's last comment that disturbed him the most. She had shown them personally to the door, but before opening it paused, her hand resting on the handle. "Bilty, Pakistani Landlords. You need to follow that up."

"Yes, I will. I understand."

"I doubt you do. What of the bigger picture?"

"It's as you said."

"Ah, but no. I only gave you the pieces to put together."

"Head's up. Mohammed was one of over a dozen Feudal Landlords who operated as a cartel. Usif was probably their leader, but maybe not.

"Asif was one of seven lieutenants Mohammed controlled in London. You now have their names. Follow that up."

"Yes of course. Anything else?"

"Yes. Do it for all the reported cases nationwide. Find the real controllers of those rackets. Up in Rochdale, do you really think 'Big Daddy' was the boss? A few miles away, say in Rotherham, there was another lieutenant, and another further afield. That tells me there is one Landlord controlling them all. The pattern repeats in Sheffield Metropolitan City, greater Yorkshire, Telford, <u>Birmingham</u> [R EP01]. Do some digging Bilty. Find the big fish behind the all of it.

"Mohammed has already told us the Landlord's names, so go after them like the bloodhound I know you to be.

"The like we just did a few moment ago, extract the demographics and apply them. This tells us the scale of abuse."

Rising to pace the room in semi-darkness, Bilty downed his drink, refilled, and stated aloud, "I will follow though. I will expose the money trail, the Landlords, the demographics, the all of this, wherever it leads.

"Cheers, Isabella!"

References

Books of fiction never contain references, except this one.

Links to supportive information are provided in full below, for those reading the printed book, or anyone having problems with links on their e-Reader. One should consider, some links being removed, is of the utmost concern.

Key: Olive Link working   Orange Access Complication   Red Link removed

Format:
Page number, Chapter number & chapter reference number, Link.

Page	Ref	Link
7	2.1	http://www.telegraph.co.uk/comment/columnists/christopherbooker/8612734/A-fathers-nightmare.html
10	3.1	http://www.telegraph.co.uk/women/mother-tongue/8339474/Couple-given-children-back-after-judge-overturns-court-ruling.html
10	3.2	https://www.channel4.com/news/by/victoria-macdonald/blogs/lost-family-told-care-granddaughter
15	3.3	https://www.gov.uk/government/news/major-changes-in-family-courts
40	6.1	Police and Criminal Evidence Act, 1984
40	6.2	Police (Detention and Bail) Act 2011
41	7.1	http://www.telegraph.co.uk/comment/columnists/christopherbooker/9434116/A-mother-is-charged-with-kidnapping-after-returning-a-runaway-daughter-to-care.html
42	7.2	http://www.dailymail.co.uk/femail/article-1308117/I-stolen-mother-The-deeply-disturbing-truth-forced-adoption.html
48	7.3	http://www.telegraph.co.uk/news/uknews/law-and-order/9370986/Minister-care-homes-like-frying-pan-into-the-fire-for-abused-children.html
48	7.4	https://forced-adoption.com/times-campaign-2008/
59	9.1	http://www.telegraph.co.uk/news/worldnews/asia/bangladesh/7073191/Rape-victim-receives-101-lashes-for-becoming-pregnant.html
67	10.1	http://www.telegraph.co.uk/comment/9383388/A-baby-comes-home-but-a-mother-remains-in-jail.html Bottom of page.

83	12.1	https://en.wikipedia.org/wiki/Domicile_%28law%29
85	12.2	http://www.telegraph.co.uk/news/uknews/crime/10057401/Oxford-grooming-gang-Only-one-carer-sacked.html
102	14.1	http://www.telegraph.co.uk/comment/columnists/christopherbooker/9075866/A-mother-on-a-visit-to-the-UK-loses-three-children-to-social-workers.html
109	15.1	http://www.telegraph.co.uk/comment/columnists/christopherbooker/7896592/Its-time-to-bring-family-law-to-book.html
109	15.2	https://forced-adoption.com/typical-case-scenarios/
111	15.3	http://www.unicef.org.uk/Documents/Publication-pdfs/UNCRC_PRESS200910web.pdf

Page since removed from the UNICEF website: Why? Appended below. It is still available from: http://www.uncrcletsgetitright.co.uk/index.php/right/file

Oh. Again unavailable. How odd. Who is covering this up? Why?

One must presume we are no longer allowed to view the 'Rights of a Child'.

| 111 | 15.4 | http://www.telegraph.co.uk/comment/columnists/christopherbooker/8363501/Parents-denied-a-voice-in-court-against-the-child-snatchers.html |
| 114 | 15.5 | http://justice-for-families.org.uk |

Website no longer available. Why? Was it shut down by Social Services?

114	15.6	http://www.telegraph.co.uk/news/health/children/9962209/A-family-who-escaped-to-a-happy-ending.html
116	15.7	http://www.telegraph.co.uk/comment/columnists/christopherbooker/9164182/Why-do-our-family-courts-rely-on-hired-gun-experts.html
116	15.8	http://www.telegraph.co.uk/women/mother-tongue/9178021/The-doctor-who-took-my-baby-away.html
121	16.1	https://en.wikipedia.org/wiki/Schutzstaffel
121	16.2	http://www.devon.gov.uk/cp_complaints_against_foster_carers_section9.pdf
124	16.3	http://www.telegraph.co.uk/women/mother-tongue/8349748/Social-services-took-my-children.html
128	16.4	http://www.frontpagemag.com/point/239615/uk-police-arrested-parents-trying-stop-muslims-daniel-

		greenfield
147	18.1	http://www.telegraph.co.uk/news/health/news/906 5998/Girls-13-given-contraceptive-implants-at-school.html
150	19.1	http://www.breitbart.com/london/2015/02/09/polic e-accused-of-helping-rotherham-abusers-mp-failed-to-act/
153	19.2	http://www.telegraph.co.uk/news/uknews/crime/1 1063874/Rotherham-sex-abuse-The-utter-brutality-is-what-shocked-me-most.html
159	20.1	https://www.theguardian.com/uk/2013/jan/15/oxfo rd-gang-girls-prostitutes-bailey
159	20.2	http://www.mancunianmatters.co.uk/content/240953 651-takeaway-worker-who-beat-raped-and-urinated-two-manchester-students-jailed
162	20.3	http://www.telegraph.co.uk/news/uknews/crime/1 0025289/Serious-and-systemic-abuse-took-place-in-Welsh-care-homes-investigation-finds.html
162	20.4	http://www.dailymail.co.uk/news/article-2526896/Revealed-Catalogue-police-failures-let-Rochdale-sex-grooming-gangs-flourish-claims-damning-police-report.html
166	21.1	http://www.telegraph.co.uk/comment/columnists/c hristopherbooker/9434116/A-mother-is-charged-with-kidnapping-after-returning-a-runaway-daughter-to-care.html Second link to this page, but different information. Paragraph three in the linked page refers.
167	21.2	http://www.dailymail.co.uk/news/article-2526896/Revealed-Catalogue-police-failures-let-Rochdale-sex-grooming-gangs-flourish-claims-damning-police-report.html
170	21.3	https://en.wikipedia.org/wiki/Female_genital_mutila tion
171	21.4	http://bullyonline.org/old/related/drugrape.htm
181	23.1	http://resources.leavingcare.org/uploads/c4f7aeaf941 cdefb8f4a18f478aa1f19.pdf Now requires login.
183	23.2	http://www.mirror.co.uk/news/uk-news/horrific-abuse-scandal-town-dubbed-8718139
183	23.3	http://www.mrconservative.com/2013/03/6673-ten-horrifying-stories-of-muslims-gang-raping-white-woman/
187	23.4	http://www.telegraph.co.uk/comment/9606161/The-

worst-scandal-I-have-seen-in-my-50-year-career.html

187 23.5 http://www.telegraph.co.uk/comment/columnists/c
hristopherbooker/9191488/Youve-suffered-care-so-
you-lose-your-child.html

192 24.1 http://www.dailymail.co.uk/news/article-
4231242/Social-workers-took-newborn-baby-
parents.html

192 24.2 http://www.telegraph.co.uk/comment/columnists/c
hristopherbooker/10485281/Baby-forcibly-removed-
by-caesarean-and-taken-into-care.html

208 26.1 http://jackiez1.typepad.com/blog/2011/03/sex-
trafficking-in-the-uk-one-womans-horrific-story-of-
kidnap-rape-beatings-and-prostitution.html

2011 26.2 http://www.adoptuskids.org/meet-the-
children/children-in-foster-care/about-the-children
[Bona fide website used as an illustration only. Imagine
'what if' a similar website was run by a paedophile –
Mohammed perhaps?]

214 26.3 http://www.forced-adoption.com/
     26.4 http://www.nfa.co.uk/
     26.5 http://www.graphitecapital.com/
          Notice, neither website admits knowledge of the other.
          Why? Is this legalised misdirection?

215 26.6 https://forced-adoption.com/recommended-
professionals/

237 30.1 http://www.dailymail.co.uk/news/article-
2413319/Father-secretly-records-moment-hour-old-
baby-taken-away-social-services.html

237 30.2 http://legallykidnapped.blogspot.com/2010/03/blog
ging-world-exposes-social-workers.html
Link no longer working, I do have to ask - WHY?
One will presume the Judge that presided, ordered the
article be removed.

237 30.3 http://www.unicef.org/crc/files/Rights_overview.pd
f

237 30.4 http://www.telegraph.co.uk/women/mother-
tongue/familyadvice/10374001/We-decide-where-
you-eat-social-workers-love-a-petty-power-trip.html

238 30.5 http://www.telegraph.co.uk/news/health/children/1
0308803/Deported-imprisoned-and-beaten-for-being-a-
parent.html

238 30.6 http://www.telegraph.co.uk/news/uknews/law-and-
order/10356274/Social-workers-damn-us-both-
ways.html

242	30.7	https://en.wikipedia.org/wiki/Queen%27s_Counsel
244	30.8	http://www.telegraph.co.uk/news/uknews/1466973/Child-porn-judge-escapes-jail-term.html
246	30.9	http://www.unicef.org/crc/files/Right-to-Participation.pdf
246	30.10	http://www.telegraph.co.uk/news/2016/10/22/what-happened-to-putting-childrens-welfare-first/
247	30.11	Rotherham: http://www.dailymail.co.uk/news/article-3844496/All-white-girls-good-sex-just-sl-gs-Eight-members-openly-racist-violent-Asian-sex-gang-raped-sexually-degraded-three-teenage-girls-Rotherham.html
247	30.12	Rotherham: http://www.dailymail.co.uk/news/article-3465306/Teenager-beaten-brothers-d-abused-Rotherham-grooming-gang-age-12.html
248	30.13	Rotherham: http://www.vice.com/en_uk/read/rotherham-grooming-security-guard-and-victims-interview-091
248	30.14	Rochdale 1: http://www.newstatesman.com/2012/08/how-rochdale-grooming-case-exposed-british-prejudice
248	30.15	Rochdale 2: http://www.telegraph.co.uk/news/uknews/crime/9446948/Rochdale-sex-gang-leader-jailed-for-22-years.html
248	30.16	Rotherham 1: http://www.dailymail.co.uk/news/article-2207756/Police-turned-blind-eye-South-Yorkshire-sex-grooming-gangs-decade.html
248	30.17	Oxford: https://www.gatestoneinstitute.org/3846/britain-child-grooming
248	30.18	Derby: http://www.telegraph.co.uk/news/uknews/crime/8157739/Asian-gang-prowled-streets-searching-for-rape-victims.html
248	30.19	Preston 2011: http://www.lep.co.uk/news/crime/40-men-in-sex-abuse-probe-1-3328295
248	30.20	Telford: http://www.bbc.com/news/uk-england-shropshire-22379414
248	30.21	Stafford:

		http://www.shropshirestar.com/news/2011/09/06/t elford-child-sex-case-collapses/
248	30.22	Halifax and Northumberland: http://www.dailymail.co.uk/news/article-2941963/Police-swoop-45-men-child-sex-grooming-Milestone-operation-sees-suspects-charged-rape-sexual-assault-trafficking.html
248	30.23	Middlesbrough: http://www.bbc.com/news/uk-england-tees-25119285
249	31.1	https://www.gov.uk/age-of-criminal-responsibility
253	31.2	http://www.telegraph.co.uk/news/uknews/crime/9 862127/Violinist-in-rape-trial-could-not-cope-with-questioning-by-woman-QC.html
255	31.3	http://www.dailymail.co.uk/news/article-2526896/Revealed-Catalogue-police-failures-let-Rochdale-sex-grooming-gangs-flourish-claims-damning-police-report.html
255	31.4	http://www.bbc.com/news/uk-england-manchester-19739073
276	35.1	http://www.bbc.com/news/uk-politics-22836634
287	36.1	http://www.dailymail.co.uk/news/article-3902838/Three-Afghan-migrants-suspected-raping-translator-Calais-Jungle-arrested-Paris-refugee-centre.html
287	36.2	http://www.dailymail.co.uk/news/article-2416586/Gangs-Asian-men-grooming-MUSLIM-girls-plying-drink-drugs.html [Read closely, and you'll conclude this was the same woman linked below.]
287	36.3	http://www.dailymail.co.uk/news/article-3944874/They-want-Islamised-despise-country-values-Translator-German-refugee-camp-says-Muslim-migrants-display-pure-hatred-Christians.html
307	39.1	http://www.telegraph.co.uk/comment/columnists/c hristopherbooker/9150659/Dubious-experts-are-paid-to-tear-families-apart.html
311	39.2	http://www.dailymail.co.uk/news/article-3884026/The-Asian-sex-grooming-scandal-Rotherham-continues-court-given-lifetime-anonymity-four-men-preyed-vulnerable-girl-years-going-on.html
313	40.1	http://www.digitaljournal.com/article/324779
313	40.2	http://biopsychiatry.com/scopolamine/borrachero.ht ml

318	40.3	http://www.aljazeera.com/humanrights/2014/08/pakistan-fight-against-feudalism-2014814135134807880.html
319	40.4	http://www.telegraph.co.uk/news/worldnews/middleeast/iraq/11110724/Isil-fanatics-fear-being-killed-by-a-woman-will-deprive-them-of-virgins-in-paradise.html
323	41.1	http://www.telegraph.co.uk/news/uknews/crime/11059138/Rotherham-In-the-face-of-such-evil-who-is-the-racist-now.html
326	42.1	http://www.dailymail.co.uk/news/article-2252733/Judges-security-family-court-rooms-spate-attacks-angry-parents.html
329	42.2	http://www.telegraph.co.uk/news/uknews/crime/10138031/Police-spied-on-Stephen-Lawrence-family-in-smear-campaign-says-whistleblower.html
333	43.1	https://victims-unite.net/child-snatching/the-musa-drama/
335	44.1	http://www.rotherham.gov.uk/downloads/file/1407/independent_inquiry_cse_in_rotherham
335	44.2	https://en.wikipedia.org/wiki/Rotherham_child_sexual_exploitation_scandal#Alexis_Jay_inquiry
337	Ep01	http://www.birminghammail.co.uk/news/midlands-news/police-knew-grooming-gangs-were-9518461

Author's Notes

347	A001	Rochdale. http://www.telegraph.co.uk/news/uknews/crime/9446948/Rochdale-sex-gang-leader-jailed-for-22-years.html
347	A002	https://www.theguardian.com/uk-news/2017/feb/09/members-of-rochdale-grooming-gang-face-deportation-to-pakistan
347	GA01	http://www.mirror.co.uk/news/uk-news/rochdale-grooming-gang-victim-speaks-824326
347	GA02	http://www.bachinese.com/forum/read.php?tid=41462
347	GA03	http://www.telegraph.co.uk/news/uknews/crime/9251920/Rochdale-grooming-trial-Girl-A-the-gangs-15-year-old-victim.html
348	2E01	http://lukesarmy.drupalgardens.com/content/rochdale-child-grooming-ring-council-and-police-had-127-

warnings-stop-abuse

349   2E02   http://www.telegraph.co.uk/news/uknews/crime/9252447/Rochdale-grooming-trial-new-generation-being-recruited.html

349   2F03   http://www.telegraph.co.uk/news/uknews/crime/9254982/Rochdale-grooming-trial-police-knew-about-sex-abuse-in-2002-but-failed-to-act.html

350   S01   https://www.thesun.co.uk/archives/news/647318/asian-sex-gang-have-ripped-my-life-apart-but-i-can-help-others/

351   A003   http://www.telegraph.co.uk/news/uknews/crime/10061217/Imams-promote-grooming-rings-Muslim-leader-claims.html

352   A004   https://www.jihadwatch.org/2012/05/grooming-gang-found-guilty-nine

352   NS01   http://www.newstatesman.com/2012/08/how-rochdale-grooming-case-exposed-british-prejudice

352   LCC01   http://www.lccsa.org.uk/news.asp?ItemID=25684
Item may still be available with membership?

353   A005   https://www.thesun.co.uk/archives/news/704133/paedo-gang-king-guilty-of-30-rapes-is-unmasked/

353   A006   Oxford.
https://www.gatestoneinstitute.org/3846/britain-child-grooming

353   A007   http://www.dailymail.co.uk/news/article-2324386/Police-chief-constable-council-chief-executive-refuse-stand-despite-catalogue-errors-Oxford-sex-ring-scandal.html

355   A008   http://www.telegraph.co.uk/news/uknews/crime/10060349/Oxford-grooming-ring-council-and-police-chiefs-should-consider-their-positions.html

355   A009   http://blogs.telegraph.co.uk/news/seanthomas/100217075/oxford-gang-rape-did-people-ignore-this-sort-of-scandal-because-racist-nick-griffin-was-the-first-to-mention-them/
This link should still be there, but access to it has changed; as has the Telegraph

355   A010   Rotherham.
http://www.dailymail.co.uk/news/article-2207756/Police-turned-blind-eye-South-Yorkshire-sex-grooming-gangs-decade.html

356   A011   http://www.independent.co.uk/news/uk/crime/five-guilty-of-grooming-teenage-girls-for-sex-2126292.html

357   A012   http://www.standpointmag.co.uk/node/3576/full

357	A013	http://www.independent.co.uk/news/uk/crime/the y-like-us-naive-how-teenage-girls-are-groomed-for-a-life-of-prostitution-by-uk-gangs-1880959.html
357	A014	Derby. http://www.telegraph.co.uk/news/uknews/crime/8157739/Asian-gang-prowled-streets-searching-for-rape-victims.html
359	A015	http://www.dailymail.co.uk/news/article-1347864/Sex-gangs-grooming-children-young-10-says-leading-charity.html
361	A016	Preston. http://www.lancashiretelegraph.co.uk/news/10661267.Brierfield_sex_grooming_gang_member_is_jailed/
361	A017	Telford. http://www.shropshirestar.com/news/crime/2013/05/10/horror-of-telford-girls-sex-abuse-ordeal/
363	A018	http://www.mirror.co.uk/news/uk-news/horrific-abuse-scandal-town-dubbed-8718139
363	A019	Bristol. http://www.bbc.com/news/uk-england-30078503
363	A020	Middlesbrough. http://www.bbc.com/news/uk-england-tees-26167790
363	A021	http://www.gazettelive.co.uk/news/local-news/ex-teesside-police-chief-issues-child-3673618
363	A022	Peterborough. http://www.bbc.com/news/uk-england-cambridgeshire-25659042
363	A023	Birmingham. http://www.birminghammail.co.uk/news/midlands-news/police-knew-grooming-gangs-were-9518461

Author's Comment
| 367 | AC01 | http://www.dailymail.co.uk/news/article-2416586/Gangs-Asian-men-grooming-MUSLIM-girls-plying-drink-drugs.html |
| 367 | AC02 | http://www.mwnuk.co.uk/ |

Author's Notes – Tales of many Trials

This section refers exclusively to the real-life events the author mirrors to greater or lesser extent, in this work of fiction. Text is reproduced as published from various sources, and is printed below as written by others, and not edited by the author of this book. This is correctly known as: *sic erat scriptum*.

Much of the early investigative journalism was conducted by Camilla Cavendish of the Times. This online newspaper has an expensive subscription, one I could not afford to consult.

Reported Fact: Rochdale 2012
[Blockquote]
During the trial it became evident the accused men had displayed a searing contempt for their victims. "You white people train them in sex and drinking," the leader told the jury during the trial, "so when they come to us they are fully trained."

Shabir Ahmed, 59, has been named as leader of a paedophile ring in Rochdale. He was found guilty of 30 child rape charges in Manchester. He was ringleader of a gang of men in Rochdale who groomed young white girls for sex and was found guilty of conspiracy, two rapes, aiding and abetting rape, sexual assault and sex trafficking. The gang targeted vulnerable young girls in the Rochdale and Oldham areas of Greater Manchester, as well as the nearby cities of Bradford and Leeds. He was jailed for 19 years.

In a second trial [R A001] some months later, he was convicted of keeping a young female of Pakistani descent prisoner. He used her as a slave, raped her repeatedly over many years, and beat her often. She was a child when she fell into his clutches. For these offences, he was jailed for 22 years, to run concurrently with his previous convictions.

Additionally, at the end of his sentence, he and others, were to be deported back to Pakistan, their British citizenship revoked. His lawyers tried many ruses by which to contest the deportation order, until the appeal was rejected [R A002].

Below is the true account of what each girl suffered in real life. Although Samantha did not give direct evidence to this court, her testimony is included as supporting evidence of a much wider web of systematic abuse.

Girl A [ref: R GA01; ref: R GA02; ref: R GA03] was 14 when she was introduced to the men by a bully and told they were friends. She was 15 when the abuse started. After falling out with her parents, she left home and started meeting men at the Tasty Bites takeaway, before she was raped at the Balti House. The abuse lasted until she was 17. She is now 19. She was singled out because she was white, vulnerable, and underage.

Unlike at home, she was allowed the freedom to come and go as she pleased, to drink and to take drugs. Looking back, she knows it was part of a softening-up process, devised by a girl (Honey Monster), who had crossed the line from victim to abuser.

After drinking heavily to try and blot out what was happening to her, she went to the Balti House and broke a counter. Police were called and she was arrested and charged. The girl told police that she had been raped and provided officers underwear containing DNA, that proved she had been raped by two men in a single attack. However, the CPS decided, on two separate occasions, not to prosecute because they considered a jury would not convict.

Afterwards, the 15 year-old's abuse continued and at its height she was being driven to flats and houses to be raped by up to five men a night, four or five days a week. Apart from central gang members, most of her rapists were unknown men who paid the gang £30 or £40 to have sex with her. Once or twice a week she was given £10 as a treat.

She said [R 2E01. Link no longer working: Why not?] at the time, that her complaints and her distress went unnoticed.

"These men would be picking me up from school — as soon as I walked out of the school gates at three o'clock — and taking me to houses," she said.

"I was getting phone calls in school asking me to walk out of school.

"I was coming into school with flea bites all over my body, dirty clothes, smelling of alcohol, smelling anyway of being unclean. I was very quiet.

"Quite a few people rang social services — school, the police, the sexual health team from Heywood. Even my own dad rang social services to get help.

"social services were already involved, but they had not done anything. Basically they had told my mum and dad that I was a prostitute and it was a lifestyle choice.

"When I found out I was pregnant, social services were informed. They threatened to remove my child at birth, but they never did anything to help me."

But it took another two years for the authorities to catch up with the gang. Rochdale's Crisis Intervention Team, an NHS clinic offering advice on abortions and sexual health to vulnerable young women, alerted police after a number of girls came to them with similar stories about being groomed for sex by Asian men.

A wave of arrests followed in December 2010, including Shabir Ahmed and Kabeer Hassan, the men who had escaped trial in 2008 because prosecutors did not think a jury would believe Girl A.

Upon her rapists sentencing, Girl A finally had the satisfaction of seeing the gang convicted, after the jury had no difficulty in believing her story, and those of her fellow victims.

Girl B was a 14-year-old in care when the abuse began. She was given "substantial amounts of alcohol" and was severely drunk when *daddy* Shabir Ahmed used her for sex. Another man sexually assaulted her.

Honey Monster was paid £200 for allowing Girl B to be raped by three men in Rochdale. The bully had already hit her hard before, and she became frightened of what the recruiter might do if she refused to have sex with the men.

Honey Monster was overheard to say that she needed the money, because another white teenager among her victims had moved away and, "the men wanted new girls."

When a victim called Girl B was being raped by one of the defendants, Shabir Ahmed interrupted, saying: "I want a turn, I want a turn."

Girl B saw him cutting his own arm with a razor blade before he threatened her with it to make her comply. She said: "I'd rather that happen than get my throat slit."

Girl C had celebrated her 13th birthday only two days before the abuse covered in the trial began. She was the youngest of the girls. She became pregnant at 13 by Adil Khan.

She said: "Pakistani men pass you round like a ball, they're all in a massive circle and put a white girl in the middle.

The prosecution described her childhood as "difficult and troubled"; she had said the men she met were her "good friends" and "nice people" who looked after her. She is now 17.

Girl D was subject to abuse when she was 15. After meeting Girl A and Girl C, she started going to the Tasty Bites takeaway. The men had already approached her before. She is now 19.

Girl E [ref: 2E01] had only just turned 13 when she first came into contact with the paedophile gang, the trial was told. Sajid took her to a house, which he said was his, and after buying vodka and cola for them to drink; before raping her. She later said Sajid and his co-defendants "treat white girls as easy meat."

Girl F [ref: 2F01 — echoed in Billie's Story]. As with all the other girls, her identity remained secret during the trial, and after sentencing. Shabir Ahmed had recruited her years before, directly off the streets. She was plied with drink and drugs, and raped by three men in a hotel. Her mother had taken her with evidence to the police, who did nothing.

Girl F became a regular sex toy and was taken to be raped all over the northwest. One day a taxi stopped to offer her a lift, only to discover the girl was her younger sister. She too ended up being raped by the gang, and so in time was the third daughter. Finally, after nine attempts, their mother got social services to put her children into child protection. This gave the gang far easier access to the girls, who's daily lives revolved around being gang-raped.

The mother of girl F showed a national newspaper evidence that suggests the authorities were aware of the abuse as long ago as 2002. An official report by a sexual health adviser, which was passed on to social workers and police in 2005, detailed the kidnap and rape of an underage girl in Rochdale, where the gang was operating, but the authorities failed to act.

The mother is recorded as stating [See above link: ref: F01], "A police officer did tell me, and a social worker has told me since, that they're frightened to do anything with the Asians because they might be accused of being racist against them."

Samantha: [ref: S01]

One girl named Samantha came forward to speak publicly of her own ordeal at the hands of the Rochdale child sex gang. Her case had come to court previously, but her harrowing tale is so similar to that of other victims.

She was only twelve-years old when one of the gang exploited her. Her attacker Shakil Chowdhury, who was 39, was jailed for just six years.

'Samantha had been walking home from school. She had just bought some ballerina pumps and had said goodbye to her friends but took a wrong turning on the way home. She knew not to trust strangers, but this man was a legitimate taxi driver, so she hopped in his cab. Afraid that she'd be late for tea, she accepted and told him her age and address while sat in the back. They made a slight detour on the way, and she was invited inside a house to wait on the settee.

Samantha said, "Another man offered me vodka, but I refused. Chowdhury forced me to go upstairs, where I was repeatedly raped by four men."

She said: "What happened to me ripped my life apart. And the worst thing is, it is still happening to other vulnerable young girls.

"My attackers were so brutal. Not only did they rape me 11 times but they beat me, mocked me, and made me hate myself.

"I wanted to die. One of them bit my chin, another bit my neck. I was left black and blue with bruises on my thighs and back."

Samantha's ordeal lasted for more than ten hours as each man took it in turns to rape her in the bedroom Chowdhury had lured her to. Chowdhury ordered her to wash herself after each rape. When her nightmare came to an end, he demanded her telephone number. "

"Her attacker was arrested and pleaded guilty to the rapes. But he was released after three years and his accomplices were never found.

Samantha said: "Chowdhury was sent to prison when I was a kid, yet he was let out when I was still a kid. How does that make sense?

"I felt very worried when he came out, but I haven't let him win. I would have liked to have seen him in prison for life, but realistically 12 or 13 years would have been just.'"

Samantha's story is further proof that male Pakistani Muslims considered they were above the law, and women [R A003] in general, especially their British victims were considered worthless.

It was patently obvious the judiciary thought they were walking on eggshells, for no mention of ethnicity or religious belief was allowed to cloud any testimony, only during sentencing did anybody put this into perspective, and that was the judge. The media only referred to them as 'Asian', which was to stigmatise many other ethnic groups who were completely unrelated, nor Muslim.

Conviction:

Of the twelve men originally arrested, all were Pakistani Muslims except for one man, who was an illegal Afghani Muslim immigrant, supposedly seeking asylum. Bail was granted, and one man immediately returned to Pakistan to evade conviction. Of the others, two would be tried later and found guilty, due in part to complications their defence council raised at taxpayers expense. However, all nine remaining were present in the dock for sentencing.

The gang received jail sentences of between four and nineteen years from a judge who said they treated their victims "as though they were worthless and beyond any respect".

In comments which appeared to conflict with police insistence that there was no "racial or cultural" element to the crimes, Judge Gerald Clifton told Liverpool Crown Court: "One of the factors leading to that was the fact that they were not part of your community or religion [R A004]."

The judge said some of the men claimed their arrest "was triggered by race."

But, he said: "That is nonsense. What triggered this prosecution was your lust and greed."

Despite the comments from Judge Clifton, Greater Manchester police denied there was a "racial or cultural" element to the gang's crimes and said it was about adults abusing vulnerable children.

The men were convicted of conspiracy to engage in sexual activity with children under the age of 16 and other sexual offences including rape and trafficking for sexual exploitation.

Sentencing:

Sentencing occurred some months later, as follows:

Shabir Ahmed, 59 — the man regarded as the ringleader — was jailed for a total of 19 years for conspiracy, two counts of rape, aiding and abetting a rape, sexual assault and a count of trafficking within the UK for sexual exploitation.

The defendant was banned from the court because of his threatening behaviour and for calling the judge a "racist b------."

The judge called Ahmed an "unpleasant and hypocritical bully."

Takeaway worker Kabeer Hassan, 25, of Lacrosse Avenue, Oldham, was jailed for nine years for rape and three years, concurrently, for the conspiracy conviction.

Abdul Aziz, 41, from Rochdale, was sentenced to nine years for conspiracy and nine years, concurrently, for trafficking for sexual exploitation. He was found not guilty of two counts of rape.

Married father-of-five Abdul Rauf, 43, from Rochdale, was jailed for six years for conspiracy and six years, concurrently, for trafficking for sexual exploitation.

Mohammed Sajid, 35, from Rochdale, was sentenced to 12 years for rape, six years for conspiracy, one year for trafficking and six years, all concurrent, for sexual activity with a child.

Adil Khan, 42, from Rochdale, was sentenced to eight years for conspiracy and eight, concurrently, for trafficking.

Mohammed Amin, 45, from Rochdale, was sentenced to five years for conspiracy and 12 months, concurrently, for sexual assault.

Abdul Qayyum, 44, from Rochdale, was jailed for five years for conspiracy.

Illegal immigrant Hamid Safi, 22, of no fixed address, was jailed for four years for conspiracy and one year, concurrently, for trafficking.

Summary:

New Statesman Overview [ref: NS01]:

'On 9 May 2012, the Rochdale grooming trial reached its conclusion. Nine men were found guilty and sentenced to a total of 77 years in prison. More arrests, and more convictions, are likely to follow. Throughout the trial, Shabir Ahmed, the 59-year-old ringleader of the gang, showed no remorse. He tore out clumps of his own chest hair in the witness box and made a female court interpreter run crying from the room. Delivering a bilious rant from the dock, he dismissed the accusations as "white lies", cursed the "bent bastards" who had brought him to trial and denounced everyone from the prosecution lawyer and Theresa May to Tony Blair and Margaret Thatcher.'

Second Conviction:

[ref: LCC01 Item may still be available with membership?]

Shabir Ahmed was convicted, at a second trial [R A005], on 30 counts of child rape. This time his victim was 'Asian'. The abuse had gone on for longer than a decade, but it was not until after Ahmed's arrest in the grooming case that his victim found the courage to give the police full details of what she had suffered.

'The girl said when she was first raped she was so young she needed to stand on a chair to reach a sink.'

§

Reported Fact: <u>Oxford</u> [R A006] **2012**
In a remarkably similar case to Rochdale, Muslim men from Pakistan, and two from Eritrea, systematically groomed white girls between the ages of 11 and 15 for sex and child prostitution. Seven were prosecuted, and six were found guilty.

Of 51 known girls identified as being enslaved to the paedophile ring, only six volunteered to give evidence in court.

Regards the child rapists and traffickers, <u>police belatedly</u> [R A007] identified 30 main protagonists within the hegemony, although only twenty-one were arrested. It is known hundreds of men from all parts of England paid a lot of money to delight in raping and abusing the girls.

Police finally put the pieces together, many years too late, under Operation Bullfinch. Nonetheless, this was not before an eleven-year-old girl became pregnant. She was given an enforced back-street abortion in appalling conditions, when she was twelve, in order for her abuse to continue undetected.

Once again, the dereliction of Duty of Care, both by police, social workers, local council officials, and the Crown Prosecution Service are paramount features of wilful neglect. Several girls reported their rapes, one even being given a medical examination by a doctor, who at the time was speaking on the phone to somebody about golf.

"Sometimes the girls were taken outside Oxford where they were sold for £600 an hour."

"During a police interview, a 15-year-old told officers she was sexually abused by Akhtar Dogar for three days after running away from a children's home in September 2006. The victim, who was raped by the gang from the age of 12 and sold for sex, told police she was sick of being treated 'like a piece of meat'. She told police that she knew other girls were being abused because 'I have seen them doing it to little girls in their uniforms'."

"Two months later, another victim was spotted by a police officer running from a room in a downmarket Oxford guest house wearing only a towel after being beaten and raped. The 14-year-old told them how the gang raped her, injected her with drugs, beat her and urinated over her."

"No charges were brought against the gang because the victim was persuaded by another girl to withdraw the allegations."

"In the same year a third victim, who was 14 at the time, told police that several Asian men had sex with her at a flat in Oxford. She told them her true age and admitted that she had run away from a children's home. But she later told them she did not want to give evidence because she did not trust them [The police] to keep her safe."

"Another girl felt brave enough to face her abusers in court, while others gave evidence from behind a curtain."

"One of the victims described how she was even threatened with arrest for wasting police time when she tried to report the abuse."

Unforgivable, yet there has been no prosecution of the police officers concerned for dereliction of duty, or aiding and abetting the commission of offences. Why not?

Girl A. In February 2006, the 14-year-old told police that she had been held against her will by two Asian men. She said they forced her to snort cocaine and left her in an unconscious state.

Then, in September 2006, the girl told police she had had sex with one of the defendants - Akhtar Dogar and another man in a park in exchange for drugs. She told police: 'They treated me like a piece of meat. They're doing it to other girls. Little girls with their school uniforms on.' The girl was examined by a doctor who found injuries consistent with 'forceful' sex.

Dogar was interviewed by police about the allegation on 13th September 2006 but denied rape, suggesting the girl had mistaken him for another Asian male.

The other girl withdrew her complaint and supporting evidence, so Girl A could not continue giving evidence in a separate trial of three men accused of raping her in 2005.

Girl B. In August 2006, the 14-year-old was taken to a flat in Oxford, and rang police after realising she was with 11 men who wanted to have sex with her. The girl was spoken to away from the men and admitted she was 14 and had run away from a children's home.

The following day, she made a statement saying nothing happened and withdrew her complaint because she was scared.

Girl C. Another 14-year-old told police she was attacked by Bassam Karrar in a guest house in Oxford in November 2006 while he was said to be high on cocaine. Police found the girl in the basement 'extremely distressed, crying and shaking'.

She told police she had been held against her will, drugged, raped and repeatedly smacked in the face. The girl was taken to a police station where photographs were taken of her injuries.

But she later dropped her complaint after pleas from another girl who was seeing Karrar at the time.

Girl D. Went missing from a care home 126 times in 15 months and staff realised she was being groomed.

In October 2007, the 13-year-old girl told a male social worker she was receiving calls from the Karrar brothers. When he answered one of the calls, a man demanded to speak to the girl and began threatening the social worker when he refused.

In January 2008, she had a meeting with a police officer and welfare officer at her school, where she told them she had been raped.

Girl E. The 14-year-old spoke to police and a social worker in June 2012 when her mother alerted them that she had been out all night.

Her clothes were seized and a DNA match to Zeeshan Ahmed was found. He was charged under Operation Bullfinch, which was set up in May 2011.

Girl F. The then 16-year-old was interviewed and admitted she had been having sex with men for a couple of years. She said Girl E had been sold to other men.

Sentencing: Due June 2012

Critique:

"Oxfordshire County Council [R A008] said it would implement recommendations from the serious case review once it had reported.

Meanwhile, figures collated by the charity Barnado's, suggested that the majority of child sexual exploitation investigations conducted by the police; did not result in prosecutions.

Out of 56 cases identified by the organisation last year [2012], only 15 went to court, with just six of those resulting in convictions."

Note:

One of the men found guilty is a Muslim Prosecutor [R A009. This link should still be there, but access to it has changed; as has the Telegraph]. This information is extremely difficult to find reference to, as there appears to be a news blackout on reporting this fact. One would seek to question why?

Observation:

Why is there not, already; a Nationwide Help-line dedicated to supporting these Girls?

§

Reported Fact: Rotherham 2010 [R A010]

Police turned a blind eye to allegations of sexual abuse of white girls by gangs of largely Pakistani men for more than a decade, it was claimed yesterday.

Research, reports, and case files also revealed that council officials, social workers, and police were desperate to cover up any racial link to the abuse of young girls.

The research shows that a string of warnings dating back as far as 2000 were ignored by the authorities. In many cases, police action was taken only against the victims.

Among the alleged crimes for which no one was prosecuted were:

A 14-year-old girl being forced to perform sex acts on five men – four Pakistanis and an Iraqi Kurd asylum seeker (and a 13-year-old girl);

A British Pakistani man was found in a car with a bottle of vodka and a 12-year-old. Both were arrested on suspicion of stealing the car. Police also found pornographic images of the girl on the 22-year-old's phone;

A 14-year-old girl missing for a week was found under the influence of drugs in a car with a man 20 years older. They had had sex but he was arrested only for drug possession;

A 13-year-old girl was found drunk at 3 a.m. in a derelict house with a 'large group of adult males' who had plied her with vodka. She was arrested for a public order offence while the men walked away.

According to previously confidential documents seen by The Times, police in Rotherham, South Yorkshire, found evidence of thousands of similar crimes and described 'networks of Asian males exploiting young white females'.

The groups were reported to have trafficked victims to cities including Bristol, Manchester and Birmingham.

Despite this, just two prosecutions of groups of men for sexual abuse have taken place in South Yorkshire since 1996.

The Girls:

The court was read three impact statements [R A011] from the victims.

One of the girls, who was aged 13 at the time, described how she was taken away from her family after the abuse emerged which "ripped my heart out" and the ordeal left her frightened.

She described how she was a little girl from a loving family, but felt her childhood had been taken away from her. She said she had been "used and abused" and the abuse had "ruined my one and only body."

The 16-year-old victim said she had to move from Rotherham to a hostel after the abuse came to light, which meant she missed out on important events with her family. She said she no longer had any confidence and was worried about future relationships with boys.

The third victim, who was also 13 at the time, described being nervous and anxious. She said she had lost weight and was upset all the time. She described herself as being "angry" and shouted at family members.

Sentencing:

As well as the rape conviction, Zafran Ramzan, 21, of Broom Grove, Rotherham, was found guilty of two counts of sexual activity with a child in relation to another girl. He was cleared of two further counts of rape.

Umar Razaq, 24, of Oxford Street, Rotherham, was found guilty of one count of sexual activity with a child - a 13-year-old girl. He was cleared of raping another girl.

Razwan Razaq, 30, also of Oxford Street, Rotherham, was found guilty of two charges of sexual activity with a child, relating to two different girls.

Adil Hussain 20, of Nelson Street, Rotherham, was found guilty of one charge of sexual activity with a child - a 13-year-old girl. He was cleared of three similar charges.

Mohsin Khan, 21, of Haworth Crescent, Rotherham, was found guilty of one count of sexual activity with a child - a 13-year-old girl. He was cleared of two similar charges and four charges of rape.

Three other defendants were cleared of all charges against them.

It is clear sophisticated grooming [R A012] techniques are employed: First selection of the target girl, followed by them becoming friends with boys their own age. Later they were introduced to the boy's older 'cousins', and plied with gifts, drink, and drugs including heroin and cocaine. They came to think of the men as their boyfriends and protectors. Most were coerced to believe they were 'In Love' with their exploiters.

Meanwhile, the men deliberately drove a wedge between the victims and their families using physical, emotional, and psychological weapons. They made threats, such as to firebomb the parent's home, or gang-rape the mother as the girl is forced to watch.

Should a girl still resist, she would have a machete placed at her neck, and with a snick, was told she would be beheaded. Every girl eventually complied with her rapist's wishes.

One of the girls [R A013], Emma Jackson, joined a charity to support girls who find themselves in similar circumstances, and in need of support—something apparently never forthcoming from British authorities.

§

Reported Fact: Derby 2011 [R A013]
This extract mainly relates to the third trial following the investigation by Derbyshire police Operation Retriever taskforce.
"

During the three court cases, 13 men from Derby went on trial at Nottingham Crown Court, and 11 were convicted. Although 100 victims were said to have been involved, police eventually identified only 27 girls.

At the third related trial, the ringleaders were prosecuted: Saddique was convicted of four counts of rape as well as two counts of false imprisonment, two of sexual assault, three charges of sexual activity with a child, perverting the course of justice, and aiding and abetting rape.

Liaqat was found guilty of one count of rape, two of sexual assault, aiding and abetting rape, affray, and four counts of sexual activity with a child.

Both men were jailed indefinitely and branded "sexual predators" by the judge.

Liaqat's brother, Naweed Liaqat, 33, got 18 months.

Another gang member, Faisal Mehmood, 24, who pleaded guilty to sexual activity with a child and got three years, has been deported to Pakistan.

Judge Philip Head told Saddique: "You are in the truest sense a sexual predator with a voracious sexual appetite that you gratified as frequently as possible in a variety of ways… Your crimes can only be described as evil."

Violence was used in some incidents and many girls threatened as the gang embarked on a "reign of terror on girls in Derby." The judge described how one typically "deeply damaged, pitiful victim" crouched down in the witness box and whimpered as she recounted her ordeal.

On 24 April 2009, a surveillance operation abruptly ended, when two tearful teenagers stumbled out of a Derby flat police were watching, and called 999. They claimed they had been raped. The officers had not known they were there.

In statements, the girls not only made forceful accusations against Siddique and Liaqat but also named other girls the pair had abused.

That became the pattern. Each victim led to more victims. Eventually police had a list of 27 teenage girls and they arrested 13 men, aged between 26 and 38.

One 16-year-old victim said, "I will never ever understand what has made them so evil and ignorant that still to this day they think they've not done anything wrong."

Det Supt Debbie Platt, who led the police investigation, said: "I was personally shocked at the scale of the abuse we uncovered. It hadn't been reported and it was happening under the radar.

"It was like a campaign of rape against children. When you see the impact these offences have had on them it is awful.

"The offenders have followed girls wearing school uniforms on the streets. They've driven into school car parks. We were incredibly shocked because we hadn't anticipated the level of offending that was going on."

Police believe no money changed hands between the dozen or so men involved but the girls were driven around the Midlands to be raped in houses, hotels and B&Bs. It was a form of internal people trafficking now recognised to be a growing problem in the UK.

The girls had been carefully groomed by their abusers. Typically they would meet them on the street, be invited out for a drive, a drink, a cigarette, or drugs. They would be driven to a secluded area, a park, or one of the rented houses the men lived in, and forced to have sex.

Sometimes five or six men would be involved and they would video the attacks on mobile phones. The rapes were often violent, some girls were locked up to prevent them getting away. Others were thrown out of the car when their ordeal was over.

Searching one of the flats, officers found extensive forensic evidence that the rapes had taken place.

Reaction [R A014]:

The inquiry was prompted by concerns at a children's charity, which patrols the streets of Derby. Safe and Sound was set up to stop teenagers being groomed for sex.

The organisation's founder Sheila Taylor said: "I was worried that we'd wind up with children seriously injured, possibly even dead.

"I think it is really widespread - there's 40-plus projects up and down the UK that are dealing with this issue. Many of them find young people are seriously damaged."

Anne Marie Carrie, Barnardo's new chief executive, said the children had 'been forgotten as discussion has focused on the ethnicity of perpetrators in high-profile cases. Children are being passed from man to man, home to home, city to city.

'It's the domestic trafficking of children for money. This problem is getting worse in that it is getting more organised, certainly the grooming is becoming more organised using technology. The children are as young as 10.'

In a report released by Europol, which co-ordinates intelligence on child trafficking across the EU, the body states that children are also sold into criminal gangs in the UK and forced to steal, as well as being abused.

The children, who are believed to be worth up to £130,000-per-year to the gangs, are subjected to 'extreme forms of violence, such as sexual abuse and torture.'

The trafficking and exploitation of these children is a lucrative business, with the children being routinely sold between different criminal gangs and the "price" based on the child's money-earning potential,' said the Europol report.

Scotland Yard's Operation Golf, which look specifically at Romany child trafficking gangs, has calculated that average price of a child in the UK is £16,000.

"

§

Reported Fact: Preston 2011
"

Operation Deter is made up of officers from Preston police, social care workers and representatives from the Children's Society, and voluntary sector group The Coalition for the Removal of Pimping (CROP). Their enquiries are unlikely to end before 2017, without any new information being forthcoming.

In the past six months [Published on 28/04/2011, 09:29], the team has protected 58 victims and dealt with 47 offenders involved in child sex exploitation.

Operation Cherish, the equivalent team in Lancashire police's southern division, which covers South Ribble, Chorley and West Lancashire, was set up in 2009 and has helped 57 victims and helped 41 offenders in the same six month period.

Among the victims Cherish has helped is a Preston teenager who was just 14 years old when she was groomed by a 52-year-old chef who abused her and fed her drugs as she worked at his takeaway.

Hossien Sabourian, who ran the Mi Casa takeaway in Blackburn, was jailed for eight years in December 2009 for engaging in sexual activity with a child and supplying class A drugs. That sentence was later reduced to four years, 10 months on appeal.

Sabourian's victim, who is now 18 years old and still piecing her life back together, said the Cherish team helped her through the ordeal massively.

She said: "They were amazing because I was always so hostile towards them. I thought they had got the wrong end of the stick and that he wasn't like that. But no matter how much I pushed them away - and I was awful to them in defence of him - they were always nice to me and they never gave up.

'(Cherish) can refer you to counsellors and things like that but really it is about getting the man put away.

'It is definitely important. Obviously I have researched it and the amount of people it happens to is amazing, especially in Lancashire'.

The victim's mother said of Operation Cherish: 'Without the help of Lancashire police and various support agencies then I don't know what would have happened.

'We had to make her realise that it wasn't a relationship it was abuse'.

A large percentage of victims in Lancashire are referred from family backgrounds as opposed to being from children's homes or in care, and

Supt Critchley said officers have been working hard to encourage children, parents, schools, care workers and others to report offences.

Many offences involve enticement of youngsters by older men using alcohol or cigarettes.
"

Related: Brierfield [R A016]girl forced by rapist to withdraw statement.

§

Reported Fact: Shropshire 2013 and 2017 [R A017]

One of the most alarming aspects of this case, so similar to others referenced above, is the fact that it was never reported in the national press. Does this indicate that the regularity with which trials of Pakistani Muslim paedophiles are coming to court, is now viewed by media as a common occurrence, one hardly worth reporting?

It is also noteworthy that the initial trial held at Stafford Crown Court was abandoned after repeated challenges by defence lawyers, that accounted for the entire first month of the trial alone, no doubt all at taxpayer's expense.

"

The jury was sworn in on 16th May, but the opening of the trial was delayed by legal discussions until 13th June. From 19th August, there was a pre-arranged break in the trial, until 2nd September, when defence counsel each made applications to the court over the case's future.

Over the 15 weeks the trial has run the court was in session for 70 days during which time there were a series of legal arguments and the jury heard evidence from just six of the prosecution witnesses.

Details of this and other previous hearings involving the seven men have been reported but the cases could not be linked until now [10th May 2013].

Many of the seven men worked for or had connections with fast-food restaurants across Telford and some of the girls were sold for sex to workers.

The men were all arrested as part of West Mercia police's Operation Chalice. Officers said the total number of girls targeted between 2007 and 2009 could be above 100. The ages of girl victims were between 13 and 17 years of age.

Det Ch Insp Neil Jamieson described many of the girls as "particularly vulnerable." He said they were groomed, receiving presents such as mobile phones to build up a sense of trust.

"What they would do is drive them around, they would ply them with alcohol, drugs, buy them things, and it would almost be a boyfriend-girlfriend scenario initially.

"It then spiralled into them being shared with other men.

"We found some of the victims had been to Halifax, they'd been to the north of the country, they'd been into Birmingham and they'd been moved around for the purposes of sexual exploitation."

Brothers Ahdel Ali, 25, and Mubarek Ali, 29, who had denied a string of child sex offences, were handed the longest sentences, of 18 years and 14 years respectively.

The trial at Worcester Crown Court heard the brothers, of Regent Street, Wellington, sexually abused, trafficked, prostituted or tried to prostitute four Telford teenagers, as young as 13.

In sentencing the pair, Judge Patrick Thomas QC said: "You have not shown at any remorse or regret for what you did. Instead you have twisted and turned to avoid justice."

Ahdel Ali was found guilty of one charge of rape, 11 charges of sexual activity with a child, three charges of controlling child prostitution, one of inciting child prostitution, a charge of inciting a child to engage in sexual activity and meeting a child after grooming.

His brother was convicted of four charges of controlling child prostitution, two of trafficking in the UK for sexual exploitation and a charge of causing child prostitution.

The judge said the elder brother had repeatedly sold one girl 'for relatively trivial sums'.

He said Mubarek's motivations went beyond profit and 'involved sheer gratuitous pleasure in the power you exercised over these unhappy girls'.

Former taxi driver Mohammed Islam Choudhrey, 54, of Solway Drive, Sutton Hill, pleaded guilty to paying for sex with a Telford schoolgirl and was jailed for two-and-a-half years at Wolverhampton Crown Court in November.

Mohammed Ali Sultan, 26, from Victoria Avenue, Wellington, was jailed for seven years after admitting having sex with two teenage girls, one of whom was 13 years old.

Mohammed Younis, 61, of Kingsland, Arleston, was jailed for two-and-a-half years for allowing his flat to be used as a brothel by allowing a man to have sex with a girl who was being controlled as a prostitute.

Mahroof Khan, 35, from Caradoc Flats, Wellington, was given a 30-month sentence after admitting having sex with a 15-year-old girl at his home, but walked free from court due to time spent on remand.

Tanveer Ahmed, 40, of Urban Gardens in Wellington, was jailed for two-and-a-half years after admitting a charge of controlling a child prostitute.

Abdul Rouf, 36, of Kingsland, Arleston, walked free from court after no evidence was offered against him, although the judge ordered that a charge of facilitating child prostitution should lie on file.
"

Telford is the Muslim grooming capital of UK [R A018].

§

Reported Fact: Middlesbrough [R A019] **2013**
The Middlesbrough grooming case, again detailed the rape of underage, white British girls by Pakistani Muslim men. Of course, none of them were charged with rape by our two-tier British courts system.
"The most deplorable thing about this case, is that it was not deemed to be important enough to be reported in national newspapers; I found this in the local rag. Above is a later BBC report that came to light.
One victim stated, "I can only conclude Paki-rape against us kids is now an accepted by the authorities, as being an acceptable part of modern British culture"
Others are listening. 'A FORMER police chief says Teessiders must be on their guard to help tackle child sex crime'.
Mark Braithwaite, who used to be a Detective Chief Superintendent with Cleveland Police, issued his alert [R A020] after the sentencing of nine men for a string of child sex offences in Rochdale.

§

And so it continues:
Bristol [R A021].
Peterborough [R A022].
Birmingham [R A023].

§

[End Blockquote]

Note:
Despite the fact that the rapists and child-traffickers were from different, if ethnically related Countries, one fact stands alone: They were all Muslim.
Here is an abstract thought:
I read this in a blog comment of a National newspaper, before it was deleted by a moderator. It may have been the Telegraph?

"Is it not time that all Muslim men in The United Kingdom, are automatically categorised as child sex offenders, unless they can prove they are not?"

I personally do not agree with it, but it provided food for thought.

Of course, the British Muslim community could stop prevaricating, and hiding it's head in the sand. But I doubt any young female victim will bother to wait for a Blinding Flash on the Road to Damascus.

They are already more than aware, that the Imam's and devout Muslim men, treat their own women as having less worth than an animal. Pubescent white girls are simply looked upon as captured infidels, slaves of a religious war.

They are used and abused by their Muslim, Pakistani 'Landlords'.

Adult Rating—18

This novel contains bad swearing and threats of extreme violence against children. There is virtually no sex in this book, and none is described in gratuitous detail. Let me be very clear upon this point.

Swearing is related to the street language they used. Words that normal people use, kids especially and often in speech. It includes the worst of words, including the 'F' word and the 'C' word. The 'N' word does not appear.

They blaspheme, and call their daily rapists 'Pakis'. That is the word on the street. I don't give a shit if it is politically correct or not. It is what most British people actually say in real life.

The violence used was extreme, gruesome at times. But is not described by the Press in any detail, except upon a few occasions. Is there is a deeper reason why not?

Generally, the violence of these heathens, is never mentioned, except as told in court. It refers to the factual reality of the lives the real girls endured. It is something most newspapers and online resources failed to do. It is important to show the brutality used to make the girls conform-- accept being slaves of their 'Islamic Masters'.

This book does not indulge in graphical sexual detail. That is horrendous, and especially given the ages of the girls concerned. It shows grooming, but at higher levels, but it follows true life.

If the reader is unsure, then be aware, the text reads like a black and white movie. One where innuendo supplants the physical fact. That is far too rare nowadays.

The novel focuses on the emotional and mental abuse the girls were forced to endure. This is both by the Muslim, Pakistani rapists, and that administered by Social Services, Family Court, the Police, and Local Authority.

Many will find this totally unacceptable in our modern society.

Author's Comment

This novel was designed to mirror real-life events.

I first became aware of these events by reading articles by Christopher Booker of The Telegraph. He detailed the SS kidnapping children into care. Then the Rochdale grooming gang became front page news, soon followed by Rotherham, and others.

I was horrified to read of events concerning both Muslim grooming gangs, and the atrocities inflicted on normal, loving families, by Social Services. I felt the record needed to be straightened, and written for posterity. I slowly began to wonder if the two were in some way linked?

In general, the national newspapers overlooked the truly horrific nature of some of the perpetrators: branding girls, urinating upon them, hitting them forcefully and with a hammer, dousing them in petrol and striking a lighter. Threatening them with a pistol. Telling them their home would be torched, their mother gang raped as the girl watched, and her father beheaded. It is all in the links above.

That is severe bullying and inhumane treatment of young children of the worst kind. But there again, the police, and Social Services, both of whom were charged with the duty to protect these most vulnerable girls, turned a blind eye.

The British police never followed-up these events as charges. Neither did they, but once, make a charge of 'possession' of illegal drugs. They did not charge the man with having sexual images of a naked 12-year-old girl on his phone. She was still in the car. Apparently, the modern police regards public acts of sex with a minor as not a crime: 'She's sucking my c**k, mate' [Derby].

I am still waiting for those officers to be charged with criminal offences. The local councils, social services, and courts propagated this miasma on our once proud society. The girls involved, now seemingly hundreds of thousands of them, deserved much more in life.

Hence, sales profits of this book will go towards supportive charities, and the places where it can do most good.

I have no Islamaphobic tendencies. There were plenty of white Christians, of apparently good social standing, involved as well. I have Muslim friends. But I do know the difference between Right and Wrong. I welcome all moderate, integrating Muslims into the heart of our British society, their presence enriches our culture.

Integration demands, these moderate Muslims acknowledge the crimes some of their men have committed, and report them to the authorities. If this is not done, then they condone what has happened: The serial rape and enforced prostitution, without payment, of extremely young, white, Christian girls. This also happens to their own children, but there is never anything said. There can be no excuses.

I also recognise that there are far more white British men who are paedophiles. Notwithstanding, when viewed as a percentage, Muslim men in UK appear to a far higher proportion.

This is a cultural issue.

It is a racial issue.

And it is most certainly, a religious issue.

I believe the time is long overdue, for the British Muslim population to take ownership of this problem, and out these misogynists in their midst. 'They are lower than a Cobra snake'.

As a final word, I also realise this is happening within the Muslim community. Is it not time for those within to speak out?

The reader may think I am an Islamaphobe. That is not the case. I have no bias against Muslims, and my balance of views is non-secular, but with Christian ethical values. But the fact remains that many of the perpetrators and ringleaders, as revealed by the Press, have been either men of Pakistani descent or the victims of their abuse who are still in thrall. Others are men who, if met on the street or in their places of business, would be assumed to be good, Christian men.

In all cases this is far from the truth. None of these perpetrators, whether Muslim or Christian by professed origin, is in fact a faithful follower of religion. There is a difference between Right and Wrong, and they follow the latter most closely. It is unfortunate that the choices of these men makes it seem as if there is a racial vendetta against them.

It is well past time for the Muslim community worldwide, to blame the rapist, and not execute the female victim of his crimes against her humanity. I repeat this link, and hope it acts as a wake-up call for those that can make a difference:

http://www.dailymail.co.uk/news/article-2416586/Gangs-Asian-men-grooming-MUSLIM-girls-plying-drink-drugs.html [R AC01]

You can learn more about what proactive, female Muslims in UK are doing about the problem, by visiting their website:

Muslim Women's Network UK [R AC01]

If you are in trouble, call their Freephone helpline: **0800 999 5786**.

My last observation, is the one that closes the book. It was so obvious to me. It was conspicuous only in its absence:

Why is nobody following the money trail?

That knowledge puts events into a different perspective. It engenders true understanding of this iniquity, as enforced upon the most vulnerable of British citizens, regardless of race or religion:

Our children.